IN BED WITH THE DUKE

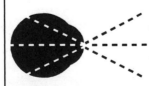

This Large Print Book carries the
Seal of Approval of N.A.V.H.

IN BED WITH THE DUKE

CHRISTINA DODD

THORNDIKE PRESS
A part of Gale, Cengage Learning

GALE
CENGAGE Learning·

Detroit • New York • San Francisco • New Haven, Conn • Waterville, Maine • London

GALE
CENGAGE Learning

LIBRARY OF CONGRESS CATALOGING-IN-PUBLICATION DATA

Dodd, Christina.
    In bed with the Duke / by Christina Dodd. — Large print ed.
      p. cm. — (Thorndike Press large print core)
    ISBN-13: 978-1-4104-2693-2
    ISBN-10: 1-4104-2693-9
    1. Women household employees—Fiction. 2. Nobility—Fiction. 3. Large type books. I. Title.
PS3554.O3175I59 2010
813'.54—dc22   2010009617

Published in 2010 by arrangement with NAL Signet, a member of Penguin Group (USA) Inc.

*For Scott and Jerry,
the little boys who wore old hats, put
broomsticks through the shoulders of old
coats, stuck straw in the sleeves, and
rode their neighborhood on make-believe
horses to fight for justice.*

*They were the
Scarecrows of Romney Marsh.*

Long may their spirit reign.

ACKNOWLEDGMENTS

Writing my first historical in four years was a labor of love, and my pleasure was intensified by the enthusiastic support of the NAL team. Leslie Gelbman, Kara Welsh, and Claire Zion, as always I appreciate you. A special thank-you and welcome to Jesse Feldman, who keeps the office running. This spectacular cover was the concept and work of NAL's brilliant art department led by Anthony Ramondo. Thank you! My appreciation to the publicity department with my special people, Craig Burke and Jodi Rosoff. My thanks to the production department, and of course, a special thank-you to the spectacular Penguin sales department. Finally, my heartfelt appreciation to my editor, Kara Cesare, who contributes so much to my work with her discerning eye and tactful suggestions.

Most especially, thank you to all the readers who, like me, love a rollicking historical romance. Here's to you!

CHAPTER ONE

Moricadia, 1849

The four-piece ensemble ceased playing, and with exquisite timing, Comte Cloutier delivered the line sure to command the attention of all the guests within earshot. "Have you heard, Lady Lettice, of the ghost who rides in the night?"

Certainly he commanded the attention of the Englishman Michael Durant, heir apparent to the Duke of Nevitt. There had been little to interest him at Lord and Lady Thibault's exclusive ball. It was an exact clone of every English ball he had ever attended, and indeed of every Prussian ball, every French ball, every Venetian ball. . . . He had made the Grand Tour, and discovered that the wealthy imitated one another to the point of boredom.

Now, tonight, the musicians played, the guests danced, the food was fashionable, and the gambling room was full. Prince

Sandre and his henchmen circulated, lending the patina of royalty to the gathering.

But of useful reports, there had been nothing . . . until now. And now, Michael knew, only because Cloutier failed to comprehend the seriousness of his faux pas. He failed to realize that by tomorrow he would be gone, thrown out of Moricadia and traveling back to France while cursing his own penchant for gossip.

With every evidence of interest, Michael strolled closer, to stand near the group of suitors surrounding Lady Lettice Surtees.

"A ghost?" Lady Lettice gave a tiny, high-pitched scream worthy of a young girl's alarm. "No! Pray tell, what does this ghost do?" Before Cloutier could answer she swung around to her paid companion, a girl of perhaps twenty, and snapped, "Make yourself useful, girl! Fan me! Dancing with so many admirers is quite fatiguing."

The girl — a poor, downtrodden wisp of a thing with a lace cap set over dull brown hair — nodded mutely. From the large reticule she wore attached to her waist, she withdrew an ivory-and-lace fan, took her place at Lady Lettice's right shoulder, and fanned her abruptly flushed and sweating mistress.

Lady Lettice complained, "It's too warm

in here. Don't you agree it's warm in here, Lord Escobar?"

Escobar hovered at her left elbow. "Indeed, you are right, señorita, an unseasonably warm summer evening."

It was a gross flattery to call Lady Lettice "señorita" — she was a widow, in her early forties, with the beginnings of the jowls that would plague her old age. But her bosoms were impressive and displayed to advantage by her immodestly low-cut, ruffled bodice, and her waist was made tiny by her stays, which had been tightened enough to impede her breathing and make the dancing, as she said, fatiguing.

None of that really mattered, because Lady Lettice was wealthy, and the half dozen men around her knew it. They jockeyed for position beside her gilded chair, offering cool goblets of champagne, smiling toothily, and, behind her back, examining the debutantes lined up along the wall, girls who were prettier and far younger, but without the necessary riches to make a good match.

"So, Cloutier, tell me about this ghost." Lady Lettice withdrew a white cotton handkerchief from between her breasts and blotted her damp upper lip.

"This ghost — he is called the Reaper. He

11

rides at night, in utter silence, a massive white figure in fluttering rags atop a giant white horse. His skin is death, his clothes are rags, and where his eyes should be, there are only black holes. A terrifying apparition, yet the peasants whisper of him fondly, claiming he is the specter of Reynaldo, dead two hundred years and the last king of Moricadian blood."

"Peasants," Lady Lettice said contemptuously. "Peasants know nothing."

"I would not argue with you there," Cloutier agreed. "But not only peasants have seen this ghost. Others who have come to this fair city to take the waters and enjoy the gaming tables have seen him, too. The rumor claims that if you're not Moricadian, and if you are unlucky enough to see the Reaper, you should flee at once, for this fearsome phantom" — Cloutier lowered his voice in pitch and volume — "is a sign of impending doom."

Michael snorted, the sound breaking the shocked silence.

At once, Lady Lettice fixed him with her gaze. "You're impertinent. Do you know who this man is?" She gestured to Cloutier.

Her paid companion might be a mouse, but she was an intelligent, observant mouse, for she squeaked a small warning and

12

flapped the fan harder.

Lady Lettice paid no heed. "He is Comte Cloutier, of one of the finest noble families in France. One does not snort when he speaks."

"One does if one is Michael Durant, the heir to the Nevitt dukedom." Cloutier bowed to Michael.

"Oh." Lady Lettice didn't bother to be embarrassed by her discourtesy. She was too enthralled by her newest prospect of a suitor. "My lord. Your grace." She fumbled, not knowing quite what to call him.

Cloutier met Michael's gaze and, knowing Lady Lettice aimed too high, did the honors. "Lady Lettice Surtees, this is Lord —"

"Please." Michael held up a hand. "In England, my name is old and honored. In Moricadia, I am nothing but a political prisoner, a nonentity, a man who has vanished from the world I knew due to the oppression of the ruling family and Prince Sandre. Call me Durant. It is the only decent title for a disgrace such as me . . . and I confess, I should be ashamed to use my family name so shabbily." His voice was a low rasp.

Lady Lettice looked appalled. "A political prisoner? I am shocked, gentlemen. Shocked! How is this possible?"

"The only ghost in Moricadia is me, my lady, for until I was allowed out for this one night, my existence has been no more than a rumor." Michael bowed and walked away, projecting tragedy with a surety that would have commanded the admiration of the stage actor Edmund Kean.

"The poor man." Lady Lettice spoke in a whisper so high as to pierce the ears. "What did he do?"

Michael paused behind a marble pillar to hear the answer.

No one replied at first; then Escobar reluctantly said, "Durant fell foul of the de Guignards. They own this country. They rule this country. The first de Guignards deposed King Reynaldo — murdered him — and now the de Guignards crush the native Moricadians beneath their jeweled heels." He lowered his voice even more. "There are rumors of rebellion and that the true king is returning to claim his throne."

"How romantic!" Lady Lettice clutched her hands at her bosom.

"Yes, except that the de Guignards accused Durant of assisting the rebels, and for these two years, it has been generally believed he was dead. Only recently has it come to light that Lord and Lady Fanchere, trusted allies of Prince Sandre, are holding

14

him under house arrest." In a mere whisper, Escobar added, "It is rumored he spent most of that two years in the medieval dungeon below the royal palace."

A silence fell as the little crowd observed Sandre. He stood across the ballroom near the dais where the ensemble played, suave and trim in his ceremonial uniform covered with medals. Sycophants surrounded him, and he played the role of noble prince with a sure hand, charming the wealthy who came to Moricadia to visit, to gamble, and to rub shoulders with easily accessible royalty.

Michael despised Sandre for what he was, and for what he pretended to be.

"But I don't understand," Lady Lettice insisted. "How do the de Guignards dare to hold an English nobleman against his will?"

"The de Guignards have always dared, and gambled." Cloutier was bitter; his family hadn't come through the last two hundred years nearly as well.

"In the case of Moricadia, they won, exterminating King Reynaldo's line . . . or so they claim, although the rebels claim differently. But for that, they seized" — Escobar waved his hands toward the window, where brightly lit villas, gambling houses, and lavish spas sprinkled the Pyrenees —

"all this. But we dare not talk of it."

"Why not?" Lady Lettice's eyes grew round with excitement.

"Because Prince Sandre has spies everywhere, and he does not tolerate dissention in his country." Escobar bowed. "Now if you'll excuse me, I see an old friend I must greet."

Michael stepped out from behind the column and nodded to the man as he hurried past. Wise Escobar. He would seek another wealthy widow, one not at the epicenter of a possible upheaval.

Mr. Graf, a well-dressed youth of twenty-two with golden curls styled across his forehead, stepped into his place.

Mr. Graf had had a run of bad luck at the gaming tables last night; he needed a wealthy bride, and quickly, before his father in Germany discovered the extent of the damage.

Of course, he granted no attention to the paid companion, still vigorously fanning Lady Lettice's neck. Nor did any of the other suitors.

Fools. The girl was nervous as a rabbit. The drab gray wool of her plain dress did nothing to complement her pale complexion, and the cut completely obscured what might have been a shapely figure, but she was thin to the point of frailty. She had typically English features, and might have been pretty, but she kept her chin down, her eyes down, her shoulders hunched as if expecting at any moment a slap across the cheek.

In Michael's opinion, any of the lords and gentlemen who hoped to capture Lady Lettice in wedded bliss would be well-advised to look to her cowed servant. Michael didn't know if the girl had always been timid, but he would wager Lady Lettice had completely broken her spirit. The girl looked as if Lady Lettice kept her on the verge of starvation. Certainly she was frightened half to death.

Yes, Lady Lettice might hide the whip from her suitors, but once wed, she would never relinquish its control.

The unlucky Mr. Graf jockeyed for position with the ambitious Count Rambaudi of Piedmont and the English Lord Bedingfield, and the result was disaster — for the companion. They bumped her arm. The fan smacked the back of Lady Lettice's head, making the curls over her ears bounce. And she turned on the girl like a rabid wolf. "You vexsome girl. How dare you hit me?"

"I didn't mean . . ." The girl's voice matched her demeanor, low and fearful, and it trembled now.

In a flurry, Lady Lettice adjusted her hairpins, and when the girl tried to help, she slapped at her hands. "Go away, you stupid thing. I should throw you out on the street right now. I should!"

"No, ma'am, please. It won't happen again." The girl looked around at the men, seeking help where there was none. None of the impoverished aristocrats and gentlemen, certainly not the ones who had caused her problem, could be bothered to care about the fate of a servant. "I beg you. Let me stay in your service."

"She isn't really sorry," Lady Lettice told the others. "She says that only because she's an orphan with no family, and she would starve without my kindness. Wouldn't you, Emma?"

"Yes, ma'am." Emma adjusted Lady Lettice's shawl across her shoulders, then took the handkerchief Lady Lettice clutched and dabbed at her cheek.

"All right, fine, stop." Lady Lettice pushed her away. "You're annoying me. I'll keep you on, but if you ever hit me again —"

"I won't! Thank you!" Emma curtsied, and curtsied again.

"Actually . . ." Lady Lettice took back the handkerchief and stared at it. Michael could almost see the spark of some dreadful mischief start in her brain. "I'd like this dampened. Go to the ladies' convenience and do so."

"As you wish, Lady Lettice." Emma took the handkerchief and scurried away.

"Watch, gentlemen," Lady Lettice said. "Here's entertainment. The stupid girl has no sense of direction. She turns right when she should turn left, goes north when she should go south. The ladies' convenience is to the right, so she'll turn left."

The men around watched as Emma walked to the door, hesitated.

Michael silently urged her to the right.

But as promised, she turned left.

The little circle of sycophants guffawed.

Michael winced.

Lady Lettice tittered. "Would you gentlemen care to wager how long it will take my stupid companion to find her way back to me?"

"Good sport," said Bedingfield. "And I wager your handkerchief will still be dry!"

The little group clustered together, making fun of a girl who had done them no wrong.

Michael, ever the fool for the underdog, quietly went to rescue the poor companion from her own folly.

CHAPTER TWO

Emma was lost. She wandered up and down well-lit corridors, stumbled into darkened rooms where couples strained to make love, then stumbled out as quickly, mumbling apologies and wishing she were back in England, where mating rituals were more restrained and less animal.

Finally she found a door to the garden, stepped out on the terrace, and looked back at the château. From here, she could hear the music from the ballroom, see the light spilling from the windows. Surely, if she studied the location, she could find her way back there and start her search again.

But then what? She still wouldn't have accomplished her mission, and she knew very well the price of disobeying Lady Lettice's commands.

Moricadia was a gorgeous little gem of a country, set high in the Pyrenees and blessed with spectacular views, bucolic meadows, and hot springs reputed to heal the sick. But Emma stood there under the stars, staring at the splashing fountain, wishing she were rich, noble, and beautiful instead of poor, common, and well educated. What good did common sense and a sharp intelligence do for a woman when her main duty was to fan a perspiring beast and, at night, to massage the beast's corn-laden feet? And if God answered no other prayer, she would think He'd at least give her some means by which to find her way from point A to point B without getting lost so that she could dampen the beastly handkerchief.

As her father had always said, she might be a timid child, but she had an analytical brain, and that was a gift from God that she should utilize to make her life, and the lives of others, better and more fruitful.

So, walking to the fountain, she dipped Lady Lettice's handkerchief into the pool until it was thoroughly dampened, then lifted it and wrung it out.

When she heard a warm, rasping chuckle behind her, she jumped, dropped the handkerchief, and turned to face Michael Durant, the tragic English nobleman.

"I came out to direct you to the ladies' convenience, but I see you found a better solution." He nodded toward the fountain.

"It's not what you think." This was her worst nightmare. He would report her to the beast. She was going to be thrown onto the street in a strange country with no resources, nowhere to turn. She was going to die — or suffer a fate worse than death. "I didn't come out here on purpose —"

He held up one hand. "Please. Lady Lettice made clear your amazing ability to get lost. What she didn't realize, I suppose, was your ability to improvise. Miss . . . ?"

"Chegwidden." She curtsied as she'd been taught in Miss Smith's School for Young Gentlewomen. "Emma Chegwidden."

In the ballroom, she had watched Michael Durant and thought him not at all lordly. Rather he was a handsome brute of a man, big-boned, tall, and raw. His black suit was of the finest material and in supreme good taste, and she would wager he visited only London's best tailors. Yet the clothes didn't fit well: The formal black jacket was tight across his shoulders, the pants were loose at the waist, and the whole ensemble gave him the appearance of a warhorse dressed in gentleman's clothing. His hair was red, untouched by gray. His eyes were bright, piercing green. His skin was tanned; he seemed like a man who followed the sun.

He bowed. "A pleasure, Miss Chegwidden. Of the Yorkshire Chegwiddens?"

"Exactly." Silly to feel relief that Durant knew of her family, respectable and impoverished though they were, but she warmed to him. "My father was a vicar at the chapel in Freyaburn near the St. Ashley estate."

"I know the area well. Very beautiful. Very wild. Do you miss it?"

"Oh, yes. In the spring, when the winds sweep across the moors and ripple the purple heather, I —" Her breath caught abruptly. She made it a point to never think about home, and this was why. A rush of silly tears could only lead to mockery.

But he said merely, "I find Moricadia is very different from England, is it not?"

"Very different." She swallowed hard, gained control, and gestured toward the east. "The city is cosmopolitan, so bright and full of wealthy visitors seeking fun and gaming."

"Actually, Tonagra is" — he took her finger and pointed in the opposite direction — "that way."

"Oh." She wasn't embarrassed by his correction. Rather, she realized how long it had been since she'd had contact with another human — or at least another human who was not intent on humiliating her. And his touch was warm, penetrating her thin cotton glove, a gentle, light directional clasp.

"But I interrupted you." He removed his hand from hers, and when she didn't immediately speak, he said, "Miss Chegwidden?"

Obscurely discomfited by her wandering mind, she hastened into speech. "Here in Moricadia, the gambling houses are large and beautifully decorated, and again, so many visitors! So much wealth! And the châteaux dot the mountain ridges like so many stars in the sky. But at the same time . . . the people are so poor, and I feel as if no human habitation or feeble effort of man can tame these towering mountains or the primeval forest that blankets them." Remembering the narrow, winding road Lady Lettice's rented carriage had taken to bring them here, the way the woods had pressed close, the glimpses of rocky peaks she had seen when they crested a ridge, Emma shivered and pulled her shawl around her shoulders.

Realizing suddenly that he watched her closely, she flushed.

In the ballroom, she had thought him a phony, another nobleman flirting with tragedy for the outpouring of sympathy and the residual gossip.

Out here, he seemed different, amused

and more than a little sympathetic to her plight. Yet he saw too much, understood too well her emotions, and in the night, with only the stars for light, he had a quality of stillness about him, like a tiger lying in wait for its prey. In her position, paying attention to details like that meant the difference between surviving unscathed by pain and scandal, and being an unwilling victim.

So she must step carefully. For all that Durant appeared kind, he could be every bit as nasty and mocking as the other gentlemen surrounding Lady Lettice, and a good deal more dangerous, for he invited confidences.

"Pay no attention to me, my lord," she said in her most self-deprecating tone. "Those are merely foolish musings on my part."

"Not at all. You show great insight."

"You have been here for a long time, then?"

"A very long time indeed."

"Is your family unable to send the ransom?"

"What ransom?"

"The one to get you released so you may return home."

"My family would be quite shocked by that request. They believe me dead."

25

"How horrible for them! Can you not send a message secretly to relieve their grief?"

"I don't choose to."

Shock and revulsion held her frozen in place. "You have a family — a mother, a father —"

"And two brothers."

"And you choose not to return to their bosom?"

"I would never ask them to send money to line the de Guignards' pockets."

She would have given anything to have her father back, paid any amount of money, would have begged and pleaded — and this man refused to send word to his relatives because . . . because . . . "So it's *pride* that holds you back? You don't wish to escape Moricadia, and you care nothing for their sorrow?"

He stepped toward her.

Abruptly she remembered that she was out in the garden. No one knew where she was. Michael Durant was a powerful nobleman. And she had just obliquely criticized him.

She retreated. "I have overstepped my bounds — but you should be ashamed of your selfishness."

"You're correct on both counts." His voice

26

was courteous and remote. "Shall I help you retrieve Lady Lettice's handkerchief?"

Glancing down into the clear water, she saw the white square floating just below the surface. "Thank you, I can do it." Without turning her back to him, she leaned down, caught it in her fingertips, and wrung it out over the pool. "So Lady Lettice did this to humiliate me." That was a bitter pill to swallow, to know everyone was laughing at her, and she could do nothing.

"She is not a gentlewoman, I believe."

"No." She wrung the handkerchief again as if it were Lady Lettice's neck.

"Nor a particularly pleasant woman." He walked up the steps and looked back at her. "Shall we go back to the ballroom?"

By that, she assumed he meant to guide her, and cautiously she followed him.

He held the door for her, *observing* her as she walked through.

She straightened her shoulders.

"This way." He gestured down the corridor, and as they walked, he continued. "I recall something about her being the only daughter of a manufacturing family, married for her fortune to Baron Surtees."

"When she was seventeen, she was reputed to be a great beauty." Emma did not say that now Lady Lettice was a great beast.

She suspected Durant, with his direct gaze, already had deduced that fact.

"I also heard that after a mere twenty-some years of miserable married life, Surtees escaped wedlock by dropping dead."

"You are uncharitable, my lord." She took a breath to avoid laughing while she spoke, and when she had herself under control, she said, "But essentially, you are correct. So Lady Lettice determined to do as she had always wished. She took his title and her fortune, which was relatively intact, hired a respectable companion from the Distinguished Academy of Governesses, a companion who had no resources, no family, and no way to leave her — that's me — and has been taking the Grand Tour of Europe."

"In hopes of meeting and marrying her next victim . . . er, husband."

His height made her uncomfortable, and as they walked, she watched his hands. Big hands. Big bones. Big knuckles. Broad palm. Hands weathered by fighting experience. A white scar sliced across one knuckle on his left hand. He had hit something, or somebody, and split his hand. And she was walking alone with him. And determinedly talking. "Originally, Lady Lettice sought out young Englishmen, thinking it would be a good idea to wed someone who could take her higher in English society, but the young men were skittish and not particularly flattering." Emma ran her finger over the raised ridge on her chin. "So she wisely moved on to gentlemen of the Continent. They have a much more sophisticated attitude toward women of her age and wealth."

"I can imagine. This way." Durant took a turn to the right, then again to the left, leading her down corridors lined with closed doors and dimly lit by sparsely placed candles.

"Are you sure?" She could have sworn they were headed back to the garden again.

"I never get lost." He sounded so sure of himself.

Irksome man. He might not get lost, but he was certainly in trouble. With more sharpness than she intended, she asked, "What did you do to get yourself arrested as a political prisoner?"

He stopped walking.

She stopped walking.

"In Moricadia, it doesn't do to poke your nose into local troubles." He tapped her nose with his finger. "Remember that."

Affronted by his presumption, she said, "I certainly would not do something so stupid."

His eyebrows, smooth and well shaped, lifted quizzically. "Of course not. You're supremely sensible."

The way he spoke made her realize — she'd just called him stupid. "My lord, I didn't mean —"

"Not at all. You're quite right. Now." He opened a door to his right.

At once, the sound of music and laughter filtered through, and, peeking in, Emma saw the dining hall where Lady Thibault's servants were setting up for a midnight supper, and beyond that, through open glass doors, the ballroom.

She couldn't restrain a sigh of relief. Relief that she had made it back in a reasonable amount of time, and would not have to face Lady Lettice's wrath. Relief that she didn't have to spend any more time alone with the enigmatic Michael Durant.

"Do you still have Lady Lettice's handkerchief?" he asked.

"I don't lose things, my lord." She showed it to him, still twisted between her palms. "I only lose myself."

"Now you are found. I'll leave you to make your own way to Lady Lettice's side." He bowed. "It's been a pleasure, Miss Chegwidden."

She curtsied. "My lord, my heartfelt

thanks." She watched him walk away, and wondered at the man. He seemed alternately kind, rescuing her from trouble, and heartless, in allowing his family to think he was dead. But still she was grateful; thanks to him, she had returned to the ballroom, the handkerchief was wet, and Lady Lettice and her nasty game had gone awry.

Of course, failure would put Lady Lettice in a foul mood, and make the nightly ordeal of unlacing the ghastly woman even more agonizing, but sometimes, regardless of the consequences, it was good to win — and now, thanks to Michael Durant, nothing else could go wrong.

CHAPTER THREE

Michael watched Miss Chegwidden hurry past the long table laden with china and silver and step into the ballroom.

She wasn't quite as unattractive as he'd first thought. When she straightened her shoulders, it was clear his supposition had been right: She did have a good figure, with a lavish bosom hidden beneath that plain and hideous bodice. Her dark hair contained hints of auburn, and her eyes . . . her eyes were unusual. Not the muddy hazel he'd first glimpsed, for when she experienced real emotion — like her indignation at his neglect of his family — specks of gold sparkled to life and the color brightened, becoming aquamarine.

No, Miss Chegwidden wasn't quite as cowed as he had imagined. She might fear Lady Lettice, but she had been free enough with her criticism of him.

He grinned. In fact, it almost felt good to

have a young Englishwoman impugning his character. Normal. As if he were home in London in the family town house, being taken to task by his stepmother for his wild embrace of adventure, by his father for not taking his role as the Durant heir seriously enough, and by his staid brother Jude for not applying himself to his duties.

His youngest brother, Adrian, had never chided Michael for this wildness. The serious boy had adored Michael, and Michael had adored him in return.

He wished he could send a message to them, to let them know he was alive. But he didn't dare. Not yet. And he prayed that no visitor from England told them the truth, for if they knew, nothing would keep them from coming to Moricadia and bringing him home.

But he wasn't finished here yet.

Yet he missed them — and how surprised Miss Chegwidden would be to know it.

Taking the long way around, he entered behind Lady Lettice and her admirers.

If anything, the crush had grown greater in his absence. The open doors had done nothing to cool the summer night, and the guests' elegance was wilting even as he watched. Icy champagne circulated on every serving tray and chilled every throat, and

33

the sounds of voices and music combined to create such a cacophony he longed to be back in his quiet room at Lady Fanchere's, staring at the bars on the window . . . and missing home.

No. He was better off here with so much to distract his mind.

He hoped Miss Chegwidden could make her way through this crowd to Lady Lettice's side. He would have guided her himself, but appearing in the ballroom with him after a prolonged absence would have done her reputation great harm. If he weren't in such a mess himself, he would see what he could do to relieve her untenable situation.

But he *was* in a mess.

As if his thought had called trouble, he glanced up, into the eyes of Raul Lawrence. He inclined his head.

Raul inclined his, and turned away.

"Do you know him?" The voice that spoke at Michael's left shoulder made him tense and swallow, trying to wet his suddenly dry throat.

But too much was at stake here for him to falter because of the memories. So he fixed a faint smile on his lips and turned to face the man who had caused so much pain. "Rickie de Guignard. How good to see you again, and in such strikingly different cir-cumstances."

"Indeed." In appearance, Rickie de Gui-gnard wasn't cut from the usual de Guig-nard cloth. He was tall and gangly, well over six feet, with abnormally long and slender limbs. His fingers looked skeletal, with wide joints and narrow bones, and Michael had reason to know his hands held strength and agility. He had a tendency to get close and peer into his victim's face, and when he was first imprisoned, Michael had thought that affectation an attempt to frighten the victim. Eventually, he decided the man had bad eyesight. In the end, it didn't matter. The sight of that forehead, broad as a gravestone, that lantern jaw, that drooping nose, had the effect of making his blood run cold.

It chilled now as Rickie bent to fix his pop eyes on Michael's. "Do you know him?" Rickie repeated.

Michael refused to back away. "I do. Raul Lawrence, bastard son of Viscount Grims-borough."

Rickie pounced like an overgrown puppy. "You know him well?"

"No. Grimsborough adopted him, then forced him down the throats of the denizens of polite society. But Lawrence is younger than I, so we are only distantly acquainted."

Michael thrust his face back into Rickie's. "Why? What do you suspect *him* of?"

"We like to gather information about people, especially people like him. He has chosen to settle in Moricadia."

"There's no accounting for taste."

Rickie reared back, his brown eyes snapping.

Michael's throat closed.

Rickie's gaze dropped to Michael's gloved hands clenched in fear. In a voice both low and menacing, he said, "You pitiful aristocrat. You wish you were back in England, do you not, Durant?"

"With every fiber of my being." Michael had never meant anything so much.

"I promise you, until you tell us what we want to know, you will never see those verdant shores again."

"Then I will never see them, because I don't know what you think I do."

"I don't believe you."

"Surely you don't imagine a pitiful aristocrat like me could have withstood two years in the palace dungeon suffering under your kind urgings?"

The fury that contorted Rickie's face both pleased and terrified Michael. This time, his hands were not tied. If Rickie struck him, he could respond in kind.

But he knew what would happen then. Imprisonment. Darkness. Death.

Then luck, bad luck, intervened.

A man's hand clasped Michael's shoulder, pushed him back, and a man's figure stepped between them — Prince Sandre, handsome, suave, wealthy, and as corrupt as any fiend in this land of corruption. "Gentlemen. Gentlemen. This ball is one of the highlights of the season. People are watching. You're making a scene."

Michael stood, knees stiff, eyes locked with Rickie's. "You have no idea what a scene I could make."

"But is it worth it to lose your freedom? Again?" Prince Sandre asked with mild curiosity.

At the pointed reminder, Michael stumbled backward. He had to play the game. No matter what, he had to play the game. "No."

"Before I am finished with you, you will give me whatever I want." Rickie stalked off, his long limbs loose and disjointed.

At thirty-five, Prince Sandre was a man in the prime of his life. He rode hard, fenced with devastating results, seduced women with careless ease. His dark hair was combed back, revealing the premature silver that streaked like wings on the sides of his head.

No matter what the occasion — a party, a bad turn at the gambling table, a bout of heinous torture in his dungeon — his dark blue eyes sparkled with humor, and he smiled as he watched the crowd avoid his cousin, like a school of small fish shunning a shark. "You do have a way of irritating Rickie."

"I try my best."

"What is it that you've done this time?" He lifted a champagne flute from a circulating waiter, took a sip; then, as if he had just remembered, he said, "Oh! That's right. He was curious to know whether you were friends with the Englishman Raul Lawrence."

Michael knew better than to avoid the question, or say one word different from what he had to Rickie. The de Guignards would later compare notes, and he didn't dare get caught in a falsehood. "We are acquainted, but he is a bastard, Prince Sandre. The heir to the dukedom of Nevitt does not associate closely with a bastard." Michael well knew his own value as one of England's top aristocrats. "If you suspect him of some nefarious deeds, you'll have to find out by the usual means — spying and deceit."

Prince Sandre did not leap into a rage in

the manner of his cousin. Instead he gave a small bow and said, "You seem to be enjoying your house arrest, my lord. Lady Fanchere says you are the perfect guest. It was she who convinced me to allow you to attend this ball."

Liar. You seek to discover what I know by subtler means, by observing to whom I speak and who speaks to me, by slacking off on the leash and unexpectedly tightening it, choking me and hoping that the pain will loosen my tongue so I tell you at last who conspires against you and your throne. "I must remember to thank Lady Fanchere."

"I would have let you have a bit of liberty sooner, but I understood your reluctance." Prince Sandre sipped again. "Your voice . . . it was very bad."

Michael touched the cravat that covered his throat. "Yes."

"I'm delighted to hear it so much improved. Pray God you are able to keep it healthy." It was a threat inflicted with skill and malice. A threat — and not a well-disguised one. But why should Prince Sandre bother to mask his intentions from Michael?

Michael was one of the few men who had seen all the way into his rotten soul. Or rather . . . one of the few men *alive* who had seen that soul. "I assure you, Prince Sandre, I would not do anything to jeopardize my . . . voice." *How he hated Sandre.*

"Yes. Because it's difficult to take your proper place in the House of Lords when you cannot speak. Harder yet when you are dead."

"Actually, Parliament is frequently so boring, the lords therein appear to be deceased. And sometimes are."

Prince Sandre laughed. "So I understand."

"Interesting institution, Parliament. Allows for input into the government. Saves on uprisings like the one that led to the French guillotining their own king."

Prince Sandre's nostrils flared — but still he smiled. "So does a secret enforcement police with a strong hand to guide them." Prince Sandre lifted his champagne flute and, in a slow, controlled motion, crushed the bowl in his fist.

The sound of splintering crystal cut the sound in the ballroom to a frightened hush. Nearby guests froze in place. Champagne dripped onto the polished wood floor.

Prince Sandre dropped the stem, and it shattered as an explosive exclamation point.

Then he pulled a shard of glass from his palm. Blood immediately stained his white glove. With his customary smile, he said,

"How clumsy of me. I hope you'll forgive me, my lord, while I seek out my hostess to bandage this."

"Of course." Michael bowed. "Prince Sandre, I hope you've done no permanent damage."

"No." He stripped away his stained glove and held it in his fist to stem the bleeding. "I always know exactly how much pressure to exert."

As if his words were a signal, waiters rushed forward to clean up the floor, the quartet picked up their instruments, the volume of voices rose again, and movement resumed.

Lady Thibault appeared at Prince Sandre's side. "If you would follow me, my prince, I will fetch my personal physician to tend to your wounds."

"As always, you're kind, but it's not worth a visit from the physician. Tend to me yourself." Prince Sandre caught her arm with his free hand and squeezed the soft flesh above her elbow.

Michael saw her grow pale, and sweat broke out on her brow.

Poor woman. Even so small an act of violence as breaking the glass had aroused Prince Sandre, and now she would pay the price.

As Michael moved back to allow the waiters to finish mopping up the mess, he caught sight of the drab gray gown Miss Chegwidden wore. She was moving with her usual stealth, head down, shoulders hunched, toward Lady Lettice, and she held the damp handkerchief in both hands as if it were the Holy Grail.

Poor dab of a thing. He would have further assisted Lady Lettice's unfortunate companion if he could, but with matters standing as they were, he could help no one else without consequences more dire to everyone concerned.

The worst of her crisis was over. She was better off without him now.

The crowds had thickened, and Emma had circled the ballroom almost entirely before she caught sight of Lady Lettice, sitting like the queen toad on her lily pad with her suitors swimming like guppies around her. Thank heavens; Emma would hate to think she had found her way into the same room but failed to locate her employer.

Walking up behind the little group of suitors, Emma heard Cloutier say, "She must arrive within the next minute, or I lose!"

The despicable little group of guppies had

been wagering on the time she would return — or if she would return. Unexpectedly, the anger she thought long crushed beneath Lady Lettice's mighty displeasure surfaced, and she stepped briskly into the circle. "Lose what, my lord?"

Cloutier said, "Ha!"

Lady Lettice jumped. Her skin turned ruddy with displeasure all the way down to her amply displayed breasts, and she snapped, "Where did you come from, you vexsome girl?"

Emma curtsied and smiled disingenuously, because she knew that whatever wager Lady Lettice had made, she'd lost. "The ladies' convenience, as you commanded." Emma extended the handkerchief.

Lady Lettice plucked it out of her palms. "It's wadded up, and too wet. You're so stupid."

Emma's brief, unexpected surge of confidence began to wilt.

"Can't you do anything right? Must I instruct you in every nuance? To think that you are the best the Distinguished Academy of Governesses had to offer is simply appalling. I shall write the director and complain. I shall!" With a flip of the wrist, Lady Lettice opened the handkerchief.

And a tiny, still-wiggling goldfish slipped out and down her cleavage.

She screamed. Leaped to her feet, slapped at her chest. Screamed again.

The music stuttered to a stop. The dancers turned to look.

Lady Lettice plunged her hand into her own cleavage, fighting against the restriction of her stays, trying to reach the tiny, wiggling creature.

The men around her burst into hearty laughter. Mr. Graf went so far as to double over with glee.

Still screaming, she lifted her skirts, revealed pudgy legs, and leaped onto the chair. Leaning forward as far she could, she shook like blancmange, but no acrobatics she performed could dislodge the fish.

Word spread through the ballroom. Dancers crowded around, hooting and pointing. Mirth blazed as brightly as wildfire.

And Emma Chegwidden backed away, hand over her mouth, whispering, "I am ruined. I am ruined."

CHAPTER FOUR

Emma stood on the lonely dirt road outside the château, shivering from cold and fear. She was alone as she had never been in her life, in a foreign country, without a way of supporting herself and without even the barest necessities — a furious and humiliated Lady Lettice had made sure of that. Emma hadn't been allowed to collect her cloak. Her meager belongings were at the hotel, miles from here. She hadn't eaten since morning. The moon was new, and the stars barely touched the sky with light. Dense woods and tall mountain peaks surrounded the château. And her thin slippers were not made for walking.

But she had no choice. She could either walk, or sit down and die. Lady Lettice had done everything — slapped her, scolded her, humiliated her — yet no matter what, Emma had refused to break. No matter how miserable her life seemed at this moment, no matter how downtrodden and hopeless she felt, she couldn't convince herself to give up. Not yet.

So she stood indecisively looking left and right, trying to remember which way they'd come in, which way would lead her back to the hotel and then to Tonagra, where she might find work and lodgings. But the carriage that had brought them had arrived as the early-evening sunlight still streaked through the trees. Everything looked different then. And while she could memorize a route, given the chance, at the time she'd seen no reason to think she would have to know. Closing her eyes, she re-created their route in her mind. They had come from the left; she was sure of it. So she turned left and walked.

Behind her, the château with its lights and music faded to nothing. The road wound along the mountain ridge through the darkest part of the forest, and even as her eyes adjusted she saw nothing but tall trees blotting out the sky. Within the stands of pines, she heard the rustling of animals. Once a dark shadow swooped toward her. She gasped and ducked. The owl hooted and sailed on.

The high-mountain temperature dropped rapidly, and she tucked her hands into her armpits in a futile attempt to keep them warm. Just when she thought she should turn back, the road plunged downward, and she well remembered the difficult climb to the château. So she was going in the right direction.

She continued on, exhausted, hungry, and half-frozen. The road got rougher. She comforted herself that the ruts were growing larger because the carriage wheels had dug them deeper, and not because water had cascaded down these slopes during the spring runoff — a runoff that had finished months ago. Deep in her heart, she knew carriages could never descend this grade, nor get through the trees that pressed closer and closer, clawing her with leafy fingers.

She stopped. Brushed her hands across her forehead.

It was so dark. It was so steep. She was so cold. And hungry. She wanted to lie down and sleep. . . .

Directly in front of her, she heard a deep, guttural snarl.

She stopped.

A pair of pale eyes shone from the thicket beside the road.

She took a step backward.

A creature slunk out of the forest, stopped

before her. The growl grew louder, more hostile.

The hair lifted on the back of her head.

The wolf lunged toward her.

She screamed. Turned and ran. Behind her, she could hear the wolf panting. Her foot slid into a rut. She twisted, fell, and leaped up again, clawing her way up the track, hoping against hope that someone would hear her, rescue her. Looking up toward the top of the rise, she saw it. Salvation. A man's form rose from the mist, blocking out the stars. With a swell of hope, she put on another burst of speed . . . and realized in horror that this was no living man.

His skin was chalky. His clothes were white and tattered, the winding sheet of a corpse. Behind him stood a horse as ghostly and unearthly as his master.

She was staring at the Reaper.

She screamed again, high and shrill. She tried to run backward. She tripped over a tree root. Her poor, abused ankle gave way, and she fell into the brush. Brittle branches scratched at her flesh and broke beneath her weight. Out of control, she rolled into the pine needles that littered the forest floor. She hit her head on a rock, and for a moment she was airborne and unconscious.

When she came to, she rested on her stomach, her face pressed into the rich loam of the forest. The scent of pine needles rose in her nostrils. Disoriented, she pushed herself up on her hands, then collapsed back into the dirt.

Her head was swimming. Every bone in her body ached. At last, after so many horrible days and so many debilitating nights, her spirit had been crushed. She had reached rock bottom, and she was going to die.

Hands clasped her under her ribs. She felt the heated rush of breath as the being turned her to face him. She looked up into that ghastly visage. It was the Reaper, and his eyes . . . were nothing but empty eye sockets.

With a quiet moan, she fainted.

Picking her up, the Reaper tossed her over his shoulder, mounted his horse, and rode away into the darkness.

Later that night, much later, the Reaper sat in the saddle, the horse warm and restive between his thighs. The stars were bright in the west, but in the east, the faintest tinge of dawn lit the sky. He watched as the long line of carriages inched down the road away from the ball. Outrunners carrying torches lit the way. Occasionally drunken laughter drifted in on the night's breeze, but for the most part it was quiet, the revelers exhausted from hours of dancing, gambling, and drinking. One by one, the carriages peeled off, taking different roads, and still he watched. Slowly at first, then with more vigor, he moved down the mountain, guided only by his plan, formed in desperate circumstances, and his thirst for revenge.

CHAPTER FIVE

"Rickie. Rickie!" Lady de Guignard shook her husband's shoulder.

"For the love of God, Aimée." He sounded half-asleep and exasperated at the same time. "It's four in the morning. Whatever foolish fit has you in its grasp now, can't it wait?"

"No. No! Do you know they say that a ghost haunts the roads by the dark of the moon?"

"Who's *they?*" Rickie sounded casual as he tried to stretch his long legs in the cramped carriage.

But she'd lived with him for twenty years. He couldn't hide the truth from her; he had gone on alert. "It was that Englishwoman Lady Lettice. She knew all about the Reaper. She told me about it in the ladies' convenience. She said the Reaper was the specter of King Reynaldo."

"So it is headless?" She couldn't see

Rickie in the darkness, but he sounded impatient and contemptuous. "Because when the de Guignards took the country, we hanged Reynaldo until he was dead, then cut off his head and stuck it on a pike in the town square in Tonagra."

Aimée gasped. "A headless specter? I don't think she knew that!"

"My God, woman, you are the stupidest . . ." His voice ground with irritation.

Lady de Guignard fussed with the lace ruffles at her throat. "If you'll look outside, you'll see it *is* the dark of the moon."

"So it is. Reynaldo's been dead for centuries. Why would he start haunting the countryside now?"

"He's the harbinger of the new king's return," she recited.

"The devil take it!" Rickie sat straight up. "How did that rumor get started? We cleaned out that rat's nest of second-rate royalty. There's no king *to* return."

"Lady Lettice said the royal family is in hiding not far from here in one of the châteaux. She said they are plotting the overthrow of the de Guignards' cruel regime, and —"

He interrupted impatiently. "You do realize 'the de Guignards' cruel regime' includes you?"

"Oh, no! It's you."

"You are my wife."

"Only by marriage."

She saw the shadow of his fist rise.

She cringed back.

The carriage lurched. Slowed.

He took a long breath and lowered his hand.

The carriage halted.

"What's wrong? Why are we stopping?" He peered out the window.

"Is it the Reaper?" Her voice quavered.

He turned on her like a striking snake. "No. It is not the Reaper. There is no Reaper. If there is, it's a man dressed up in a ghost costume designed to scare the ignorant. Which is why it is working so well with you!"

"Why, Rickie." Tears filled her eyes. "That was mean."

"Mean? No. That wasn't mean. You don't know what I'm capable of," he muttered. Slamming the door open, he said, "I'm getting out to see what's going on."

She fluttered like a peahen. "Be careful!"

"Not even these ignorant peasants are fools enough to play games with me." He swung out, shouting, "Let's get rolling. I'm in need of my bed!" His voice faded as he tromped off into the darkness.

Lady de Guignard huddled into the corner of the carriage and whimpered softly. No matter what Rickie said, she believed in the Reaper. She believed Reynaldo had returned for his revenge. And although she pretended to be ignorant, and Rickie thought she didn't know of the duties he performed in the dungeons of Prince Sandre's palace, she knew it all, and shivered when he touched her with those freakishly long fingers and covered her with his tall, skeletal body.

At the same time, she knew all too well that Rickie was her only safety in this degenerate land, and she waited tensely for his return.

But gradually the wine she'd consumed and the lateness of the hour worked irresistibly on her, and she relaxed against the seat. She closed her eyes for a minute, just a minute. Then another minute, then . . . with a start, she woke up. The carriage had started moving again.

Rickie must have straightened out the problem. They were never in real danger. Because she knew he was right; none of the Moricadian peasants would dare hinder him in anything he wanted to do.

Everyone was afraid of Rickie de Guignard. Everyone except Prince Sandre, and although she wasn't a clever woman, and although she had never seen proof, she knew Prince Sandre was worse than her husband . . . and that was very bad indeed.

"What was wrong, Rickie?" she asked sleepily.

No one answered.

"Rickie?" She groped in the seat beside her, then the seat across from her.

Rickie wasn't here with her.

Had he decided to ride out with the coachman? That seemed so unlike him. He was fastidious, and liked his elegant clothing to remain pristine.

She rapped on the roof of the carriage and called, "Halloo! Are you up there?"

No one answered.

The carriage continued down the road. She peered out the window. Dawn was breaking, a lightening of the gray mist. A movement at the top of the hill attracted her attention, and she looked up, up, up . . . and saw a ghostly figure in white rags on a white horse.

He had holes where his eyes should be.

She flung herself backward, her back hitting the far wall of the carriage, and crumpled in a heap onto the floor. She covered her eyes, whimpered, and moaned, fear writhing like a worm in her belly.

Then, slowly, she crawled onto the seat.

Staying low, she crept back toward the window and, in the greatest act of bravery of her feeble life, looked out again.

The figure of the Reaper had disappeared.

But as they drove past the gibbet on the crossroads, she saw a tall figure dangling there, his feet still performing the dance of death.

She screamed in terror.

It was her husband.

It was Rickie de Guignard.

CHAPTER SIX

In a rush of panic, Emma opened her eyes and stared around her.

She lay prone on a feather bed with clean linens and brocade bed curtains. The room itself was small, but well-appointed, with rugs on the floor, a chest with a mirror, and, beside the bed, a table with a basin and water jug. Cheerful afternoon sunshine streamed through the open windows, and from outside, she could hear the birds chirping.

She didn't know where she was.

She didn't know how she got here.

She lifted her arm and looked at the white sleeve, heavy with lace at the cuff, and felt her neck where buttons secured the neckline.

This was not her nightgown. It was too nice to be her nightgown.

She must have died and gone to heaven.

But no. That was impossible. In heaven,

she wouldn't have awakened with the need to use the ladies' convenience.

Abruptly she sat up.

That left only one answer. At last she'd come to the pass that she'd always feared: She was in a house of ill repute.

"Please, Miss Chegwidden." A young woman dressed in a clean and ironed maid's costume bustled forward, and in a marked French accent, she said, "You're not to get up. M'lady's orders."

Emma stared at her wildly. "Who are you? Who is m'lady?"

"I'm Tia, and you're in the home of Lady Fanchere."

Lady Fanchere's name sounded vaguely familiar, but Emma didn't know why. "Is she the madam of this establishment?"

The maid took her shoulders and pressed her down onto the bed. "I don't understand what you mean, miss."

Tia's accent wasn't French, Emma realized, but Moricadian, and Lady Fanchere was . . . she was . . . Emma knit her brow as she tried to grasp the vague thread of memory.

Last night. She'd been at the ball, fanning Lady Lettice, when someone had said, *Lord and Lady Fanchere, trusted allies of Prince Sandre, are holding him under house arrest.*

Who was being held by Lord and Lady Fanchere?

The answer snapped into her mind.

Michael Durant, heir to the Duke of Nevitt.

Memories of last night were fuzzy, but Michael Durant was crystal clear in her mind. The red hair, the green eyes, the fine clothes, the cavalier manner in which he dismissed his family's worry at his absence, his kindness to her . . . He was a very odd man, and she didn't know whether to scorn him or like him.

She remembered something else, too. Something that nudged at the edges of her mind and sent chills down her spine . . . "There was a wolf!" she said.

In a soothing tone, the maid said, "Yes, miss, of course there was. I'll call Lady Fanchere and you can tell her all about it."

Emma was so wrapped up in her thoughts she scarcely noticed when Tia slipped from the room.

She certainly noticed when the bedroom door reopened, and a lady bustled in, Tia trailing behind.

The lady was of medium height, anywhere between thirty and forty, with handsome features and a shapely figure. She was also the epitome of a chatelaine. She wore good, but serviceable clothing, a large ring of keys at her belt, and a competent expression. Her glossy blond hair was pulled back into a chignon and wrapped in a net, and her large brown eyes examined Emma and made a judgment Emma feared was not flattering. She stopped at the foot of the bed and slipped her hands into her apron pockets. "So. You're awake at last. Miss Emma Chegwidden, I believe?"

Emma sat up. "That's right."

"I'm Lady Fanchere, daughter of Bernardin de Guignard and wife of Lord Fanchere, minster of finance to Prince Sandre."

Still in a sitting position, Emma tried to bob a curtsy.

Lady Fanchere waved the courtesy away. "Tia, bring Miss Chegwidden her breakfast tray."

Tia placed a tray on the table beside the bed, fluffed the pillows behind Emma's back, then put the tray over her lap.

The smell of fresh bread and hot tea made Emma almost faint with hunger. But she couldn't dine in front of the mistress of the house.

Lady Fanchere must have been a mind reader, for she said, "I didn't order a breakfast tray to torment you, Miss Chegwidden, or test your self-restraint. I do not starve my people. Eat. Then we can talk."

Walking to the window, she looked out into the sunlight.

With trembling hands, Emma lifted the slice of bread and took a bite. The crust broke into stiff crumbs, the white interior was faintly sour, and someone had trickled lavender honey in a thin stream across the yeasty surface.

Each bite tasted like satisfaction. She finished the slice, ate ham sliced thinly and rolled around a slice of melon, and dabbed at her lips with her napkin. Tia handed her the cup of black tea sweetened with sugar and pale with cream, and she sipped like a worshipper at the altar of Englishness.

When she looked up, Lady Fanchere had turned to watch her, and she was smiling. With the instinct she'd cultivated in service, Emma deduced that Lady Fanchere was a woman who liked to care for others. Finishing the tea, Emma put the cup down and folded her hands in her lap. "Thank you, Lady Fanchere. That was most reviving."

Lady Fanchere gestured to Tia, who pulled a chair to the side of the bed. As Lady Fanchere seated herself, she said, "Tia, would you please remove Miss Chegwidden's tray and get us a new pot of hot tea?"

Tia's bright face dimmed, but she took

the tray, bobbed a curtsy, and moved swiftly out of the room.

Lady Fanchere waited until the door shut behind her before asking, "Could you answer a few questions now, Miss Chegwidden?"

"Of course. I'm delighted to do so."

"Do you remember how you got here?"

"No, I'm sorry. I . . . I remember some of last night, but then . . ."

"The wolf?"

"Yes." The memory of pale, glowing eyes burned in her mind. "There was a wolf!"

"There are few wolves left in the Pyrenees, and the ones that remain are far into the wilderness."

"I *was* far in the wilderness!" Seeing Lady Fanchere's cocked eyebrow, Emma added unsteadily, "I think."

"Tell me what you know, starting with" — an unexpected dimple quivered in Lady Fanchere's cheek — "the fish."

Appalled, Emma put her hand to her temple. "The fish? At the ball?"

"Exactly."

"I hope you don't think badly of me for that. You see, Lady Lettice wanted her handkerchief dampened, and I got lost. I found my way into the garden, which was very dark, wet the handkerchief in the fountain —"

Lady Fanchere gave a gurgle of merriment.

"— and apparently a small, very small fish found its way into the linen folds. I fear I must have stunned it when I wrung out the excess water. I handed Lady Lettice the handkerchief, not knowing . . ."

Lady Fanchere chuckled through every word.

Distressed, Emma said, "Lady Fanchere, please believe me. I didn't do it on purpose. I would not be so foolish as to jeopardize my only employment in a strange land!"

"Ah, yes. You English girls are too sensible for that." Lady Fanchere leaned forward, eyes dancing. "But is it true the fish slid down Lady Lettice's cleavage?"

"Yes, it did, and then . . ." The remembrance of Lady Lettice's nimble jig as she tried to dislodge the fish rose in Emma's mind, and unexpectedly, hilarity caught her by the throat. She giggled, stopped herself, tried to apologize, and giggled again.

Lady Fanchere waved her to silence. "I beg you, don't say you're sorry. It was the highlight of the dullest evening of a completely dull season! I thought I would die laughing. Lady Lettice is all wig and no hair, if you comprehend me, and while I'm not

one to judge someone by their intelligence
— one of my dearest friends is Aimée de
Guignard, a darling and the greatest ninny
in all Christendom — one cannot say the
same about Lady Lettice. That woman is
venal in her gossip and her clever cruelties.
She wouldn't be accepted in society at all,
but here in Moricadia all one needs is a
fortune to be Sandre's best friend." She bit
her lower lip as if regretting that last comment. With a determination Emma admired,
Lady Fanchere changed the subject. "Now,
tell me what happened after you left the
ball."

"After I was thrown out like a strumpet?"
The humiliation added a surprising bite to
Emma's tone. "I walked and walked. It was
cold. I was afraid I was lost, and afraid to
turn back for fear lights and warmth were
around the corner, and then that wolf
stepped in front of me. It was a wolf. It was!
I am not mistaken about that."

"All right. I believe you," Lady Fanchere
said in a soothing tone. "How did you get
away?"

"I turned. I ran. And then . . ."

"Then?"

"I don't know. I don't know!" Emma
rubbed her head with both hands, trying to
coax some vestige of remembrance from her

brain. "There's nothing. I don't know how I escaped being a wolf's late-night meal. I most certainly don't know how I got here."

"You have a bump on the back of your head. Do you know how that happened?"

With cautious fingers, Emma explored her scalp and winced when she found the lump. "I must have fallen. Did someone find me in the woods?"

"You were left unconscious on our doorstep like an orphaned child." Lady Fanchere watched as Emma absorbed the news. "You truly don't remember?"

Emma shook her head in bewilderment.

"There was no rescuer that you recall?"

Emma frowned. Something stirred in her brain. Some vague recollection of hands turning her to face —

A strong whiff of ammonia brought Emma to consciousness with a jolt. She opened her eyes to see Lady Fanchere leaning over her, holding the smelling salts and wearing a troubled expression.

"Thank heavens," Lady Fanchere said. "I've never had anyone faint during a conversation before."

"I'm sorry." Emma tried to struggle back into a sitting position.

"Please lie back." Lady Fanchere seated herself again and waved the smelling salts under her own nose. "We're both shaken. Let's calm ourselves and make sure there are no repeats of that incident."

Emma sank back onto the pillows. "I must have hit my head harder than I realized."

"I think you are right." Lady Fanchere rested her hand on her waist above the curve of her belly. "Well! You may know the Englishman Michael Durant is our prisoner —"

"Yes, I met him last night."

"So he said."

"Did he have something to do with my presence here?" If that was true, she owed him a very great debt.

But Lady Fanchere waved that suggestion away. "Not at all. I was fatigued, so we returned early from the ball. As you may know, Michael is under house arrest, and we're responsible for his custody. Last night, he went to his bedroom in the dowager house" — she waved a hand out the window — "which I assure you is luxurious and befitting his station despite the bars at the windows and the door, and we locked him inside."

"Ah." It was silly of Emma to scorn Durant's easy acquiescence to his imprisonment. Obviously any resistance on his part would be futile and lead to his injury. But to go like a lamb to the shearing . . .

"This morning, after we had discovered you on the doorstep and identified you as Lady Lettice's companion, Michael suggested, and my husband concurred, that *I* need a paid companion." Amusement cut a quirk into Lady Fanchere's cheek. "All the highly fashionable ladies have them."

"I am grateful, my lady." The thought of having a secure future with this woman brought tears to Emma's eyes. But . . . "If you don't mind my saying so, you don't appear to be the type of person to, er —"

Lady Fanchere interrupted, "Care about keeping up with all the other highly fashionable ladies? No. I don't care. But Lord Fanchere's lineage is not so exalted as mine, and he does. So I indulge him."

Emma inclined her head in reply and in thankfulness. "In that case, let me assure you I am well versed in a companion's duties, as well as trained in many aspects of medical care."

"Really?" Lady Fanchere lifted her brows. "Where did you learn that?"

"My father's parish was poor, didn't merit the attentions of any kind of physician, and the barber-surgeon in our little town was a drunkard. So Father taught himself to be the de facto physician and I was his assistant. As I grew older and we dealt with females, we discovered women preferred to speak with me of their problems and seek my help. So I am very good with rubbing away backaches and helping dispel pains in the head and feet. It was for those reasons Lady Lettice kept me in service." Emma experienced a deep satisfaction in knowing Lady Lettice would miss those ministrations. "Although my bag of medical supplies was left in Lady Lettice's room and, I fear, is irretrievable, let me assure you I am especially good with ladies who are with child, so I can be of special assistance to you."

Lady Fanchere rocked back in astonishment, and asked fiercely, "How did you know that? How did you know I am breeding?"

Oh, heavens. Had Emma put her foot wrong already? "I'm sorry. Have I spoken out of turn?"

Lady Fanchere stood, walked to the window, and looked out for a long moment. Finally, she faced Emma. "I've been married almost twenty years, since I was eighteen, and I have always failed to conceive. I've been to spas. I've prayed at shrines. I've tried every remedy medical science and the Church could suggest. And at last, our dearest desire has come true and I . . ."

"You fear to tell the world of your joy before it has come to fruition."

"Exactly. I can't keep it a secret forever, of course, but until I'm sure I'll carry the baby to term, I have been most discreet. So again, I ask — how did you know?"

"As with all happily increasing women, you have a glow about you." Emma smiled at her. "May I say that in my experience, a woman who is slow to conceive does not necessarily have trouble producing a healthy child."

"Thank you for that." Lady Fanchere nodded. "I think you and I will do very well together, Emma Chegwidden."

A knock sounded, and before Lady Fanchere could call permission, the door opened. A man of perhaps fifty stood there, tall, bald, and distinguished. Emma pulled the sheet up, but for all the attention he paid her, she might as well have not been in the room. Instead, he extended his hand to Lady Fanchere. "My dear, I bear sad news."

She rose and hurried to his side. "What has happened?"

He put his arm around her waist, pulled her in to lean on him, and looked into her eyes, his deep concern obvious. "Your cousin Rickie was killed last night . . . by the Reaper."

CHAPTER SEVEN

"One more time, Aimée. Tell me what happened to my cousin Rickie."

"I've told you a dozen times since this morning, Your Highness." Aimée sat huddled in a straight-backed chair in the middle of the antechamber in the royal palace, weeping from fear and exhaustion. "Why won't you believe me?"

"Because what you have told me is absurd." Prince Sandre could barely contain his fury. Aimée had always been a pretty fool, the woman his cousin had married for her fortune and her body and then talked about killing to rid the world of that high, thin voice.

Prince Sandre had always stopped him — no one would have believed it an accident, and the de Guignard family already had a shady reputation. But the irony of having her outlive Rickie had not passed him by.

Sandre knew only that if he yelled at her

or threatened her, she would collapse in a damp heap of panic and he would never get the information he needed. So, keeping his voice low and kind, he said, "Now, Aimée. You were riding in your carriage on your way home from the ball."

"I was telling Rickie about the Reaper." For the first time in Sandre's memory, Aimée's distinctive auburn hair was badly mussed, her plump cheeks looked drawn, and her ivory complexion was blotched.

"He informed you there was no Reaper."

"That's what he said, but I knew he was wrong, and this *proves* it." She lifted her head and stared pitifully at Sandre. "Do you think that by denying the existence of the Reaper he raised its ire?"

"If there is a Reaper, then it is a man in a silly costume, and I will find him and make him sorry he ever dared to ride my roads and kill my cousin."

"Rickie said that, too."

"What?"

"That the Reaper was a man. But he couldn't be. No mere man could have put my husband to death."

She had a point. Who in Moricadia had the nerve to lure Rickie de Guignard, tall, strong, and cruel, out of his carriage with the intent to hang him?

Sandre intended to find out. "I must ask how a ghost could tie a noose and string Rickie up?"

"Maybe he frightened Rickie into committing suicide."

Sandre wanted to take Aimée's skull between his fingers and crack it like a melon, and see whether there were brains inside, or simply a jingling bell.

She continued. "I saw his body. The only bruise he has is around his neck. How else do you explain his death?"

Sandre flicked a glance at his guards. Two Moricadian men stood immobile beside the door, holding swords, with loaded pistols in their belts. They went everywhere with Sandre. Their jobs were to keep him safe. And Sandre secured their loyalty by keeping their wives and children within easy reach — the whole family lived and worked in the palace. So while he never doubted they would defend him to the death, he did not intend that they would go back to their wives and whisper that the Reaper was the ghost of the old king, or a harbinger of the new king's arrival, or that the Reaper had a vendetta against the de Guignards . . . and had killed the most fearsome of them all.

Oh, Rickie. We had such fun together.

The world felt as if it had tilted on its axis,

73

but he was not a man who allowed a ghoul to strike down him and his regime. Stroking the bandage that wrapped his palm, he crooned, "Tell me everything that happened."

"I already told you." She wore black crepe, the garb of a new widow. She dabbed at her blue eyes with a lace handkerchief. Yet all the public markings of mourning could not convince Sandre she had nothing to do with Rickie's death. Not deliberately, of course. She was too stupid for that. But as an unwitting dupe to be used in a scheme to take down the de Guignard family.

That would not happen on Sandre's watch.

"Tell me again." He paced across the room.

"We got in the coach at the party. Everyone was leaving."

"Other guests saw you leave?"

"Of course they did! The main road was crowded. It wasn't until we took the turnoff that it got quiet and . . . and dark. Which made me remember what Lady Lettice had told me about the ghost. So I told Rickie, and that I had a horrible premonition that something awful was about to happen." Aimée took a breath and looked around, all too obviously worried that Sandre wouldn't believe her.

He flicked his fingers at her. "Go on."

"The carriage stopped. Rickie got impatient — you know what he's like — and got out."

She was talking about her husband in the present tense.

"My premonition grew stronger. I begged him not to go."

Her melodramatics were growing stronger, too.

"But he insisted and disappeared into the dark. I was left alone, and I sat and trembled in fear for my husband's life."

"The first time you told me this story, you said you fell asleep."

Impatient at having her monologue interrupted, she said, "I might have drifted off. A little. Maybe once. But I knew something awful was happening and . . . and it haunted my dreams!" Aimée had started to enjoy the attention. "When the carriage began to move, I came to complete consciousness and I called for Rickie. He wasn't there, so I looked out the window and . . . ."

Sandre saw the moment it became real to her again.

She paled, collapsed back in the chair, and her voice became a whisper. "I saw him at the top of the hill, the Reaper, his winding sheet fluttering in the wind. He was staring down at me. . . . I jumped backward and screamed, just . . . I screamed. When I looked out again, he was gone and there was Rickie, hanging by his neck from the tree."

"Was he alive?"

"No. He was hanging by his neck from the tree." She repeated herself as if Sandre were stupid.

"When they're hanged, men don't immediately die. Some hang there for an hour before they find their release . . . unless their necks are broken."

"How would I know that?"

"We have public hangings in this country." Rebellious and rotting Moricadians decorated the lowland valleys where the peasants lived. It was good to remind them how easily and painfully life could be extinguished. "So you did nothing to help Rickie?"

"He was dead! I think. His head was crooked. I pounded on the ceiling of the carriage, so the coachman whipped up the horses and we raced home."

"Last time you told me, you said he whipped up the horses and then you pounded on the ceiling of the carriage."

"I don't remember which came first," she

76

shouted.

One of the guards gasped.

That caught her attention, made her realize what she'd done, and in a soft, conciliatory voice, she said, "I beg your pardon, Your Highness. I am distraught. But I don't remember which came first. I only know that Rickie is dead, and the Reaper killed him."

Out of the corner of his eye, Sandre saw the guards glance at each other. In a hard, cold voice, he said, "I asked that your coachman be brought in for questioning, and do you know what? Your driver was found bound and gagged in Thibault's hayloft by the stable hands this morning. What do you suppose that means?"

She gasped like a fish out of water. "The carriage was driving itself under the command of the Reaper?"

No woman could actually be so stupid.

But Aimée was. Sandre knew she was, although he had to draw several long, patient breaths to cool his rage. "No. Someone jumped him, tied him, and took over the task of driving you home precisely so this 'ghost' could murder Rickie." Before she could come up with some other stupid explanation, he said, "Your ghost has accomplices who do as he bids when he goes forth on his murderous missions."

"Oh." She clasped her hands under her chin, her blue eyes wide with excitement. "Has the ghost killed other men?"

"No. Not yet." Sandre's tone was clipped with annoyance. "For the most part, he poses in his silly costume to terrify the credulous and gullible. But last night, he turned deadly, and I promise you I'll unmask him, and hang him and every man who assists him."

"You can't hang the Reaper. He's already dead," she told him.

"I will find the man who attacked your coachman and kill him by slow inches until he reveals all he knows." Sandre was speaking to the guards.

Aimée wasn't smart enough to realize that, and answered with that lopsided logic. "The servants of King Reynaldo are all long dead, too."

"They're alive! The Reaper and his assistants are living men!" Before she could say more, he snapped, "As a sign of my affection, we're burying Rickie tomorrow in the royal de Guignard plot."

"I hate that cemetery. It's spooky."

"Rickie would wish to be buried there."

"Yes. It fits him, doesn't it?" Aimée bit her lower lip. "I need protection."

"From whom?" he asked sharply. He would never have suspected Aimée was smart enough to know her days were numbered.

"The Reaper will kill me for daring to speak of him."

Did the woman never listen? Was she oblivious to her own safety? She might have saved herself if she agreed the Reaper was merely a man masquerading as a ghost, but her insistence on his supernatural powers had fed the peasants' hope — and doomed her. "I'll have the Reaper in custody before he can harm you."

Aimée hugged herself, her arms protectively around her chest. "May I leave now? I want to go home and get my maid."

"And go where?" he asked cordially, wondering all the while if she intended to leave the country.

"To Lady Fanchere. Eleonore is my dear friend. And your cousin. I need her. *Need* her." Her voice wobbled pathetically.

Lord and Lady Fanchere were his supporters in all things. Eleonore had been his companion when he was a boy, and still believed he retained his youthful ideals. Fanchere was not so blind to Sandre's faults, but he knew on which side his bread was buttered.

Yes, Aimée would go to them and tell her fantastic tale. Eleonore would kindly laugh at the story, and that would be the end of that. In addition, it would be good for Aimée to be seen in their company after this visit with Sandre.

"Then by all means, you should go to Eleonore." He glanced at the window. "But it's a long drive, and it's getting late. Remain here until morning."

"No! I mean . . ." Aimée wildly looked around. "I'm not prepared. I don't have my maid. No clothing . . ."

He almost smiled to see her squirm like a worm on a hook. "Nonsense. This is the palace. We have hundreds of rooms, ladies' clothing of every size, seamstresses for alterations, and maids who are eager to serve. Quico's wife is one of our maids, isn't she, Quico?"

One of the guards nodded stiffly.

"Her name is Bethania. A lovely woman. Very respectful. Very responsible. She lives to please. Isn't that right, Quico?"

Quico nodded again, once, his face blank.

"See? Here you will have your own personal guard to protect you and your own personal maid to give you whatever you wish. Most important, you can't travel in the dark."

"I can. Really."

"You're afraid of the Reaper," he reminded her.

"Yes, but . . ."

Aimée wasn't as stupid as she seemed.

Putting his hands on her shoulders, he helped lift her to her feet. He kissed her forehead. "Tomorrow you may go to Eleonore. For tonight, I insist you stay here. I couldn't bear the guilt if I allowed you to leave and you were killed, too."

She watched him, her eyes wide and unblinking with terror.

"So you will stay. I command it." He waved his hand and Quico opened the door for her. As she tottered out of the room, he said, "You may rest assured, in Rickie's name, I will bring this Reaper to justice."

She cast him one last, petrified glance, and with Quico at her back, she disappeared down the corridor.

At once a new guard took Quico's place.

Sandre's congenial smile faded. He wouldn't kill her tonight. That would be too obvious. He rang for Jean-Pierre de Guignard, his newly anointed second in command.

"How may I serve you, Your Highness?" Jean-Pierre was a lesser cousin, the son of a sot who had died when he broke his neck

81

riding drunk down the meanest street in the old capital, and a noblewoman famed for her expertise in the French style of love — and her willingness to practice it on many men consecutively. So although Jean-Pierre was clever, well-read, and skillful, he was not welcome in the finer homes of Moricadia, not even those of his de Guignard relatives.

For those reasons alone, Sandre knew he could depend on Jean-Pierre to do everything to prove himself worthy of Sandre's trust.

But there was more. Jean-Pierre looked like a de Guignard — dark hair, handsome face, muscular build — yet his eyes were a curiously pale blue. There were theories about why they were that color, most of them amusing, vulgar, and involving his mother and the results of her promiscuity. But Sandre had his own theory. He believed that Jean-Pierre was like a dog on the verge of rabies, and that his eye color was a warning provided by nature to protect the unwary. He believed that Jean-Pierre could be trained to be the deadliest man alive. As long as Sandre held the chain, he would be glad to provide the training.

Now Jean-Pierre bowed low, a little too overcome by his promotion, a little too obsequious. This son of a whore understood the precariousness of his position, and he intended to do whatever he needed to secure it.

Sandre liked the ambition, fear and neediness. He could make use of that.

In a low tone, but loud enough for the guards to hear, Sandre said, "I will not have anyone spreading rumors of the Reaper and his revenge. Carefully, tactfully, silence Aimée."

"As a lesson to all?" Jean-Pierre asked.

Sandre thought of Eleonore and shook his head. "I won't have trouble in the family. But she must be a lesson to others who put their hopes in a royal family that the de Guignards defeated long ago." He gazed at the guards, sending a message to them, their friends, and their families.

They didn't cower. Instead, they looked stoically back.

They had hope — a hope that would have to be quashed.

If his theory was right, Jean-Pierre was just the man to do it.

CHAPTER EIGHT

The next morning, Emma's eyes opened wide. Her heart beat fast; her breath labored in her lungs; she was trapped in the twisted sheets, damp with her fear and sweat.

She'd been dreaming. Of the Reaper. A nightmare of confused images — of a forest with branches that clawed her like fingers, a wolf with glowing white eyes and a ghoul without eyes. Of apprehension and pain and . . . and . . . what? She didn't know.

Sitting up slowly, she freed herself from the panic and her voluminous nightgown.

The nightmare must have been caused by yesterday's news, overheard in a private moment between husband and wife. The Reaper had murdered Lady Fanchere's cousin, hanged him by the neck until he died.

Poor Lady Fanchere had been shocked, but she hadn't forgotten her responsibilities. She had ordered Emma to stay in bed, had Tia return to watch over her, and every time Emma woke she was served small meals designed to tempt a deprived palate.

So yesterday's frailty was vanquished. To dwell on a nightmare was foolish, and she was not foolish. She had been given a chance to make a different life for herself, and she wouldn't fail. This would not be like last time, when she had left England as a companion to Lady Lettice, wide-eyed and enthusiastic at the idea of seeing foreign lands and historic monuments. Instead, she had found herself trapped in one hotel room after another, waiting in dread for Lettice's return.

Emma could serve Lady Fanchere flawlessly — she knew she could — and so she climbed out of bed, steadied herself, then looked around.

The morning was far advanced, the sun shining, and she saw today what yesterday had escaped her attention.

For a servant's chamber, the room was large and well-appointed, and she wondered if, now that she had recovered, she would be sharing it with other serving women. Walking to the window, she looked out at the back of the estate. A sweep of well-tended lawn dropped down to a cliff, precarious in its nature, and there, clinging to the edge, stood a small, old castle — the dowager house that imprisoned Michael Durant. The stones looked cold, but Emma had no doubt that Lady Fanchere had made him comfortable within.

Clean clothing had been hung in the highboy in the corner: undergarments, petticoats, and an attractive blue cotton gown, and on the floor, a pair of simple black leather shoes. She dressed quickly, attaching the white, starched collar and cuffs, finding the waist a little large, the hem a little short, but the material good and — she peeked into the small mirror placed atop the bureau — the color flattering. Her complexion, except for the abrasion on her jaw, glowed like alabaster lit from within.

Abruptly, she stood up straight. She had no reason to be vain. She had always been thin, and her sojourn in Europe had pared off more weight. Her hair was so intensely brown it was almost black, freakishly dark against her fair skin. Her face was oval, starting with a widow's peak in the middle of her forehead and ending in a chin pointed as a witch's, so Lady Lettice said, and Lady Lettice said she had a deplorable habit of allowing her emotions to kindle in her changeable eyes — and those emotions had not been complimentary to Lady Lettice.

For that, Emma had paid, and more than once.

A tray of sliced bread, cheese, and fruit had been left on the bureau, and she ate a quick, satisfying meal, then walked briskly to the door. Opening it, she found a flight of stairs that descended to the second level. She stood there uncertainly, not knowing whether to turn right or left, when a stately gentleman came around the corner.

A second look proved she was wrong. Not a gentleman, but the butler dressed in formal black and white. Middle-aged, tall, and stout, he carried himself with such palpable dignity she identified him as English even before he spoke.

"Miss Chegwidden, I presume." He bowed. "I am Brimley. You're seeking Lady Fanchere?"

She curtsied. "A pleasure to meet you, Mr. Brimley. If you could give me direction, I would be most appreciative."

"Follow me, and while we walk, I'll apprise you of the situation in the household."

"Thank you." He wanted to put her in her place, to impress on her her station here. She didn't mind; as Lady Fanchere's companion, she had become an important cog in the Fancheres' home, and he, as butler, was responsible for keeping that home running smoothly.

Leading her along another corridor lined with closed doors, he said, "You and I are the only two English people in the household. Are you at all familiar with Moricadia?"

"I'm afraid not. I arrived less than a week ago with Lady Lettice, and as you have probably heard, that employment did not end well." She hunched her shoulders and waited for Brimley to make it clear he would not allow any occurrences such as that in the future.

But he had other information he wished to impart. "I've been with the household a little over three years, and found the differences here in Moricadia to be both puzzling and intriguing. As you know, the country is a French protectorate, exotic in its isolation and almost feudal in its society's divisions. Unfortunately, the de Guignards deposed the Moricadian king by hanging him — they are quite fond of hanging. The de Guignard family, led by Prince Sandre, has turned it into an international destination for the noble and wealthy. The poor arc so very poor; the rich are so very rich; there are no native merchants or storekeepers; all money-making ventures are owned by the de Guignards, who rule with an iron hand. I, of course, do not recall the circumstances that led up to the revolution in France, where they beheaded their king, but I do believe the de Guignards have created that situation here. There are no nobles except for the de Guignards and their relatives. There is no parliament. Here, civilization seems to have stopped its progression."

"A harsh assessment."

"Yet true. During my tenure here, I have tried, time and again, to gain the trust of the servants working here. Yet the Moricadians are clannish, distrustful people. Given the betrayals of the past and the dreadful consequences for any perceived traitor to de Guignard's rule, this is perhaps justified." He walked on toward a dazzling light at the end of the corridor.

Emma followed him into the gallery overlooking the massive foyer, and caught her breath in awe and amazement.

The marble floor was one level below, an intricate mosaic of pale peach, gray, and black. The ceiling rose with cathedral-like magnificence to the third level, held erect by pillars of white marble that ended in gold-painted finials. A crystal chandelier glittered. The two front doors were tall and covered in bronze. The multifaceted windows faced south, overlooking a rolling green lawn and neat gardens. Beyond that, the vista opened to reveal the long valley where, Emma knew, a river ran wildly and the old capital brooded in the shadows of the Pyrenees.

The house was rich beyond her wildest imagining. The view was glorious, breathtaking, overwhelming. She turned, wide-eyed, to Mr. Brimley.

"Yes, it is grand." He lowered his voice. "But what I'm trying to tell you, Miss Chegwidden, is that although we live a life of privilege in a spectacular setting, at any moment the powder keg on which we sit may explode."

CHAPTER NINE

At Brimley's warning, Emma's heart quailed. All she wanted from life was employment caring for someone quiet and subdued, perhaps an older woman. Emma could read her stories, look after her in the fading years of her life. . . . When she got back to England, she would ask the Distinguished Academy of Governesses for that kind of position.

When she went to work for Lady Lettice, she had wanted adventure. But not danger. She had never been foolish enough to want danger. If danger existed, she should leave this place.

Then she heard voices from below, ladies' voices, and the clatter of crockery. She heard Lady Fanchere's voice and thought of her worrisome pregnancy, and knew she couldn't leave. She was needed here. Smoothing her skirt, she looked into Brimley's eyes. "Perhaps that is true, Mr. Brimley. Perhaps I will live to regret my decision to stay, but, you see — I have nowhere else to go."

His brown eyes warmed. "I thought that was what you would say. The English do not run from a challenge."

A "challenge"? He considered a revolution a "challenge"? She stared at him with wide eyes. Obviously, Brimley was constructed of stern materials.

He moved toward the stairs. "Lady Fanchere likes her servants to be well treated, and since I am in charge of this household, I urge you to come to me with any needs or concerns."

She hurried after him. "Thank you, I will."

At the top of the steps, he turned to face her and lowered his voice. "However, you are a young person and undoubtedly love intrigue and adventure."

"No!"

Brimley paid her no heed. "Let me caution you against involving yourself in anything resembling conspiracy. Stay away from those Moricadians who appear to be plotting anything. The de Guignard family is ruthless when it comes to maintaining their hold on the country, and they would not hesitate to incarcerate you, Miss Chegwidden. You might be English and female, but they have dared more than imprisonment in the pursuit of those plotting this revolution." He indicated the foyer. "Do you see him?"

A man dressed in a proper black suit made his way across the marble floor. His reddish blond hair was precisely trimmed, and she thought, from this angle, his face looked as if he were perhaps twenty-five or at the most thirty. Yet he moved like an old man, his gait crablike, and one dark sleeve was pinned up, concealing the stump where a hand and arm should be.

"That is Durant's valet. He's Moricadian, and twelve years ago he was accused of assisting a boy to play a prank on Prince Sandre. The boy escaped. Rubio did not." All too vividly, Brimley was showing her the consequences of unwise action. "The de Guignards tortured him on the rack."

"That's medieval!" She watched Rubio disappear into a long corridor.

"Exactly. Before, he walked with confidence wherever he wished. Now each step is agony."

"And his arm?"

"They mangled it so thoroughly that gangrene set in, and to save his life, amputation became necessary."

"Poor man!"

"He's a competent valet, but nevertheless, most gentlemen would not use him. It's kind of Mr. Durant to do so, for if he did not, Rubio would be begging in the streets, and charity is hard to come by in Moricadia."

Fervently, she said, "I understand, Mr. Brimley, and I assure you, I am the last person on earth who seeks anything resembling exciting activities."

"Very good." He led her down to the foyer. "Also, I would appreciate it if you would forget we had this conversation."

"Of course, Mr. Brimley."

"If you would follow Henrique" — he gestured to the uniformed footman moving at a stately pace, tea tray balanced in one hand — "he will guide you to the ladies' tea party."

"Thank you." Henrique led her through the conservatory, a glass-roofed structure filled with roses and their heady fragrance. Here, white roses twined around the gray marble pillars, while red blossoms covered the shrubs clustered around their bases. Down the middle of the room, pink roses climbed on arches surrounding the avenue that led to a sitting area of small tables and dainty chairs where eight elegant ladies spoke in explosive bursts.

"The ghost of King Reynaldo . . . he's come back for revenge."

"He's a harbinger of doom for everyone who sees him. . . ."

"Lucretia laid eyes on him and she's been half-crazy since. . . ."

"Always half-crazy anyway . . ."

"Silliness, all those rumors, he's nothing but a criminal who should be captured, drawn and quartered, then . . ."

"A murderer who'll kill us all in our beds!"

Emma stopped at the entrance, unsure whether to proceed, but Lady Fanchere, obviously desperate for a distraction, caught sight of her and gestured her forward. "Emma, come and assist me."

The talking stopped as Emma hurried to do Lady Fanchere's bidding.

An older woman with a monocle examined her from head to toe, then turned to Lady Fanchere. "My dear, isn't that the girl who put the fish down Lady Lettice's bodice?"

"I've hired her as my companion." To Emma, Lady Fanchere indicated she was chilly.

Emma gathered the shawl off the back of Lady Fanchere's chair and drape it over her shoulders.

"Are you mad?" The lady dropped the monocle. "If the chit will put a fish down

Lady Lettice's bodice, what will she do to you?"

"Lady Lettice was impertinent," Lady Fanchere said.

"A loutish woman," the older woman agreed.

"Exactly, Lady Nesbitt, and she deserved her comeuppance. The fish idea was mine." Lady Fanchere's smug smile both challenged Lady Nesbitt and put Emma in awe of her falsehood, and of the panache with which she delivered it.

Lady Nesbitt first looked shocked and offended, then reluctantly laughed. "I fear our Moricadian society will never be held in respect by other nations while we allow — nay, encourage — vulgarians like Lady Lettice to join our inner circle."

"So true. English noblemen come to Moricadia to gamble and indulge in other, insalubrious activities, yet their noblewomen stay well away. It is only English women of Lady Lettice's inferior quality who visit for a chance to do those activities they would not dare while in England."

As the women in the room nodded and murmured their agreement, Emma took up her position at Lady Fanchere's right shoulder.

Lady Fanchere continued. "Since Lord

Fanchere was most desirous that I have a companion to tend to my needs, and I discovered Emma had been recommended to Lady Lettice by the Distinguished Academy of Governesses . . . You do know of the Distinguished Academy of Governesses, do you not, Lady Nesbitt?"

"I don't know that I do, Lady Fanchere." Lady Nesbitt looked annoyed as only a woman who liked to be on the cutting edge could be.

Lady Fanchere smiled and toyed with the fringe of her shawl. "In 1839, the Distinguished Academy of Governesses was founded by three gentlewomen with the intent to educate and place other impoverished young gentlewomen in positions as governesses to respectable families. When those three women married well — married very well — they sold the academy to Adorna, Lady Bucknell, who as you know is above reproach in every way."

The ladies nodded, mesmerized by Lady Fanchere's recitation.

"Lady Bucknell . . . works?" Lady Nesbitt pursed her lips in disapproval.

"Lady Bucknell holds such an exalted position in English society she does as she wishes, and that includes the expansion of the Distinguished Academy of Governesses into other careers suitable for young women of exceptional birth." Lady Fanchere placed her hand on Emma's arm. "Women like my dear companion."

Emma was equally mesmerized by the realization that Lady Fanchere not only knew about the Distinguished Academy of Governesses and its fabled patroness, but that in this group of women, Lady Fanchere held such a position of respect that no one questioned her absurd tale of how she acquired Emma's services.

"Are there other companions from the Distinguished Academy of Governesses in Moricadia?" one of the younger women asked.

"No, Alceste, but they're getting an international reputation for quality help, and I'm sure you could send to England. . . ."

Alceste was shaking her head even before Lady Fanchere finished her sentence. "Yves would be most displeased at the extravagance. He is a good man, but he squeezes the gold eagle tightly enough to make it squeal."

The conversation shifted to the subject of husbands and their stinginess.

Really, Emma thought, it was better to leap at once into her duties. She wouldn't have time to brood about the loss of her belongings left in Lady Lettice's hotel room. She knew full well Lady Lettice would never consent to give them up, and it wasn't as if any of them had any value other than sentiment. The miniature of her father. The worn copy of *Pride and Prejudice* owned by the mother she didn't remember. The small glass figurine of a spaniel she had bought in Venice, broken in one of Lady Lettice's rages and now minus a leg. The wool shawl woven by the ladies in Freyaburn and given to her as a going-away present. Her bag of tools and medicines . . .

She realized she was blinking away tears, and wondered when she had become such a cowed creature as to cry at the loss of a few meager possessions. Had Lady Lettice and her cruelties really made her so feeble?

"Michael!" Lady Fanchere's voice sounded with quiet delight. "I'm so glad you chose to join us."

Emma looked up to see a tousled, genial Michael Durant posed in the doorway with all the careless grace of Adonis before his worshippers.

"My dear Lady Fanchere." He strode forward to kiss the extended hand. "And my dear Lady Nesbitt." Another hand. "Lady Alceste." Another. And so on through the room, showing clearly that he had spent the time of his house arrest ingratiating himself to the females in Moricadian society.

Emma watched as each lady smiled and fluttered under his admiring gaze, and again Emma fiercely and silently condemned an Englishman too lazy to escape this luxurious prison, a man who renounced his own family to lounge about in a foreign society.

Briefly his gaze brushed Emma, and it was as if the night before had never been. He bowed briefly, then took the chair at Lady Fanchere's side.

Henrique brought a fresh tray of pastries.

Emma began to disperse delicate china plates, and offered linen napkins embroidered with a white "F."

"Have you eaten?" Lady Fanchere poured Michael a cup of tea. All too obviously, she doted on him like a hen with a favorite chick.

"I had a small repast when I woke." His voice was lower and raspier than it had been the evening before.

"Did you enjoy your first ball after so many days and nights of" — Alceste glanced from side to side — "imprisonment?"

Lady Nesbitt sniffed warningly. "Listening ears, my dear Alceste. Spies are everywhere." Taking the laden tray from Henrique, she held it under Durant's nose and gestured to Emma. "Here, dear boy, you're too thin."

Emma presented him with a plate.

Durant accepted it. He held the tea in one hand, balanced the plate on his knee and filled it from Lady Nesbitt's tray. He looked pleased and abashed . . . and tired. Dark circles ringed his eyes, his cravat was loosely tied, and his hair was attractively disheveled. "Last night's ball was glorious."

"It was kind of the prince to allow you attend, was it not?" Lady Nesbitt prompted.

"Prince Sandre defines kindness in a way no other man could." Michael's mouth curled sardonically.

Alceste laughed, an abrupt snort of appreciation.

But when Emma glanced at her, her face was smooth, expressionless.

Michael's cheek quirked. "House arrest under Lord and Lady Fanchere's care could not be kinder. I have bars on the window of my room" — he challenged them with his gaze — "but I come to tea. I am under suspicion of traitorous activity, but I am allowed the services of my valet. I cannot leave Moricadia, but I attend its finest balls."

"Sandre instructed me to allow you as much freedom as I thought reasonable," Lady Fanchere said. "And he kindly suggested you would be entertained by our social gatherings."

"I am wounded, my lady." Michael placed his palm on his chest, fingers splayed. "You obviously don't consider me a rascal or a villain, capable of stealing the Fanchere silver or, even better, absconding with a Moricadian maiden."

The women began to giggle.

"You are absurd." Lady Nesbitt tried to sound stern, but a smile tugged at her mouth.

"Am I so tame a creature that ladies yawn behind their fans at my appearance? Could I not conceive and execute an evil plan to change the palace guard's uniform from blue and red to stylish mauve, or . . . or . . ." He sputtered to a stop.

The women were laughing.

"Or ride about the night-clad countryside dressed like a ghost?" Alceste joked. Then with abrupt embarrassment she slapped her hand over her mouth and gazed, eyes wide with horror, at Lady Fanchere.

Lady Fanchere gestured her forgiveness.

Michael at once stepped into the breach. "Yes! I could be the Reaper. Only a few obstacles stand in my way. My regrettable tendency toward cowardice." He smiled at Alceste.

She dropped her hand away from her face and smiled gratefully.

He continued. "My lack of a worthy horse — my own steed is aged and plodding. The key with which I am locked into my bedroom at night. Accomplices . . ."

Everyone was smiling once more.

For reasons Emma didn't understand, Durant and his smooth charm made her want to roll her eyes and snort. He'd been pleasant the night before. He'd tried to save her, although her own recklessness had put her on the road and her lack of direction had sent her into the forest to face a wolf and . . . a ghostly face with no eyes. She froze. The sounds in the room faded. The plates tumbled from her nerveless fingers. They fell slowly toward the floor, hit the hardwood, and shattered.

Abruptly, she could hear again, move again. One glance around the room proved that everyone was staring at her, some with disdain, some with impatience. "I'm sorry. So sorry." She knelt and tried to pick up the biggest pieces.

Lady Fanchere said, "Emma, leave that. I'm warm."

Taking a fortifying breath, Emma rose and removed the shawl from Lady Fanchere's shoulders.

"Are you sure she's from the Distinguished Academy of Governesses? She certainly doesn't seem to have the necessary graces to be a paid companion," Lady Nesbitt said.

Emma hunched her shoulders.

"She is exactly what I wanted," Lady Fanchere said firmly.

"Are you well, dear Lady Fanchere?" Alceste leaned forward in concern. "First you're chilled; then you're warm."

In the exact opposite reaction, Lady Nesbitt leaned back as if avoiding contamination. "You're not coming down with anything, are you?"

Lady Fanchere placed her hand to her forehead. "I don't know. . . ."

"You *are* looking a little flushed," Durant said. "I heard the plague had broken out in the low town."

His pronouncement had the effect of getting the ladies on their feet, expressing concern as they rushed to the door, leaving Lady Fanchere, Emma, and Durant alone in the study while two footmen cleared away the plates and cleaned the room.

Lady Fanchere chuckled and waved Emma to a seat. "Thank you, Michael. That was very crafty. I was growing weary. Now — I have a job for you. Would you go with

Emma to gather her belongings from Lady Lettice?"

"Oh. No." At the thought of facing Lady Lettice again, Emma wrung her hands. "There's no need —"

"There is every need. I want you to be comfortable and have your belongings. Your clothes. Your mementos." Lady Fanchere looked directly into Emma's eyes. "Your medical supplies."

CHAPTER TEN

"I apologize for the effort you've been forced to make on my behalf." Emma sat in the small cart, gloved hands in her lap, and watched as Durant picked up the reins and urged the pony forward on the road that wound away from the Fanchere estate and toward the glittering resort city of Tonagra.

"I'm under house arrest. I have few pleasures and fewer duties, so accompanying you on this jaunt is a pleasure." He tossed his tall hat into the corner by his feet.

She faced straight ahead with the brim of her bonnet protecting her from his gaze, but she thought she heard the echo of amusement in his voice. "I would not call it a jaunt; nor will it be a pleasure."

"This is a lovely summer day. The setting is gorgeous." He swept an arm around at the mountains towering above the winding road. "The company is charming. If the errand turns arduous, then we'll have paid for our joys." In a voice quite different from his usual laughing amusement, he said, "When a man spends a lifetime in the dark, he learns what's important in life, and he seizes it in both hands."

Turning her head, she observed him in surprise. Did he mean that?

It seemed he did. Before they started, he had removed his jacket and placed it in the hamper hooked on the back of the cart, and now, without his hat, with the breeze ruffling his hair, he looked not at all like a proper English nobleman. Not that Durant was improper. He held the reins with one hand, controlling the pony without effort, yet he took his ease against the seat, lounging carelessly with legs outstretched and one arm draped over the edge of the cart.

She sat with stiff attention, making sure the movement of the cart didn't accidentally make her sway in his direction, taking care that her shoulder didn't bump his. "What is it you would seize?"

"A sunny day. A good glass of wine. A child's smile." He turned to her, his green eyes serious. "My one chance at love."

Was he flirting with her? Surely not.

Then she remembered his captivating performance during Lady Fanchere's tea, and realized he probably was. For this

English lord, flirting was apparently as necessary as breathing. So in repressive tones, she said, "Admirable sentiments. Would you not seize your chance at freedom?"

"I take what blessings I can, thank God for them, and while I enjoy my current seeming liberty, I'm intelligent enough to know that escape from even so small a country as Moricadia is impossible in a pony cart with a beast such as this pulling it." He pointed with the whip.

Emma was forced to admit he had a point. The pony was round as a barrel, with a lethargic disposition and a pink bow in her mane. If she could gallop, and Emma saw no reason to suppose she could, her legs were so short a greyhound would pass her in the first hundred yards.

"If I were to try to escape, it would be faster on foot, and my boots are too worn for that." With a laugh, he showed her his sole.

She was shocked to realize she could see his sock through the hole in the leather. "What? Why?"

"I was wearing them when the prince in his infinite wisdom commanded I be sent to prison, and since then, they became . . . shabby."

She considered what inquiry to pose next. *Don't you have another pair of boots? Can't you have them resoled? Have you considered cutting several sheets of paper to a size larger than the hole and placing them inside?*

Instead she blurted, "What did you do wrong?"

"To be arrested, you mean? Nothing. However, I was *accused* of assisting the enemies of the de Guignard regime, and I was told I would be held until I gave up the names of the conspirators."

She remembered Brimley's admonition about staying away from intrigue, remembered too that he had said the de Guignards never hesitated to arrest anyone they suspected of plotting treason. It was Durant of whom he was speaking. "Why didn't you?"

"Do I *look* like the kind of man who knows any conspirators?"

She had to admit he didn't. Any man too lazy to fix his boots or buy new ones was too lazy to bother with the messy business of insurrection. "Why did they let you out?"

"They hope I'll lead them to the conspirators."

"While you're under house arrest?"

"They watch my movements, study anyone with whom I dare speak or spend time." He smiled at her. "You should be frightened

109

to be seen with me. Perhaps they'll believe *you're* a revolutionary."

"A revolutionary?" She gave a choked laugh. "No one would ever believe that of me."

"Because you're female?"

"No, because I'm a coward."

"At the Thibaults' party you were not at all a coward."

"I swear to you, sir, I didn't put that fish down Lady Lettice's bosom on purpose."

"I realize that. I was referring to your flight into the forest."

Her heart leaped in alarm, and she turned on him. "What do you know about that?"

He leaned away from her, looking surprised. "I know that you have a propensity for getting lost, and that you were put out on the road and weren't seen again by any of the guests leaving the party, so I assume you turned the wrong way and got lost."

"Oh." For the first time on this drive, she relaxed against the seat. "I'm sorry; I don't quite remember what happened." Pressing her hand to the bump on her head, she closed her eyes and tried to conjure up the scene in the woods. There was a wolf and something that frightened her even worse than the wolf. . . . a face . . .

"You don't remember?" He sounded

astonished, even avid. "You don't remember how you got from the wilderness to the Fancheres' doorstep?"

Opening her eyes, she stared straight ahead. "I know I sound insane, but truly, until this incident, my memory was excellent."

"Well." He shrugged. "Your arrival is a fortuitous mystery, then."

"Yes." Her gaze fell to her hands, clenched into tight, white-gloved fists.

She didn't want to talk about it anymore.

The road wound along the long ridge that ran through woods and meadows and almost the length of the country. Off to the right and above was a string of grand châteaux like Lord and Lady Fanchere's, sumptuous in their excesses, overlooking a series of valleys below. As the pony cart rounded a bend, another view came into sight. Here the cliff disintegrated into a series of stair steps, the foundation of Tonagra, the capital city. Here the finest hotels, spas, and eating establishments existed for the sole purpose of attracting the moneyed wanderers who traveled Europe to see its culture and taste its wonders.

Here Lady Lettice had taken her rooms in the Hotel Moricadia, and Emma shivered at the thought of confronting her. "Maybe she won't be in," she said.

Durant followed her train of thought without problem. "Maybe not, but I do hope she is. I would like to justly compensate her for her treatment of you."

In alarm, Emma said, "Sir, I do not seek vengeance." Suddenly uncertain, she added, "I mean, if that is what you intend."

"Vengeance is a very strong word, and certainly I wouldn't dream of hurting Lady Lettice in any . . . meaningful way. But I hate bullies."

Emma chewed on that, trying to decide if he meant that he intended to create a scene more awful than the one she imagined, or she was making more of his words than he intended. She glanced at him and found his gaze fixed darkly up and slightly behind. The road had turned away from the valley and toward the upper elevations, and, following his gaze, she saw a sight that had escaped her before.

Elevated on a gray pinnacle, set higher and separated from the rest, a medieval castle grew from the rock. It was tall and craggy, primal as a hunting hawk, with spires and crenellations like claws tearing at the bright blue sky. "What is that?"

He brought the pony to a halt outside the massive iron gates opening onto a rolling estate. "That is the royal castle of Moricadia and long the home of the Moricadian royal family . . . and now of Prince Sandre."

"It looks as if it could withstand a siege right here and right now."

"Absolutely. No guests uninvited by Prince Sandre can reach the castle. The road to the drawbridge winds up and down and around that pinnacle, and at any point, he could easily repel an assault. Of course, in this modern age, no one tries to assault the castle, but even for so simple a thing as to attend a party, the road requires a team of good horses to pull the carriage."

"And that's the only way up?"

"There's a path up to the postern door, too, where the shopkeepers bring the supplies for the kitchen . . . and the bodies are carried out."

"Bodies?" She laughed uncertainly.

"Below the kitchens are the dungeons. They aren't a pleasant place." He smiled, a stretching of his lip muscles to show his teeth.

She watched him in fascination. Never had she seen a man so nakedly show his fear and loathing. "That's where they kept you?"

"Yes."

"Did they hurt you?"

Now he looked genuinely amused. "No. Of course not. I'm a subject of the British Empire. They wouldn't dare."

His assurance comforted her, helped her settle back once more.

He slapped the reins against the pony's back and it trotted on, indolent and genial.

The breeze blew in her face. The air smelled of forest and grass. The sun was warm on her shoulders. This would be the ideal drive . . . "If only . . ."

Again he followed her thoughts. "I assure you, I won't let Lady Lettice hurt you — which I think she has done, has she not?"

"She can be unpleasant in a temper." A mastery of understatement. "You must think me a poor thing to be frightened of a mere woman."

"No. I of all people understand how a bully strips away every bit of courage and leaves you trembling before the fear of pain and death."

She thought about that. "I thought you said they didn't hurt you."

"A dungeon is a disagreeable place to pass two years of your life."

She suspected that he, also, was a master of understatement.

They rounded the corner, passed through

the medieval gate and into the city, crammed with gaming establishments, hotels of all sizes, and spas that bragged of their natural springwater and its healing properties. Emma's heart drummed faster as they approached the inn where she had lodged with Lady Lettice. To face her again, after all the abuse and the humiliation of the other night . . . Emma could scarcely breathe.

Durant stepped from the cart, handed the reins to the doorman, and set the step. She put her hand in his and climbed down; then, at his slight bow, she walked ahead of him into the lobby. With the assurance of a man who knew himself to be welcomed anywhere, Durant walked to the front desk and introduced himself to Bernhard, the desk clerk, then said, "I've come to fetch Miss Emma Chegwidden's belongings from Lady Lettice. Is she in?"

"Yes, my lord, but she has decided to vacate her room and is now in the process of packing for her return to England." Bernhard was a German immigrant, with a pronounced accent and the militant attitude necessary to run a large hotel.

He scared Emma to death, yet with Durant at her side, she found herself asking incredulously, "She's packing for herself?"

Bernhard recognized her, and met her gaze with exasperation he clearly expected her to share. "Ha. No. She has four of our chambermaids collecting her belongings, and has kept them working for more than five and three-quarter hours. She doesn't seem to realize that the girls are not for her sole use, that the other guests have need of services, and that we need to clean that room for our arrivals tonight!"

"Lady Lettice is not a woman of large understanding," Emma said.

"No. She is not!" Bernhard was fuming. "She complained so vociferously of the fireplace smoking, we brought in a chimney sweep and kept him waiting for three hours this morning. I finally sent him up in the hopes the soot will drive her out."

"So since Lady Lettice is packing and we need Miss Chegwidden's possessions, we should go up." With a decisive nod, Durant turned to Emma. "Which room is hers?"

"She took the whole second floor," Emma said faintly.

"Of course." He offered his arm.

Bernhard drew himself up, offended. "My lord, I can't allow you to visit an unmarried lady's room."

"I suspect you had no idea where I intended to visit when I came into the lobby,"

Durant suggested.

Bernhard considered that. Heard a pounding from above like someone was stomping on the floor. And said, "You are right. I didn't."

The climb up the stairs took hours, yet was over too soon, and Emma led him to the lioness's den. Louvers at the top and bottom of the door allowed for ventilation in the summer heat, and from inside, they heard a repetitious rasping noise.

They exchanged puzzled glances.

Durant raised his hand to knock — and they heard a thump, a scream of agony, and Lady Lettice's voice shout, "Get that filthy beast out of here before he does any more damage!"

CHAPTER ELEVEN

A second scream pierced the air, and before Michael's gaze, Emma transformed from a timid, proper English girl into a steely-eyed Amazon. Turning the doorknob, she strode into the luxurious suite of rooms.

There, in the sitting room, holding his arm and rolling in agony on a soot-covered sheet placed before the fireplace, was a young boy no more than seven.

Lady Lettice was in her nightclothes and cap, wrapped in a white velvet robe now spotted with black, dancing up and down and shouting at the boy and the chimney sweep, who in his turn stood shouting at the boy.

The four maids crowded into the doorway of the bedchamber, watching with wide, dark eyes and exclaiming in the Moricadian language.

Emma paced into the middle of the chaos, pushed the chimney sweep aside, pulled off her gloves, and tossed them on the side table. "Get me my medical bag," she told Lady Lettice.

"Get you your medical bag? What medical bag? Nothing here is yours. Nothing!" Lady Lettice shrieked at a decibel so high Michael knew dogs howled for miles.

Emma knelt, her knee in the powdery black soot, caught the boy by the shoulders, and spoke softly in his ear. Somehow she made him focus his gaze on hers, and when she had his attention, she took his forearm in her hands. Carefully, she slid her fingers over his skin, shook her head, and murmured, "Broken."

Michael couldn't take his eyes off her. How did she know? When had she learned so much? Turning to Lady Lettice, he intended to demand Emma's medical bag.

Before he could move, Emma bounded to her feet and turned on the woman like a virago. "Give me my medical bag. Now."

Lady Lettice's bosom and chins quivered with indignation. "I will not. You made a fool of me. You made me a laughingstock."

The words spilled forth from Emma like water from a broken a dam. "Lady Lettice, you need no help to be a laughingstock. You are an older woman courting younger men. You are of low morals and without gentility.

Society laughs because you deserve to be laughed at. So, madam, give me my bag and I'll let you leave Moricadia without telling everyone of your disreputable peccadilloes."

Lady Lettice reared back, lifted her hand, and prepared to swing.

Michael caught her arm. "No." A simple word, spoken forcefully.

Lady Lettice looked at him, looked at Emma's blazing aquamarine eyes, and crumpled. "Your medical bag? I lost it. I gave it away. I threw it in the garbage on the street of this lousy stink hole."

Emma walked around her, pushed past the maids, and entered the bedroom.

Michael held on to Lady Lettice's wrist while she turned her pleading gaze on him. "You have to understand. I was good to her, and she was nothing but an ungrateful slut who went behind my back and frolicked with the gentlemen who might have wanted me for their wife. It is her fault I am held in disrespect."

Emma came out of the bedroom with a carpetbag clutched in her hands.

Lady Lettice had apparently convinced herself she spoke the truth about Emma, for she had tears in her eyes.

Emma didn't care. All her attention was on the child. "Michael, I'm going to need help," she said, and he thought she would be shocked to realize she used his Christian name and a command tone.

Certainly Lady Lettice was shocked when he obeyed the unspoken summons, going to kneel beside her in the soot and wrap his arm around the boy's shoulders.

"What's your name?" Emma asked the child.

The boy didn't answer, and the chimney sweep flushed with anger. "Answer the lady, you miserable churl!"

Emma lifted her head and looked at the man. "Get out." She was using that voice again.

But the chimney sweep was the type of man who equated obeying a woman with weakness, and he snarled, "I paid for that kid and I'm not leaving her alone with some madwoman who wants to coddle her because she fell and got herself hurt."

Emma looked at the sweep, and the gold in her eyes had vanished. They were now as hard and cold as green crystal. "This is a *girl?*"

"They're thinner, smaller, and they're always worried about the little ones at home, so they work harder. They're motivated, you might say." His voice rang with pride at his perceived intelligence, and he laughed. He didn't even see the danger until Michael's fist was an inch from his face.

Then it was too late to duck.

Lady Lettice screamed.

The sweep stumbled back, smashing into the wall, leaving a black mark that looked like a giant mosquito had been swatted there. His flailing arms brought down the Chippendale side table, the Chinese vase, the fresh flowers, and the lace scarf. The reverberation made the painting in its gilded frame swing wildly, then fall off and smack the sweep on the head. He slumped, unconscious, to the floor.

The girl under Emma's hands chuckled hoarsely; then in rough, accented English, she whispered, "Elixabete. My name is Elixabete."

"Elixabete, did you fall from the chimney?" Emma made eye contact again.

The child nodded.

"Your arm is broken. I'm going to wash it off; then this gentleman and I will straighten it. I won't lie to you: It's going to hurt very badly, but afterward it will feel much better, I promise. All right?"

Elixabete nodded, her eyes shockingly blue in her blackened face, her hopeful gaze fixed onto Emma's.

Emma pointed at one of the maids. "Bring

me water and a towel. Michael, hands here on her shoulders." Emma laid out a clean cloth, then removed from her bag a corked jar, two sticks, and cloth torn into strips.

Elixabete didn't stir, but she watched all the movements in the room.

With calm efficiency, Emma washed the arm, murmuring to the child all the while, reassuring her. Then, eyes half-closed, she felt along the bone with careful movements. She gave Michael a warning glance, took a long breath; then in a smooth, assured movement, she adjusted the arm.

Elixabete screamed. Tears leaked from her eyes and ran in rivulets down her sooty face.

Lady Lettice drew in a sharp breath, and fainted in an ungraceful heap on the floor.

Bernhard strode into the room, with one glance took in the unconscious chimney sweep, his unconscious guest, and the coal dust and water that stained the rug and the wallpaper, and broke into excited German that condemned the morals of everyone's parents in the room, most specifically Michael's.

As far as Emma was concerned, Bernhard might not have been there. She again felt the broken bone, then, with a satisfied smile, plastered the arm with a grainy white material, splinted it, secured the splint with strips of cloth, and looked around. The long lace scarf that had draped the table caught her eye. She caught one end of it.

Bernhard grabbed the other and screamed like a girl. "No. No, you may not!"

They played tug-of-war over the scarf until she turned a cold look on him and asked, "Would you like to find yourself in the same position as those two?" She nodded at Lady Lettice and the sweep.

Michael rose.

Bernhard took one look at Michael's clenched fists and let go of the scarf. "I will call the prince's men now!"

"You should," she said cordially. "But before you do, you have a guest who's insensible on the floor. You should tend to her before she wakes and discovers you've been indifferent to her needs. I assure you, Lady Lettice would make her displeasure known."

Bernhard wavered, then hurried to Lady Lettice's side and knelt, slid his arms under her, and lifted her off the floor with an audible, "Oof!"

Lady Lettice groaned, stirred, and curled her arms around his neck.

At Bernhard's horrified expression, Michael grinned. *Yes, my friend, you are in trouble now.* He spoke to one of the maids, still trapped in Lady Lettice's bedroom, then leaned against the wall and watched Emma's deft handling of the situation. Apparently he had misread Miss Chegwidden. She was not the limp biscuit he had first perceived — or she seemed to think.

Emma wrapped the scarf around Elixabete, immobilizing her arm.

When she was finished, Elixabete said in a tone of surprise, "It does feel better!"

"Good." Emma smiled at the child, her face warm and kind. Then she looked up at Michael, and determination shone through the dust and sweat on her face. "We need to get her home."

Michael sobered. "As you say."

But he knew Emma was not prepared for the sights she would see.

CHAPTER TWELVE

As the pony cart descended into the old town, the roads got narrower and narrower, the houses taller, the shadows darker. The old town stank of garbage, and sewage ran in open gutters. People, unwashed and hostile, stopped to watch Durant, Emma, and Elixabete as they drove by.

Emma clutched the child closer, murmuring reassurances, while she wondered if they would be attacked for their shoes or her medical kit or the cheerful ribbons woven in the pony's mane.

Yet Durant seemed to know where he was going, driving with assurance through the twisted streets to a gray, empty courtyard surrounded by tall tenements. Jumping out of the cart, he called, "Damacia!"

At once the shutters on the fourth floor swung open, and a young woman with an old face looked out. At the sight of the child, she paled.

"Mama!" Elixabete called faintly.

Durant started to speak, but Emma called, "She's going to be all right. Her arm is broken, but it set well."

Damacia covered her eyes briefly, then disappeared into the room. In only a few minutes, she appeared in the doorway on the ground level and ran to the side of the cart.

Elixabete leaned forward, wordlessly begging to be held.

Carefully, with Durant's support and Emma's assistance, Damacia picked Elixabete up. "You foolish lass, I've told you to stay home or you'd come to trouble." She scolded her and at the same time cradled her against her chest.

"The baby's crying all the time. She's hungry." Big tears filled Elixabete's eyes. "We need my wages, and now . . . now what?"

Emma had never heard such despair, and from such a small child.

"Shh." Damacia lifted her chin. "We'll make do."

Durant met Emma's eyes and shook his head briefly, urgently. He didn't want her to offer . . . anything.

Pride. These Moricadians were too proud to accept help, yet how desperately they needed it!

Other people appeared in windows and around the fringes of the courtyard, and two women ventured to the well in the center to draw water, all the while staring and observing.

"Thank you for bringing Elixabete home," Damacia said. "Thank you both. Ever since Rickie de Guignard was killed, we've barely stirred out of our rooms for fear of the prince's men catching us and asking their questions. Once they've held you, you might as well die of the shame."

One of the women at the well thumped her bucket on the cobblestones. "Quiet, Damacia. For the sake of your children."

Damacia shook her head fiercely. "This is the *Englishman*."

Both women inhaled sharply. They seemed to know Durant by that title.

One bobbed a curtsy.

The other one, the one who offered a warning, edged away.

Emma watched, trying to understand, and thinking, *This is a society broken and divided by fear.*

Durant lowered his voice. "Has retaliation been bad?"

"Not too bad. *They* don't really think it was any of us. *They* think we're not smart enough to make a plan to be the Reaper. *They* know we haven't the money for a fast horse, and *they* know most of us have never ridden. *They* imagine we're too cowed to try to kill a pig like Rickie de Guignard." Damacia's voice vibrated with outrage. "Maybe we are, but we're glad he's gone."

"Damacia. Quiet." The other woman at the well spoke urgently.

Durant and Damacia paid her no heed.

"I heard that the Reaper is frightening away the gamblers who bring their money and squander it at Prince Sandre's tables," Durant said.

"Good." Damacia laughed harshly. "I heard that Prince Sandre is angry because his men can't catch and eliminate the Reaper, and he's afraid he'll become the butt of all the jokes in Moricadia. Our prince does not like to be viewed as a fool."

"Then he shouldn't try to catch the Reaper. The Reaper is the ghost of King Reynaldo, and ghosts can't be captured." Durant looked quite serious, as if he believed in ghosts.

Emma didn't believe in ghosts . . . or she hadn't until she came to Moricadia. Now a barely remembered skeletal face made her so faint with fear she dropped plates and wondered if she had been hallucinating.

"I heard that rumor, too. Maybe he is. I don't care. Rickie de Guignard killed my husband." Damacia spoke to Emma now, as if Emma would understand.

"I am sorry," Emma said.

"He left Tiago's body hanging at the crossroads for the birds to pluck out his eyes. I'm glad Rickie suffered the same fate, and I hope the birds had a chance at him before they cut down the body."

The violence of Damacia's sentiments shocked Emma, yet at the same time . . . if she had someone to love, and he had been so unjustly taken from her . . . She wasn't without emotions. Surely she would be angry. Maybe even unforgiving.

She didn't know. It had been so long since she allowed herself to feel anything but dull acceptance, she didn't know what she would feel.

Durant lowered his voice. "I also heard that Reynaldo's ghost is the harbinger of the true king's return."

The two women edged closer, straining to hear.

Damacia stared at him. "Is it?" Her words were no more than a breath.

"Of course, it would be worth more than your life to repeat such a report." His eyes glinted as he spoke.

Damacia nodded without taking her gaze from him. "Yes. That would be very dangerous. I won't repeat it."

But the two ladies at the well stood transfixed, and Emma thought that if Durant was trying to start a rumor, he'd done a good job.

In a more normal voice, he said, "Elixabete seems to be an intelligent young lady. After a few days of recuperation, send her to Lady Fanchere's. She has a position open for a scullery maid, and I know Miss Chegwidden would be glad to recommend her."

"Indeed I would." Emma smiled warmly at Damacia and her child. "Do you need assistance taking Elixabete to your rooms?"

"No, I thank you. My friends will help." Damacia backed away from the cart. "Elixabete, say thank you to Miss Chegwidden."

"Thank you." Elixabete tried to smile, but her face was pinched with pain.

"Oh, wait." Emma opened her medical bag and rummaged among the jars tumbled by Lady Lettice's careless hand. She found the one she wanted and offered it. "Boil a spoonful of ground white willow bark in water, let it steep for thirty minutes, then have her drink it. She'll feel better tomorrow."

Durant climbed into the cart and slapped

131

the reins on the pony's back.

Emma turned back and called, "Keep that arm immobilized!"

She waited until they had driven out of the cesspool of lower Tonagra before bursting out, "Why is it like that there?" He started to answer, but she didn't wait. "This country is so rich. So much money comes in from the rich visitors. And the native Moricadians live like that? Why?"

"Because the de Guignards and Prince Sandre have the power to hold the wealth, and they do."

"That's what Brimley said. But it's a small country. The de Guignards could share the tiniest bit of what they have, and what a difference that would make. Leaving people to live like that" — she gestured back toward the tenements — "it's criminal!"

"Yes."

"Can nothing be done?"

"I was in prison for two years because Sandre thought I knew something about a conspiracy. So no. Nothing can be done." He stared straight ahead, his expression stern, aristocratic. "Miss Chegwidden, keep your nose out of Moricadian business."

Outrage almost lifted her from the cart. Two years in prison, yes. That was horrible in a way she knew she couldn't comprehend.

But to speak so coldly of this outrageous neglect, to say there was nothing to be done, when he was so pleasantly situated!

"Miss Chegwidden. You will not get involved with the Moricadian people." His tone made it clear he was giving an order. "It's hopeless. There are too many. You are no crusader, so don't start now."

She looked around. The Moricadian countryside embraced them, beautiful, rugged . . . cold, cruel, and hard. If Lady Fanchere turned her out, she would be on that road into the forest again, back toward a fate composed of fear and starvation.

Her indignation collapsed. He was right. Courage was a luxury she couldn't afford, and didn't have anyway. In a small voice, she asked, "Does Lady Fanchere really have an opening for a scullery maid?"

"She's very kind, so yes, soon it will come to her attention that she needs another child to scrub the andirons."

He wasn't so bad, really. He was generous in a careless way, and he'd helped her set Elixabete's arm without hesitation. She needed to stop judging him so harshly. After all, he was no more of a coward than she was herself . . . although he did have family and wealth to support him, should he choose. And for the life of her, she didn't know why he didn't choose that oh-so-easy life. Michael Durant was a bit of an enigma.

For the first time since they'd walked into the chaos of Lady Lettice's room, Emma looked at Durant, really looked at him, and saw a man streaked with coal dust. "You're a mess!" she said.

"My dear girl. That's the pot calling the kettle black. Literally." With two fingers, he wiped across her cheek, then showed her the soot that colored his skin.

In horror, Emma looked down at her gown, the handsome gown she'd found waiting for her this morning. Black stained the material over the knees. She had soot on the bodice and all over her right arm, and somehow, somewhere, she'd torn her white cuff off completely. "This is the second gown I've ruined in two days. Do you think Lady Fanchere will notice?"

Leaning his head back, he roared with laughter; then, when he had stopped, he leaned back and looked at her. Just looked at her, but the expression in his eyes was different. Interested, or intrigued, or . . . something. "I think she will. And very soon." Still smiling, he turned the cart into the Fancheres' estate.

"Can you take me to an entrance where I won't be seen going into the château?" She spread her hands in her lap. Her nails were stuffed with soot, and somewhere she'd lost her gloves.

"Of course. The château is full of passages and entrances." Driving her to a small side door, he stopped the cart before a stoop. "Before the Fancheres moved the kitchen, this served as the servants' entrance. It will take you on the shortest route to your room." When she prepared to climb out, he stopped her with a hand on her arm.

She looked at it warily. What did he intend?

"Listen carefully while I give you directions to the servants' quarters," he said.

She relaxed. "Thank you." So he had had a peculiar expression in his eyes when he looked at her. He had been a perfect gentleman. She was foolish to imagine anything else.

She listened as he told her which stairs to take and how many corners to turn. She assured him she could find her own room, although she was none too sure of that, and allowed him to help her to the ground. She hurried toward the château.

His voice stopped her. "Miss Chegwidden."

She turned, once more on edge.

He opened the hamper at the back of the

cart and brought forth her medical bag.

"Thank you!" She had almost forgotten it. She turned away.

Again he called, "Miss Chegwidden."

She swung back to see him holding another bag, her old, worn travel bag that seemed stuffed with . . . "My clothes! How did you get them?"

"I had the maids collect them while you were busy with the child."

"Thank you, you've saved my life!"

"No, Miss Chegwidden, I did not save your life, and let us both pray I never have to try."

"True. I wouldn't like that, either." Because she didn't believe he could do it.

Opening the travel bag, she found her second-best gown crammed within and undoubtedly wrinkled, but at least clean. Beneath that was the wool shawl the ladies in her village had woven for her, her father's miniature, her mother's copy of *Pride and Prejudice.* "You have done a great many services for me today," she told Durant. "I will remember, and I promise, somehow, I'll repay you."

"I'll hold you to that." When she looked at him, startled and abruptly worried, he smiled with well-practiced insouciance and slouched against the cart. "Do you remember my directions to your room?"

"Yes. Thank you again!" With a wave, she hurried into the château.

He watched until the door closed behind her.

Before his arrest, he had been carried away by pleasure, by anger, by the love of adventure. Wherever his feelings took him, he willingly went without prudence or forethought. His brother had complained about Durant's excess, telling him that sooner or later, it would get him in trouble.

Jude had been right, and someday, Durant intended to tell him so. But for now . . . On his release, Durant had discovered the dungeon's dark loneliness had pressed away his capacity for delight.

How fascinating that, after so long, a woman as cautious and jumpy as a kitten should make him feel real emotion. Miss Chegwidden made him laugh. That laughter felt familiar, as if something in him well remembered when he took joy from every day. At the same time, the amusement that bubbled up in him felt new, as if he'd never felt the sunshine on his face, smelled the cut grass, experienced the pleasure of listening to a pretty girl.

Miss Chegwidden was right to be wary. He had a mission to accomplish, and then . . . and then, she would discover the manner of man Michael Durant had become.

CHAPTER THIRTEEN

Emma recited Michael's directions to herself while dodging maids and footmen, and made it all the way to the servants' quarters without being seen.

Then her luck ran out.

Lord Fanchere paced up and down the corridor. He looked worried, running his hands across his bald head, ruffling the tufts of hair around his ears, and she thought — she wasn't certain, but she thought — he had staked out her bedroom door.

She picked up speed. Had something happened to Lady Fanchere?

Catching sight of her, he burst into speech. "Thank God you have returned. Where have you been?" Before she could even try to answer, he gestured dismissively. "Never mind that. Come at once. I want you to take my wife and her cousin to the spa to take the waters."

"Your wife and her cousin . . ." What he

said was so very different from what she had expected. "Lady Fanchere is well?"

"Very well, but she must go to Aguas de Dioses at once."

"I . . . I don't understand. If she is well, why must she . . . ?"

"Aimée is crying because her husband is dead, God rot him. She says the Reaper killed him, and that Prince Sandre is going to kill her for saying so."

Emma nodded as if she understood, when all the while her mind was racing to put together the clues. . . . The Reaper had killed Rickie de Guignard, so this Aimée was Lady de Guignard, Rickie's wife. Or rather, his widow. "But why is Prince Sandre perturbed by Lady de Guignard's declaration? I thought the Reaper *had* killed Rickie de Guignard."

"Don't *you* start saying that. If Sandre's official story is that the Reaper doesn't exist and didn't kill Rickie, then anyone who contradicts him could suddenly disappear. Do you comprehend me?"

"Yes. Yes, I fear I do." Had she not been told this already today?

"Eleonore likes you, she's become attached to you, and your disappearance would distress her." Lord Fanchere pointed a finger at her. "I won't have her distressed.

Aimée is saying things that will bring San-dre's wrath down upon us, *and* ruining Ele-onore's serenity. I want Aimée muffled and distracted. Ergo . . ."

"The spa. But . . . is not Lady de Gui-gnard in black crepe and deepest mourn-ing? For her to go out in public at such a time will surely create a scandal."

"She's wearing black. But I assure you, she is not in mourning, and Aguas de Di-oses is a place where ladies go to take the waters, to bathe, and to recover from grief and disappointment. No one will gossip." He seemed very sure.

But Emma was still doubtful. In England, this plan would be unacceptable. But more than once since she'd arrived in Moricadia it had been forcibly borne in on her that she was not in England any longer. "Very well. Let me clean up and change my gown —"

"No time for that." He caught her wrist and tugged her down the corridor. "Come on!"

Horror-stricken, she tugged back. "My lord, I can't go to your wife in this state."

He glanced at her, and for the first time seemed to see her and the stains that cov-ered her from head to toe. "What did you do? Fall in a chimney pot?"

"Something like that."

"Perfect." He walked on again, dragging her after him. "Both women will be aghast at your plight."

He seemed a very odd man, but worried to death about his wife, and for that, Emma liked him. But to appear before Lady Fanchere and Lady de Guignard in such a state . . . "This isn't proper."

"This is Moricadia. Propriety takes a backseat to profit, to expediency, and especially to survival." He glanced back at her with a pitying eye. "I know it's hard to believe, in light of the luxury that surrounds us, but we live balanced on the narrow blade of a sword, and one wrong move could be fatal. Right and wrong have become muddled in this country, so please, Miss Chegwidden, for your own sake, say as little as possible and don't get involved with matters of conscience."

"You're the third man to give me such a warning today."

"Take that as a sign." He stopped before a wide double door.

From within, Emma could hear loud weeping.

He placed his hands on the doorknobs. "Now, remember. Your task is to move them to Aguas de Dioses. So . . . distraction.

142

Distraction. Distraction!" Flinging open the door, he called, "Eleonore, Miss Chegwidden seems to have gotten herself into trouble again. Can you and Aimée help her?"

The trip to Aguas de Dioses was accomplished with relative ease. While Lady Fanchere and Aimée exclaimed over Emma's spoiled gown, their maids packed their bags. By the time Emma was bathed and dressed in yet another new gown, the traveling coach was at the door. Lord Fanchere handed the ladies, and Emma, into the coach and admonished them to relax and enjoy themselves. The road was good, the coach well sprung, and when they arrived at the spa in the early evening, Emma exclaimed in surprise and delight.

Aguas de Dioses was more than a place to take the waters. Set in a tiny, verdant bowl of a valley, the spa was a whole town built around the warm springs that eased from the earth, rich in iron and sulfur, and the cold water tapped from a bright blue glacier near the top of the mountain. The assembly rooms were its beating heart, and glowed pink and white with marble from Italy.

Tall, luxurious hotels bookended the springs, and wide streets wound up from there, full of shops that sold breads, cheeses, hats and gloves, fine lace . . . anything a bored lady or gentleman of leisure could desire. Below the assembly rooms, narrow streets led to homes where lived the maids and footmen who worked in the shops, the hotels, and the impressive assembly rooms.

Lord Fanchere had sent them to the smaller and more exclusive of the two hotels, and their arrival was greeted by a gathering composed of the manager, the butler, the housekeeper, the chef, the concierge, and five maids, two assigned to each of the ladies and one to Emma.

In her travels with Lady Lettice, Emma had visited a great many hotels, but never had she been given a maid whose instructions were to make sure she needed for nothing. "I am very impressed," she said as she watched the maid take her small valise up to her room on the fourth floor.

Lady Fanchere laughed. "It is beautiful here, one of my favorite places in the world." She took Aimée's arm and strolled through the lobby, gesturing for Emma to follow. "We can relax here, can we not, Aimée?"

"Oh, yes. Prince Sandre is far away, and surely the Reaper can't find me here." Lady de Guignard's voice shook with little quavering tremors. "Can he?"

"Now, don't start that again," Lady Fanchere admonished.

The first time Emma heard Lady de Guignard mention the Reaper, faintness had once again overcome her. But she'd recovered, for she had heard the same plaintive moan all the way to Aguas de Dioses.

Yet she couldn't dislike Aimée de Guignard. Lady de Guignard was a petite woman with rich auburn hair, a plump face, and blue eyes made sad by too many years spent with the wrong man. She seemed not to have a speck of sense or discretion, but when she saw Emma's soiled gown and heard the story, she had been kindness itself, insisting that Emma try one of her day dresses, then giving it to her because, *By the time I'm out of black crepe, the fashion will have changed, and anyway, the color doesn't flatter my coloring at all, but the violet makes your eyes sparkle like jewels!*

Emma smoothed her hand over the polished cotton. She straightened the white lace insert that ran from the bodice to the waist, then down the skirt in a panel, and she swore to herself she wouldn't ruin this dress as she had ruined the others.

Lady de Guignard babbled on, uncaring that the housekeeper arranging the flowers or the footman carrying the luggage could

145

hear every word. "The Reaper is the ghost of King Reynaldo, so as a phantasm, can he go wherever he wishes? Or is he tied to the area around the castle where the de Guignards hanged him?"

"The Reaper is not a ghost," Lady Fanchere said.

"I saw him. He glared at me through empty eye sockets." Starch crackled as Lady de Guignard clutched the fall of ruffled lace at her throat.

"He's not a ghost," Lady Fanchere repeated patiently. "He's a man dressed like a ghost."

"That's what Sandre said, too, and he got quite angry with me about the matter." Lady de Guignard took a shuddering breath. "I don't know how my death will come, but I know it's imminent, either from supernatural means, or because Sandre will murder me."

"Sandre would not harm a lady, much less a lady who is his relative." Lady Fanchere had lost her patient tone.

Lady de Guignard came to a halt. "You didn't hear what he said to me."

"But I know Sandre." Lady Fanchere was firm.

"You think he is the same boy with whom you played as a child, and he takes care to keep you in that belief." Aimée's voice began to rise. "He isn't. You know what Rickie always was, and what Sandre did with Rickie in that dungeon is the stuff of nightmares. Now Sandre wants to silence me. But I can't lie about how Rickie died. I saw him. I saw his body hanging on the tree, and the Reaper on the rise behind him, waiting to guide his spirit to hell —"

"Shh." Lady Fanchere patted her hand and glanced behind at Emma, silently summoning her to help.

Remembering Lord Fanchere's admonition — distraction, distraction, distraction — Emma hurried to Lady de Guignard's side. "I see the dining hall is this way, and the servants have put cloths on the tables for the evening meal. I know it's early, but our dear Lady Fanchere is looking pale and in need of sustenance. Lady de Guignard, can you help me take her there?"

On cue, Lady Fanchere staggered slightly.

Lady de Guignard sniffled, glanced at Lady Fanchere, and at once agreed that she should be coddled because she was — Aimée spoke in a piercing whisper that carried throughout the lobby — increasing.

Apparently, Lady Fanchere had shared her secret with Lady de Guignard, and from the exasperated expression on Lady

147

Fanchere's face, she now knew it would be a secret no more.

By the time Emma had cared for the ladies — made sure they were fed, taken to their third-floor adjoining suites, helped them into their nightgowns, and put them to bed — she was glad to adjourn to her own small, neat room, one of the three dozen rooms in the attic assigned to the personal maids and companions who accompanied the ladies to the spa. Apparently the spa had thought matters through, assuming that servants living in comfort would encourage their employers to stay longer.

Here under the eaves, the daytime sun had created an uncomfortable heat, so Emma went to the window, opened it, and let the nighttime air wash over her. It was four stories to the ground, and only the occasional dormer broke the slope of the steep, slick slate roof. Overhead, diamond stars twinkled in a sky so deep and dark, it looked like eternity. The lights of the town sparkled in the midst of a forest, dense and primal, that pressed close to the edges of the town.

As if on cue, Emma's heart picked up speed. She broke into a sweat. She had walked into the wilderness. Been menaced by a wolf. And been rescued by . . . by . . . she didn't know who. Or what. She could *not* remember, but when she did, she knew it would mean . . . something.

Faintness overcame her. She yanked her head inside and covered her face with her hands. Hidden in her brain was something she did not want to confront, something she feared so much. . . .

Taking a long breath of the fresh night-time air, she gained control of her wayward emotions.

The maid had unpacked Emma's bag, hung up her second-best gown, and put her underwear into the drawers of the tiny dresser, leaving Emma with nothing to do but comb out her long hair, braid it, and change into her white cotton nightgown. The sleeves covered her from her shoulders to her wrists. The length covered her from her throat to her toes. Yet the amount of material was deceptive, for the nightgown was so old and thin, it was like tissue. She wrapped herself in her beloved wool shawl and, candle in hand, threw back the covers and examined the sheets. They were clean and white. The comforter was also white, thick and full of down. She climbed into bed and sank into the deep, plush feather mattress. She fluffed the pillows at her back and sighed with relief.

It had been a very long day.

Her mother's worn copy of *Pride and Prejudice* rested on the nightstand beside the burning candle; she lifted it with the resolve to read only a few pages.

Five chapters later, it was midnight and she was so involved in the story she had forgotten where she was. A breeze from the window ruffled the pages of the book. She glanced up, disoriented, as a rumble of thunder snatched her back from Regency England. The soft *snick* of a turning latch made her stare, still caught up in her longing for Mr. Darcy, as with the creak of hinges, the door swung wide to reveal — the Reaper.

Emma dove out of bed and prepared to scream — then her breath caught in her throat.

CHAPTER FOURTEEN

Emma recognized the pale, corpselike figure. . . . She remembered him!

The Reaper leaped across the small room to the bed, clapped his white-gloved hand over her mouth, held her tightly, and shook his head in silent warning.

She stared, wide-eyed, at the figure that had inspired so much fear and loathing.

He stood over six feet tall, clothed in a white shroud and ragged winding clothes. A dingy white hood covered his hair; a pale mask concealed the upper half of his face. White powder dusted his broad jaw, his generous lips, and the hollows of his cheeks, while streaks of charcoal, carefully placed, created a skeletal illusion. In the flickering light of the candle, with the storm gathering overhead, he was a frightening creature.

But Prince Sandre was right: The Reaper was not a corpse, but a man.

In her mind, memory bridged the gaps

created by fear, and the recollection of that night in the forest now sprang fully formed into her mind.

The Reaper had saved her life.

That night in the forest, half-crazed with terror, cold, and hunger, she had run from a wolf right into the arms of the Reaper, then turned and fled again. She had fallen, and while she was barely conscious, he had picked her up off the ground, lifted her onto his horse, and ridden with her to Lady Fanchere's, delivering her to the doorstep and leaving her there like an unwanted newborn.

Never, not once, had he spoken, but he had covered her with his cloak, cradled her in his arms, cared for her as no one had cared for her since her mother's death. He had been more than conscientious. He had been kind.

Slowly, incredulously, she pushed his hand away from her mouth.

Beneath his mask, the skin had been darkened to create the empty eye sockets that had so frightened Lady de Guignard, but his eyes glinted as he observed her with the caution of a man who knew his existence hung by a thread.

She started to speak.

He put his finger on his lips.

She indicated her understanding, then watched as he made his way to the door and quietly shut it. He put his ear to the panel, then shook his head, and through the mask and the powder, she saw fear and determination.

Treading softly, he went to the window and looked out. She knew what he saw — four stories to the ground and a steep slate roof. He might be able to leave in that direction . . . or he might fall to his death. Certainly it wasn't a climb she wanted to attempt.

In the distance, lightning flashed and thunder rumbled.

Outside the door, she heard men shouting. A dozen boots running up the stairs.

She owed this man her life.

In a soft voice, she said, "They're after you."

He nodded and prepared to climb out.

"You'll slip, especially if it rains." Thunder rumbled again. "And it sounds as if it will. Let me hide you." More than gratitude guided her offer. Today she'd been to the lower city, seen the poverty there, heard Damacia's satisfaction in knowing that the Reaper sought vengeance for a reason. Odd and frightening as he was, Emma knew he was a crusader — and he needed her help.

He looked around the room, then at her. Far beneath the holes of his mask, she could see the glisten of his black-rimmed eyes, and she could almost see the skepticism that directed his every move.

"I won't betray you. Come on." She lifted the covers and indicated the feather mattress, depressed in her shape. "Get in. I'll get in beside you, pile the blankets over you, and if anyone comes in, I promise I will save you."

Doors down the corridor opened and shut. The shouts grew louder.

Frantic, she said, "Now!"

The Reaper leaped across and into the bed, getting as close to the wall as he could.

Stretched out straight, he filled the bed from top to bottom, but as she'd planned, he sank into the deep mound of feathers that stuffed the mattress. "On your side," she said.

He turned to lie on his left side, facing her. In his right hand he held a knife, long and sharp-tipped.

All right. This was dangerous. She knew it was, but somehow, the sight of that knife made her realize what a perilous game she played.

After all the warnings she'd heard today — Brimley, Michael, and Lord Fanchere had all said to stay out of trouble — now she was helping a wanted man to evade the law. But nothing could change the fact that she owed him her life.

Glancing around, she made sure he had tracked nothing in, that nothing about the room would betray his presence, then climbed in beside him. She pulled the sheet over them both, piled the feather comforter over him to conceal the lump he created, fluffed one pillow over his face and another behind her shoulders. She checked to make sure her buttons were fastened all the way to her throat, then arranged her braid over her shoulder and onto her chest. She picked up her book and, with an assumption of ease, began to read.

Up and down the corridor, she heard doors opening and closing. Most of the rooms were empty, she knew. Those were easily searched, so the men were moving quickly. Her heart beat faster as the sound of the boots got closer. The heat of the Reaper's body pressed against hers from her toes to her spine. In a soft voice, she said, "Remain absolutely still and silent, and we'll get through this."

Right on cue, three men burst through the door, three men clad in riding clothes. Two held pistols. One she recognized — Prince

Sandre, dark haired, blue eyed, trim and athletic, holding a long sword in his left hand and a knife in his right.

With a girlish scream, she dropped her book and sat straight up. The sheet fell to her waist, and she knew very well what she exposed.

Her nightgown covered everything, but the material was so worn, her breasts were clearly visible, and when a sudden breeze from the window brought a cool draft, her nipples sprang to attention. She blushed, but the men didn't notice. They stared at her chest, and from their expressions they didn't even know she had a face.

"Why are you here? What are you doing in my room?" She gazed at Prince Sandre, silently pleading to the man in charge, and she put her hands over her breastbone, playing peekaboo with her own nipples.

His eyes became the dark, intense blue of desire. Drawing in a hard breath, he pointed toward the door. "Out!" he roared at his men.

The two guards backed toward the door, still distracted by her revealing nightgown. Which was exactly what she intended, but to be alone with Prince Sandre . . . Belatedly, she realized this could be trouble, more than she could handle. Trouble for

156

her, and trouble for the Reaper.

The prince's men stepped into the corridor, and before the door shut behind them, she heard one laugh coarsely.

Sandre took a step toward her.

She gasped in panic and pulled the sheet up to her chin. "This isn't proper!"

He halted in midstep. The intensity faded from his gaze, and confusion replaced it. "It isn't?"

"You must know it is not! I pray you, please leave. I am Lady Fanchere's companion, a gently bred female, and I dare not risk my reputation with this intimacy."

"Lady Fanchere! You're Lady Fanchere's companion? That changes matters. Lady Fanchere's companion must be above reproach." Hastily he holstered his pistol, sheathed his sword, and bowed. "Don't be alarmed. I am Prince Sandre of Moricadia." He pronounced his name with a verbal flourish.

"Your Highness." She inclined her head.

He paced away, then paced back. "Lady Fanchere is my cousin. I hadn't heard she was visiting Aguas de Dioses."

"We arrived today."

"Still, I expect to be informed of these matters."

"She has come to take the waters, and I

157

beg you, sir, please leave at once!"

"First I must inform you of my mission here. I'm chasing a most desperate scoundrel who calls himself the Reaper." As Prince Sandre spoke the name, his blue eyes grew as cold as the glacier far above on the mountain.

She glanced around her small room, then back at him, and lifted her eyebrows as if to invite him to tell her where the Reaper could be hiding . . . and all the while, she was aware of the warm, long form pressed against her hip.

What had seemed like a brilliant idea five minutes ago now seemed likely to get her killed.

But Prince Sandre was oblivious to the man-shaped lump in her bed. He was too focused on her face and form to notice any discrepancies. "You haven't seen him, then? He is a very dangerous criminal, a murderer and a traitor. He would not hesitate to hurt you. To . . . have his way with you."

Beside her, the Reaper tensed. She could almost feel him projecting scorn at Prince Sandre, and reassurance to her.

"I haven't seen him," she said.

"By pursuing the Reaper, I risk my life for the safety of others."

"That is good of you." Her voice quavered

without artifice. "But, Your Highness, men aren't permitted on this level." Fear brought tears to her eyes. "Please, Your Highness. You must leave at once!"

"I will." A smile slashed his handsome face. "As soon as you tell me your name."

"Miss Emma Chegwidden of England."

Lightning flashed. Thunder boomed.

She jumped nervously.

"Miss Emma Chegwidden of England, are you frightened of the storm?" He seemed amused by the idea, and worse, interested in her thoughts.

"Yes." Of the storm, and of him.

The tempest came closer. The lightning grew more frequent. The thunder was a tumult, and wind gusted through the window. Her candle sputtered, almost went out, but Emma didn't dare reach out to cradle it. If she moved too much, might not Prince Sandre observe what was so obvious to her — the unmoving lump in her bed?

As if the swirl of fresh air brought an idea to his mind, Prince Sandre strode to the window and looked out, from one side to the other and up above, using the flickering lightning that revealed . . . nothing.

So for all his chivalry, he didn't believe her when she said she hadn't seen the Reaper. Not really.

If he didn't leave pretty soon, she would faint from tension.

He bowed again, and in a voice infused with romantic meaning, he said, "Miss Chegwidden, I will see you . . . again." Backing out the door, he shut it gently behind him.

She heard him shout in a snarling tone, "Keep searching, you scum, keep searching!" She heard doors open and shut down the corridor, heard boots moving away from her. She waited a few minutes to make sure they were really gone, then leaped from her bed and ran on tiptoe to the door and turned the key.

As soon as the lock clicked, the Reaper threw back the covers and rose. He sheathed the knife. Going to the window, he opened it again and, like Prince Sandre, looked out. As he did, a torrential rain started, cool and wet, driven on the wind.

From below, she heard men shout about getting out of the storm.

Of course. Prince Sandre had stationed guards below. They were abandoning their posts, slipping back under the eaves or into the lobby. If the Reaper could get out of her room, down the stairs, and out a window undetected, he could possibly escape.

He turned.

She smiled at him.

He stared hard at her, examining her as if he did not understand her at all . . . and behind his mask, and in his stance, she saw something more — desire.

"I'm fine." Her pulse was settling down to a steady, rapid beat . . . rapid because, once again, she was aware of herself in the flimsy nightgown, and of being alone with a man . . . a man who was very much attracted to her.

She knew nothing of this emotion. She had never desired a man, and there had never been a man who desired her. But logic told her his appearance here was no coincidence, and instinct told her he had sought her out not to put her in danger, but to warn her.

So she wasn't worried or offended. For all Prince Sandre's ominous warning, she knew she could trust the Reaper. He had proved himself to her.

He strode to her side, took her hand, and bowed over it, touching it lightly with his lips.

"Are you leaving?"

He nodded and went to the door, listening with his head pressed to the panel. He pointed up.

The boots had moved up to the narrow

attic that ran the length of the hotel. She could hear the prince's men overhead.

The Reaper began to turn the lock —

And she knew that if she let him go like this, she would regret it forever.

CHAPTER FIFTEEN

"Wait!" Emma called.

The Reaper turned to face her, query clear in his form and movement.

She stepped up to him. "You found me in the woods. You saved my life. And I want to thank you . . . thank you. . . ." Gathering her nerve, she took his face between her hands, rose on her toes, and pressed her lips to his.

She had no experience, but she put all her appreciation in that one kiss. His lips were warm and surprised, and then warm and . . . ardent. His breath touched her, quickening as she slanted her face to his, yet he held back, not touching her, waiting for her to make a move.

But she didn't know what move to make.

So she listened to the instinct that crept up from the quiet place within her where it had been hiding, repressed and afraid. Wrapping her arms around his neck, she leaned against him. Not her whole body, not the lower part; she didn't have the nerve for that. But her breasts and shoulders. That was . . . very nice.

He radiated heat and strength, smelled of hard riding and horse, and towered over her. She took a breath, delighting in the differences between them, then kissed him harder, mashing her lips to his.

The thought had just occurred to her that kissing was not as exciting as she'd hoped, when everything changed. Something — her eagerness, perhaps? — drove him beyond control.

He swept her up, one arm around her waist, one arm cradling her spine and head. He tilted her backward. And he *kissed* her.

This wasn't some tentative, inexperienced press of lips to lips.

This was a swashbuckling kiss. This was a passionate kiss. This kiss was running through an exotic jungle, splashing into a warm, tempestuous sea, stepping into the storm outside and inviting the lightning to strike and set her ablaze.

The wind from the open window swirled around them, wet and cool, lifting the hem of her nightgown and tangling it around his boots.

Emma strained against him, absorbing this

man's love of adventure, of justice, and of . . . her? His lips parted hers; his tongue swept into her mouth. He tasted her and wordlessly invited her to taste him, his soul, his being. He supported her and wanted nothing more than for her to allow him the privilege.

For the first time in her life, she *yearned,* her nipples pressed against his chest, hard and tight, her heart thumping with a ferocious rhythm. Foolish with longing, she skimmed her hands up his arms and over his chest. There she found strong muscle and tough sinew, and against her open palm, his heart beat with a fervor to match her own.

With a soft, wordless murmur, he lifted his lips from hers.

She rested in his arms, breathing heavily, recovering from the brief, brilliant tempest. Opening her eyes, she looked up at him, bewildered and embarrassed. "Oh, my heavens. Oh, my heavens. We just . . . I just . . ."

His eyes beneath the mask scrutinized her, not critically, but as if he wanted to reassure her. He nodded and touched her cheek, then pulled a clean handkerchief from his pocket. Carefully, he dabbed at her lips, then showed her the folded linen.

Sometime during that turbulent kiss, he'd transferred the white powder on his face to hers. Now his skin, touched by sun, peeped forth from beneath his disguise, reassuring her that he was, indeed, a man.

Holding his gloved hands at the ready to catch her, he gradually stepped back. When he was sure she was steady on her feet, he bowed, his face solemn, turned, and opened the door as if sure he would pass through the corridors without incident.

Would he? Above them, she could still hear the boots of his pursuers thumping on the floorboards. But perhaps Prince Sandre had left a guard. . . .

"Be careful," she whispered.

He turned, his shroud swirling like a cloak, placed his hand on his chest, and bowed again.

Like a silly girl at her first ball, she bobbed a curtsy in return.

His eyes warmed. He shut the door. And he was gone from her sight.

Never once had he said a word or made a sound.

She stood staring, wide-eyed, hands loose, breathing hard, with no thought in her mind except desire. Then lightning struck, outside and in, and she realized he was somewhere, racing through the hotel, dodging the prince's pursuit. She ran to the door and listened, then ran to the window, opened it all the way, and stuck her head out.

The rain washed across her face. The wind whipped her hair. Lightning flashed, giving her brief glimpses of the courtyard below.

Nothing moved.

Nothing moved. Then . . . there he was, sprinting across the cobblestones, a dark cloak covering his disguise. She held her breath, terrified she would hear a shout of discovery.

All was silent.

He reached the tree line undetected. At the last moment, he turned and faced the hotel. She thought he raised a hand to her.

She waved frantically in return, knowing he couldn't see her, but unable to remain still.

Then he was gone.

Reluctantly, she pulled herself inside. She shut the window all the way. Then, claustrophobic, she opened it a few inches. Taking a white linen towel, she dried her face and rubbed at her hair, looked down at herself and laughed a little in embarrassment. With her nightgown wet, she indeed might as well have been nude. A good thing for her the Reaper didn't see *that*.

A better thing Prince Sandre had not.

Going to the door, she locked it again, then walked to the bed and sank down on the mattress.

Only this morning, with complete solemnity, she had promised Brimley she would avoid involvement in the Moricadian revolution. And now she had hidden the Reaper in her bed! She had attracted the attention of Prince Sandre! Who was she? Timid companion or foolish heroine?

And what was worse — the danger she faced, or her wanton behavior?

Michael stood watching the sunrise through the bars on his window, and everything in him vibrated with tension and excitement.

Tonight had been a close call, the closest so far. Ever since Rickie had been killed, Sandre had flung all his resources into catching the Reaper.

But the Reaper would not stop. Not until he had vengeance. Not until he had justice.

Michael had accepted the fact that the Reaper would probably be captured, probably die a horrible, agonizing death.

Before it hadn't mattered, but now . . . after so much suffering in the cold, damp, close dark, the Reaper had found a reason to live.

Her name was Miss Emma Chegwidden.

Turning to Rubio, Michael said, "Send a message to Raul Lawrence. Invite him to visit me here today."

"What if he's busy?" Rubio asked.

"Tell him it's a favor for an old friend."

CHAPTER SIXTEEN

"You're looking very rosy today, Emma." Lady Fanchere smiled as they strolled through the assembly room. "Moricadia agrees with you."

Emma blushed, her mind very much still on the danger she'd faced last night, and the kiss that had followed. "Yes, Lady Fanchere. I'm happy here." And ecstatic to discover, after tactfully questioning the maid who brought her hot water this morning, that the Reaper had escaped capture.

"The surroundings are lovely, are they not?"

Emma viewed the spacious interior of this noble building: its marble columns holding the arched and painted ceiling, its large windows facing out into the valley, and its stone fountains, one that ran with steaming hot water from the earth, the other icy from the glacial melt. Both were reputed to have healing powers, and as the morning progressed, the wealthy gathered to sip from marble cups, walk slowly or sit elegantly, and be seen among the modish surroundings and in the sunny atrium. "It's not the surroundings that make me happy, Lady Fanchere; it's being in your employ."

Lady Fanchere laughed musically. "A graceful compliment, until I remember where last you worked."

Emma smiled, too, so at ease with Lady Fanchere she knew she was being teased.

"But I swear it's true." Lady Fanchere would not be dissuaded. "You're almost blushing. What could be the cause?"

"Perhaps the altitude?"

"After that storm last night, the air is very fresh here," Lady Fanchere agreed.

Emma felt her face go from rosy to hot. She ought to tell Lady Fanchere about Prince Sandre breaking into her room last night. If she didn't, Lady Fanchere would find out some other way, and that would put Emma's character and virtue in doubt. Yet Prince Sandre's appearance was bound in her mind with the Reaper, her own astonishing courage, and that kiss. She found herself saying, "I might have gotten too much sun."

"Did you take off your bonnet during your ride with Michael?" Lady Fanchere asked sternly. "With your fair skin, you should be more careful."

"You're right, I *should* be more careful." In every way. Emma should keep soldiers and princes out of her bedroom, and never, ever should she kiss a ghost.

But still, remembering the night before, and the sensations that kiss had caused, she could find no regret in her heart — or other places.

"Eleonore. Eleonore!" Aimée hurried toward them, looking once more overexcited.

A footman holding three cups balanced on his tray followed.

A diversion for Lady Fanchere. *Thank heavens.*

"Aimée is so kind, so well-intentioned." Lady Fanchere rubbed her temple with her gloved hand. "But I only wish that for one moment, she would stop talking, especially about —"

Aimée reached them, out of breath. "Have you heard?" She handed them the cups of steaming water straight from the hot springs, then shooed the footman away. "The Reaper was spotted last night. Here! In Aguas de Dioses!"

Emma froze and held her breath.

"Oh, no." Lady Fanchere sighed.

"Yes." Aimée clutched her throat. "He has come for me!"

"Aimée, that's not possible," Lady Fanchere said.

Aimée ignored that with a determination that was impressive. "Drink your water, Eleonore. It's good for the baby."

Lady Fanchere touched the cup to her lips.

"Emma, you should drink yours, too. You're all flushed." Aimée peered into Emma's face. "You're not coming down with the plague, are you?"

"I don't believe so, Lady de Guignard. My health is most robust."

"Good." Aimée reverted to her favorite topic without pause. "The Reaper was here, in this very hotel. That handsome Irish scoundrel, Mr. Gillespie Cosgair, said he heard the commotion." She leaned forward and cupped her gloved hand beside her mouth, and whispered, "They say Countess Martin is here also, and there have been nocturnal visits between their rooms."

"The Reaper and Countess Martin?" Emma exclaimed in dismay.

Aimée *tsk*ed. "No, dear! Mr. Cosgair and Countess Martin. She's a famous strumpet, but not even she would sleep with a ghost!"

"He's not a —" Lady Fanchere took a

breath. "Aimée, if your only verification was a stranger's account of some brawl, then that's a rumor, not the truth." Her exasperation seeped through her usual calm demeanor. "You must stop repeating gossip, especially about the Reaper."

Aimée drew herself up to her full height, which still meant she was several inches below Lady Fanchere. "I don't know about Mr. Cosgair and Countess Martin, but the tidbit about the Reaper is not gossip, Eleonore."

"How do you *know* that?"

"Because Prince Sandre arrived hot on his heels."

Lady Fanchere's tone became quiet pleasure. "Sandre was here? Is still here?"

"Yes! Yes!" Aimée jumped up and down with excitement.

Oh, no. Emma wanted to sink through the floor. If Prince Sandre was nearby, if he hadn't left Aguas de Dioses, then Emma really needed to acknowledge the incident last night. "Lady Fanchere, I have a confession."

Aimée didn't pause. "I'm telling you, Eleonore, Sandre was after him, but the Reaper summoned the storm and vanished in a bolt of lightning!"

"Oh, Aimée." Lady Fanchere sounded as

if she were in despair.

"I am doomed to die at the hands of either the Reaper or Sandre. They're stalking me across the countryside!"

"Lady Fanchere, it would be best if you could spare a moment of your attention," Emma said.

But Lady Fanchere was completely focused on Aimée. "You have done nothing! Why would either one of them want to kill you?"

Emma sighed. She put the cup to her lips; then when the smell hit her, she pulled it away with a moue of disgust. "This is vile!" she exclaimed.

Both women paused in astonishment.

"Yes," Aimée chirped. "Didn't you know?"

"Why would anyone drink this?" With a straight arm, Emma held the cup out.

"It's good for you!" Aimée said.

Lady Fanchere grinned, collected the cups, and gave them to a passing servant.

"So, it's not the Aguas de Dioses water that put the roses in your cheeks?" Lady Fanchere asked Emma.

"It is most definitely not the water, my lady." Emma wanted to scrape her tongue.

"Yet Miss Chegwidden looks so fetching this morning," said Prince Sandre from behind them.

In a flurry, the three women turned and curtsied.

Emma kept her gaze down and wished desperately to be somewhere, anywhere, but here.

A quick glance at Aimée proved she felt exactly the same.

"Now, now, cousin." He opened his arms and embraced Lady Fanchere, and kissed both her cheeks. "You needn't be so formal. We're family!"

Lady Fanchere hugged him with obvious delight. "It is good to see you, Sandre. It's been too long."

"You've been reclusive. Why is that?" He held her hands.

"She's increasing," Aimée piped up.

Prince Sandre started, eyes wide with surprise, then smiled broadly. "Is that true?"

"It *was* a secret," Lady Fanchere said crushingly.

"But such good news. Congratulations to Fanchere at last." He kissed her cheeks again, then turned to Aimée and embraced her, too. "As for you, little cousin — still saying too much about that which should be kept silent. Such indiscretion could get you killed."

He sounded genial, but the words were

cold, and Aimée shrank as if he'd slapped her.

Emma shrank, too, at his public reprimand of Aimée, and because she recalled last night and his visit and the way his eyes had turned to ice when he spoke of the Reaper. The more she heard, the more she realized Sandre was a truly frightening man.

Lady Fanchere put her arm around Aimée's shoulders. "I don't mind, Sandre. The truth will be obvious soon enough, and dear Aimée has been nothing but kind and helpful since she arrived at my home, saddened by Rickie's death."

Prince Sandre's mouth tightened. "Yes, Rickie's death was a tragedy, and one I promise will not be repeated. We almost caught the Reaper last night. The net is closing."

"So it's true? He was here?" Lady Fanchere looked suddenly tired, as if that news were more than she could bear.

Emma took her arm. "My lady, if you would . . . You've walked enough, and there are seats in the atrium. Let's go there, and I'll find you a cup of water, cold water, from the glacier."

"That would be pleasant," Lady Fanchere acknowledged.

"Let me clear the way." Prince Sandre

walked briskly toward a group of Moricadians relaxing on chairs in an alcove. He spoke to the occupants. They scattered. And in only seconds, Emma was able to place Lady Fanchere in a cushioned chair with a view of the glacial wall of ice and the stream that raced from beneath its icy toes.

"Thank you, Sandre. That was very good of you." Lady Fanchere rubbed the small of her back.

Aimée chafed her hand.

Emma put her shawl around her shoulders.

"I'm not an invalid, you know," Lady Fanchere objected.

"No, just well loved." Aimée's plump, pink cheeks and sunny smile made a mockery of her black mourning gown.

Lady Fanchere lightly touched her arm. "You're a dear. Now." She turned to Prince Sandre, and her eyes were unexpectedly severe. "Emma tried to tell me something earlier, and I wasn't listening. But you seem to know my dear Emma, and I wonder how."

Emma winced and said, "I should have told you immediately, but —"

Lady Fanchere interrupted, "I asked Prince Sandre for his explanation."

Emma subsided, so embarrassed at the reprimand and the coming tale, she could do nothing but sit with her hands twisting in her lap.

But Prince Sandre was more than glad to answer Lady Fanchere. He posed, a hand on one hip, and said, "It is true. Coward that he is, last night the Reaper chose to hide among the weakest and gentlest of the people in Moricadia. He ran upstairs into the servants' wing —"

"Where you are housed, Emma?" Lady Fanchere asked.

"Yes, my lady," Emma said in a small voice.

Almost without pause, Prince Sandre plunged on. "And I ran after him, my men on my heels. He hid —"

Lady Fanchere interrupted again. "But not in your room, Emma?"

"I heard the boots thumping as the prince's men searched," Emma said.

"Although we searched all the rooms," Prince Sandre continued, "we didn't find him. He escaped, and now it is up to us to bring him down."

"You can't take down a ghost!" Aimée said. "He's ephemeral."

Prince Sandre turned on her, his face savage with impatience. "I have a plan."

Emma lifted her head and considered him, eyes narrowed. A plan? He had a plan?

179

"Dear Aimée, don't be silly." Lady Fanchere pressed Aimée's arm with her hand, and at the same time stared reproachfully at Sandre.

Once more, he donned the facade of the noble warrior. "Silly Aimée. You're so childlike in your belief, almost as if you were Moricadian yourself."

Aimée tried to speak again.

Lady Fanchere shushed her.

Emma took a breath. Took another breath. Then inserted herself into the conversation. "Your Highness, won't you tell us about your plan to capture the infamous Reaper?" She was surprised to hear herself sound so calmly interested and so . . . so . . . composed, as if she regularly made conversation with royalty and noblewomen. Had it been only three days ago that she'd massaged Lady Lettice's feet?

Yet Lady Fanchere cast her a grateful glance, as if Emma had planned her intervention to save Aimée from censure.

And Prince Sandre smiled at her, a man proud of his intentions and the woman who invited him to proclaim his wiliness. "A good question, Miss Chegwidden. Tonight and every night until we hold him crushed in our fist, my men will wait at the crossroads between the lower city and the castle.

They'll place a rope across the road, wait on either side, and when they see the Reaper galloping close, they'll pull the rope tight. The horse will fall, the Reaper will be flung to the ground, and we'll capture him. And hang him, of course." He paused, waiting for praise.

Aimée was shaking her head.

Emma couldn't speak for dismay. Would Sandre's scheme work? Would the Reaper die, leaving the Moricadian people without a champion?

"A sound plan, Sandre," Lady Fanchere said. "I hope that brings an end to this terror that has stalked the land."

Her turn of phrase displeased Prince Sandre. "The Reaper is not a terror. He is a foolish, measly coward, and I will have his head."

In a cold, clear voice, Aimée asked, "If he's a foolish, measly coward, then what are you that you've let him roam free for so long?"

Sandre turned apoplectic red from his starched white cravat to his forehead.

Emma wanted to moan. How could Lady de Guignard be so wise and so foolish at the same time?

"Aimée, I think it would be best if you went to rest. I believe you have a headache."

Lady Fanchere sounded coldly angry.

Aimée seemed startled by Lady Fanchere's tone. She glanced up at Prince Sandre and whispered, "Oh. Yes. I do." Standing, she curtsied, turned, and scuttled away.

"I do not know how you stand that woman," Prince Sandre said.

Without pause, Lady Fanchere attacked. "You were in Emma's bedroom last night?"

He sighed theatrically. "I'm afraid so, but let me offer my assurances that your companion was completely safe in my company."

"Emma wasn't alone with you," Lady Fanchere said. "You said your men were there."

Emma half closed her eyes, wondering if Prince Sandre would lie, and half hoping he did.

"It wasn't proper for my men to be in a young lady's room, so I sent them out."

Lady Fanchere abruptly stood. "Sandre, if you would, I'd like a moment of your time."

Prince Sandre nodded as if Lady Fanchere's request didn't surprise him. He bowed to Emma, took Lady Fanchere's arm, and led her away.

CHAPTER SEVENTEEN

Emma glanced at Lady Fanchere and Prince Sandre, knowing full well she was the subject of their conversation, wondering what Lady Fanchere would say to him . . . but although her future depended on this conversation, it wasn't what occupied her mind. Instead, she wondered how she could possibly pass a warning to the elusive Reaper.

"Miss Chegwidden?" A stranger's voice made her turn and stare. His English was flawless. He was handsome, but in an intense, brooding way that made her think he would be an uncomfortable companion. He wore a dark suit and white linens that looked as if they had come from London's finest tailor — and he looked not at all familiar.

"I'm Miss Chegwidden," she acknowledged.

"How good to see you again." He bowed

with the seamless elegance of a gentleman born.

So she had met him. But where? "I fear I don't recall . . ."

"You don't remember me. Of course, why would you?" He smiled at her as if expecting nothing more, although why this man should be modest, she didn't know. "I'm Raul Lawrence, the son of Viscount Grimsborough. You and I met briefly at a gathering at St. Ashley. You were very young then, but somehow we had a chance to visit, and you know one of my sisters — from school, I believe."

"Of course." Still she didn't recall him, or his sister, either. But she had certainly attended gatherings at St. Ashley, at Christmas and on May Day. And at her boarding school, she had met many noblewomen who noticed her only in passing. Some were kind to the rector's daughter, others less so. Apparently his sister was one of the kind girls, so Emma pretended recollection. "How very good to see you again. Are you visiting in Moricadia?"

"I live here."

"Here?" She looked around the assembly room. Her gaze rested on Prince Sandre and Lady Fanchere, and once again she wondered what was passing between them that made Lady Fanchere look so solemn and Prince Sandre speak so persuasively.

"Not *here*. But in Moricadia. I own a villa not far from Aguas de Dioses. It's a bit of a rattrap, I fear, deep in the woods without another dwelling for miles, but I make do." He indicated the promenade. "Shall we?"

She didn't really know him. Yet this was a public place, and he was an Englishman. This was proper, and just because she had a niggling of unease didn't mean she shouldn't accept his invitation. Rising, she joined him and the other members of Moricadian society as they strolled around the huge room, chatting and drinking their vile water. "What made you settle in this country?"

Mr. Lawrence waved off a footman who offered a cup-filled tray. "I'm in exile, actually. My father's a bit of a tyrant and I take ill to his hands on the reins. For all that he successfully shoved me down everyone's throat for years, I'm not well received among the *bon ton*."

He sounded like a misfit, like her. Like the Reaper. "Why is that, Mr. Lawrence?"

"I'm a bastard," he said bluntly.

He had her full attention once more.

"I'm sorry; I've left you speechless," he said. "But it's true. So I live here among a society that is more tolerant of reprobates and gamblers."

"Is that what you are?" she asked solemnly.

"Yes. I'm a bit of a rebel, actually." He paused significantly.

When that sank in, she turned her startled gaze on him. *Rebel?* Did he say *rebel?* Did he mean what she thought he meant?

He smiled and inclined his head. "Yes, I think you and I are both rebels."

She stopped cold.

He put his hand on her arm and gave a little yank. "Keep walking, Miss Chegwidden, and look pleasant and *slightly* interested."

She moved with him, thinking furiously, trying to put all the pieces together. Was Mr. Lawrence a friend of the Reaper's?

But no. He was cruelly handsome, darkly charming. He exuded such ruthless sensuality it made her nervous to walk beside him. He was surely not a good man.

So was he a spy for the de Guignards? Had someone who had seen the Reaper run from her bedroom reported her? Was Mr. Lawrence seeking information only she could give him?

But no, for, still smiling, still suave, he said, "Last night I believe you had a lump in your mattress."

"How do you know that?" she asked in a low, incensed undertone.

"Perhaps I'm the Reaper."

"No, you are not." She didn't know how she could be so certain, but she was.

Raul Lawrence laughed deep in his chest. "Then perhaps I'm a friend of his. Because only he or a friend of his would know where exactly you hid him."

"That's true." So was she wrong in her reading of his character? Again, she thought hard and long, because she had to get this right. A man's life — *her* life — depended on it. "Or perhaps you work for Prince Sandre, and have taken him and have tortured him to make him reveal that information."

"If Prince Sandre had taken the Reaper, you would be currently inhabiting the royal dungeon," Mr. Lawrence said flatly.

Already she knew enough about the de Guignards to believe that. Glancing once more at Prince Sandre and Lady Fanchere, she thought their conversation was winding to a close. Certainly Prince Sandre had noticed that she was walking with a man, and was not pleased, for while he listened to Lady Fanchere, he watched them with a frown.

"Can you pass a message to the Reaper?"

She kept her voice low and urgent.

"Keep walking, Miss Chegwidden."

She forced her feet to move.

"Smile as if we're old friends exchanging minor recollections."

She fixed a smile on her face.

"And . . . yes, I can."

"Prince Sandre has a scheme to trap him the next time he rides." Quickly, she outlined the plan.

"Thank you, Miss Chegwidden. You're most helpful. I promise this will reach his ears. And now" — raising his voice, Mr. Lawrence said — "Mrs. Andersen said she'd rather be hung for a sheep than a lamb!" He laughed aloud.

Her voice quavered when she laughed, but she did laugh, and wasn't surprised when Prince Sandre spoke behind her.

"What a pleasant surprise to find you two know each other."

"Your Highness." Mr. Lawrence turned in simulated surprise. "We do indeed know each other. One of my father's estates marches across the estate where Miss Chegwidden's father was rector."

Prince Sandre smiled with chilly intent. "Then you are old friends."

"Acquaintances, rather. Miss Chegwidden is far too proper a lady for me."

Prince Sandre seemed to like that thought. "She is, isn't she?"

"But it's good to hear an English voice in this strange land." Mr. Lawrence bowed. "Since I live so close, I frequently visit Aguas de Dioses, so I hope to see you again, Miss Chegwidden."

"And I you, Mr. Lawrence." She smiled and inclined her head, and acted the lonely expatriate as if she'd been born to the role.

"Are you homesick?" As Mr. Lawrence left, Prince Sandre slipped into his place on the promenade, walking at her side as if they were two normal people in society.

Yet Emma looked around and saw people staring. Lady Fanchere had returned to the chair she had vacated earlier, and watched with a smile. The best society of Moricadia were watching and gossiping about the prince and Lady Fanchere's foreign companion, and Emma hated to imagine what kind of speculation ran rampant in this room . . . and beyond. "I do miss England," she said. "But Moricadia is a country of unsurpassed beauty, and I've enjoyed my stay here."

"Your diplomacy is exemplary." He looked ahead and smiled, as if she'd passed some unexplained test. Still in that congenial voice, he said, "I forgot to ask you last night

— did you enjoy your trip to the lower city?"

"My trip to the lower city?" Emma stopped, turned to him, stared.

People walked around them as if they were pebbles in a stream.

"It was very good of you to set that child's arm. What is her name? Elixabete? So sad that she lost her father tragically."

Emma was horrified at this demonstration of the reach of his knowledge, and afraid he knew what Damacia had said about him, and that he would take action against her.

But he laughed amiably. "Come, Miss Chegwidden, I *am* the prince, after all, and it *is* my business to know everything that goes on in my own country."

No. It really isn't.

Who in that tenement courtyard was one of his spies? Which one of those ladies at the well had sold her soul to keep her children fed?

Emma glanced around, for the first time uneasy in this place.

Who in this room was one of his spies? Who watched and listened and reported any unusual activities to the prince and his henchmen? The thought made the back of her neck itch. "Your Highness, I just did not realize that you would trouble yourself with something so unimportant. Now, if you would excuse me . . ." She sounded abrupt, she realized, but he didn't know her. Perhaps he thought her always so tactless.

She walked away from Prince Sandre, going against traffic, blundering past ladies trailed by their maids, and gentlemen so surprised they dropped their monocles.

She had no one else to blame but herself for this conundrum. She had chosen to rescue the Reaper. She had sat up in bed, knowing full well she was revealing herself in an enticing way, and she had attracted the attention of the most powerful man in Moricadia.

Now she had to pay the price. And she would do it gladly, because now Prince Sandre was moved to confide in her — no, *brag* to her — and she might be the one to save the Reaper from vengeance at the prince's hands.

Prince Sandre trailed Emma to Lady Fanchere's side. "You're taking this too seriously. To not discover what my people are saying and doing is to neglect them."

"I'm not one of your people," Emma said.

"I would like to change that," he answered.

Oh, God. She wasn't ready to move at this speed.

He caught her hand. "Do I repulse you?"

"No! Not at all. But you're a prince and

I'm only a servant."

He tugged her closer. "I'm a man and you're a woman."

A woman who was very unused to such attentions, and yet quite aware that he sounded as if he were reciting a line in a play he had acted many times.

She pulled free. "Your Highness, to speak so to me is inappropriate." Conscious of Prince Sandre watching her intently, she turned to Lady Fanchere. "My lady, you expressed a wish to walk outside. We should find Lady de Guignard and proceed so that you both may enjoy luncheon all the more, and your rest this afternoon."

Lady Fanchere smiled as if amused by Emma's careful planning. "As always, Emma, you're the perfect companion."

"Perhaps I might join you in your walk," Prince Sandre suggested.

But Lady Fanchere was firm. "Tomorrow you may join us, Sandre. Today is our first full day here, and time for us ladies alone."

Prince Sandre's eyes flashed with impatience, but he sounded pleasant enough when he said, "Enjoy your day, then, and I look forward to tomorrow."

CHAPTER EIGHTEEN

Lady Fanchere watched Prince Sandre walk away, then took Emma's arm and headed toward the door. "Come on. We have to find Aimée."

"Yes." Because Aimée had a sensible attitude about Prince Sandre, and Lady Fanchere had a militant gleam in her eyes.

They marched out the door, through the square, and to their hotel. There they found Aimée sitting in the lobby, looking miserable and worried.

Uncharacteristically, Lady Fanchere seemed not to notice. She put her hand under Aimée's arm and hauled her to her feet. "Come on. We're going to Madam Mercier's establishment."

Aimée's eyes lit up. "Shopping?"

"Yes. Come on, Aimée! You know I treasure your advice in these matters." Lady Fanchere walked back out the door, energized in a way Emma had not yet seen.

"What are we shopping for?" Aimée asked.

"Clothes for Emma." Lady Fanchere led them down the street, then up toward the upper city.

"What? Why?" Aimée hurried to catch up with Lady Fanchere.

"Why do I need more clothes?" Emma smoothed her hands over the skirt of her gown, the gown she had treasured. The gown she had worn for two whole days without tearing or covering with soot.

"You can't go to the palace dressed like that!" Lady Fanchere said.

Aimée took a breath. "Eleonore, why would it matter what she wears when she goes to the palace? She's merely your companion." Aimée cast an apologetic glance at Emma.

Emma nodded, not at all offended. Aimée's frank assessment needed to be said.

"That is not true." Lady Fanchere swung to face them both, stopping them in the middle of the street. "Emma, I suspect you know I was speaking to Sandre about you."

"I thought perhaps that was the case." Emma bit her lower lip. "My lady, he came into my room and I begged him to leave, told him it wasn't proper. I've done nothing of which I should be ashamed."

"I believe that, Emma; however, some-

194

times, when a man is rich and spoiled, a girl doesn't have to do anything to attract his attention. In your case, Sandre saw you in your bedclothes —"

"I wish he hadn't!" Emma said fervently.

"— and was charmed by your beauty and your modesty," Lady Fanchere finished. "I told him that you were a young woman of admirable character and I would not have him seducing you. He assured me his intentions were honorable."

"Honorable?" Emma's heart sank. How bad a situation had she created? "What do you mean?"

Lady Fanchere spelled it out. "If you are amenable, he would like to spend time with you with the intention of discovering whether the two of you could make a match."

"A match!" Aimée's blue eyes went wide with horror, and she put her hand over her heart.

"A match. Do you mean . . . to marry?" This was not what Emma intended when she had hidden the Reaper in her bed, nor when she thought to encourage Prince Sandre to tell her of his plans. This was serious.

Lady Fanchere smiled, her eyes dancing. "You look stunned."

"I am. You must know I am." Emma

almost choked. "I'm a . . . a paid companion!"

"Eleonore, have you lost your mind?" Aimée was almost shouting. "Emma can't marry the prince!"

People on the street turned to look.

Emma tucked her chin close to her chest and wished fervently to be elsewhere.

"Shh, Aimée. Be quiet." Lady Fanchere took their arms and led them up the hill once more and into a small, elegant shop.

A stylish female of middle age, dressed all in black, looked up from bolts of silks, satins, and cottons. Her eyes lit up, and she hurried forward. "Lady Fanchere, Lady de Guignard, welcome. Welcome! What can I do for you?"

"Madam Mercier, this is Miss Chegwidden." Lady Fanchere indicated Emma.

Madam Mercier assessed and dismissed Emma with one glance. "Hmm. Yes?"

"I want you to create a new wardrobe for her."

Madam Mercier looked to Aimée for guidance.

With a matter-of-factness that seemed foreign to her nature, Aimée said, "For what reason, Eleonore?"

"No. Please, Lady Fanchere." Emma was squirming with guilt, with embarrassment, with the desperate need to escape this rapidly escalating situation.

"Don't be silly." Lady Fanchere put her arm around Emma's waist and smiled at Madam Mercier, the kind of smile that imposed a noble will on a person of lesser station. "You should think of Miss Chegwidden as my daughter, one I wish to prepare for her first series of balls and parties."

Emma objected: "You're not old enough to be my —"

"Yes, I am," Lady Fanchere snapped. More calmly, she looked into Emma's eyes. "Yes, I am, and I want to do this. It will be fun, something I've dreamed of doing all my life. Indulge me."

What could Emma say to that? "I appreciate your kindness and will never forget the debt I owe you, Lady Fanchere, but —"

Lady Fanchere wasn't interested in *buts*. She said, "Good! Then, Madam Mercier, let us see what you have in mind."

Madam Mercier exchanged another telling glance with Aimée, then bustled forward and tapped her chin as she circled Emma, staring as if she were a mannequin. "Yes. Yes. She's young. Good hair. Excellent figure. The eyes . . . hmm. Witch's eyes. Stormy. Unpredictable. The color changes with her mood. In medieval times, she would have burned. Lady Fanchere, I will make Miss Chegwidden lovely. Er . . . what amount should I . . . ?"

"Spare no expense," Lady Fanchere instructed.

Madam Mercier curtsied again, and again, and Emma saw the glint in her eyes. She had just stumbled into a gold mine. She hustled toward the back room.

"Eleonore, what are you doing?" Aimée asked fiercely. "You wish to present Miss Chegwidden — an innocent! — to Sandre?"

"Sandre is not so bad as you think, Aimée, and even if he might be, he is of an age — thirty-five — to look for a wife. Certainly I have urged him in that direction. Additionally, he's in the enviable position of not needing to care whether his intended is wealthy or titled."

Emma had never meant anything so much in her life as when she said, "I am neither, and this honor would be too much for me."

"You're of respectable birth and have shown yourself to be resilient, kind, and intelligent, all requirements for a princess," Lady Fanchere said.

"Don't mislead Emma. She deserves better than that!" Aimée faced Emma, her eyes bright with indignation. "Sandre can't get a bride who's wealthy or titled because none of the nobility of Europe will have him. He's like Henry the Eighth of England — after you've killed enough people, no one wants to lose her head to you. Sandre has a reputation for consorting with criminals and scoundrels in the name of profit. Not that nobility doesn't consort with scoundrels, but the scoundrels grovel to them. The criminals bow to them. Sandre will bow to anyone to keep his gambling houses going. Furthermore, the nobility of other countries have learned from the French Revolution, and at least pretend a concern for their common people. Here the misery is so great, Sandre's policies are an embarrassment to us all."

"Aimée, your grief over Rickie's death has unhinged your mind." Lady Fanchere's eyes shimmered with tears, and she looked like what she was — a woman torn between two loyalties.

"I am not unhinged; I am . . ." Aimée caught her breath. "Look, Eleonore, Madam Mercier is waiting with a bolt of cloth in her arms. I think she wants to consult with you."

Lady Fanchere stared at Aimée.

"Go on." Aimée shooed her away. "You worry too much."

Because Lady Fanchere loved her friend and cousin, and trusted her, she walked to Madam Mercier and engaged in an intense conversation about style.

In a low, rapid voice, Aimée said, "Don't do this, Emma. I beg of you. Eleonore wants this because of Sandre. She hears the rumors about him, but she doesn't want to believe them. She wants to think he's a decent man, but more and more she's had to face that he isn't. She has urged him to marry, believing the love of a good woman would bring him back from the brink of damnation where he now teeters."

Emma kept her eyes down, her hands folded, and spoke as softly. "That's a big role for one woman to perform."

"Exactly. Now he wants you, and *you're* a good woman, just what Eleonore wanted for him. Dear girl, don't take this badly. I'm going to be blunt, but I know Sandre. I know men like him, and I know the worms that twist and turn in their minds."

Aimée was talking about Rickie, Emma could tell.

"Yes, Sandre is attracted to you because of your pretty face and lovely manners. But more than that, he wants you for your virtue, because you've never had another man and he won't have to try to satisfy you.

He wants you because you have no fortune or nobility, so you will be grateful for the elevation. He wants you because you have no family at all and few friends here, and he'll have complete control over you. Emma" — Aimée took Emma's hands in her own and looked into her eyes — "you are better off poor and alone than trapped in a marriage with that man."

Aimée gave desperately earnest advice, no doubt learned from some horrible experiences in her past, and she made Emma want to cry. But nothing changed the facts: Emma had to stay and play this game to its end. The Reaper's life depended on it — and who knew how many other lives depended on him? To Aimée, Emma said, "My lady, I take your advice in the spirit in which it was given, and I do believe you. I will do everything I can to avoid this fate, but right now, circumstances compel me to stay here."

"Do you need money?" Aimée asked urgently. "I can give you money to return to England."

"It's not that." Emma glanced at Lady Fanchere, still engaged by the couturiere.

"Oh, of course." Aimée's eyes filled with tears. "It's my dear Eleonore. She has confided her previous infertility and her fear she cannot carry this child, and you feel responsible. You are such a kind girl!"

What could Emma say? *No, it's not that?* Because it *was* that. But it was also the Reaper, and Damacia, and Elixabete . . . and after a lifetime of being the vicar's daughter and then a repressed and oppressed paid companion, this was Emma's one chance to live passionately and fully!

In the end, she said nothing, but tried to look modest and concerned, and she must have succeeded, because Aimée sighed and dabbed at her eyes with a handkerchief.

And when Lady Fanchere called, "Emma, come here. Madam Mercier is ready to fit you now," Emma wanted to die of guilt.

At the same time, while she spoke to Lady Fanchere and listened to Madam Mercier's suggestions, her heart beat heavily in her chest, because all she could think was . . . would *he* return tonight?

CHAPTER NINETEEN

Emma sat on her bed in her room, propped up on her pillows, her book open in her hand.

Everything was as it had been the night before. Her nightgown was white, clean, and worn, and buttoned up to her throat. Her hair was braided and carefully arranged over her shoulder. As before a storm growled in the distance, inching closer, sending wisps of wind swirling through the open window.

But Emma wasn't really reading. She was listening. Listening for a man's step in the corridor.

The hotel was silent. Sleeping.

She shouldn't want him to come. Her actions today had been foolish in the extreme. It was one thing to feel as if she had a debt to pay to the man who had rescued her from certain death.

Last night she had paid that debt.

So why had she so eagerly listened when

Prince Sandre told of his plot to capture the Reaper? Why had she so desperately wanted to find some way to pass that report to him?

She could tell herself it was because she was appalled by the conditions in the lower city and wanted to help. That was true. But her tense anticipation tonight proved she had another motivation.

She wanted to see the Reaper again. She wanted him to feel gratitude to her. She wanted him to escape Prince Sandre so he could return to her arms and kiss her as he had kissed her last night. Because last night she had discovered a whole new, unsuspected facet to her personality. She was shallow and easily swayed by passion — she, a rector's daughter!

She laughed softly to herself.

The candle flickered in the breeze.

She glanced at it, then realized — a still figure, clad in a shroud, stood in the shadows.

She should have been prepared. Instead she gasped. Jumped. Gave a little scream. "It's you." Putting her hand over her thumping heart, she said, "It's you. You frightened me!"

He didn't answer.

"How did you get in?"

Of course, he still didn't answer . . . but he moved into the light.

He glided with eerie soundlessness, almost as if he really were a ghost, when she knew very well he was not. Last night he had proved that.

"Did you get my message?" she asked.

There was a flash of glee rapidly subdued. He removed his white gloves, tucked them in his belt. Putting his hand over his heart, he bowed.

She relaxed against the headboard and smiled back. "Good." She had helped him. "Mr. Lawrence is your friend? You sent him to me?"

Again the Reaper bowed.

His bare hands, she saw, were long fingered, broad palmed, tanned, and capable. The sight of them stirred her; it was almost as if he had revealed one of his secrets, showed her a part of himself no one else knew.

"I'm going to spy for you," she said.

He shook his head, an emphatic no.

"I want to. Really, it's easy. All I have to do is flatter Prince Sandre, widen my eyes, and ask if I'll ever be safe from the big, bad Reaper" — Emma pouted seductively, a skill she didn't even know she had — "and he'll tell me anything."

The Reaper frowned, and again shook his head.

"Why not? He has spies everywhere. I visited the lower city and he knew about it. He knew whom I had visited and he knew what I had done. Someone there told him, and that's not fair. You need to know who his spies are."

I will find out.

She understood him so well, even without words. "I want to help you." She didn't have to tell him about Prince Sandre's request to court her, and how much he frightened her. Let the Reaper think this was easy for her. "I *did* help, didn't I?"

Outside, the thunder rumbled, coming closer, and the candle once again flickered in the breeze.

He nodded. He moved his lips as if to speak, then put his hand to the cloth over his throat. Then, in the first awkward move she'd seen him make, he swung around and stumbled toward the door.

"Wait!" She scrambled out of bed.

He turned back, eagerly, she thought.

She came to a halt three feet away from him. "Don't you want to kiss me?" she blurted.

He froze.

She closed her eyes in embarrassment.

Had she really said that?

His boots scraped on the floor. The scent of the Reaper, of leather and horse and man, filled her head.

Her eyes flew open.

He stood directly in front of her. His hand hovered over her head, and as if he couldn't resist, he lightly touched her hair. Slowly, he slid his fingers along her dark braid, following it over her shoulder to the place where it rested on her chest.

She put one bare foot on top of the other.

He watched her face as if he couldn't look away. He watched her intensely, passionately. He watched her as if she were the most enchanting woman in the world, as if he wished nothing more than to live this moment with her.

She took a long breath, dragging air into her lungs.

His gaze shifted to her breasts, pressed against the thin material.

His hand was close, so close, holding her braid. He took a slow breath to match hers. He wanted her; she knew he did. . . .

He seemed to recollect himself, shook his head, once, firmly, and started to step back.

She grabbed his hand and pressed it against her chest.

His palm flattened.

The heat in her flared. It seemed the cotton between them dissolved, and she was left naked and trembling with desire. She wanted him to move his hand lower, to cup her breast, to stroke her nipple, to somehow make that swelling sensation get better . . . or be *more.*

His broad palm moved, lifted her, pressed her yearning flesh. He took her nipple between his forefinger and thumb and lightly squeezed.

Shock sent her reeling backward.

He caught her, his arm around her waist, and brought her back, forcing her to stay in place while he squeezed again, then set in motion a slow, steady thrum of pinch and release, pinch and release.

He wasn't hurting her. But he was driving her mad. The sensation of wanting grew in her breasts and her loins. Her heartbeat escalated, throbbing in her throat and chest. He was branding her with his touch, his scent. . . . She gazed at his face. If only she could see him, really see him, but as before, the mask covered his upper face and drooped over his cheeks; his stark cosmetics, white and black, gave him the bone structure of a ghoul; and a hood covered his hair.

If she met him in the broad light of day,

she wouldn't recognize this man. And he held her breast in her hand, held her passions in thrall. "Please," she whispered.

He leaned forward and kissed her lightly on the lips, a mere brush of promise.

Her lips opened on a sigh.

His unspoken pledge became reality. He slanted his head to hers, smoothly matching their lips, exploring with his breath and his tongue until her eyes closed and she gave a whimper of need.

Lightning flashed, bright on her closed lids. Thunder boomed, a cacophony of glory.

Still he held her away from him, trapped in his embrace, held, but not held close.

She moved closer.

He moved back.

He was teasing her, caressing her breast endlessly, building a dark torment that flashed with the brilliance of the lightning outside.

At last, unable to bear it any longer, she grabbed pieces of the winding sheet that circled him and pulled herself close.

He laughed soundlessly against her lips. His hand left her breast, moved to her throat, and, with deliberation, he opened the row of tiny buttons that closed her nightgown.

The opening revealed nothing. Most

dresses had a wider neck than this. But they were alone, at night, in her bedroom, and beneath the tissue-thin cotton, she wore nothing. When he spread his fingers inside her collar, sliding along the frail bones at the base of her neck, she felt naked. "Please." This time it wasn't so much a plea as a breath of self-consciousness.

Even she knew it was too late for that.

He pushed her against the wall, nudged her head back, and kissed her throat. He slid his mouth behind her ear, ruffling the delicate skin with his breath. His chest, his costume rubbed against her, and her nipples gathered tight, overwhelmed by sensation.

Awareness built. Of him, playing her with his touch. Of herself, growing frantic and needy. Tears of longing pressed at the backs of her eyelids.

He thrust his thigh between her legs, lifting her, setting her to ride him.

The shock of contact made her back arch, made her shudder and sink her fingernails into his shoulders. This was indecent, to have a man, this man, know so much about her body and so expertly exploit her longings, and at the same time . . . Oh, God, the rocking motion forced fire to the ends of her nerves, to the tips of her fingers, to her breasts and deep inside. She burned. She panted. She grew faint from self-consciousness, from desperation, from the abrupt feast of sensation when she had been starving for so long.

It seemed she had waited forever to experience this madness, and yet . . . until this moment, she hadn't known such frenzy existed.

Softly he bit her earlobe . . . and that single, bright, tiny jolt of pain was the lightning strike she needed. Pleasure assaulted her. Unprepared, she shuddered, pressing herself onto his thigh and ever closer to him, moaning as she galloped through the tempest of lightning-bright bliss, of tumultuous gratification, and all the while she held on to him for dear life, closer to him than she had ever been to another human being.

Finally, the violence was spent and she went limp in his arms.

As her breathing grew measured, as her scattered senses returned, she was aware once more of the rain-washed breeze blowing through the open window, of being in a tiny room with him. . . . He had stopped pressing his lips to her skin, tilted her upright, put her on her feet. She clutched him again, not wanting this bliss to stop, but he loosened his hold on her. He held her, running his hands up and down her back, until she had recovered her breath — and he had recovered his.

She glanced at the bed.

He shook his head, but a tiny smile crooked his cheek. It wasn't a cruel refusal. More regretful than anything else.

"Will you come back tomorrow night?" Did she even have any pride? Any finesse? If she did, it had boiled away in this rush of heat.

He lifted his hands helplessly.

"I know. You have other things to do. People to help. Injustices to fix. But I'll see Prince Sandre tomorrow."

The Reaper shook his head.

"I have no choice. He's Lady Fanchere's cousin." *He wants to pay court to me, and Lady de Guignard said it was for no good reason.* "So I might as well listen to him. If I see you, I can give you the information." Then a terrible thought occurred to her, and she added hastily, "But if you think there's danger, don't come. I could tell Mr. Lawrence instead."

The Reaper nodded.

"All right." She smiled and tried to look as if it didn't matter one way or the other. "Please have a care for yourself."

He made a gesture that she easily read:

And you.

"I will."

He opened the door and slipped out so quietly she never heard the latch close.

The wind picked up, lifting her nightgown to dance around her ankles. The storm roared around the hotel, closer and more violent. Lightning blistered the air.

And good sense returned to her.

What had she done?

She had indulged in sin. She had wallowed in passion. She had luxuriated in scandal.

Furthermore . . . she wanted to do it again. With him. With the man whose face she had never seen, whose voice she had never heard, but whose bravery she admired and whose body she worshipped.

Would he return tomorrow night?

Or would he die tonight?

CHAPTER TWENTY

Emma woke to bright sunshine and a rapid knock on the bedroom door.

She sat up, her heart pounding.

They had killed him. They had killed the Reaper.

"Emma?" It was Lady Fanchere's voice. "Are you well? It's very late, and we expected to see you sooner."

She sounded so normal.

Emma looked around. Noted the sun was high. Realized she had overslept, that of all people, Lady Fanchere would not be bringing her that particular piece of bad news; Emma had no reason for panic. She took a deep breath to calm herself and cleared her throat. "I'm sorry; I think I . . ." Pushing back the covers, she climbed out of bed. "My lady, is all well?"

"All is very well. Aimée and I are here to help you dress."

Emma stared at the door as if it were

speaking in a foreign language. They were here to help her dress? "I can dress myself."

"We brought you some different garments."

Emma donned her robe. She should have gone to sleep earlier, but she'd been worried about the Reaper's safety and excited by . . . well, excited. She was paying the price now.

In a low voice, Aimée said, "I told you she would think this odd."

"She's just tired," Lady Fanchere said firmly. "She'll appreciate this later, when she sees the prince."

Emma searched the room, searching for any sign the Reaper had been there, then jerked the door open.

The two women stopped squabbling and fixed smiles on their faces.

"Come in," Emma said.

Lady Fanchere brushed past her.

Lady de Guignard lifted a carpetbag. "We gathered a few things from our trunks." She brushed past, too.

Emma peeked out, looked up and down the corridor. Empty. So she pulled back inside and shut the door, then leaned against it and considered the two ladies.

They were both unpacking their finds, spreading them on the bed, and crowing like roosters over the sunrise. Obviously, they did enjoy dressing her as if she were a doll. She might have enjoyed it, too, if she didn't know they were doing it for Prince Sandre. "What do we have here?" she asked.

"After your fitting yesterday," Lady Fanchere said, "I asked Madam Mercier if she had a gown that might fit you that hadn't worked for another client."

"The gown Lady de Guignard gave me is more than sufficient!"

Lady Fanchere pretended she hadn't heard. "She didn't have anything, but she had this instead!" She lifted a long drape of lace from the bed. "It's a shawl of Belgian lace with an inset of Indian silk."

"It's gorgeous, but not appropriate for a paid companion." Emma could be as firm as Lady Fanchere.

Lady Fanchere capitulated. "You are correct, of course. You have an impeccable sense of propriety, and that would be an asset for Sandre." Seeing Emma draw back, she added, "Of course, what happens next is totally your decision. So we'll put this shawl aside and bring it out only for the evening. Now, look at these cuffs and this collar. They will change your gown from pedestrian to celestial."

Indignation made Emma snap, "I love that

gown, and I appreciate Lady de Guignard's kindness in giving it to me!"

"I liked it, too, Eleonore." Aimée sounded hurt.

"Ladies, we know the criticism any woman gets for wearing a gown more than once. We must disguise this reuse until Madam Mercier is done with Emma's wardrobe." Lady Fanchere looked so eager, Emma and Aimée exchanged glances and submitted.

By the time they were finished, Emma was clad in Lady de Guignard's gown, with white lace collar and cuffs, her beloved old shawl, a new bonnet of violet velvet decorated with fresh pale blue flowers, and soft black leather shoes. When she peered in the mirror, she thought she looked like a young lady in her debut year, young and innocent.

She felt like a lamb to the slaughter.

She dragged her feet all the way down the stairs, along the street, and into the assembly room.

People turned and nodded at Lady Fanchere and Lady de Guignard, casual greetings to two of their own, but when they saw Emma in her finery, they put their heads together and gossiped.

Emma wanted to squirm in embarrassment. Instead she tried to walk, as she always had, one step behind the ladies.

Lady Fanchere would have none of that, but pulled her between them and linked arms. "You're right, Emma. With your bright eyes and pink cheeks, you need no decoration."

Prince Sandre walked in, looked around, and, when he caught sight of them, made a beeline toward them.

Yes. A lamb to the slaughter.

"Smile at Sandre," Lady Fanchere instructed.

Emma couldn't. Then she did, because she had promised the Reaper she would spy for him.

But the smile felt more like a stretching of lips across her bared teeth.

Prince Sandre didn't notice. Maybe he was used to smiles like that. Maybe he couldn't tell the difference.

Maybe he didn't care.

He bowed and smiled, suave and sure of himself. "Good morning, Eleonore, Miss Chegwidden." His gaze skimmed Lady de Guignard. "Aimée."

They all stopped. They all curtsied.

But Emma felt Lady de Guignard press closer, as if simply being in his presence frightened her, and squeezed Aimée's arm comfortingly.

"May I accompany you on your promenade?" His request was a formality; he fell into place beside Lady Fanchere. "Miss Chegwidden, you look very bright today, considering how late you were up."

"I beg your pardon?" she said.

"Your candle was lit very late last night." He watched her from beneath heavy-lidded eyes.

Pressing her lips together, Emma turned her face away. She was not going to give him an explanation, not even a false explanation.

"You did sleep in this morning," Lady Fanchere said. "What were you doing so late?"

Now Emma had no choice. "I was reading, my lady."

"As you were reading the other night." He deliberately reminded her of those moments in her bedroom. "I hope you're not a bluestocking. Too much intelligence is unattractive in a lady."

As if she knew that Emma's hand itched to slap him, Aimée held her arm tightly at her side.

"For heaven's sake, Sandre, you're medieval!" Lady Fanchere laughed. "It's not as if she's reading scandalous literature. For a female author, Jane Austen is quite respected."

"That's true, and as long as a lady doesn't muddy up her mind with serious works of literature, I can approve." He nodded pontifically, then sighed and in a lowered voice said, "I beg you ladies to bear with me. Mr. Gillespie Cosgair and Countess Martin are walking to greet us. He's Irish, wild, rich, and careless, and I fear you may be subjected to rough language in his presence. Also, Countess Martin is a difficult woman."

Aimée murmured in Emma's ear, "Countess Martin is so well-known for her affairs. How could she not be? Her husband behaves like a maniac each and every time."

Mr. Cosgair was fair skinned and dark haired, with eyes as green as spring grass and the figure of a young god all wrapped up in the finest of fashionable garments. Emma could hardly take her gaze off his knee-height glossy black boots or the jacket that fit his shoulders so well and tapered to his narrow waist.

Countess Martin was his match in beauty and fashion, and the exact opposite in coloring: dusky skin, dark eyes, and fair hair. She was also clearly a woman who exulted in her sexuality. Her hips rolled as she walked, her bosom was temptingly displayed almost to the nipples, and her lips were stained with red. She stared at Prince Sandre, challenging him with a lift of her chin.

Again Aimée murmured in Emma's ear: "The countess has a reputation as an oracle."

Emma looked at Aimée, surprised out of good sense. "An oracle? Do you mean she's a fortune-teller?"

"Not like someone who requires you to cross her palm with silver and then tells you you're going to go on a long journey and find true love. She's got marks on the palms of her hands that look like . . . like eyes, and this uncomfortable way of going all unfocused, then grabbing your arm and telling you to stay away from cliffs." Aimée shuddered, but she rattled on as if nothing were wrong. "She was once Sandre's mistress. She's never forgiven him for discarding her, and she is fabulously outspoken."

"Ah," Emma said. That explained Prince Sandre's stiff demeanor.

Lady Fanchere poked them both and glared. "Behave!"

Mr. Cosgair bowed to the prince.

Countess Martin did not. She trailed her black-gloved fingers across Prince Sandre's cheek, kissed his lips, and, in a glorious contralto, said, "Greetings, my darling. Have you heard? Last night your men set a trap for the Reaper."

Emma froze, every muscle in her body tight, waiting . . . waiting. . . .

"On my instructions," Prince Sandre answered stiffly.

"That is a tragedy." Countess Martin laughed softly. "Have you heard what happened?"

"I have!" Mr. Cosgair waved a hand. "Your men strung a rope across the road. In the dark, the rope was invisible. The Reaper rode up the road, looking like a cadaver, or so I understand, and these soldiers of yours jerked the rope taut. And he jumped it as if he had always known it was there."

Prince Sandre stiffened. "He escaped?"

"Oh, yes, Your Highness." Countess Martin almost purred with pleasure. "When he leaped the rope, he waved his arm and the rope broke in two." Her gaze shifted to Emma and it seemed to Emma that she was speaking right to her. "It appears the Reaper is as magically powerful as rumor says he is." She transferred her attention back to the furious Prince Sandre. "My darling, you have failed once more."

Prince Sandre rode up the steep grade to the palace, slashing at his horse until its flanks ran with blood and sweat. From above, he heard the guards shouting, "Open the gate for the prince. Open the gate now!"

Yes, they could tell he was in a fury, and none of them wanted to be the one he took it out on.

As he got close, the gate creaked open. He galloped into the yard, sawed at the reins, and before the stallion had even come to a stop, he leaped out of the saddle.

He stumbled as he landed; he imagined the onlookers sniggering, and that fed his rage. The grand doors to the palace opened as he approached, and he stormed inside. "Where is he?" he shouted to his groveling staff. "Where's Jean-Pierre?"

In a trembling voice, the butler said, "He's in the master guardroom, Your Highness."

Sandre wheeled and turned into the ancient part of the palace, where the decor was centuries old, the servants were housed, and his personal guard ate and drank in their off-hours. As he walked, his riding boots echoed loudly on the stone floors, his spurs jingled, and his temper rose with each step.

No one waited at the entrance to the guardroom. He paused, then pushed against the door enough to open it slightly and peer within.

His loyal men lounged on benches, leaned on tables, drank wine, and laughed. *Laughed!*

With a grand gesture, he slammed the door against the wall.

Everyone froze, turned. And cowered.

But Jean-Pierre, the traitor who should have run, who should have hidden himself, stood before the fire and stared as if he didn't comprehend what awaited him. And maybe he didn't. Maybe he was such a big fool, he honestly didn't.

Sandre stalked across the floor, measuring each step, using his innate sense of drama to guide his actions. "You. You dare look me in the face?" In a sudden move, he lifted his arm and slashed at Jean-Pierre.

He caught his cousin by surprise. The skin broke across Jean-Pierre's nose, across his cheek, across his jaw, in one giant, bloody slice. For one moment, he looked murderous.

Sandre raised his whip again, the murderous expression vanished, and Jean-Pierre did what he should have in the first place — he lifted his arm to protect his face. "Your Highness! Stop!"

"Stop? You dare tell me what to do? After you humiliated me in front of the whole country? In front of the *world?*"

Jean-Pierre retreated across the room.

The guards scattered like cockroaches.

"I gave you a plan to rid me of this Reaper. And what did you do with my plan? You ruined it, and at the same time, you built his reputation." Sandre slashed and slashed.

Jean-Pierre ducked and ducked.

"They're talking. Everybody's talking."

"Who?"

"The whole country. About how the powerful, superior Reaper leaped the rope in the dark and broke it with a wave of his hand. You *fool!* Did you check the rope before you placed it? Did you watch to see which of these men, of my *guard,* sabotaged it in favor of this Reaper?" Sandre stopped, chest heaving. His arm dropped.

One of the guards actually dared to *speak.* "No, Your Highness, we would never betray you."

"You believe that the Reaper is the ghost of King Reynaldo, come to take revenge on the de Guignards. You want everyone to believe the Reaper is the harbinger of the king's return. And you want the ignorant to believe it, too."

"I'll find out who did it," Jean-Pierre said.

"Don't bother." In a cold, clear voice, Sandre said, "Twelve lashes each." He looked at Jean-Pierre. "You administer the whip. Do it now. Do it before you care for your face. Maybe that way, every time you look in the mirror, you'll remember what it costs to fail me." He strode away, leaving shock and silence behind him. At the door, he turned. "Get me the Reaper, Jean-Pierre. Get him soon, and don't fail me again. The gibbet is high and hungry, and I love to watch a man dance as he hangs."

CHAPTER
TWENTY-ONE

For Emma, the week that followed was oddly pleasant, a time out of mind.

Prince Sandre had walked away from the scene in the assembly room, and he hadn't returned. Word, via Countess Martin, claimed that he'd returned to the palace to direct Jean-Pierre and his men in the capture of the Reaper.

Every day, a gown arrived from Madam Mercier for Emma to wear, and while part of Emma was appalled to be so indebted to Lady Fanchere, the other part, the part that had never been indulged . . . that part was thrilled each time she donned a new gown of green velvet or one of chocolate brown silk.

Lady Fanchere ate, took her naps, and went to bed early, and Emma's belief in her ability to carry this child grew with every passing day. When the next six months were over, Lady Fanchere would present her husband with a healthy child; Emma felt sure of it.

Lady Fanchere and Lady de Guignard refused to allow Emma to return to her role as paid companion. They treated her like a young relative in training for her first season, and introduced her to members of international society staying in Aguas de Dioses. Such was their cachet that Emma was courteously treated by almost everyone — everyone except old Mrs. Mortensen, who offered her a position as her companion and snorted rudely when Lady Fanchere said Emma was no longer working as a common girl. "Once a commoner, always a commoner, I always say," Mrs. Mortensen had said. "Blood will tell."

Countess Martin drifted by and said, "Miss Chegwidden is a direct descendant of William the Conqueror. Her blood is purer than yours, Mrs. Mortensen, with a strong Danish influence." And she drifted away.

"Humph!" But Mrs. Mortensen said nothing more.

Countess Martin had repeated a much-treasured Chegwidden family tale. Emma didn't ask how she knew.

She didn't ask because nothing that happened in the daytime mattered very much.

What mattered were the nights, when the Reaper appeared in her bedchamber. He didn't come for information; with the prince gone, she had none to give him. He came for her.

He appeared silently in a gust of wind, and once, in the distance, thunder growled. She ran to him, flung herself into his arms, and they kissed, passionately, yearning, touching each other with ever-increasing boldness. He caressed her ears, her shoulders, the base of her spine, and the peaks of her breasts. He pressed her against the wall, holding her there with his body, while they grew ever more frantic with need.

But every night, despite her invitation, he left her alone to dream deeply of him and a passion so bold her dull life was transformed.

She worried about his safety, of course, but she began to think he truly was a phantom, capable of slipping past guards and into her arms.

So when, on the morning of the eighth day, Lady Fanchere and Aimée knocked on her door, she opened it eagerly.

The maid Emma had been assigned was there, standing behind the ladies.

Lady Fanchere was smiling.

Aimée was not.

To the maid, Lady Fanchere said, "Pack Miss Chegwidden. Pack her up! We're leaving today!"

"What?" Emma's bright mood evaporated in an instant. "We're leaving here? Now? Why? Where are we going?"

"We're going home. To prepare."

"For what, my lady?"

Lady Fanchere handed her a stiff piece of paper, folded and sealed with purple wax.

Emma broke the seal, opened the paper, and read, *To Miss Emma Chegwidden: Prince Sandre of Moricadia requests your presence at a ball in the royal palace.* . . . She looked up at the ladies. "But this is tomorrow night!"

"Yes, isn't it wonderful? I thought Sandre had gone back merely to capture the Reaper — and I'm sure that has been his primary focus; he is very concerned about our safety. But he also arranged for an event wherein all Moricadia can meet you!"

Emma looked between the two ladies, seeking some kind of reassurance when she knew there was none, when she should be glad to be back in touch with Prince Sandre so she could spy for the Reaper.

"I know what you're thinking," Lady Fanchere said confidently.

"I doubt that," Emma replied.

"But I already spoke to Madam Mercier, and she has your wardrobe ready, all except your ball gown, and she's throwing all her resources into that. She'll deliver it herself tomorrow." Lady Fanchere turned to Aimée. "Have you decided? Are you going to return with us?"

"Isn't she going to the ball?" Emma asked in alarm.

"I didn't receive an invitation." Aimée smiled tightly.

"She's so recently a widow, it wouldn't be proper for her to attend so frivolous an event as a ball." Lady Fanchere wrapped her arm around the obviously un-grief-stricken Aimée. "But Fanchere would be glad to host her if she wishes to remain here among the beauties of Aguas de Dioses."

"I believe it would be safer to come with you," Aimée said.

"Aimée!" Lady Fanchere glared reproachfully. "You aren't still imagining that Sandre —"

"Yes. So I'll return with you and help Emma to prepare for her debut into Moricadian society." Aimée sounded weary and quite unlike her usual cheerful self.

"That would be lovely, Lady de Guignard. I would appreciate your support," Emma answered honestly, truly wanting Aimée's kindness. Yet at the same time, she wasn't really thinking of the ball or Lady Fanchere's hopes or Prince Sandre's courtship.

She could think of only one thing — when she disappeared from Aguas de Dioses, would the Reaper be able to find her?

CHAPTER
TWENTY-TWO

"You've returned." Lord Fanchere helped the ladies out of the traveling coach. As he kissed his wife, he said, "You appear to be blooming."

Lady Fanchere laughed and returned his kiss. "It was a wonderful retreat. Aimée no longer feels burdened with grief."

Lord Fanchere kissed Aimée's forehead and nodded as if he had never believed that to be an issue. "I was almost glad to hear the prince had ordered a ball, knowing that would bring you home to me." His gaze shifted to Emma, and he nodded brusquely. "And with a new project."

Lady Fanchere tucked her hand in his arm. "I can't wait to tell you all about it."

"I've heard rumors," he said, and led her into the house and up the stairs.

Brimley directed the flow of trunks into the house.

Emma curtsied to him.

He seemed not to notice.

Aimée and Emma entered the grand foyer. Servants flowed around them, carrying garment bags and hatboxes and everything new from Madam Mercier.

As they removed their hats and handed them to a maid, Aimée drooped with discouragement. "Now I have to decide what to do. Countess Martin spoke to me again, and warned me to stay away from cliffs and high places. Look around!" She gestured out the window. "All of this country is cliffs! Nowhere is safe for me. Except here. I never want to leave. As long as I'm with Eleonore, he doesn't dare hurt me. But I can't stay forever!"

"You're speaking of Prince Sandre?"

"Yes. As long as I stay in Moricadia, my life is in danger. I know Eleonore doesn't believe me, but it's true. Sandre is going to kill me."

"*I* believe you." On the ride back, Aimée's unhappiness had become increasingly apparent, and Emma had pondered her plight. "If I understood correctly, when you married Rickie de Guignard, you had a fortune."

"I was an heiress."

"Do you know, is the fortune intact?"

"I don't know anything about it. He never allowed me that knowledge."

"Perhaps you could ask Lord Fanchere to find out, and if there is a fortune, you could ask him to help you send funds ahead so you could go to Greece, or England, or anywhere beyond Prince Sandre's reach."

Aimée stared at Emma, dumbfounded. Slowly, a sparkle grew in her eyes. "I could do that, couldn't I? I've always wanted to go to Italy."

"You have no children to hold you here. Why not go and spend the winter wrapped in sunshine?"

"He would help me, I know he would, and that is the exact right solution!" Aimée embraced Emma. "You are the smartest, kindest girl in the whole world! I'm not even going to unpack, and when Fanchere is finished greeting his wife" — she winked — "I'll speak with him!"

Emma watched her trot up the stairs, and drew in a sigh of relief. At least she knew she'd done one thing right. Removed from Prince Sandre's influence, Aimée would live a long and happy life.

"Miss Chegwidden?" A young girl of perhaps eight or nine curtsied before her. She was a pretty thing in a miniature maid's costume, with a white mobcap too large for her small head, and a large white apron tied around her waist twice.

Emma couldn't place the girl until she saw the sling that bound her arm against her side. "Elixabete! How good you look. How clean!" Perhaps not the most tactful thing to say, but without the grime that had encrusted her, Elixabete was a handsome child, if still far too thin.

Elixabete wasn't offended. She grinned, showing strong white teeth.

"Lady Fanchere employed you, then?"

"Yes, ma'am, and Mr. Brimley has been most solicitous of my injury."

Remembering the spy who had reported her visit to the city, Emma asked, "Is your mother well?"

"She is most well, thank you, and she told me to tell you something." Elixabete glanced around and lowered her voice. "If ever you need help with anything, call me. I will do anything for you. You saved me, my mother, and my sister, and we pay our debts."

Emma stared at the child. She was so young, so small, and yet she understood the need for subterfuge, for secrecy, and most of all, she understood loyalty. Emma wanted to assure her that she would never need anything, and yet . . . she was involved, so involved, in the troubles of this country. Someday, perhaps she might need to pass a message or send for help, and although her conscience might prick her, she would do it . . . to save the Reaper. "Thank you, Elixabete. I will remember that."

"You're back!" Michael Durant stood in the door of the library. His voice was low, scratchy, but he projected it across the breadth of the entryway.

"My lord, how good to see you." Emma folded her hands primly before her.

"You look well." He surveyed her from head to toe, noting her new garments. "You look very well. Aguas de Dioses must have agreed with you."

"Yes, thank you, it did."

"Go on, Elixabete." Durant pointed toward the servants' quarters. "Before someone sees you speaking with Miss Chegwidden. You know it's better if you appear not to know her."

What an odd thing to say. Or perhaps not so odd; Durant seemed to comprehend Elixabete's situation better than anyone.

"Yes, my lord." Elixabete curtsied and whisked away, a sprite in a big brown dress.

"What brought you back?" He advanced on Emma, curiosity dancing in his lively green eyes.

"Lady Fanchere received an invitation to the prince's ball tomorrow night, and so we returned to prepare." She hesitated, reluctant to tell him everything, but what was the use of hiding the truth? He was going to find out somehow, and better if he heard it from her. "Actually, I received an invitation, too."

"You did?" Imperiously, he gestured her into the library.

She found herself obeying him without question. He had an air of command about him, and she remembered he was, after all, the son of a duke and a privileged member of English society.

He indicated a love seat by the window.

She placed herself in one corner.

He placed himself in the opposite corner, not three feet away. In a stern tone, he asked, "Since when does Prince Sandre invite a paid companion to one of his royal dances?"

She felt as if she were facing a strict older brother. "He wishes to court me."

"Have you lost your mind?" His voice rasped with dismay.

She expected him next to point out the chasm between a prince and a serving girl.

Instead, he said, "Have you not heard of his cruelties, his excesses? You can't marry a man like that. You would be miserable living with him, and die an early death while under his thumb. Believe me. Many have."

She stared at him, wondering at the way he leaned forward, at the shadow that darkened his eyes and the intensity with which he spoke. She wanted to assure him she knew all those things, and that she had an ulterior motive.

But how would that improve matters between them? He'd warned her about getting involved in the situation here. He would hardly approve of her helping the most wanted man in Moricadia.

Most important, she could never hint that she had met the Reaper.

"Lady Fanchere is quite enthusiastic about Prince Sandre." Emma was very good at being noncommittal; she had learned the art while working for Lady Lettice.

"Lady Fanchere is a kind woman who sees the best in everyone, and she's related to your beloved prince."

"I know." Emma glanced out the window. The sun was starting to sink below the horizon. She needed some privacy, some time to prepare in case, just in case, the Reaper somehow managed to follow her here. "I comfort myself that the prince can court me, but I don't have to accept."

"Once Prince Sandre has indicated his intentions, and the rest of the country knows about it, do you believe you can walk away from him?"

"Until I agree —"

Durant snorted. "My dear, even you can't be that naïve. If you dared refuse him, he would hunt you down and bring you back, and make you pay for humiliating him."

He chided her so passionately, she wavered, then remembered again — the Reaper. She was doing this to help the Reaper. "Surely it's not so desperate as you paint it." Jumping to her feet, she said, "I must go. It's bedtime."

Durant looked outside in astonishment. "It's still light!"

"I'm tired. From the journey."

He stood tall, unsmiling, forbidding. "I suppose you want a good night's sleep so you'll be fresh for the ball tomorrow night."

"Of course." *Good excuse.* "Yes!"

"You know, at one time, I had thought of courting you myself."

"Don't be silly." She laughed.

He didn't. "But what's a man who will someday inherit a dukedom when compared with a prince of a small country?"

Her amusement faded. "I don't believe you, but even if I did — why would you imply such a cruel thing?"

"Cruel? For what other reason than the desire for wealth and security would a

woman like you marry such a man as Sandre de Guignard?"

The scorn with which he spoke caught her
by surprise, and so did the rage that lifted
her like a wave rising on the incoming tide.
Lunging at Durant, she said, "You know
nothing of what a woman *like me* desires.
You've never been so poor that if you didn't
obtain a position, you would have to work
the streets as a prostitute. You've never
rubbed a minor noblewoman's smelly feet,
knowing full well that when she was satisfied, she would kick you away. You've never
wandered in the forest, so cold and lost that
lonely death beckoned and you wanted to
run to its arms." She gestured widely. "Yes,
you were in prison for two years, but you
put yourself there. Women *like me* are
placed in this prison of poverty and desperation through no volition of our own, and we
live and die there without hope of ever
escaping. So don't judge me, my lord. You
know nothing of my motivations."

"Emma . . ." His hand rose as if to cup
her cheek. He stared into her angry eyes. . . .

And for a moment, she had the oddest
feeling of familiarity . . . and fear. What was
it about this man that made her react so
violently to his disdain?

Then the wave of fury crashed around her,

241

and she didn't care. Turning, she flounced
out of the library.

CHAPTER
TWENTY-THREE

As Emma hurried to her bedchamber, she wiped a few angry tears off her hot cheeks.

How dared Durant speak to her so critically? What did he know about women "like her"? His whole life had been one of privilege. Or at least, until the last two years it had been a life of privilege. Stupid to care about his opinion when he stayed here in Moricadia, lazing about, doing nothing to relieve his family's worry; he was a man of little honor or loyalty.

Yet she couldn't forget that he had been kind to Elixabete and Damacia, and she knew that in another time and place she would have been enchanted by his interest in her.

Oh! She couldn't make sense of that man. First he was indolent. Then he was kind. Then he implored her to stay away from Prince Sandre for her well-being. Then he accused her of being nothing better than a strumpet, trading her body for money.

She started up the second stairway to her bedroom in the servants' quarters when Tia stopped her. "Miss Chegwidden, do you remember me? I'm the maid who helped you on your first day here."

"You're Tia." And Tia was acting oddly, not looking at Emma, pretending to be subservient to the extreme. "What's wrong?"

"Thank you for your graciousness." Tia curtsied. "I'm here to assist you. Your chamber has been moved."

"Moved?" Emma scrubbed her handkerchief over her red eyes. "Why moved?"

"Those were my instructions, ma'am. If you would follow me . . ."

Emma glanced up the narrow stairway, then hurried to catch up. "All right, but I'll need to get my belongings. . . ."

"I transferred everything to your new chamber. There was not so much that I needed help." Tia said the words with such a lack of inflection, they were a criticism that made Emma wince.

"No, I suppose not."

The maid led Emma down a broad corridor hung with oil paintings and gilt-framed mirrors, and stopped before a wide door. Opening it, she waited while Emma entered.

Emma gaped at the large, sumptuous room. An oriental rug of brown, red, and cream covered much of the polished wood floor. A mirror hung over the dressing table covered with creams and cosmetics. A red velvet chair sat on one side of a fireplace set with wood.

While Emma watched, Tia knelt and lit the fire. "It's warm for a fire," she ventured.

"As the sun goes down, the evening will grow chilly, and you'll want the heat after your bath."

After my bath?

Tia closed the amber drapes of velvet hung at the windows and opened the bed curtains to reveal the massive bed. Going to the tall wardrobe, she opened it and said, "I've hung your gowns here, and your under- and nightclothes are here." She showed Emma the drawers. "I've taken the liberty of laying out one of your nightgowns and a robe." She gestured toward the bed.

Emma gawked at the white lace-trimmed garments.

A soft knock rattled the door.

"That would be the water." Tia let a procession of serving maids carrying steaming buckets into the room. Two burly scullery maids followed lugging a huge tub.

Brimley stood in the entrance, holding a cold supper laid out on a tray. He handed it to Tia, who placed it on the table beside the bed. Then as she directed the placement and filling of the bath, Brimley asked, "Is all to Miss Chegwidden's satisfaction?"

She stared at him, horrified.

He used his most proper stuffy-butler tone, and he wouldn't look at her.

This was why he hadn't spoken to her as she entered the château. Clearly, he was indicating his loss of respect for her.

He had come up especially to indicate his loss of respect for her.

And she didn't want that. She liked Brimley. *She* respected *him.* But like Durant, he had warned her against getting involved in Moricadian affairs. How could she explain her actions in a way that would make Brimley accept them as wise? In his book, what she was doing was the *epitome* of unwise.

So in a faltering voice, she said, "Yes, thank you. All is most satisfactory."

"Tia pleases you as your lady's maid?"

Emma darted a glance at Tia. The girl stood, hands folded before her in the manner of a docile servant — in the manner Emma had so often used herself — and stared at the floor. "Tia pleases me, yes."

"Very good, ma'am." Brimley bowed, head

246

turned away, turned on his heel, and left.

The rest of the servants left with him. None of them looked at her — she was being snubbed by her peers. Because she was above herself? Or because it was the despised Prince Sandre who paid her court?

Only Tia remained, and she helped Emma out of her clothes and into the tub. While Emma bathed, the maid bustled around, building the fire higher, warming the towels, warming the sheets, pouring a crystal glass of deep red wine. She helped Emma wash her hair, and when she was finished, she helped her out, dried her, and held the nightgown so Emma could slip it over her head and the robe so she could put her arms into it.

Tia never spoke. Never looked at her.

Emma broke the stifling silence. "You may have the bath removed; then leave me to enjoy my solitude until the morning."

Tia looked surprised, as if she had expected Emma to break under the unspoken criticism. But she did as she was told, placed the wine and the food tray on the table before the fire, and in only a few minutes, Emma was alone.

In the distance, she could hear the deep rumble of thunder, like a criticism about everything she thought and everything she did. In this large room, she felt small and dirty, and cheap. She had bought this luxury under false pretenses, and while she knew she was doing the right thing, she also knew how her acceptance of Prince Sandre's courtship looked to everyone except the optimistic Lady Fanchere. She did look like a strumpet grasping at her chance to escape the hopelessness of her life. Not that women hadn't done exactly that for all of history, but few had had to face so degrading and cruel a bridegroom as Prince Sandre.

Sitting down on the velvet chair, she pulled her comfortable old shawl around her shoulders, picked up her comb, and began to work the tangles out of her hair.

As he had for so many nights, Jean-Pierre sat on his drowsing horse, quiet, immobile, concealed by the brush beside the main road. He was alone; for too long the Reaper had evaded him. And the prince would not wait forever.

As he had so many times before, Jean-Pierre touched the whip slash that had opened his face to the bone. It was red, infected, a reminder, as Prince Sandre had hoped, of his failure.

So Jean-Pierre had shed the company of his men, the men who grew impatient with the long hours of waiting, who gossiped among themselves about Sandre's obsession with catching the Reaper and, with their gossip, let servants know where they were going and what they were doing.

Now Jean-Pierre slept by day, and by night he watched the road, his rifle loaded and at the ready.

Tonight it was after midnight. The shadows were thick. The half-moon sailed high in the sky. In the distance, he heard the inevitable thunderstorm, and cursed viciously.

Every night, another storm rose over the horizon, bringing gusts of windblown rain and lightning flashes to set the world on fire. As if the damp weren't miserable enough, he knew the peasants pointed to the tempests as proof that the Reaper controlled the weather. For didn't he always appear in a clap of thunder and disappear in a flash of lightning?

Superstitious serfs.

He stiffened.

Nearer at hand, he heard the *clop-clop* of a horse galloping down the road.

Silently, he slid the rifle from the leather holster.

The rich Irishman, Mr. Gillespie Cosgair, rounded the corner, leaning over the neck of his gelding, glancing behind and urging him on as if in a panic.

In a panic? Because he was being chased by the Reaper?

Jean-Pierre put the rifle to his shoulder.

Another horse came around the corner in hot pursuit.

Count Belmont Martin raced down the road, his eyes fixed on Cosgair's back, his face contorted in a killing rage.

Once again, Martin's wife had made him a cuckold.

Jean-Pierre slid his rifle back into the holster.

And waited.

CHAPTER TWENTY-FOUR

The Reaper slipped into Emma's room through the door that connected to the next-door sitting room, and moved soundlessly to the middle of the room.

She sat before the fire, wrapped in her favorite old shawl, leaning forward to capture the heat of the flames and sliding her comb through her long, dark hair. The sight of her pensive silhouette made his heart melt even while the fire backlit the thin material of her nightgown and showed him the outline of her long, slender legs.

She put her comb down. Took a sip of wine and ate a handful of grapes. The shawl slipped off one shoulder, and he saw that she wore a new nightgown with lace straps and a lace bodice. Lace! As if her beauty needed any enhancement.

Unbidden, a raw sound escaped him.

She turned and saw him, clad in his costume of rags and shredded scarf, mask and white powder.

Slowly, she straightened. The other nights, his appearance had given her joy. Not tonight. Tonight she seemed uncertain, and rushed into explanation. "We had to leave suddenly. I didn't dare leave a message, and I was afraid you couldn't find me. I didn't want you to think I was . . . that I was avoiding you."

He wished he thought that. He wished she were less honorable, less determined to do what she thought was right.

He wished he desired her less. He wished . . . he wished one of them could walk away. Instead, they met in secret, drawn together by mutual desire.

He strode to stand before her. Taking the comb out of her hand, he ran it through her dark hair, lifting it as if he were spinning ebony.

Outside, the thunderstorm rumbled closer, flashing heat and light into the soil, igniting trees and slashing the earth with hail.

She sighed and relaxed, as if his ministrations gave her pleasure. "When I left England, the length was down to my hips, but when I realized how difficult Lady Lettice would be, I cut most of it." It hung down just past her shoulder blades now. "As Lady

Lettice said, it's not as if it's a pretty color."

Dropping the comb to the floor, he put his knee on the wide seat beside her. Gathering handfuls of her hair, he crushed it in his fists like a miser with his gold, then used it to tilt her head back for his kiss. He probed her mouth, seeking pleasure in the taking.

She tasted of red wine and ripe fruit. She smelled of lavender soap and warm woman.

God, he wanted her. It seemed as if he'd always wanted her, that all his life he'd been waiting for her, for the moment when they would meet and fall in love, and he would take her in his arms and make her his.

He ran a fingertip across the low, off-the-shoulder neckline, then lightly touched each nipple as they strained against the lace inset. He observed the blush that rose from beneath her neckline, felt the press of desire, and knew that only his restraint kept them apart. She was in love with him, had fallen easily for the romance of his deeds and his dark masquerade. But she loved an illusion, and until he could reveal himself, he had to hold back from the final claiming.

She tilted her head back, silently inviting him to touch her with his lips, to take what was his.

He had to leave now, before he succumbed to her enticements.

He turned away.

She stood and grabbed his arm.

He looked back.

She shook her hair away from her face and glared at him, one hand clutching his arm, the other lifted in a fist. "You kiss me. You caress me. But it's a game with you. You always run away, and you always leave me frustrated. Why should I think tonight is any different?"

He wanted to answer, but he couldn't break his silence.

"I won't be here tomorrow night." She lifted her chin, angry and defiant.

He turned back, spread his hands to ask why.

She threw off her shawl. "I'm going to the prince's ball."

This silence that imprisoned him drove him mad. He wanted to speak to her, to beg her not to go, to forbid her to pursue this dangerous course. But he couldn't.

So she kept talking. "That's why we came back from Aguas de Dioses. I'm going with Lord and Lady Fanchere as the prince's guest."

He shook his head.

"You know why I'm going to the ball. This last week . . . every night with you, it's been wonderful. But every morning I wake up, terrified you've been shot, imprisoned, killed. You don't even . . . You wear white. White! At least you could wear a black cape over your costume while you ride. The tourists would still see you, hear about you. They'd still be afraid. They'd still run away, depriving Prince Sandre's treasury of their gold. But no. You won't listen to me. You *have* to stand out as much as possible, be the brightest target you can be. I can't stand it." Her fingers gripped him more tightly. "I know you don't like it, but I will continue to encourage the prince — I must know what his plans are. It's the only way."

Taking her shoulders, he shook her. *No.*

"You can't stop me. You exist only at night." She was taunting him as she had never done before.

He knew why. He kissed her. Caressed her. Made her mad with passion, and every night left her alone to suffer. She was in love with a man who didn't exist and with whom she could never have a real relationship, never marry, never carry his children. . . . He had given her hope, and at the same time taken it from her.

So she said, "I'll dance with the prince tomorrow night. I'll smile at him; I'll drink with him; if he asks me to be his dinner partner, I'll dine with him. And I'll do it for you — but I'll enjoy myself, too."

His hands trembled on her shoulders; he fought to contain himself.

"Because some people believe women like me will do anything for security." Her voice broke on a bitter laugh. "Perhaps I'll marry the prince to keep you safe."

No. No, you can't.

Even through the mask, she must have seen his anguish, for she smiled, a cruel Delilah.

Finally, frustration and lust drove him mad, and he cracked. Turning to the bed, he ripped the covers off and flung them to the floor before the fire. He pushed the thin lace sleeves off her shoulders. The gown slithered down. She stood before him clothed only in firelight and defiance.

She'd gained much-needed weight while working for Lady Fanchere, yet still her belly was flat and muscled from the labor she'd performed for so many years. Her waist was narrow, her hips lush, her legs long and lean. And below, a small dark brush of hair guarded her passage.

Lifting her, he laid her on the floor, on the crinkled mass of velvet and goose down he had tossed.

She sank into the plush coverings, her hair

wild about her, and she glared at him as if he had done something wrong. "Are you teasing me again?" she snapped.

Wait, he gestured. Reaching into the depths of his costume, he loosened the ties that bound the top and pulled them apart. He shed the wrap of shroud and winding rags.

She gazed at his chest, tanned from his hours in the high mountain sun. "Beautiful," she whispered.

He wanted to laugh aloud. There had been a lot of women in his life, experienced women, women who taught him skills, women who enjoyed those skills, Englishwomen, continental women, noblewomen, and commoners. None of them had ever called him beautiful.

But Emma's awed gaze made him feel . . . beautiful. Strong.

She made him forget the nightmares.

He opened the ties at his waist and discarded the cleverly sewn trousers. The boots and socks went next, and he was naked. Naked except for the wrap around his throat, his hood, his mask, and the white powder that disguised his face.

He dropped to his knees beside her.

Her expression had changed. She was no longer haughty and angry. Rather, she looked curious and amazed and frightened and eager and wary.

She looked like a girl who faced her first lover, and found the reality more than she had ever imagined.

If he could have laughed aloud, he would have, for her startled gaze flattered him, made him grow harder, longer . . . made the press of passion imperative.

He had cupped her breasts, brought her to orgasm with his caresses. He knew the shape and texture of each sweet tit, yet to see them, full and firm, nipples pointing at him . . .

Cold? Nerves?

He didn't know. He didn't care. All he knew was that he wanted to stroke them, suck on them, until she writhed in desperation and begged him for his cock inside her.

Leaning down to her, he gathered her into his arms and kissed her. She yielded as always, but his shoulders seemed to have acquired heat, for she touched him as gingerly as she might have touched a hot iron. And when she found the brand on his upper right back, her eyes grew big and she explored with her fingertips. "What is it?" she asked.

He looked away.

She sat up and looked at the red, raised

mark in the shape of an eagle. "Oh, Reaper." She kissed the brand, a soft caress that healed him even as she branded him with her own lips.

He took her down again, leaned against her breasts and slid his chest back and forth; she froze, closed her eyes, and breathed. Just breathed.

He'd learned so much about her body in the last week. She was sensitive and easily startled, innocent, with an instinctive knowledge of what would please him . . . and her.

Armed with that knowledge, he went to work.

CHAPTER
TWENTY-FIVE

The Reaper slid his palms down the sides of Emma's waist and over her hips, over and over, soothing her as if she were a lion and he the tamer.

As he caressed her, her ire faded, and she focused on him. On his face, hidden by the mask that, even now, he didn't discard. On his body, magnificent and layered with muscle, smooth and tanned from the sun. On his intentions . . . Her eyes half closed.

He was generating new passions in her, building a madness that stripped away her control, and with nothing more than those long, slow strokes of comfort. Then his hands began to wander, to slide up to her wrists, lifting them above her head, exposing the tender undersides of her arms. Then down her thighs, where the skin perceived his passion and warmed at his touch. Her skin grew sensitive to the air, to the light, to his breath as he leaned toward her to kiss her lips.

Finally, *finally,* she had provoked him into giving her what she wanted. Finally. It was happening. She wanted to shout with joy, to twirl with excitement.

She wanted to be joined with him for all eternity, and if that wasn't possible, she wanted to be joined with him *now.* Because although she knew nothing about men and women, she knew this: The Reaper had a way of walking, of standing, of *being,* that assured her he would not rest until she fell exhausted and satisfied into his arms.

This was nothing like her youthful imagining. She had thought making love would be romantic, something done between two people that would propel them into a gossamer world full of moonbeams and perfume.

Instead they were naked, and the very newness of this had her feeling shy and gawky, brought a sudden return of Miss Emma Chegwidden, paid companion, whose only real skill was foot massage. And according to Lady Lettice, she hadn't even done *that* well.

It all came down to this: She had been raised in the country. She knew how farm animals mated. She'd been midwife to many a mother and baby. She understood how this was going to work, but she hadn't expected him to be so . . . real.

She could smell him, smell soap and sandalwood and the desire in his veins. She could feel the heat he generated, and how seeing her, touching her, raised his temperature another degree. She could hear his harsh breath, the smooth sigh of their bodies as they moved together.

Could he smell the desire on her? He leaned close and took a long breath, as if he needed her scent to live. Could he feel her heat? Her skin glowed with warmth, with need. Could he hear her heart beating in anticipation? Could he hear the panting of her breath as he twined their fingers together, as she kissed his hand, his shoulder, his cheek?

She had no secrets . . . and for that very reason, she grew shy and wary.

They'd embraced, yes. They'd caressed. He had brought her pleasure every night. Yet every moment they had remained clothed.

Now he put his mouth to her breasts, and she pushed against him in instinctive denial.

He paid no heed.

Then, as joy began to grow, her hands smoothed along his shoulders, exploring the muscles she'd previously found only under his costume.

Silently, he encouraged her, lightly lapping at her areola, at the underside of her breast, at the upper slope. When her fingernails scratched him softly, he responded by pulling her nipple into his mouth and sucking strongly, rhythmically, until her back arched and her legs moved with desperate uncertainty.

The fire burned beside them, providing a glossy warmth to his skin. Outside, she could hear thunder ripping the curtain of night.

Inside she heard her heart pounding in her head, heard the crackle of flames and the rustle of goose down shifting beneath their combined weight.

He assaulted her with caresses. He stroked the lobes of her ears as he nudged her legs apart; then lifting her legs and opening them wide, he looked *there,* until she writhed with embarrassment and . . . oh, desire, too, for a dampness grew under his appreciative gaze.

"Don't," she whispered. "Please."

Still holding one leg, he slid his fingers up and down her cleft, lightly, the same kind of stroking he'd done on her sides, on her arms.

But this was not the same; in that other

stroking there had been an element of comfort. There was no comfort in this. Agitation, yes. Passion, yearning . . . the need to demand . . . things . . .

If he would just press a little harder, caress a little deeper . . .

And he read her mind, pushing his finger inside, gliding along, using his thumb to circle her clitoris. . . .

She lifted her hips, whimpering, moaning, whispering pleas that he must have heard and understood, for he carefully, oh, so carefully, worked another finger inside her, stretching her to the point of discomfort, and then, as the constriction eased, pulling out and working his fingers in again.

He was manipulating her, using his skills to make her feel *more* than she expected or wanted.

She moved her hips, trying make him do what she wanted, to build her need into something greater.

But he took his hand away, pressed his chest to hers, applying weight like a tool designed to make her malleable, and used his thighs to spread her legs wider again. His fingers moved between her legs; then it was no longer his fingers, but his cock, long and thick, pressing inside, and she discovered the truth.

He was bigger than his fingers, and he hurt her.

"Wait!"

He didn't.

She fought, shoving against him, trying to throw him off, but if anything, her motions pushed him deeper. He held himself still, let her struggle, let her wiggle, and when she was finished, he was all the way inside.

"It burns!" And she was mad about it. All that lush and glorious promise, vanquished by him. By his size and determination and refusal to quit.

He didn't seem concerned about her anger. No, he *smiled,* a slow smile of promise.

Startled, she focused on him, on his face, his body, his scent, his strength. . . . How could he hurt her and at the same time make her want what he promised? What was he doing that made this more than the act?

He put her hands on his shoulders and shifted, slowly sitting up and back on his heels, holding her hips, bringing her with him. Lifting her as if she weighed nothing.

She was in his lap, face-to-face, looking into his eyes beneath the mask. She was straddling him, her legs around his hips, her feet planted flat on the floor. He was so far inside her it felt as if they could never be parted.

Had the burning sensation bonded them together?

No, because she could still move. With her feet under her, she could lift up . . . and she did.

And when she was almost free, he caught her hips and pushed her back down. She tried again, and again he pushed her back.

He watched her, smiling, challenging her.

She stopped, panting, angry and in pain and wanting . . . wanting what he'd tacitly sworn he would give her. With more finesse and without his help, she rose and fell, once, twice, stroking herself on him, riding him as if he were a stallion.

His smile vanished. His muscles grew taut. He leaned back, braced himself on his hands, and gave her the freedom of his body.

Self-consciousness became self-centeredness. Pain became desire.

Before, he had made her aware of everything around her. Now she was aware of only him, only her. Where they touched she felt the throbbing of desire, the desperation for release, a desperation that increased with each stroke. She could see the tension in his shoulders as he fought to hold himself in control.

He was sweating, grinding his teeth, trembling with the compulsion to move.

She was stroking faster and faster, not knowing what was she doing, not knowing where she was going, aware only that she drove toward satisfaction.

Her satisfaction. And his.

When at last climax swept her, when spasms of irresistible pleasure took her, she felt her body taking his, squeezing him.

He grabbed her, tilted her backward until her shoulders touched the floor. He knelt, held her hips up to him, and thrust into her, deep thrusts that claimed her and demanded she yield everything to him.

And she cried, and clasped him between her thighs, and welcomed him inside, and made him hers.

CHAPTER
TWENTY-SIX

"For the ball gown, I had a difficult choice. Our little English rose has a fair complexion, dark hair with auburn highlights, and most unusual eyes. By themselves, the eyes, they seem to be hazel with starbursts of gold — the eyes of an enchantress."

Hands wrapped around a bedpost, Emma listened while Madam Mercier spoke, and held on for dear life while Tia pulled the strings on her corset tight. Behind her, she knew Madam's seamstresses were straightening the tangle of her new petticoats, while Lady Fanchere and Aimée hovered by the fireplace and watched Madam Mercier personally unpack Emma's ball gown.

It was evening, time to prepare for the ball, and Emma felt numb with anxiety and wild with excitement. It was as if she were making her debut in society — Emma Chegwidden of Freyaburn in Yorkshire. And as if that weren't enough, while she was making her debut, she was also spying for the man she loved . . . the man whose body she had worshipped, but whose face she had never seen.

She was tired and sore, happy and worried.

Madam Mercier continued. "Miss Chegwidden's eyes change colors with the clothes she wears. A blue cotton and they appear sky blue. A green satin and they're pea green. So I wanted a material that would allow her unusual coloring to shine without influence. I decided on this."

Emma heard a rustle of silk, and Lady Fanchere and Aimée *ahh*ed in delight. Emma strained to see, but Tia hissed at her and pushed her around to face forward again, and the seamstresses hissed at Tia to hurry.

"I sent out runners to Madrid, asking for this particular silk. I didn't know when it would arrive, and then, the prince's sudden decision to throw a ball proved a challenge beyond even my humble services. I doubted we would be able to make it up in time. Then I realized — the richness and color of the silk is usually worn by women of, shall we say, experience. Miss Chegwidden is young and virginal, so to contrast with the material, the gown itself needed to be simplicity. That, we were able to do, and on time." Madam Mercier sounded as pleased as a purring cat.

"It's perfect," Lady Fanchere said.

Tia turned Emma to face the room. She got a glimpse of a dark gown laid across the bench; then Tia lifted her arms and the seamstresses threw the petticoats over her head. By the time she had fought her way out of the starched and rustling confinement, the gown had been hung behind her and the ladies were discussing which jewelry she should wear.

Madam Mercier forbade them anything but a simple pair of earrings and a thin silver ring. "No! No! Simplicity. Trust me. You'll see!"

At last Emma was trussed into the undergarments, and Madam Mercier herself pulled the gown over Emma's head.

Emma looked down, trying to view what had so pleased the ladies.

Madam Mercier took the long braid of hair at the back of her neck and pulled. "Young lady, no peeking! You may see in a moment. *Fils*, fasten the buttons; then I will do her hair."

The girls seated her on a low stool.

Madam Mercier took the comb away from Tia and said, "I was a lady's maid."

Which she might have been, but she'd lost any subtlety in the years since, for she tugged Emma's hair back so hard Emma's eyes felt slanted, and used hairpins with such precision Emma felt as if she were the donkey in the children's game.

When Lady Fanchere said, "Perhaps fresh flowers . . . ?" Madam Mercier said, "*Non!* Diamond hairpins placed here . . . here . . . and here, like stars in the midnight sky."

Everyone *ooh*ed.

Emma itched with starch and curiosity.

Tia placed ballroom slippers on Emma's feet, and she was allowed to stand.

The seamstresses made fussing noises as they straightened the long, slim sleeves and adjusted the low neckline.

Lady Fanchere and Aimée clasped hands and gazed at her, tears in their eyes.

"Turn, mademoiselle. Turn!" Madam Mercier had Emma spin in a circle. At last she, too, smiled. *"Bon!"* She pushed Emma to stand in front of the full-length mirror.

Emma stared. And stared.

"You see, I am right. The material is Japanese silk, completely new to the continent. The color is a rich maroon shot with silver thread. In the daytime, it would be garish, but in candlelight . . ." Madam Mercier kissed her fingertips.

271

Emma turned her head to see the upsweep of dark hair gathered at the base of her neck, and the twinkle of diamond pins among the strands.

"You'll note the way the silk shimmers as Miss Chegwidden moves, a jeweled setting for her beauty." Madam Mercier's satisfied voice bounced along the surface of Emma's consciousness. "With her hair drawn back from her face and secured at the back, her hairline is revealed. The widow's peak on her forehead is echoed by the heart-shaped neckline. With the plain bodice, the plain sleeves, and the gathered waist, every male will be transfixed by her magnificent figure."

"Hush, madam." Lady Fanchere put her hand on Emma's sleeve and spoke to her. "You're very quiet, my dear."

"Don't you like the gown?" Aimée asked gently.

The room grew silent.

Emma stepped toward the mirror and touched the reflection of her face. "You have made me beautiful."

Madam Mercier laughed a little laugh that broke in the middle. "*Non.* It is *le bon Dieu* who did that."

Emma looked at the women, who were beaming at her in pride.

"Then . . . *I'm* beautiful?" She looked back

272

the mirror. "I'm beautiful."

A single tear ran down her cheek, and she hastily wiped it away.

She wished her lover could see her like this . . . and he never would. He never would.

CHAPTER
TWENTY-SEVEN

The herald thumped the floor with his staff.

"Lord and Lady Fanchere." His sonorous voice echoed out over the long, marbled, opulent ballroom, up to the towering ceiling, and over the people who crowded the perimeter of the empty dance floor.

Lady Fanchere indicated to Emma that she should stay where she was, and they descended the stairs into the chattering, noisy crowd.

"I'm Emma Chegwidden," she whispered to the herald.

"Oh, I know who you are," he answered, and once more thumped his staff on the floor.

To Emma, the sound was ominous.

"Miss Emma Chegwidden," he called.

She started down the stairs and realized . . . the ballroom had fallen silent.

She glanced up. Every person in the ballroom was frozen in place. Every face was turned to stare at her.

She faltered. Was stricken by stage fright. Saw Lady Fanchere standing at the bottom of the stairs, her dark gloves gesturing, *Come down here to me.*

Emma took a breath and resumed her journey. But now, each step was an agony of fear and self-consciousness, while she prayed she wouldn't trip and humiliate herself.

Why was everyone gaping at her?

Not because she'd discovered that in the right clothes and with the right coiffure, she could be beautiful. No, that wasn't it.

They watched her because Prince Sandre had indicated his interest.

She looked down at her feet, then up at the crowd, and saw Prince Sandre moving toward the bottom of the steps, a smile on his lips that frightened her more than the crowd's silence.

Durant's cynical comment echoed in her head. *Even you can't be that naïve. If you dared refuse him, he would hunt you down and bring you back, and make you pay for humiliating him.*

She had known she had embarked on a serious mission. She hadn't realized she could be trapped in it.

She wanted to reach the bottom, to be off

this showcase where she was trapped, and at the same time she writhed at the thought of putting her hand in Prince Sandre's and allowing him to guide her through her first ball.

But she had no choice. The stairway ended. Prince Sandre bowed and offered his arm. She put her hand on it and, with a glimpse of Lady Fanchere's beaming pride, she walked at his side across the empty dance floor toward some unknown destination.

"I had hoped to start the dancing with you tonight." His charm was light and practiced.

And she was wiggling like a fish on a hook. "I would remind you, Your Highness, that I'm really a paid companion. My dancing skills are rusty and perhaps would embarrass you."

"I would remind *you* that *I* am a prince and have been taught to lead the young ladies with a firm hand."

He meant dancing, of course, but also something more. Probably he meant to thrill her. He frightened her instead.

A brief, intense pang of longing struck at her heart. If only she could be with the Reaper now, have him hold her close and somehow let her know that everything would be all right. *Please. Somehow, make everything all right.*

But her prayer was not to be answered, for the prince brought her to a halt in the middle of the empty floor.

Now? He meant for them to dance *now?* She felt ill with horror.

He lifted his gloved hand.

The orchestra played the opening bars of a waltz.

He bowed.

And what else could she do? She curtsied.

He put his arm around her waist.

Off they swirled, around and around in nauseating circles that should have felt like flying but instead felt like a tree swing hooked to a broken branch. She saw faces reel past her, people standing on the edges of the dance floor, staring malevolently or with amazement or with sour amusement.

One face, affable, encouraging, caught her attention, and every time she circled, she looked over the prince's shoulder at Michael Durant, standing on the sidelines and nodding encouragement.

That one friendly face eased her tension, and she wanted to somehow tell him, *Thank you.*

But Prince Sandre swung her around and around, and said in her ear, "Smile! You

277

look as if I'm tormenting you."

She took a breath — she'd been holding it for far too long — and decided she must not throw up. Digging into her acting repertoire, she produced a pleasant expression. "I'm simply overwhelmed by the honor you offer me, Your Highness."

He laughed, delighted. "Have you ever been to a ball before?"

"No, this is my first. After this magnificence, how will I ever attend another?" She fell easily into the role of sycophant, and she discovered she could keep up a light patter of flattery and dance at the same time.

As the waltz progressed, other couples joined them on the dance floor until it was crowded with colorful gowns and smiling gentlemen, and the notoriety that so bothered her was diminished. The song ended; they stood politely and clapped; then Prince Sandre took her arm and led her back toward Lord and Lady Fanchere.

And there, near the edge of the floor, sat Lady Lettice, surrounded by her suitors.

Until this moment, the thought of once more seeing Lady Lettice hadn't occurred to Emma. She'd been too busy hiding the Reaper, worrying about Prince Sandre and his intentions, assisting Lady Fanchere and

Aimée, being fitted for gowns and facing the disapproval of her peers.

Now, suddenly, fate had offered her a chance for the smallest bit of revenge, and even knowing this was shallow, weak, and petty, she seized it.

She leaned against Prince Sandre's arm, unobtrusively guiding him in that direction, and when they strolled past, she started in simulated surprise and said, "Lady Lettice, what a surprise to see you."

Lady Lettice came to her feet, compelled by royal directive.

But Emma could see her struggling, *struggling* with the demand that she curtsy — for that curtsy would be a courtesy not only to Prince Sandre, but to Lady Lettice's own former paid companion.

Prince Sandre seemed not to realize the interplay between the two women, but he did realize, all too clearly, that Lady Lettice was not offering him the respect he demanded. So he stopped. Stared coldly. "Well?" he said.

With a sob that sounded like fury, Lady Lettice sank into a reverent curtsy.

Mollified, Prince Sandre said, "I hope you're enjoying your visit to our fair country."

"Yes, Your Highness." Lady Lettice remained in the curtsy, eyes cast down, the picture of submission.

Of course. As long as they stood there, she couldn't rise.

So Emma said, "I had thought you were leaving, Lady Lettice."

"I am!" Lady Lettice said.

"Moricadia will be desolated by your departure," the prince said.

A small tremor started in Lady Lettice's straining knees and worked its way up to her corkscrew curls.

"She fears the Reaper," Emma informed the prince.

Lady Lettice cast her a look of loathing.

She smiled sunnily.

"You have no reason," Prince Sandre told Lady Lettice. "He is as good as dead."

Then Lady Lettice made her fatal mistake. She snapped, "Of course he's dead. He's a ghost!"

Prince Sandre went from pleasant to frigid in a second. "He's a criminal, and he will be brought to justice." He walked on.

Emma walked with him, delighted to hear a groan behind her, wondering only if Lady Lettice had managed to get up on her own or whether her suitors had had to hoist her to her feet.

"She looks vaguely familiar. Who *is* that

wretched woman?" Prince Sandre asked.

"That is the lady who dropped a fish down her bosom," Emma pronounced with deep satisfaction.

Throwing back his head, he laughed aloud. "I remember now! That was fabulously funny. I wish I could see it again."

"I don't think I could manage that," she said with a sly wit that sailed past Prince Sandre.

He was too busy smiling at the tourists and nodding to his sycophants.

He delivered Emma to Lord and Lady Fanchere.

"What a lovely couple you make!" Lady Fanchere said.

He bowed to both the ladies, and shook Lord Fanchere's hand. "I hope to claim Miss Chegwidden's next dance, also," he said.

In England, such an occurrence was as good as a betrothal.

Emma couldn't allow that. "Thank you, Your Highness, but I must excuse myself from the ballroom. I will return soon."

He understood her code; she wished to use the ladies' convenience. He summoned a servant for her, and swiftly she was whisked from the ballroom and into the depths of the palace. A long, dim corridor led her to the brightly lit lounge. With a curtsy, the maid left her there. And inside sat Countess Martin, leaning into a mirror and staining her lips with red.

Emma curtsied and hurried into the inner chamber. She lingered there, hoping Countess Martin would depart, but when she returned, the woman still sat there, overwhelmingly sensuous in red satin and black lace.

She lolled in her chair and watched Emma splash her hands and face with water, then handed her a linen cloth and said, "You're afraid of me."

"Yes. No. That is . . . yes."

"Because Lady de Guignard told you I can read the future?"

"Lady de Guignard is quite whimsical. I know that."

"But it's true."

The lady was blunt, too blunt, and frightening in her own way, and Emma didn't know how to blunder her way out of the conversation. Tentatively, she said, "She said you had marks on your hands."

"That's true." Countess Martin stripped off her gloves and showed Emma. Eyes drawn from dark lines stared from her palms, eyes that looked Egyptian and exotic.

"Family birthmark?" Emma asked faintly.

"I don't know. I was abandoned as a baby, left on the grave of King Reynaldo. Some old man found me. He wanted nothing to do with an infant, so he carelessly handed me over to the nuns in the orphanage. They tell me when the report went out that I had marks on my palms, he came back for me, claiming to be my father and wanting me back. They didn't believe him; wouldn't give me to him. They believed I was marked by the devil — or for the devil; I never managed to make that out — and they were determined to beat the evil out of me." She recited the tale without self-pity, without even much interest.

And her very lack of expression made Emma feel the weight of the tragedy. She pulled up a chair. "I'm sorry."

Countess Martin chuckled as if she were weary. "I think you are. Compassionate, even though you've had none too easy a life yourself."

"What happened?"

"I was lucky. I grew up to be beautiful. That's a helpful tool when you're trying to crawl out of the gutter — or the convent. I caught Count Martin's attention first, and he has complained that I bewitched him, but he is pleased to be bewitched. I set my sights on Prince Sandre next." Countess

283

Martin smiled, her teeth clenched together. "I got him, but I didn't keep him. I think, knowing what I now know, it was a lucky escape."

Emma nodded.

"I reach out for others, take them when I wish; then when I'm bored, I tell my husband. But I touch none of them except with my gloves on."

"What do you mean?"

"When I touch a person, I know their future. Pitiful, brief, tragic, sopping with liquor or doused in laudanum, gout ridden or dwindling to a poor, sad end. I don't want to know, so I keep them at a distance and hold Count Martin close. He's boring, but he will live long and die a sudden death in his sleep." Fervently, Countess Martin added, "Lucky bastard."

Emma stared at her, stricken by the realization that knowing the future was to know tragedy.

"But something about you calls to me. I *want* to know your future, or I'm meant to tell you your future. Or something like that. I never comprehend why I'm called, only that I am." Countess Martin offered her bare hands. "Come. Let's see what I'm told."

Tentatively, Emma placed her palms in

Countess Martin's.

The countess's eyes went out of focus; she was here, but she was not, and in a dreamy voice, she said, "Ride for honor. Ride for justice. But don't ride for friendship." Her hands tightened on Emma's. "If you give in to the anger, disaster will follow, and only the bravest deeds can save you from cruelty, from the everlasting dark . . . or a grave that will hold your soul forever. . . ."

Emma swallowed and wished she were anywhere but here, facing a crazy countess babbling nonsense about Emma riding when she could barely sit a horse. "If I will make you less unhappy, I promise not to ride at all," she said.

Countess Martin snapped back to the present. She scrutinized Emma from top to toe, and laughed. "I'm sure that you mean that promise, but I fear you'll not keep it. Very well." Standing, she waved a dismissive hand. "Give Sandre my best."

Emma stood, too.

Countess Martin started to leave, then returned. With a tight smile, she said, "I try to shake this feeling, but I still worry about Lady de Guignard. Tell her . . . tell her again to avoid high places. The fall is very far."

The intensity with which she spoke made Emma feel ill with fear. "I'll tell her," she

285

promised.

"Good girl." Countess Martin chucked her chin as if she were a child. "And remember what you already know — Prince Sandre is foul in every way. Run from his attentions." She laughed. "But of course. I forgot. You can't. The Reaper holds you in place." She swept from the room.

Emma stared, dumbfounded.

How did the countess know that? What did she know about the Reaper?

Could she tell Emma what was going to happen?

"Wait!" Emma leaped to her feet and ran into the corridor.

But Countess Martin was gone.

With a groan, Emma started her trudge back to the ballroom.

CHAPTER
TWENTY-EIGHT

Emma was lost. Lost in the royal palace.

She had stepped out of the convenience, found herself alone, and, without even thinking, she had turned left.

Apparently, she should have turned right, for the palace was a rabbit warren of passages and stairways — and she was the rabbit. She wandered through the dimly lit corridors, looking for someone to direct her. Failing that, she sought a brightly lit corridor that would lead to a public area.

She'd had no luck.

Now she saw a glow and walked eagerly toward it, then realized she had located the terrace and the glow was the moon in the clear, dark sky. She moaned and collapsed against the wall, staring out the window and wondering whether anyone would come looking for her, or if she'd be lost forever in this horrible parody of the Cinderella fairy tale.

The corridor turned left here. At intervals, a single candle burned in a sconce. Doors opened all along that corridor, and in each doorway she could see moonlight. So the corridor ran parallel to the terrace, and she started down it, peering into the dark rooms. Seeing a door onto the terrace, she hurried to it and stepped out, walked to the rail, and looked around.

The palace was built on medieval lines, with the kitchens below and the living areas above. She stood on the second floor; the cliff dropped off below her, and although the view was magnificent, there was no stairway, no way down to the lower level, where she might find the kitchens and servants and be directed, at last, to the ballroom.

The breeze ruffled her hair. Over the horizon, lightning flickered, eerily silent, illuminating the sharp profile of the peaks.

She lingered for a moment, wondering where the Reaper rode tonight. Would he be safe?

Her heart picked up speed.

When could they twine together, chest to chest, heart to heart, strain and pant and love? She put her hand to her mouth, bit the tip of her finger, and tried to wipe the smirk off her face. It was outrageous, but all day, at odd moments, she had been swept up by memories of their union. The pain, the glory, the sense of feeling, for the first time, like part of someone else.

When would he come to her again?

Never, if she didn't get to that ballroom and urge Prince Sandre to tell her his plans for capturing his nemesis.

Determinedly she turned away, found her way back to the corridor. Briefly, she spared a thought to Michael Durant. If he were here, she would be safely on her way back to the ballroom, for he would direct her.

Once again, she walked, glancing in the doors. Each room was lit by nothing but moonlight, but she saw luxury here. She passed room after well-appointed room, and realized that somehow, she'd found her way into the royal chambers.

And through the windows, out on the terrace, she glimpsed the swiftly moving figure of a man walking in the same direction.

She stopped, stared, but he was gone.

So she hurried on, and glanced through the next doorway.

Again she saw him, a black cloak rolling behind him.

Again he disappeared toward the next room.

Lifting her skirts, she raced to the next

doorway.

He was there; then he was gone. The man was keeping pace with her.

No, not a man, a *ghost,* for beneath the cloak, a ragged shroud fluttered as he walked.

The Reaper.

She ran to the next doorway and saw him pass, ran again and saw him again.

At the next doorway, she saw no sign of him.

She waited. She ran forward. She backed up.

He was gone.

"No!" She rushed into the moonlit chamber, skirting the furniture, and ran to the window. She pressed her cheek to the cool glass, seeking a glimpse of him.

He was gone.

"Come back," she whispered.

A hand snaked out from behind her, covered her mouth and her gasp of surprise, and for a moment, her heart leaped in anticipation, for surely it was the Reaper. Then she was pulled hard against a man's tall figure, and anticipation became terror.

Who was this gentleman who held her so roughly against him? For he was a gentleman. He smelled not of leather and horse, but of soap and clean linens.

She gave a muffled scream and fought him.

"Shh." The warning was almost silent, roughly delivered in her ear.

He spun her around to face him.

Mask. Costume of white rags.

The Reaper. He had come for her.

For one moment, a single thought possessed her.

He could speak.

Then other thoughts crowded her mind.

He wore a mask, but not his usual white mask. This one was dark, and in this dim light, it appeared that the pale powder he usually applied to his skin was missing.

He looked different, his face thinner, his jaw more determined, his nose more decisive.

He didn't smell right. He didn't look right.

Uneasy, she asked, "Is it really you?"

He laughed, a rough chuckle of mirth. Taking her chin in his fingers, he lifted her face and kissed her.

Oh . . . She relaxed. . . . It was him, all right. She knew his taste, the way he parted her lips, the swirl of his tongue against hers. Her hands groped their way up his arms and clung to his shoulders as she pushed closer to press her breasts against his chest.

Still kissing her, he picked her up and set

her on a small table, twelve inches by twelve, against the wall.

It rocked precariously.

She squeaked like a mouse and grabbed the sides.

"Shh," he said again.

"What are you doing?"

No reply.

"How did you find me?"

No reply.

Instead, he lightly ran his fingers down her forehead, over her cheek, over her lips, down her throat, and lingered over the swelling mounds of her breasts.

There was possessiveness in his touch, a reminder of who held her heart.

The moon was bright, but they inhabited the shadows. The room was silent except for the ticking of a clock. The table beneath her bottom was hard and cold, and her feet dangled, but didn't reach the floor.

"You can talk," she said. "So tell me —"

He put his hand to his throat, wrapped as always in a long white scarf, and made a rough, painful sound.

Yes, even last night, when their bodies were entwined, he had kept that scarf in place. "All right," she said. "But someday will I be able to hear your voice?"

He nodded.

"And someday I'll see your face?"

This time he put his hand to his heart. That was his hope.

Lifting her wrists, he held them away from her body. He looked at her as if he couldn't quite believe it.

She thought she knew what he must be thinking — that this elegant gown was not the gown of the simple companion he had first met. "I dance and smile," she whispered. "It means nothing. I do it so I may discover his schemes to capture you."

The Reaper hissed in annoyance. And jealousy?

"I won't stop," she said. "He's frantic to get you and prove to everyone he holds the country in an iron grip. It's become more than a matter of pride. If he doesn't succeed, he's shamed."

Behind the mask, the Reaper's eyes watched her face as his hands wandered over her bare shoulders and down her arms. He lifted her fingers to his lips and kissed them, one at a time.

She leaned her head against the wall and watched him kiss the palms of her hands. Each touch of his mouth, each whisper of his breath against her skin made her own breath quicken.

"We can't make love here." She cupped

his jaw and reveled in the clean feel of his bare skin. "It's too dangerous."

He pointed to her and to him.

"Yes," she said. "To us both."

He smiled . . . and lifted her skirt.

"No." She tried to push it down. "Really. It's not possible."

He took her fingers in his, pressed them to the edges of the tiny, precarious table, and indicated that she should stay still. Kneeling before her, he once again lifted her skirt. The silk and starched petticoats rustled, and she gave a stifled shriek as he slid beneath.

She tried to clamp her legs together. "No," she said, frantic with embarrassment and confusion. "No."

He caressed her calves, smooth and warm in their silk stockings. He toyed with the tie just below her knees, the one that held them in place. His hands crept up, slyly advancing regardless of her protests, and slid along the delicate skin of her inner thighs.

She tried to lunge away, but the table wiggled beneath her weight, and again she grabbed it to steady herself.

What did he think he was going to do? He seemed to have a definite direction in mind, for he pressed the flats of his palms hard against her knees, separating them, then lifted her thighs into the crooks of his elbows and kissed her ankle. Then her knee. Then . . .

She had never been so shocked in her life. "No! Please!"

Possibly he couldn't hear her. Probably he didn't care.

And after a moment, she didn't care, either.

The man who seduced her with a single kiss on her mouth now used his tongue and lips to drive her mad. He nuzzled her, kissing her softly at first, then more insistently, putting pressure against her closed cleft. Then, with his tongue, he explored, probing here and there with a leisurely determination that seemed to indicate that he . . . he was enjoying himself.

She was not enjoying herself. She had pressed her spine against the wall as hard as she could, trying to get away.

Or to steady herself.

But mostly to get away.

Really.

Because this was shocking beyond anything she'd ever imagined, and she was uncomfortable knowing he was tasting her . . . and discovering that she was growing damp.

"No," she whispered again, and rolled her

head against the wall as if he could see her denial.

He licked her, a slow, catlike lick of enjoyment, as if savoring the flavor of her . . . displeasure. His tongue probed her, inside her, and involuntarily her inner muscles clamped down as if to keep him inside.

He laughed. She couldn't hear him, but each nerve had grown so sensitive she could feel his face lift in amusement, feel the slight rasp of his teeth against tender flesh, feel the gust of his heated breath enter her.

She almost came right there.

But no. No. This wasn't right, to have him doing these things to her while she perched, helpless, unable to touch him or move or do anything but take this kind of ruthless pleasure he forced on her.

She tried to kick at him.

The table shook as if an earthquake rumbled beneath the palace.

He held her hips, keeping her in place, and as he sucked her clitoris into his mouth, she felt an earthquake indeed. It started small, as he used his lips to massage the tiny, sensitive piece of flesh. It grew as he sucked harder, pulling at her, making her gasp and scrape her nails beneath the table. Finally, encouraged by a single tiny, tender bite, the earthquake blasted through her, shaking her so hard she forgot the precarious table, her embarrassment, the ball, the prince, even the danger she should have so desperately feared. All that existed was her own pleasure and the man who forced it on her in touches of silk and kisses of ecstasy.

Her back arched. Tears ran down her cheeks. She whimpered and moaned. She came. And came. And came until finally her overloaded nerves no longer could receive pleasure, and she went limp, barely capable of holding herself on the table.

He gave her a last kiss and slid from beneath her skirts, his hands lingering on her legs as if the touch of her skin gave him pleasure. He stood and steadied her with his hands at her waist. He brushed the tears off her cheeks. He kissed her lightly, and she tasted herself on his tongue.

That humiliated her. And pleased her. It was as if she had branded him in a way so personal only the two of them would ever know.

He waited while she recovered, until she no longer moaned softly with each breath.

Lifting her off the table, he set her on her feet. Again he waited until her legs could support her and her knees no longer buckled.

He wrapped his arm around her waist and

led her to the entrance. He put his finger to his lips and opened the door. He looked out, then with a nod led her into the corridor.

They walked, she didn't know where, until at last she could hear music and voices. They rounded a corner and she could see the lights of the ballroom. She stopped and stood there, staring, knowing she had to go back, but wanting nothing more than to stay here with him, where she could be herself, where she was safe and loved. So well loved. "Reaper . . ." She turned back to him.

He had left her side, was returning to the darkness from whence he came.

"Remember . . ." The word was a single low breath.

Then he was gone.

CHAPTER
TWENTY-NINE

The Reaper watched from the shadows as Emma, still unsteady on her feet, entered the ballroom.

She was beautiful in her silvery gown, and more beautiful without it. She was his, and he could scarcely bear to see her go back to Prince Sandre's side. But he had a mission.

Swiftly, he returned to the room they had so passionately occupied.

He had recognized it right away. The de Guignard shield decorated the double doors; this was the prince's office, and he felt a deep satisfaction in knowing he had pleasured Emma on the prince's decorative table.

Inside the room was dark, yes, but the moon was out, and years of practice had taught him to see well in the dark.

He searched the desk: the official papers strewn on top, then the contents of the desk drawers.

In the top right-hand drawer, a pistol.

He pulled it out and examined it. Loaded. Yes, if a person lived as Prince Sandre lived, it was a good idea to keep a pistol handy.

In the second drawer, a list caught his eye — names, written neatly, with notations of payment beside them. *The* list of Moricadian citizens used to spy, willingly or unwillingly, for the prince. He read it, committed it to memory, then returned it to its place.

Still searching, he opened the bottom drawer and heard metal rattle. He froze.

He knew that sound.

With the caution of a man handling a venomous snake, he pulled out an iron ring. On it dangled two huge, old black keys.

They were medieval, and should have been rusty with time, yet they were polished and smooth, well used and well cared for.

They were Prince Sandre's personal keys to the dungeon.

Revulsion gripped the Reaper, and the keys trembled in his hands, clinking like death's own herald. He wanted to take them, fling them off the terrace so Sandre could never again go down to the dungeon to torment another poor soul.

But that wouldn't save the prisoners, and the Reaper didn't dare let Sandre know he'd searched his study.

With steely self-control, he replaced the keys, shut the drawer, and made his way into the depths of the palace to replace his costume with the formal attire of a gentleman attending a ball.

What had started for the Reaper as a coolly plotted attempt to signal the beginning of the end for Prince Sandre and the de Guignards had now become a desperate race to end their regime before Sandre found out the truth about Emma — that she was no meek, gentle, proper companion, but a woman who would fight like a wildcat for the man she loved.

The Reaper was that man. The stakes were too high. He had to win this game, and soon.

Emma stood on the perimeter of the ballroom, smiling slightly, nodding as people greeted her, pretending to look for Lord and Lady Fanchere.

Her lover had risked life and limb to find her; it perhaps spoke ill of her that she should be so flattered. But she was. Even more remarkable was that his insistence that he make love to her in such a novel, embarrassing, fabulous way should make her feel mellow and pleasured and more at ease in the palace than she could have ever imagined.

Additionally, she now suspected something that had not occurred to her before.

In real life, the Reaper was a gentleman.

She swept the crowd, looking for him.

It made sense. He could afford a fast horse; that took a good income.

On the other nights he had visited her, he'd ridden to her side, and so he carried with him the odors of saddle and horse. Tonight he'd come into the palace as one of the guests, for he smelled of soap and clean linens.

He could speak, but wouldn't. Because he had an accent? Was he Moricadian? Or German or French or Italian? Or perhaps his voice was high or low or . . . Was he in this room now? Was he watching her?

She straightened her shoulders, lifted her chin, preened for a man who might not be here.

"Miss Chegwidden, I had hoped to speak to you tonight, but you disappeared for so long, I was in despair. Were you lost again?" Durant laughed hoarsely.

She glanced at him, annoyed that he'd broken into her fantasy. "Yes. Yes, I was lost."

"I'm sorry I wasn't there to guide you. But somehow you found your way back."

"I did. Yes." She wanted him to go away. He was blocking her view of the room.

"Be careful where you wander. Some places in this country are dangerous ones to stumble upon." He looked different than she remembered ever seeing him. Not more serious. She'd seen him serious. This was more . . . intense.

"I remember." She looked into his eyes, and for one moment, there was a dizzying sense of connection.

Then —

"Miss Chegwidden. I've been looking for you." Prince Sandre picked up her hand as if he had the right to touch her. "Where have you been?"

"She was lost," Durant said. "It's a chronic situation with Miss Chegwidden."

The prince turned on him with a ferocity that made Emma gasp. "Get away from us."

Durant shrank back, fear as real and sharp as knives. Turning on his heel, he fled, leaving her alone with the prince.

Any feeling of connection vanished. Her pity welled up, and all she could think was, *Poor man.* She didn't care what kind of assurances he'd given her. Something horrible had happened in that dungeon, and Prince Sandre had been there to do it.

Prince Sandre swung back on her. "Where

were you?"

"As Durant said, I was lost. I turned the wrong way and wandered for a long time." That was true, as far as it went, but she blushed when she remembered where she had gone and whom she had found.

He scrutinized her face, and guests scattered as he pulled her into an alcove. "For an hour? You were lost for an *hour?*"

"I saw much of the palace. I fear I intruded on your privacy."

"Where were you?"

She didn't like his tone. "If I knew, I wouldn't have been lost!"

His blue eyes went frigid, and he squeezed her fingers hard enough to dig the simple silver ring into her flesh.

She stiffened under the lash of pain, and said rapidly, "I was in a long corridor with rooms opening off it. I saw a terrace, white in the moonlight. I went out in hopes of finding my way down to the kitchens, but no."

His grip loosened. "You were in my personal area."

"I thought so. Even in the dark, the rooms were luxurious."

He mulled over her explanation. "How did you get back?"

"I tried what felt like the wrong way, and

here I am." She wanted to add that she was sorry to be back, but although the fury in his eyes was fading, he still held her hand, and she was afraid.

"Everyone was asking where you were. I was worried."

Worried that she'd run away and left him looking like a fool. But she nodded. "I was worried, too. I had no idea the palace had so many rooms."

Lord and Lady Fanchere stepped into the alcove.

"Sandre, this privacy is not proper." Lady Fanchere's voice was severe.

"I had to speak to Miss Chegwidden about the proper way to behave when one is invited to a royal ball." Prince Sandre smiled, but it looked more like a baring of teeth.

Emma wanted to slap him, or contradict him, but her hand hurt. She eased it away from his and glanced down. He'd squeezed hard enough to cut her with her own ring; blood was drying, sticky and brown, between her fingers.

Lady Fanchere noticed, and probably guessed at the cause, for she took Prince Sandre's arm and turned him toward the ballroom. "I suppose you've heard what Aimée's doing now?"

No! Emma started to take a step forward, to stop Lady Fanchere.

Lord Fanchere caught Emma's arm and shook his head. *Too late,* he mouthed.

Prince Sandre sighed in exasperation. "What crack-brained scheme has Aimée come up with now?"

Lord Fanchere offered Emma his arm, and they followed the cousins.

"She's decided to go abroad." Lady Fanchere was delighted and obviously expected Prince Sandre to be, too.

His head snapped around. "What?"

Lady Fanchere was oblivious to his displeasure. "She's going to Italy first for the winter, then moving on to Austria for the summer. It is exactly what she needs, and she's as excited as I've seen her for years."

They strolled through the crowd, and all the while, Emma strained, wanting Lady Fanchere to stop talking.

"How is she managing this?" Prince Sandre asked with elaborate interest.

Lord Fanchere stepped forward. "I'm setting up an account for her to draw on while she's abroad."

"Are you?" Prince Sandre flicked him a glance.

"Eleonore asked me to," Lord Fanchere said.

"Yes. I suppose you must do what Eleonore says." Prince Sandre chuckled as if it were a joke.

But Lord Fanchere treated the matter seriously. "She asks me for so little, and I would do much more." Taking his wife's hand, he kissed it. "Because she has given me so much."

"There you go, Miss Chegwidden, the secret to getting your own way in a marriage. Ask for little and you'll get whatever you want," Prince Sandre said.

She thought, *I do not care what you think.*

She said, "I'll remember, Your Highness." With the intention of changing the subject, she turned to Lady Fanchere. "I was lost in the palace, and found the terrace. I had no idea the view was so dazzling."

"The old royal family chose their location well, wouldn't you say?" Prince Sandre seemed willing to brush aside his interest in Aimée's plans. "They say the only way this stronghold can be taken is by treachery from the inside."

"I believe that's how your family did it, is it not?" Lord Fanchere asked.

Emma looked at him in astonishment. He was so calm. So staid. So quiet. Yet he wasn't stupid, and to say that to Prince Sandre . . . Was he, too, trying to distract the prince from Aimée's plans?

"It's true, Sandre — our ancestors were not admirable people." Lady Fanchere shook her head sadly.

"I don't know the story," Emma said.

"The Count de Guignard was invited by the Moricadian royal family to visit the palace," Lady Fanchere told her, "and before his arrival, he placed his people in key positions in the serving hall. He brought wines from his lands as a gift, and poured freely, and when the royal guard was insensible, he gave a prearranged signal. His people opened the postern door and let in the soldiers, and they slaughtered every member of the royal guard and all their servants, and violated the women, and dragged the king out and hanged him."

"Horrible," Emma whispered.

"The Trojan horse is a time-honored way to win a war." Prince Sandre was remarkably unconcerned with his ancestors' villainy.

"They broke all rules of hospitality!" Lady Fanchere retorted.

"Ah, but look what they gave to us, their descendants." Prince Sandre gestured across the glittering, noisy ballroom. "The palace, the lands . . . the money . . ."

Emma saw her chance. "From the terrace,

it's clear your country has very difficult terrain. No wonder the Reaper has escaped you." She held her breath for a moment, waiting to see if he would take the bait.

"Not for long." Prince Sandre looked grimly pleased. "I had to clearly express my wishes to my cousin Jean-Pierre, and he has made the matter a personal concern."

"Where is Jean-Pierre?" Lady Fanchere glanced around.

"He's hunting." A smile slipped across Prince Sandre's lips, and it terrified Emma.

"For the Reaper?" she asked in an admiring tone.

"Yes. He is my best marksman."

Emma felt the color drain from her face. "He's going to shoot him? He's going to kill him?"

"A good thing," Lady Fanchere said. "That Reaper scared Aimée to death."

"That Reaper killed Rickie," Prince Sandre snapped.

"Perhaps the Reaper killed Rickie; perhaps someone else did. For all that he was our cousin, Rickie was not well liked." Before Prince Sandre could contradict her, she added, "God rest his soul."

"Regardless, the Reaper is going to hang," Prince Sandre said. "For villains like him, I like hanging."

Desperation made Emma bold. "I thought your cousin was going to *shoot* him."

"You are a bloodthirsty little thing, aren't you?" Prince Sandre approved. "No, I want the Reaper alive, and I will make an example of him. We'll keep him alive until we can string him from the gibbet." He bowed. "He should suffer for frightening a lady as lovely as you."

"Yes," she said, and because he seemed to think that was a tribute, she added, "Thank you."

"Enough of this serious business. This is a ball. I've waited over an hour to dance with you again, Miss Chegwidden." Prince Sandre offered his arm. "Let us waltz!"

Emma stared at him, repulsed by everything she'd learned of him, struck by the realization that, even for the sake of the Reaper, she couldn't continue on this course.

"Miss Chegwidden?" He lifted a surprised eyebrow.

Emma couldn't touch him. He made her flesh creep. She couldn't *bear* it.

Lady Fanchere put a hand in her back and gave her a push.

A contralto voice, musical and amused, saved Emma from disaster. "Sandre, darling." Countess Martin stepped into the little circle, edged Emma aside, and caressed his face. "Have you heard the rumor that's sweeping the ballroom? The Reaper has been seen here!"

"Here?" Sandre jerked his head aside.

"What do you mean, here?" Emma asked.

Countess Martin ignored her as if she didn't exist. "He's in the palace, darling Highness. Tonight! While your men are hunting the countryside for him. Now you have to admit, *that's* amusing!"

CHAPTER
THIRTY

Jean-Pierre sat on his horse, watching the horizon while lightning flickered along the peaks like Zeus's sharp blessings. The prince had given a ball, but had made it clear Jean-Pierre was not welcome. Not because of his mother, whom Prince Sandre laughingly called a slut with a talented mouth, but because Jean-Pierre hadn't yet caught the Reaper.

The wind picked up. A cloud obscured the stars as it formed, grumbling in its growing pains. The smell of rain grew fresh in the air.

Confounded thunderstorm. It was coming, and coming fast.

Jean-Pierre was sick and tired of sitting in the old royal graveyard on the road to the palace, getting drenched every night. He intended to attend the next ball.

The slow *clip-clop* of a horse's hooves brought his head around. He watched with negligent interest as a white horse rounded the corner from the palace.

On his nightly mission, he'd seen a lot of white horses. The rider wore a black cape.

But the rider reached the straight stretch of road and urged the horse forward. As he did, a brilliant flash of lightning illuminated the landscape.

Jean-Pierre straightened in the saddle.

A black cape . . . and a black mask . . . and when the cape rippled back, Jean-Pierre saw it — a white shroud and winding clothes that fluttered as he rode. So what if the description didn't precisely match the reality? Everything about the Reaper had been obscured in gossip and legend.

Lightning blazed, thunder snarled, and Jean-Pierre pulled his rifle from the holster.

The Reaper's horse was cantering now, gaining speed, smoothing its gait into a gallop.

Jean-Pierre steadied his aim at the Reaper's right shoulder. He waited for the next flash of lightning and pulled the trigger.

As he did, the Reaper leaned into the horse's neck.

Jean-Pierre heard the blast of the shot, saw the puff of cloth, flesh, and blood as the bullet struck the Reaper high between the shoulder and the neck.

The Reaper sagged in the saddle. Recovered. His horse leaped forward, riding around the bend and out of sight.

Jean-Pierre cursed, thrust his rifle into his holster, and slapped his horse on the rump. The Reaper would not escape him now.

But as he cleared the bushes and hit the highway, the heavens opened. Rain fell in buckets. The temperature dropped. Hail battered the ground, shredded the trees, and pummeled him. He rode, knowing the Reaper faced the same conditions, but he couldn't see. He urged his horse faster. The beast balked, reared, and threw him out of the saddle.

Jean-Pierre splashed into an icy puddle.

The horse reared again, his hooves precariously close to Jean-Pierre's head.

Jean-Pierre ducked and rolled across the mud.

The horse ran, head outstretched, back up the road toward the palace.

Cursing, Jean-Pierre came to his feet. He looked up and down the road.

It was empty. Of course. What fool would be out in this weather?

As he trudged after his horse through the torrents of rain and blasts of wind, he knew the story that would sweep the palace.

The Reaper had called the storm and used the lightning to defeat his enemies.

Well, maybe so. But Jean-Pierre had seen that bullet strike.

The Reaper was wounded, cowering somewhere in pain, and Jean-Pierre would find him and bring him in.

Emma walked into her bedroom, holding her candle high, looked around, and wanted to cry. Tia was nowhere in sight, Emma had buttons up the back of her silk gown, and unless she trudged all the way down to the kitchen, she would have to sleep in this dress — and the corset.

She pressed her palm to the stays that held her spine rigidly erect and nipped in her waist.

She couldn't do it. She would have to find help to undress.

On the other hand, after Prince Sandre left the ball early to direct the search for the Reaper, Lady Fanchere had admitted she was tired, and Lord Fanchere had brought them home through a blinding hailstorm. All of which meant that Emma did not have to dance a second dance with Prince Sandre.

Emma considered that a victory she could celebrate.

Outside, the storm was rumbling away at last.

She fumbled with the diamond pins that held her coiffure in place — one thing she had to say for Madam Mercier: Nary a strand had dared escape — when a male figure limped out of the shadows at the back of the room. "Miss Chegwidden."

A week ago she would have screamed. Tonight she pulled a pin from her hair and held it like a weapon.

The man held up an arm. "I am not here to harm you. I am Rubio, Durant's valet."

She had seen him from above before; now she looked into his face.

He was older than she by probably five years, but his eyes were the eyes of a man who had seen horrors no one should see, had experienced pain no one should experience. As before, he was dressed with a gentleman's precision in a black suit with white linens. One sleeve was neatly pinned up; his arm was gone. And tonight his reddish blond hair was rumpled, and a spot of blood stained his cuff.

She lowered the pin. "Yes?"

In an urgent voice, he said, "He's been shot. He needs you."

She stared at him, confused, her mind tumbling, trying to understand whom he meant. Not Durant. So . . . "The Reaper?"

"Yes. They shot him. You can fix people up. Come and help him."

She grabbed her medical bag, picked up her skirts, and said, "Lead me."

"You go." Rubio started limping toward the door. "He's in the dowager house."

So the Reaper was with Durant? But she didn't wait to ask questions. She raced out and down the stairs, out the back door, and across the wide expanse of lawn. It was wet. Pieces of hail rolled beneath her leather slippers.

The door stood open.

She rushed in.

The dowager house was old, a primitive castle decorated to disguise its age. She hurried up the winding stone stairs to the second story, then walked toward the open, lighted chamber.

She paused in the entrance of the bedroom.

Michael Durant sat on a chair in front of the mirror, writing on a piece of paper. His red hair dripped water. A soggy black mask was discarded on the table. His face was drawn with pain, and blood oozed from the bullet wound that creased his muscle between his shoulder and his neck. A soggy white scarf wrapped his throat. Damp white trousers were decorated with winding rags. He was bare chested . . . and she recognized that chest. She recognized that chin. She recognized *him.*

At last she knew the truth.

Michael Durant was the Reaper.

CHAPTER
THIRTY-ONE

"You bastard," Emma breathed.

Jean-Pierre had shot the Reaper. He had shot Michael Durant.

She wanted to kill Durant herself.

He glanced up, met her eyes in the mirror. "I told him not to tell you. Why did he tell you?" He dipped his pen into the inkwell and went back to writing.

His voice was hoarse, distinctive.

Oh. Of course. No *wonder* the Reaper had spoken only one word to her. It wasn't an accent he was trying to disguise. It was that distinctive rasp.

The deceitful bastard.

She diagnosed him with a glance. "Because you're so white you look like you're in disguise, you've got blood all over your chest and back . . . and you can't lift your left arm?"

He couldn't. She could tell by the way his hand rested limp in his lap, palm up, and by the faint blue hue of his flesh. And by the fact that he didn't deny her accusation, but sat weaving in his seat.

"Lie on the bed while you can," she said brusquely. "I've got to get that bullet out of you."

"The bullet went through. And I have to finish writing this list of informers before I forget."

"Before you die?"

"That, too." He seemed remarkably unconcerned with that prospect, or with her discovery of his true identity. Probably he figured she was going to find out eventually. Probably he figured she'd do what she always did and take it with a proper British stiff upper lip. Probably he figured she wouldn't kill him.

Not yet, anyway.

Opening her bag, she found her towels, her tweezers, her small container of sulfur water drawn from a spring in France. She soaked a linen strip, laid it on his wound, and smiled as he flinched and said, "By God, woman. That hurts!"

Served. Him. Right.

"And it stinks," he added, but he wasn't really paying attention.

"The sulfur will help stop an infection." She took the strip away and examined the

320

wound. "You're going to need all the help you can get. The bullet blasted the costume and the shreds have adhered to the muscle."

With a sigh, he put down the pen and looked at her, really looked at her, for the first time since she'd walked through the door. "Emma, this is important."

If he told her he loved her, she was going to say she didn't care.

"That paper contains the list of informants, either willing or unwilling, to Prince Sandre. You *must* promise me you'll make sure Rubio gets this list to Raul Lawrence."

Hadn't she already realized she was a fool? And now she knew she was a hopeful fool, clinging to the expectation that he was going to declare his devotion to her. She wanted to slap herself.

No, she wanted to slap him.

"Emma, will you promise?"

"Of course. I've given my all to the cause. I'm hardly likely to fail you now."

His voice deepened, and he crooned, "Emma . . ."

Oh, now he realized she was upset. And he was turning, if possible, even whiter.

She didn't care. *That bastard. If he dies, I'll kill him.* "Lie down on the bed."

"I dream of you saying that to me, but under different circumstances."

Did he imagine he could charm her *now?*

He stood up. He swayed.

She leaped forward and wrapped her arm around him.

He leaned against her heavily, then straightened.

The stupid, bullheaded, strutting, pulling-the-wool-over-her-eyes rotten bastard.

"What did you say?" he asked.

She was a vicar's daughter. She hadn't really thought any of that. She certainly hadn't said it out loud. "I *said,* lie down."

"I thought so." How dared he sound amused here? Now.

She helped him to the neatly turned-down and waiting bed.

Earlier tonight. Earlier *tonight* he had kissed her beneath her skirt; then, not half an hour later, he had conversed with her in the ballroom, pretending that none of that had happened, that he hadn't been in her bedroom the night before and every night before that. And the night before that, and the night before that, and that he hadn't convinced her to seduce him into making love to her, and hadn't made her stay awake nights worrying about him.

She was so angry. She was shaking with rage. It sure wasn't worry that he would die of this measly little wound that had blasted out a chunk of muscle, leaving his arm limp and him with an infection she could see coming a mile away.

"How did you pull this off?"

"Tonight or . . . ?"

"All of this. Your costume, your horse, the freedom to ride at night when you're supposed to be locked away or under supervision?"

"Rubio is a miracle with clothing and costumes. When I went into the dungeon, my Moricadian friends saved Old Nelson for me."

"Old Nelson is . . ."

"My horse. There's a stable in the cave below the dowager house." His voice grew weaker, the rasp more distinct.

"So you have all the ingredients to be the Reaper except freedom, and — let me guess. Fanchere's guards are Moricadian, and none-too-vigilant when it comes to caging the Reaper." She wasn't really guessing. Brimley had warned her there was more to the Moricadians than met the eye, and allowing Michael to roam the roads was neatly undermining the de Guignards' fortune and prestige. Of course the servants wanted him to ride. "Fanchere is Moricadian. Is he also a party to this deception?"

"Perhaps." But Michael nodded thoughtfully. "We've never spoken of it, and if he is, it's more of a blind eye than active assistance."

Emma inclined her head.

"Don't be angry with me," Michael whispered. "I know what you think I've done to you, but it's not true."

"You don't know what I think." She went to work with her tweezers, pulling threads of his black cape and his white shroud out of the mangled, bleeding muscle.

He didn't answer. He had passed out.

Good. He couldn't feel the pain, although why she cared, she didn't know.

She ran her hands along his arm. It felt cool and lifeless. The bullet had done something dreadful: ripped his nerves, destroyed an artery — she didn't know, and for all her furious ill humor, she didn't want to amputate his arm.

She glanced up as Rubio finally made it through the doorway.

If Durant were conscious, she would get Rubio over here to tell him about living with an amputation. Just to scare him. Just to let him know how close he was to death and dismemberment.

Rubio limped to the bed. "How is he?"

"He's fine." She continued working the shreds of his costume out of his shoulder.

"Then why are you crying?"

"I'm not crying." She wiped the tears first with one shoulder, then the other. "There's a list on the table. It's important. You're to deliver it to Raul Lawrence."

He limped over and looked, folded it, and put it in his pocket.

"What did he think he was doing?" she burst forth.

"Riding, you mean? As the Reaper?" Rubio grinned and showed two chipped teeth. "He had to. When he was in the dungeon, he planned a way to undermine the de Guignards' reign. And God bless him, it worked."

When she thought about the danger into which Durant had put himself, and the way he had used his disguise to seduce her . . . "What did he think he could accomplish?"

"He intends to destroy Sandre."

"By dressing up as a ghost?" She poured her scorn into her voice.

"To transport information to the new king. To send the tourists running and Sandre's income to perdition. To spread the rumors of the true king's return. To fight if he has to, and kill for vengeance."

She looked at Rubio, then went back to work on Durant. "Get him out of his wet trousers," she ordered. When Rubio hesitated, she cast him a look of burning scorn. "I've seen it all before, and he's chilled to the point of hypothermia. Get him out of these trousers and wrap him in warm blankets." Without looking at him, she started unwrapping the scarf at his throat.

Rubio peeled Durant out of his trousers and covered him. He looked at her and saw the way she was staring at Durant's throat. "When he got out of the dungeon, he couldn't speak at all," Rubio said.

He couldn't speak? *She* couldn't speak.

The marks on Durant's neck looked as if someone had hooked a chain around him and dragged him behind a horse. The skin was red, scarred, broken across his Adam's apple. The disfigurement covered him from his jaw to his collarbone. . . . It was barely healed. It would never heal. "What caused it?"

"The de Guignards love hanging."

"I've heard that before." Earlier tonight, in fact. From the prince.

"Because it's true. They love to put rope around a man's throat, pull him up, and let him dangle, kicking and choking, grabbing for his throat while death creeps up on him so slowly he can count the beats of his heart."

"They hanged Michael? So what saved him?"

Rubio laughed roughly. "Their desire to hang him again. If you leave a man up there for fifteen minutes, you can cut him down and let him recover, then hang him again and enjoy his struggles all the more. It's a rough thing, knowing you're going to die with their laughter ringing in your ears."

She looked at his throat and saw similar marks rising above his stiff collar.

"I was no one. They didn't care whether they mutilated me. So they hanged me and they cut me up and put me to the rack. Him" — Rubio jerked his head toward Durant — "they cared about. Because his family has money and influence. Because he wouldn't break. Because he gave them a lot of entertainment. Because they believe he knows more than he will admit."

"Does he?"

"I don't know. But if he does, he's fought off the fear and the pain to keep his secrets." He sounded as if he admired Michael.

Of course, he was a man, simple and direct.

And she was a woman betrayed.

She went back to work on Michael's wound. "Get me warmed sandbags. We need to pack his arm to keep his blood moving."

"I'll do it." She heard the heels of Rubio's boots on the stone floor as he limped away. Step. *Step.* Step. *Step.* The boots stopped. "Someone needs to don the Reaper's costume and ride while he's wounded."

"Then find somebody."

"It can't be a Moricadian. Moricadians used to be the best riders in the world, but now none of them can afford a horse, and if one of them is caught, they'll be hanged seven times before they die."

"Then the Reaper's role will go unfilled." She concentrated on the task at hand.

"The Reaper has ruined the prince's income by frightening away the gamblers. The Reaper has created hope in the common people — they believe his appearance is the harbinger of the true king's return. Best of all, the Reaper has made the prince look like an incompetent fool." Rubio laughed hoarsely. "He's made Sandre a laughingstock. The Reaper's done a lot of good here. You can't let his efforts go for naught."

She shot him an annoyed glance. "I'm not listening."

But she heard him.

Inside his study, the prince sat at his desk, working in his leather-bound book of accounting. Flames flickered in the fireplace, dispelling the chill of the sudden, icy storm. Quico's wife, Bethania, moved with quiet grace around the room, dusting the furniture. It was a cozy, peaceful scene . . . probably the last Jean-Pierre would ever gaze upon.

He stood in the doorway, dripping on the floor, shivering with cold . . . and fear.

"Yes?" Sandre didn't look up.

"I shot the Reaper, my prince."

The prince placed his pen on the blotter, looked up from his desk, folded his hands, and smiled. "Not fatally, I hope."

"Not fatally, no." Jean-Pierre regulated his breathing to keep his voice even. "He got away."

Sandre's smile faded. "He got *away?*"

"My liege, I was careful not to kill him — too careful, I fear." Jean-Pierre hurried on to the next bit, the good part. "But I saw the bullet hit, saw the impact take out the shoulder of his costume. I saw him sway in the saddle, and the blood spray in the air. He is hurt. He can be found."

Sandre stared at Jean-Pierre. Just stared at him. Stood. Opened his drawer. Reached in. And pulled out a pistol.

Jean-Pierre was going to die.

Sandre lifted the pistol, aimed it at Jean-

Pierre — then swung it around and shot Bethania.

She screamed and fell to the ground, writhing on the carpet, holding her thigh.

Calmly, as if he did this every day, Sandre put the pistol back in the drawer and shut it. Raising his voice to be heard above Bethania's shrieks, he said, "Since the Reaper started making his appearances, there has been a decided drop in income from the gambling halls and the hotels. And do you hear that sound?"

Jean-Pierre glanced at Bethania. "Yes, Your Highness." How could he not?

"I don't mean her. That other sound. Listen!" Sandre cupped his ear.

Jean-Pierre strained, but he could hear nothing above the woman's pain-fed sobs.

"It's the sound of Moricadia laughing. Do you know whom they're laughing at?"

Jean-Pierre shook his head.

"They're laughing at me. They're laughing because the Reaper still rides." Sandre dropped his hand to his desk and leaned forward. "No one laughs at Prince Sandre de Guignard."

"No, Your Highness."

"Tell my guards to go and find the Reaper. Every three days that they don't find him, another wife or child will be shot."

330

Jean-Pierre couldn't believe Sandre.

The prince was crazy.

The prince was going to get his way. This would galvanize the guard as nothing else could.

"Take her out of here." Sandre rubbed his temple. "Her screaming is giving me a headache."

Jean-Pierre rushed in, gathered the writhing woman in his arms, and started out the door.

"Jean-Pierre!" Sandre called.

Jean-Pierre turned back.

"From now on, *you're* going to be the one shooting their loved ones. You'd better find the Reaper fast, or you'll never dare fall asleep again."

CHAPTER
THIRTY-TWO

"Do you suppose I should take this with me to Italy?" Aimée smoothed her hand along the white-painted wood of her grand piano in the echoing music room of her imposing mansion.

"Do you play?" Emma eyed the nine-foot length with trepidation.

"Oh, no." Aimée wiggled her short fingers. "I don't have the reach."

"Then I think you should rent one when you get there." Lady Fanchere had sent Emma to help Aimée pack her belongings and close her house, and now Emma knew why. As Aimée sorted and discarded the paraphernalia of her life, someone had to be the voice of reason.

But Emma had spent the last two nights awake, caring for Michael Durant as he lay in the Fancheres' dowager house, tossing with fever. While she was away from him, Rubio cared for him as tenderly as if they were brothers, yet every moment she spent helping Aimée, she worried, and that infuriated her.

Why was she concerned about the fate of a man who had lied to her? Seduced her? My God, he had even reproached her for allowing Prince Sandre to court her when he knew perfectly well why she was doing it, and he'd taunted her with the prospect of courting her as Michael Durant, the heir to the Duke of Nevitt, when he knew he'd made her fall in love with the Reaper. With himself!

If he didn't die from this infection, she was going to kill him.

"Dear, are you all right? You look upset!" Aimée looked upset, too.

"I believe I'm perhaps a little weary." Not a good excuse, but truthful, and the only one of which Emma could think.

"Sit down here." Aimée pulled the sheet off one of the chairs. "Elixabete, run and get Emma a glass of water."

Elixabete stood stock-still, her eyes wide and frightened.

Emma took pity on the child. "No, truly, that's not necessary. If I could rest for a moment, I'll be fine."

Lady Fanchere had sent Elixabete to assist them, to fetch and carry, but the child hadn't been the help Emma had hoped. Not that Emma blamed Elixabete. Maybe it was Emma's exhaustion that made her oversensitive, but Aimée's home was spooky. It was huge, larger than the Fancheres', with dual curving stairways climbing from the massive marble foyer up to the second-floor gallery and into the corridors lined with doors and rooms and more rooms and more, until a person felt as if she could get lost and never find her way back.

Everything — the marble on the floors and the columns, the walls, the furniture, the vases and accents — was white and pristine. The paintings were watercolors of faded gray, and even the servants were dressed in white, pale ghosts who slipped silently through this horrible parody of heaven.

When Emma had tactfully asked about the decor, Aimée had said, "It's Rickie's doing. He wanted the house to look clean."

In Emma's opinion, the house didn't look clean; it looked barren, unwelcoming . . . haunted. As she directed Aimée's servants to cover the furniture with sheets and Lady Fanchere's servants to carry Aimée's trunks to the cart, she constantly found herself looking behind her, convinced someone was watching. Once she saw Elixabete turn suddenly, fists up, prepared to defend herself against . . . nothing.

Even Aimée's bedchamber was washed-out, without color or character of any kind, and that, more than anything, told Emma what Aimée's life had been with Rickie. This lady who loved flowers and bright clothes and laughter had been regimented while in the confines of her own room.

Apparently Aimée saw nothing wrong, packing, trotting up and down the stairs, chatting merrily. Perhaps the sight of her prison meant nothing now that she had made her escape. She decided what to keep and what to throw away in a slapdash manner, and so far nothing white had made the cut.

Taking the sheet off another chair, Aimée seated herself, then pulled the footstool close and patted it.

Elixabete hurried to her and curled up on the stool, huddling as near as she could into Aimée's skirt.

"When I get to Italy," Aimée said, "I was thinking of getting a kitten. I've always wanted a kitten, but Rickie said they shed — and worse. I always thought *worse* was worth it for the joy of having a little thing that jumped in my lap and twined around my ankles."

Emma watched her smooth her hand over Elixabete's hair over and over, an unconscious gesture of comfort and closeness. "You seem like the kind of woman who would own dozens of dogs and cats."

"Yes, I am that kind of woman." Aimée brightened. "Maybe when I get to Italy, I'll get a dog, too. Fanchere did rent me a villa; there should be lots of room for pets."

On impulse, Emma suggested, "And maybe a lover?"

All expression smoothed from Aimée's face, leaving it blank and still, and she didn't look at Emma or speak.

Emma was embarrassed; she knew she should never have suggested such a thing; it was too daring for an unmarried woman to say. But she so badly wanted Aimée to be happy, and she had a vision of her in her villa surrounded by flowers and pets, in the arms of a tender man who loved her for all the caring, wonderful, silly things she was. "I apologize," Emma said. "That was bold and uncalled-for."

"Not at all, dear!" Aimée smiled, but without her usual joie de vivre. "But as to another man in my life — no. Once was enough."

Emma's heart hurt for Aimée, even while she understood completely. Because loving someone was too much trouble and too much anguish, and somehow, when she had Michael Durant cured and on his feet again, she was going to flee Moricadia and never look back.

"Maybe I will come to be your paid companion in Italy," Emma said.

Aimée's hand stopped in midair and her true smile blossomed. "I would like that." She offered her hand to Emma. "I would like it better if you came as my friend."

Emma was so touched, tears sprang to her eyes again. She took the outstretched hand and squeezed. "I would like that, too."

Aimée hugged Elixabete with her other arm. "And she'll bring you, Elixabete, and we'll teach you to read and write and make a great lady out of you. Shall we do that?"

Elixabete nodded and smiled.

The three of them pushed the cruel ghosts away, and joined in a moment of peaceful companionship.

Then Elixabete stood. "If we're going to go to Italy, we've got to finish packing!"

CHAPTER THIRTY-THREE

Jean-Pierre was here at last, attending a royal ball.

But he wasn't enjoying himself.

He stood holding a glass of champagne and watching the guests flow into the ballroom. None of them looked wounded or feverish. None of them even looked tired.

Well, of course not. That would be too easy. Instead he would have to examine the guest list, find out who didn't come, and go search their homes in the hopes he could at last make an arrest and end his hunt for the Reaper — and he would do it before tomorrow night, when Sandre's three-day deadline expired.

"Jean-Pierre! How good to see you. Where have you been hiding yourself?" Lady Fanchere hugged him and offered her cheek.

Taken by surprise, Jean-Pierre at first stood stiffly, then touched his lips to her face. He'd been under so much strain, he'd forgotten how truly loving his cousin Eleonore was. He shook hands with Fanchere, who was standing, as always, at Eleonore's right shoulder, stoically silent, and said, "I've been on the prince's business." He sounded clipped, he realized, not like a guest at a ball but like the hated policeman Sandre had created. So he smiled, but the expression felt more like a grimace.

Eleonore cupped his face and gazed searchingly into his eyes. "You look worried to death. I'll have to speak to Sandre about working you less."

"No. Please!" *God, no.* "Say nothing. I live to serve His Highness."

She paid no attention, but lightly touched the still-infected whip slash. "That looks painful. You should have had it tended."

"I was busy."

"Our little Miss Chegwidden has quickly made herself indispensible in the household as our physician. Next time, I'll have her look at it."

Jean-Pierre felt his interest stir. "Miss Chegwidden cares for the wounded?"

"She does what needs to be done. Her father was a vicar in a country parish in Yorkshire, so she became indispensible to the people of his flock, and thus indispensible to me." Lady Fanchere smoothed her hand across her thickening waist.

"Ah. Congratulations are in order then." Jean-Pierre kissed her cheek and shook hands with Fanchere again, but he didn't really care that his cousin was increasing. Right now, that wasn't important. What was important was the possibility that Miss Chegwidden was involved with the Reaper and his exploits. For what did they really know about her? Only what she had told them.

"Miss Chegwidden is quite the paragon, then, if all you and Sandre say is true." Ever since Jean-Pierre had announced he'd shot the Reaper, Sandre hadn't asked when he was going to be captured, or spoken of Quico's wife, or mentioned the rapidly rising tension in the palace. He had spoken only of the silly chit with whom he'd fallen in love, boring Jean-Pierre half to death.

Perhaps Jean-Pierre should have been paying more attention. "Is she caring for the injured now?" He faked a mild curiosity when in fact he was straining to hear the reply.

Which Sandre interrupted. He appeared dressed in the uniform of commander of all Moricadian troops — troops he had never seen, as far as Jean-Pierre knew. He kissed Lady Fanchere's cheek, but his gaze searched behind her. "Where is the lovely Miss Chegwidden?"

"I sent her to help Aimée pack up her house and the poor girl came back exhausted, so I ordered her to stay home tonight."

Jean-Pierre's excitement collapsed. Even this slim lead had failed him.

Sandre pulled a long face. "You shouldn't weary Miss Chegwidden with such minor matters. Send a servant with Aimée. Better yet, send her home to pack." He flicked a meaningful glance at Jean-Pierre.

Jean-Pierre could scarcely contain his irritation. *Yes, yes, I know. I'm to murder our cousin Aimée for you and make it look like an accident. But I'm busy right now, and Aimée is in Eleonore's care. You wouldn't like to have Eleonore's illusions about you shattered, would you, Sandre?*

"Aimée is very important to both Emma and me, and we wish her to enjoy at last a little of her life. If I could help her close her house and pack, I would do so, too."

If Jean-Pierre could feel amusement — and he was beyond that — he would have felt it now, watching Sandre squirm under Eleonore's gentle reproach.

"Yes, of course. I wish her Godspeed, too." Sandre delivered that line with a little

341

too much fervency.

Every minute, Jean-Pierre's men were out searching feverishly, looking in every cave and every hovel, dragging the sick and injured out of bed to see if they had been shot, because every minute that ticked by brought them closer to Sandre's deadline and the moment when someone's wife or child would have to be shot. By him. By Jean-Pierre.

Meanwhile, the guests circulated, the champagne flowed, and in the gambling halls, travelers lost their wallets to Sandre's dealers.

So as far as Sandre was concerned, all was right in the world. And for everyone in Moricadia, that was all that mattered.

Lady Fanchere patted Sandre's cheek. "You'll see Miss Chegwidden in three days at the Petits' afternoon tea. You can wait that long, can't you?"

"If I must." Sandre bowed gracefully.

But Sandre's eyes glowed with a peculiar combination of love and lust that meant Miss Chegwidden would suffer for every moment Sandre had to wait, and if Jean-Pierre had had any pity to spare for anyone but himself, he would feel sorry for Miss Chegwidden.

They were both caught in the claws of

a monster.

"Bring them in. Bring them in." Sandre waved to the mercenaries he'd hired to protect him from his own guard. "Don't dawdle. I'm a busy man."

Jean-Pierre stood, his back pressed against the wall in the guardroom, and watched as the families of his men were herded inside. Women. Children. Sobbing quietly or loudly or standing white faced. Mothers with babes in their arms and one old lady, Tavercse's mother, because Taverese had no other family for Sandre to hold hostage. She was a goodhearted soul, and even before this, she'd been nice to him. In the last three days, they'd all been nice to him, offering him food, service, sex if he would only spare their sons, their daughters.

They were like cattle to the slaughter.

And he was the killer.

Behind the line of mercenaries, the guard watched the scene.

Sandre had had them searched before he let them in. The revolution was not going to start here and now, he assured them.

No one — not the guard, not the women, not the children — could look away from the pistol Jean-Pierre held in his hand.

He'd searched long and hard for this

pistol. It held small bullets, mere specks of round iron, the kind, he hoped, that would do the smallest amount of damage to muscle, bone, and nerve.

But he was gazing at a lineup of three-year-olds, of gawky adolescent boys and women who looked fragile from overwork. A small bullet . . . that could still kill, especially if he weren't skilled. If his aim was off.

"Line up against the wall." Sandre sounded brisk and cheerful.

Of course. Sandre had been looking forward to this for three days.

Jean-Pierre wanted to close his eyes and shoot. But he didn't dare. He might kill somebody. A kid. A wife.

Instead, he picked his target carefully. He pulled the trigger.

Taverese's mother slammed into the wall, blood pouring from her arm.

Taverese shrieked and cursed, and had to be restrained by the other guard from attacking Jean-Pierre.

And Jean-Pierre knew Sandre was right.

Jean-Pierre would never dare sleep again.

CHAPTER
THIRTY-FOUR

Another two nights of searching with no sleep and no success made Jean-Pierre want to shout at the brightly gowned, gregarious, and cheerful crowd at the Petits' afternoon tea. Did they not realize the gravity of the situation in Moricadia? The prince was insane, the Reaper was unfound, and Jean-Pierre had one more night and one more day before he had to shoot another one of his guards' family members — and there were no more old ladies to sacrifice in place of a wife or child.

Jean-Pierre took a long drink of absinthe. The old lady was still alive, but if Jean-Pierre shot somebody's kid, he didn't know how much longer he would be.

Hey, look. Here was Sandre, swaggering over in his uniform, come to ask if Jean-Pierre had yet to see his little flower blossom, Emma Chegwidden. And here were Lord and Lady Fanchere, dressed in their afternoon finery, headed to intercept the prince — and Miss Chegwidden was nowhere in sight.

Here was trouble.

Jean-Pierre moved into position to overhear the conversation.

"Eleonore, you promised me Miss Chegwidden would attend this party. Don't tell me she didn't." Sandre didn't sound princely. He sounded petulant.

"No, Sandre, I'm sorry." Lady Fanchere did look apologetic.

"Because of Aimée? She's not here because of *Aimée?*" His voice rose when he said her name.

"That's not it at all," Eleonore said in a soothing tone. "Aimée took her maid and went to her house alone, for I was told one of our staff was injured and Miss Chegwidden was forced to stay back to care for him."

Sandre breathed heavily, clearly angry, yet restraining himself in front of his cousin . . . and the other guests. A few tourists and their servants had been roughly handled by the guard. Amid rumors of instability, a steady stream of travelers was leaving Moricadia, taking their wealth with them. Sandre couldn't afford to offend any more by throwing a royal temper tantrum. "I hope, Eleonore, your servant's injury is not serious enough to inconvenience you."

Jean-Pierre finished his drink and found a tray of fresh absinthe thrust under his hand. He didn't glance at the footman. He didn't care who he was. All he cared about was the answer to his question. Stepping forward, he asked, "Who was hurt?"

"I don't know. I didn't ask." She pressed her hand to her stomach. "Lately I've found myself squeamish when faced with the sight of blood."

"So it *was* serious?" Jean-Pierre exchanged his empty glass for a full one.

"I believe so," she said. "But why?"

Jean-Pierre looked around. "Where's Durant?" He hadn't been in the inner circle two years ago when Sandre imprisoned Michael Durant, but he well remembered that Durant had been cocky, laughing, dashing, charming the women, outfighting the men, and winning every gamble — just the kind of man to take on the role of the Reaper.

"The last ball was too much for his voice, poor fellow." Suddenly she seemed to comprehend the direction of his questioning. With a reproving glance at Jean-Pierre, she turned to Sandre. "My prince, when he is not in our company or, with your permission, at a party, Michael Durant is locked in the dowager house, watched by our servants and guards."

"That is true, Your Highness," Fanchere said.

Jean-Pierre raised his eyebrows. It took a lot to move Fanchere to speech.

"You trusted me with his custody," Fanchere said in his slow, precise voice. "I'm not fool enough to fail you."

Precise and to the point, Jean-Pierre judged. In two sentences, Fanchere reminded Sandre that Sandre had faith in him, and subtly suggested Fanchere stood in fear of the prince and his brutal reprisals. Which, Jean-Pierre now knew, he should.

"Quite right," Eleonore said. "We all know who holds my husband's trust. In addition, before night, Aimée will return to our home and be there as chaperone to Miss Chegwidden, and of course, Miss Chegwidden would never do anything that she believed was wrong."

Sandre laughed. He actually laughed. "That Michael Durant could be the Reaper might have occurred to our cousin Jean-Pierre, but I know that pitiful aristocrat. He cowers at the sight of me. And I assure you, he would not approach the woman who interests me."

"But you put him in the dungeon because you believed he had information about the revolutionaries," Jean-Pierre said.

Sandre turned on him impatiently. "Yes. So?"

"You never got that information from him. So he either didn't have it, or he's held out on you." Jean-Pierre saw Eleonore flinch. He glanced at her.

She was looking at Sandre as if she could see him all too well, and didn't care for the view.

"That has nothing to do with this," Sandre said in a savage undertone. "I have no worries about him and Miss Chegwidden. Even if he dared, out of spite, to court her, no woman wants a broken man."

The footman was still there, holding the tray, and Jean-Pierre put his glass down and quietly turned away.

Everyone knew the English were fools for the underdog, and Emma was an independent Englishwoman with the ability to heal the sick, living in a house full of Moricadian servants itching for revolution who were led by an English butler. And housed under their roof was an English nobleman who had already been involved with the revolutionaries and most certainly desired revenge.

He was glad Sandre thought Durant had been reduced to a shadow of his former self. Jean-Pierre wasn't so sure.

Someone shook Emma's shoulder and whispered in her ear, "Miss Chegwidden. The prince's man is on his way."

Emma opened her eyes and looked stupidly at Elixabete. "What?"

With increasing urgency, the child said, "Jean-Pierre de Guignard is on his way here."

Durant's fever had finally broken last night. He would recover, and after spending the night putting water down his throat and helping Rubio change the sweaty sheets, Emma had fallen asleep on his bed with him. Now she was tangled in his arms, staring at Elixabete, trying to make sense of what the child was saying. She eased herself free of Michael's embrace and quietly asked, "How do you know this?"

"The servants at the palace heard what was said, realized what he intends, and they delayed him while one of the stableboys rode to warn us."

So the servants in the palace hated and feared Jean-Pierre, and dared what they could to thwart him. And they dared even more to protect the Reaper?

Yes. Probably only a few knew the truth,

but those Moricadians who did would help if possible. "Why is Jean-Pierre coming?" Emma asked.

"He's searching for the Reaper. He heard you're a *curadora* and that you'd canceled two parties this week, so he became suspicious."

Emma pushed her hair out of her eyes. "How do you know this?"

"Mr. Brimley has his ways."

"Our esteemed butler has some sort of network? Never mind. What are we going to do?" Emma looked down at the still-sleeping Michael.

"Mr. Brimley says he'll take care of everything. But he sent me after you. You need to come in, change and clean up, and be ready to tell the story he has concocted."

"Yes. I will." She slid out of bed and ran with Elixabete to the house.

Tia grabbed Emma's hand as soon as she walked into the house and tugged her toward the stairs. "Mr. Brimley says I must help you to look calm and radiant."

"All right." Emma already thought she looked calm, but perhaps after a fearful night of caring for Durant, she looked less than radiant.

They rushed to her bedchamber. Tia removed Emma's crumpled dark blue gown.

Emma washed her face and hands and pinched her cheeks to bring the color up. Tia pulled a light blue gown over Emma's head — "Mr. Brimley specifically said you were to wear the light blue gown; it turns your eyes a trustworthy blue" — and buttoned it. Emma loosened her hair and ran a comb through the tangles, and sat to allow Tia to form it into a soft swirl at the base of her neck. "Mr. Brimley said it should look slightly mussed."

Apparently, Brimley had thought matters through.

They rushed back toward the staircase, but before they reached it, Tia stopped her. "Wait here." She tiptoed toward the gallery. "Is it safe?" she called softly toward the top of the stairs.

Elixabete was on guard. "Yes. Come on."

Now they all raced down to the main level, then down more stairs to the lowest level.

The kitchen was hot, and crowded with sobbing serving girls and grim-faced footmen. Cook had her apron pressed to her mouth. One of the scullery maids was passed out on the floor while another fanned her with a paper fan. A path opened to let Emma through, and Brimley called, "Miss Chegwidden, I have need of your services."

For all the seeming madness that permeated the room, Brimley's voice was calm, as always.

But it also seemed to make the serving girls sob harder.

Emma hurried toward the long wooden table where he was seated . . . and slowed as she took in the scene.

All around him were rags and towels covered with blood. *He* was covered with blood, his formal white shirt and collar splattered with it as if he'd stood too close when Cook wrung a chicken's neck.

A meat cleaver rested beside his right hand.

"If you would, I requested that your medical bag be brought here for your use, for this is bleeding a little more than I expected." He lifted his left hand. "Additionally, we haven't a lot of time to make this look as if it happened earlier."

Brimley's little finger had been severed.

CHAPTER THIRTY-FIVE

Emma examined the finger. It was a clean cut, done decisively, leaving only the joint closest to Brimley's hand.

The footman, Henrique, held the medicine bag open for Emma.

She removed a thin, clean rag, wrapped the rag around the base of the finger, and tightened it to form a tourniquet. "Mr. Brimley, what happened?"

Before Brimley could respond, Cook took the apron down from her mouth and started talking. "He comes down, calm as can be, and announces we've got to have a serious injury to show, because that grandmother-murdering bastard, Jean-Pierre de Guignard, was on his way to find the Reaper. And we Moricadians, we know what's what out there in the dowager house, but we didn't realize Mr. Brimley did. Once we figured out he knew, we thought . . . well, we thought . . . He's so good at assigning work, and we thought he'd decide on which one of us should do ourselves an injury."

Emma gazed at him, aghast that the Moricadians knew about Michael, aghast that Brimley knew about Michael, aghast at the deed Brimley had performed to save them all. "You picked up the meat cleaver and cut off your own finger?"

He steadily gazed back. "I would never ask my staff to do something I would hesitate to do myself."

And this was why English butlers were the backbone of civilized society.

"Get me icy cold water," Emma told Cook. "Mr. Brimley, do you still have the rest of the finger?"

"Yes." He pulled a bloody handkerchief from his breast pocket and offered it to her.

"We're going to put it back on," she said.

"Won't it rot?" One of the skinny message boys was wide-eyed and gruesomely fascinated.

"Probably," she told him, "but it's an effort worth making. If it doesn't succeed, we can always amputate later."

"If you put it back on, how will that prove anything to that baby-killing swine Jean-Pierre de Guignard?" one of the gardeners asked.

"We'll unwrap it very carefully and show

him." She plunged Brimley's hand into the basin Cook placed beside them. "All of you act as if this Jean-Pierre is worse than the prince."

"De Guignards are all devil's spawn. But this one has eyes so light they're almost white." Cook shivered, a huge mound of flesh quivering like jelly. "He's shooting his own people in the palace. He's a spooky one, he is."

"Everyone!" Brimley twitched as if he wanted to clap his hands to get their attention. "De Guignard will be here at any moment. Get this mess cleaned up. Put the bloody rags in the trash right here; don't throw them in the rubbish heap outside. Should he look for them, we need them close as proof that this happened. I appreciate you young ladies crying over my little finger, but it was, after all, only a little finger, and I am, after all, only British."

In a choked voice, Tia said, "Not anymore, Mr. Brimley. Now you're one of us."

The maids started wailing again.

His hand twitched. "I appreciate the sentiment, but enough of that! If you must cry, go to your rooms. We must appear to be back to normal. Now, scatter! Go do your jobs, and if you can't, when de Guignard appears, stay out of sight! Remember, the

Reaper's safety depends on *you*."

Within a minute, the kitchen was empty except for Cook, her three assistants, and the two scullery maids, all working in harmony on their preparations for the evening meal. One of the assistants was sniffling, for which Cook rewarded her with a slap on the cheek. One of the maids came over to the table with a bucket of sand, wet rags in hand, ready to scrub away the crimson stains. She took one look at the stump of Brimley's finger, still slowly oozing blood, turned away, went to the slop bucket in the corner, and unloaded her dinner.

Emma sympathized and dried his hand.

"I should have thought of a tourniquet ahead of time," Brimley said. "Of course, we did want to maximize the bloody display."

"We didn't have to use yours. There are animals aplenty in here, Mr. Brimley," Cook called from the stove.

"I should have thought of that, too," he said.

"Perhaps you were distracted by your intentions." Emma carefully placed the severed finger back onto the joint. "I'll sew it later when I have time. For now, we'll wrap it." Which she did, taking care that the two parts would touch within the bandage.

Henrique ducked in the door. "De Guignard is riding up the drive."

Brimley nodded. "Young man, remember what I've taught you. You are a proud representative of the Fancheres, and as such, you move slowly and with dignity."

Henrique returned the nod in exact imitation of Brimley's stately manner, turned, and paced up toward the foyer.

"Henrique will go far." Pride rang in Brimley's voice. "Now, Miss Chegwidden, if you would go to the library, seat yourself in an obvious location, and appear to be reading, I believe that would be the correct strategy."

"You should be in bed, Mr. Brimley," Emma said.

"I find my legs are surprisingly unsteady" — and he did look surprised — "so if Cook will fix me a cup of tea, I believe this placement will have to suffice for our confrontation."

Emma stashed her bag under the table, cast a long glance at the bandage around Brimley's finger — she hated leaving it in such an unfinished state — and proceeded upstairs to grab a book at random and take her place in the library.

Just in time — Henrique opened the front

door and intoned, "Please come in, Mr. de Guignard."

Jean-Pierre came in, his boots stomping fiercely on the marble floor. "Where is she? Where's Miss Chegwidden?"

Emma watched out of the corner of her eye as he stormed past, hat pulled low, black cape fluttering behind. He didn't look like the devil's spawn.

"She's in the library, sir, and if you will allow me to announce you —"

She heard his cloak crack as he whirled around, and she looked up with simulated surprise.

Jean-Pierre stood in the doorway, examining her up and down, and Cook was right — his eyes were pale, with dark pupils in the center that looked like holes. "Miss Chegwidden?" He didn't remove his hat.

"Yes, but I'm not acquainted with you, sir," she said.

"I'm Jean-Pierre de Guignard."

"Prince Sandre's cousin?"

"I'm flattered that you've heard of me." He couldn't have made his sarcasm and contempt clearer. "What are you doing?"

She turned the book over and glanced at the spine — she was holding something called *When the World Was Young: A History of the Chosen Ones* — then looked at him as if concerned about his powers of observation. "I'm . . . reading?"

"I was told you were taking care of someone who was hurt in this household."

So Brimley's report was right. "I did. I am. Our butler, Mr. Brimley, was injured this morning. At this moment, he requires none of my services." She put down the book, rose, and paced toward him.

He smelled of absinthe. He'd been drinking, and in her experience, drink made a man unstable and explosive.

She kept her tone firm. She maintained eye contact. She did not retreat. "Why this cross-examination, Mr. de Guignard? What is the problem?"

"Show me this injury you stayed home to tend."

"As you wish. This way."

Henrique moved into place, and led them down the stairs and into the kitchen at a pace so solemn Emma hid a grin and Jean-Pierre snarled, "Hurry up!"

"There's no rush," she told him. "I don't believe Mr. Brimley will be going anywhere soon. He's lost a lot of blood."

The kitchen, when they entered it, smelled, sounded, and looked exactly as the kitchen of a château should look — pots bubbling on the stove, Cook yelling at her underlings, supper well in hand.

But in the trash can, Emma was glad to see, bloody rags peeked up, and the scullery maid still hadn't removed the stains from the table.

Brimley sat exactly where Emma had left him, drinking a cup of tea. He looked up inquiringly when they walked in. "Sir!" He tried to rise, then sank back down. "Pardon my dishevelment. I never expect to receive guests in the kitchen." He glared balefully at Henrique as if he were at fault.

Henrique bowed. "I apologize, Mr. Brimley. Mr. de Guignard insisted he see you at once."

"I was told you were injured." Jean-Pierre's eyes glowed with frustration.

"I'm afraid in a misguided attempt to show Cook the correct way to cut up a chicken, I removed my little finger with the meat cleaver." Brimley held up his bandaged hand.

Jean-Pierre walked close. "Your finger looks fine to me."

"That's because I have hopes that it will reattach. If you insist, I can unwrap it. . . ." Emma started to move toward the table.

"Never mind. I can do it myself." Reaching out, Jean-Pierre ripped the bandage away.

Blood spurted.

Cook screamed.

Two squeamish scullery maids fainted.

With the first moan Emma had heard, Brimley doubled up in pain.

"Mr. de Guignard!" Emma ran to Brimley, pulled rags out of her bag, and attempted to stem the flood. "Have you lost your mind? What have you done?"

Jean-Pierre examined Brimley's finger, then tossed it back on the table. "It's true then. Pardon me, Miss Chegwidden, for doubting you. And you, Mr. Brimley" — he bowed slightly — "my apologies for the pain caused. I was just doing my job."

When he had walked out, Brimley said faintly, "As was I."

"I would say you did your job above and beyond the call of duty," Emma told him; then to Cook, she said, "Get me some strong young men. We need to put Mr. Brimley to bed."

To her surprise, the strong young men immediately appeared — gardeners, for the most part. Maids and footmen trickled in. Henrique and Elixabete took their places among the crowd. By the time Emma had the bleeding under control, the kitchen was as full as it had been when she had first entered. She exchanged a bewildered glance with Brimley, then turned to face them.

"If you, either of you, ever need anything, you ask any Moricadian," Cook said, her voice hoarse with sincerity. "We will do anything for you. It will be our honor to save your lives as you have saved our hero, and our country."

And as one, the maids curtsied and the men bowed to Brimley and to Emma, heartfelt tributes that left Emma blinking back tears.

For the first time since she had left England, she was at home.

CHAPTER
THIRTY-SIX

Although Brimley stoically objected, he was swiftly taken to his room on the servants' level and placed on his bed. Emma sewed his finger into place, bandaged it again, gave him a sleeping powder, and told Henrique to make sure someone was with him at all times.

"We will," Henrique said, and for the second time she heard the phrase, "He's one of ours now."

"Good." It had taken the sacrifice of a finger, but Mr. Brimley had achieved what he sought — his place as integral head of the Fanchere servants.

And she . . . she was no longer a pariah and the prince's whore. She had earned her place of respect in Moricadia.

She headed downstairs to make sure Jean-Pierre de Guignard was out of the house, because if he wasn't, she was going to kick him out herself. Or just kick him, she didn't know which.

But as she descended to the main level, she heard male voices from the library, a deep rumbling that sounded as if Jean-Pierre was speaking with . . .

But no. That was impossible. Because Michael was asleep in the dowager house, used up and weak with fever, not sitting in the study chatting.

Stepping carefully, making no sound, she sneaked over to the door and peered in.

Jean-Pierre sat in a chair opposite a casually dressed and laughing Michael Durant, seated on a long couch.

"Do you want to see them again?" Michael was saying. He slipped first one shoulder free of his shirt, then the other. "See? No bullet wounds."

Jean-Pierre shook his head as if he couldn't believe it.

So did Emma. Because she'd seen Michael over and over for the past six days, and he definitely had a nasty red divot between his neck and his shoulder joint. Where had it gone?

"Are there any other parts of me you want to see?" Michael grinned nastily at Jean-Pierre, doing a good imitation of an angry and insulted lord. And maybe it wasn't an imitation. "You want to see a rib or a thigh?

I know — let me drop my pants and show you my buttocks."

"No. That won't be necessary." Jean-Pierre stood. "I'll leave you now. Enjoy your evening."

"I intend to."

With not nearly the confidence and fury with which he had entered the house, Jean-Pierre walked past Emma. He bowed, started to speak, then bowed again. Still he didn't move.

"Yes?" she asked frostily.

"Nothing," he said. "Now if you'll excuse me, I have to go kill a child." A footman, not Henrique this time, opened the door. Jean-Pierre strode out, mounted his waiting horse, and rode away.

She stared, wondering if the madness she'd glimpsed in him was caused by more than drink.

Then a faint call from the study made her forget all about Jean-Pierre de Guignard.

"Emma?" Michael's voice was faint.

She hurried in. "How did you do that? Where's your wound?" she demanded fiercely, and, "What are you doing up? And dressed?"

Michael smiled up at her. "Rubio is a genius with wax, clay, powder, and color. He makes my face into a skeleton, and he made my bullet hole disappear. And I may be dressed, but I'm not up." The color slid from his face, and he slithered sideways on the couch to lie prone.

"Blast you, Michael." She had forgotten her ladylike language. She forgot she had sworn to keep him at a distance and called him by his Christian name. She forgot everything that was right and proper around Michael Durant . . . but she didn't forget how angry she was at him. It was hard to forget when she knew he'd been using her for a trollop, and laughing all the while.

Still she put her hand on his forehead and was thankful to realize it was cool and unfevered.

"Is he all right?" Rubio stood in the doorway.

"So far." She bit off the words in irritation. "Why did you let him do this?"

"He heard Elixabete tell you Jean-Pierre was here hunting for the Reaper. He decided he needed to put in an appearance to calm Jean-Pierre's suspicions. Do you think I can stop Durant when he's resolved to do something?" Rubio summoned the half dozen broad-shouldered young men who had transported Brimley up to his bed. They now lifted Michael and carried him out of the study, out of the house, and down to the dowager house. When they placed him on the bed, he was trembling with exhaustion, and by the time Rubio was finished removing the wax from his wound and Emma had rebandaged it, lines of pain bracketed his mouth. She gave him a glass of willow bark soaked in water, and expected him to go right to sleep.

But when she would have walked away, he caught her hand. "You're angry with me for being the Reaper. You must forgive me for my deception of you. I couldn't tell you the truth."

She didn't care how sick he was; she refused to allow him his pretense of innocence. "You couldn't tell me that you were the Reaper. I understand that. But after that first night when I hid you in my bed, you didn't have to return to me. You didn't have to show me the meaning of romance."

"I didn't mean to take it so far." He tried to look boyishly mischievous, but he was long and lean beneath the sheet. His shoulders were bare and muscled.

And she remembered far too well the power of his body as it moved on hers. "You are a cad and a despoiler, and I'm embarrassed I was fool enough to fling myself at your head."

"You're mad about that bit of fun in the palace, are you?"

"You ass." She yanked her hand away from his. Was that all he thought she was mad about? Was he really so insensitive?

"I might have enjoyed fooling you a little too much," he acknowledged.

She stormed toward the door.

"No, Emma." He struggled to escape the bed and come after her. "Listen." He thrashed around.

She heard something hit the floor, water splash, glass break. Turning back, she realized he had fainted.

She liked him better this way.

Rubio came running, and with a grimace of disgust, he said, "He's knocked his recovery back a week."

"Yes."

"Someone needs to ride," he said again.

"Yes." Because no matter how angry she was with Michael, the Reaper had advanced the Moricadian cause. Emma had a responsibility to Elixabete, to Henrique, to Tia, and to Cook — a responsibility to continue his work. They had sworn to serve her, and she was now bound to them. "Prepare a costume. I ride tonight."

CHAPTER THIRTY-SEVEN

The costume was too big. The saddle was too big. The horse was too big. All Rubio's assurances that Old Nelson was a broadbacked, gentle gelding whose main desire was to carry his rider didn't help when Emma faced riding astride for the first time in her life, not that she had ridden that often. She cantered out of the cave beneath the dowager house — wine cellar and stable in one — and onto a path that wound through the darkened woods.

Rubio stood in the doorway. "Give Old Nelson his head," he shouted. "You'll be fine."

Rubio was the genius behind the Reaper's costume and makeup. To fit her into the clothes, he had cinched up the trousers, stitched up the sleeves, found her a pair of white leather gloves, and made a mask — and he'd done it in an afternoon. He had painted her face with such skill, she had gasped at the stranger in the mirror, and he'd hoisted her onto the horse while keeping up a patter of advice and praise.

But where was he now?

Back in the stable, making his slow and painful way up into the house.

Meanwhile, she was alone. Branches slapped her. In the woods, wild animals cawed and howled and watched. She couldn't see anything but starlight through the trees. For all she knew, Old Nelson might be carrying her to face off with another wolf. Who would rescue her with Michael upstairs suffering a recurrence of his fever? And . . . and — *Oh.*

She broke off her fretful litany.

Old Nelson slipped out of the woods and onto a road.

She didn't know where she was. She didn't know where the road would go. But Old Nelson seemed to. He trotted, bouncing her up and down until her teeth rattled. Then his gait smoothed out, and he was running, running through the moonlight.

She clutched his reins and his mane, terrified she would fall the long, long way to the ground. She closed her eyes, hung on to the saddle with her butt cheeks. His hooves struck the road in a soothing rhythm.

And still she was in the saddle, while cool

night air rushed past her.

Taking a breath, she opened her eyes.

The moonlit landscape spread before her, forest on one side, cliff on the other.

She shut her eyes again. Opened them again.

The road was a pale ribbon ahead. A billion stars illuminated the velvet sky. The road curved and turned into the depths of the forest, and as they passed a meadow, she saw a deer lift its head and stare, saw an owl swoop out of the trees and soar on midnight's breeze.

She passed a carriage and waved, and laughed at the terrified faces pressed to the window, then leaned into Old Nelson's neck, urging him on. Because it was beautiful, and she was alone with the horse and the night and the wild that permeated her soul. . . .

When she finally returned to the stable near dawn, she told Rubio she was late because she got lost.

Old Nelson had always known the way home, but in a way, she was telling the truth.

For the first time in her life, she had been lost in freedom.

"She rode out as the Reaper?" Michael held Rubio's collar and stared into his eyes, and wished Rubio had both arms.

"Three times in the past four days," Rubio said with pride. "With no problems at all."

Because as it was, Michael couldn't pound him to a pulp. And that was what he wanted to do. Pound Rubio.

He'd woken this morning with the strong sense that something was wrong. Emma hadn't come to him in the night to see if he was still breathing. When he'd been really sick, her touch had been the only thing that soothed him. Then he realized she hadn't come on any of the recent nights, and when she did come, it was early in the morning, and she had smelled like . . . like leather, like horse, like . . . the Reaper.

Why it all clicked in his brain now, he didn't know. Maybe because he felt well enough to discover the truth. Maybe because something about her pink cheeks and bright jewel-toned eyes had put him on alert.

So he had thrown on trousers and a shirt, his scarf and a cloak, and come down to the stables to find Rubio awaiting her return.

"Someone had to ride as the Reaper while you were down. The Moricadians were getting anxious and Jean-Pierre was getting suspicious." Rubio spoke with great conviction.

"She could get hurt."

"No." Rubio scoffed. "You know Old Nelson is a sensible horse."

As if that were going to calm Michael's ire.

"She could get killed. The prince's guard is on the hunt!"

"She hasn't had a lick of trouble, and because of her, there have been Reaper sightings. The tourists are fleeing Moricadia, and rumor says Prince Sandre is going mad with fury." Rubio jiggled Michael's hands. "You want to let go of my collar now?"

Stunned and appalled, Michael loosened his grip, walked to the door of the stable, and looked out at the dim path winding its way through the forest and, he knew, onto the road that ran past châteaux and the palace on its way to Tonagra.

He wanted to pound Rubio for encouraging her with this madness almost as much as he wanted to chase after Emma. Chase after her and teach her that a woman's proper place was in the home, because she didn't seem to realize she wasn't supposed to put herself into danger and make him worry like a parent with a truant child.

But he couldn't chase her — Old Nelson

was his, and the only horse to which he had access.

Rubio came to stand at his side. "She's returned every time before dawn, looking all happy. That Emma, she's a smart one."

"It's getting light." Michael turned on Rubio. "So where is she *now?*"

"Ah. Dunno. Well." Rubio scratched his stubbly cheek. "As long as you're here and feeling as well as you are, I suppose I don't need to stay to help Miss Chegwidden groom Old Nelson and change out of her costume —"

Michael bared his teeth.

Rubio started backing away. "— so I guess I'd better go see what Cook has for your breakfast. You know you're her favorite."

"Where's Emma?" Michael shouted after Rubio's limping, fleeing figure.

"Breakfast!" Rubio shouted back. "Need to keep up your strength! Her, too!"

Devil take him! Devil take them all! Michael paced into the stable, then out.

He had plotted his revenge on Rickie, and when he hanged him, he'd exacted retribution for countless other lives lost.

Yet still Sandre lived and ruled, and until Michael completed his vengeance, he couldn't leave.

Time was running out. He knew that. He

knew his family would hear about his resurrection soon, and send someone to verify his existence. In fact, they wouldn't send someone — he'd be lucky if his father, his stepmother, and both brothers didn't descend on Moricadia and make Sandre sorry he'd ever dared to imprison a Durant.

But more than that, because of Jean-Pierre's good aim, Michael had now unwittingly involved Emma in his masquerade.

He paced around the cozy stable scented with leather and hay and the deep, rich smell of surrounding earth.

He opened the gate to Old Nelson's stall. Rubio had already cleaned it out, so Michael set out the currycomb, the body brush, the hoof pick.

He glanced in the stall next door, where he always changed, and there was a pile of clean straw, a saddle hung on the wall, a basin and pitcher set on a wooden box. Emma's walking boots were placed neatly on the floor, directly under the hook where her clothes hung — a dark green gown, starched and ruffled petticoats, and a lawn chemise so fine he could almost see through it.

Rubio had prepared everything for her return.

Irresistibly drawn, he unhooked the chemise and crushed it in his hands as if it were a stalk of lavender and he was releasing its scent. Holding it close to his nose, he breathed. Just breathed. And as always, his libido stirred, responding to the faint, feminine perfume of Emma.

His imprisonment had created degenerate needs in him.

No, wait. When he was released, he hadn't suffered from this constant torture of want and need.

It was Emma who had created the degenerate in him.

Yes. It was Emma.

Tenderly he hung her chemise up. He checked the pitcher to make sure it was full of water and placed the soap beside the basin. He paced back to the outer door.

The sun was peeking over the horizon.

Where was she? Flung over Old Nelson's head and unconscious on the ground? Trapped by Jean-Pierre and his men? Shot and bleeding and dying . . .

At last, faintly, he heard the *clop-clop* of a horse's hooves. He tensed, staring so hard his eyeballs hurt.

There she came, mask hanging on her arm, makeup smeared on her chin, blithely trotting along, patting Old Nelson's back and crooning.

He walked out to the edge of the forest,

put his hands on his hips, and frowned. "Where have you been, Emma?" He had the satisfaction of seeing her jump.

But his meek little companion didn't cower from his displeasure. She frowned right back. "What are you doing out of bed?"

"I'm fine." And he was. Getting up to face Jean-Pierre had caused a temporary setback, but Michael was eating huge meals and moving without pain, and his wound had closed without any sign of infection. "What are you doing on that horse with that ridiculous outfit?"

"Are you saying I look like an ass?"

"Exactly!"

"Then that's something for you to remember in the future when you don the costume." She ducked as Old Nelson entered the stable.

The horse headed right for his stall.

Michael followed.

She slid off onto the mounting block, then picked up a rag.

Michael took it away from her. "I'll wipe him down. Go wash your face and change."

"Fine," she snapped at him, and headed into the next stall.

He needed to be patient. She was tired from her ride. She had probably been frightened all night long, alone in the dark on roads she didn't know, always worried that someone was going to shoot her. And he had to remember that this was the first time he'd had a chance to talk to her, calmly and rationally, since she'd discovered the Reaper's real identity. When she'd seen him, she'd been angry, and he'd been transcribing the list of informers, and once that was done, he'd collapsed.

He did owe her an explanation, no doubt about that. But she was a reasonable woman. Once he explained why he'd done what he'd done — become the Reaper and kept secrets from her — she would understand.

So as he groomed Old Nelson, he said, "I know it's been a rough night for you."

"I had no problems whatsoever," she said. "You're not the only one who's competent to ride a horse, and you're not the only one who sees reasons to shake up the de Guignard rule." Something smacked the wall, shaking the wood.

The top of the Reaper's costume? "I didn't mean that you would have problems or that you don't have the same strong sense of justice. I meant that you . . ." He trailed off.

If she'd thrown the top of the costume,

what was she wearing?

"That I what?"

Michael tore his mind away from the thought of her half-naked body, picked up the body brush, and went back to work on Old Nelson's neck. "It might be a good idea if I told you why I became the Reaper."

She didn't answer.

He heard the sound of splashing.

Was she washing her face, her body? Was she naked from the waist up? Or naked all the way? Were tiny rivulets of water slipping down her neck, her chest, and clinging to her nipples before dropping to the ground?

Old Nelson turned a knowing eye on him, and he realized his hand was suspended in midair.

"I'm listening!" She sounded thoroughly annoyed.

With a grimace at the horse, Michael discarded his scarf, pulled off his cape, and tossed it over the top of the wall. "I just got too warm." He went back to work. "It was for revenge."

"On Rickie, for what he did to you?"

"On Rickie, for what he did to us all." Michael hadn't told anyone the details of his imprisonment. He never wanted to see the pity in their eyes. But Emma couldn't see him, and he couldn't see her, and she was so aggravated with him he doubted she would feel anything but exasperation.

Exasperation he could handle.

He continued. "Two years is a long time, especially spent alone in the dark. Nothing to do but think and sweat and fear . . ."

"Sounds awful." The straw rustled as she moved about, undressing, dressing. . . .

"Yes. Do you know what it's like to make a friend you never see, who is nothing more than a voice in the darkness, but you know him because he eats the same gruel you eat, suffers the same pain you suffer, cries the same tears you cry?" The rhythm of the grooming soothed Old Nelson, and soothed Michael, too, for the memories seemed more remote, and the words came more readily. "Then he no longer cries. No longer speaks. You know he's still alive: You can hear him breathing; you can hear the guards taunting him; they drag him out for torture . . . but his spirit has died. Finally, one day, they drag the body out of the cell, put it in a bag, and carry it away. You've never seen him, but you've lost a friend."

"Oh, Michael." Pity. He heard pity.

He didn't want that, but now that he was talking, he couldn't stop. "It happens again and again, until one day they put someone new down there, and he calls out in panic and fear, wanting only to hear another human voice . . . and you don't answer. Because you haven't got a heart anymore. It's been taken out of your chest, piece by piece, and carried away in those body bags."

He heard a sob, muffled, as if she were pulling her petticoats over her head, then more clearly, her quavering voice repeating, "Oh, Michael."

"During all the hopeless days and nights of my imprisonment, I listened while my fellow prisoners begged for pity, screamed in pain, sobbed in loneliness . . . and silently died." He didn't know why, but it felt good to tell her these things. She listened, she saw into the dark places of his soul, and she didn't seem to think he was weak or heartless. She understood. "That's why I plotted my revenge on Rickie — and Sandre. That's why I ride as the Reaper."

He definitely heard a sniffle.

She had softened toward him. Good. In this case, he could use her pity to manipulate her. "So you comprehend — you have no such reason to put yourself in danger, and I forbid you to do so again."

CHAPTER
THIRTY-EIGHT

Emma stared at the damp, tearful handkerchief clutched in her hand, and she couldn't
believe her ears. "What?"

"I said —"

"*Forbid* me? You *forbid* me?" She had
donned her petticoats and chemise before
sitting down to cry over Michael's ordeal,
but now hot rage dried her tears and drove
her around the partition. "Because I have
no reason to wish for justice? *You're* the one
who took me to the lower city. *You're* the
one who showed me the misery the de
Guignards have caused in this land."

Old Nelson stomped his feet.

Michael put down the body brush and
threw a blanket over the horse's back.
"You're upsetting him. He doesn't like having a virago behind him."

"You dare." Michael was not the lonely,
pitiful prisoner she'd been imagining. He
might have been once, but now he was tall

and handsome, healed and sure.

She backed up to let him out of the stall, and helped him shut the door and lock it. "Should I not want Damacia to have vengeance for her husband's death?" she demanded. "Should I not help Elixabete to have a better life?"

"There are other, safer ways to accomplish that than by riding as the Reaper while the prince's guards scour the countryside."

"Not while you're sick unto death because you've taken a bullet, there aren't." She shook her finger at him. "Should I stand by and do nothing while Prince Sandre's men come and drag you away because they've discovered you are the Reaper? Who are *you* to forbid me to do anything? Who are *you* to judge me to be meek, afraid, and incompetent? How can *you* have the temerity to condemn me to a life of regrets because I could have taken action and did nothing?"

Head down, he grasped the edge of the gate, his chest heaving as if each of her words lashed him.

And she hoped they did. She really hoped they did. "You may be the heir to the dukedom of Nevitt," she said, throwing her bitterness in his face, "but you have *no* rights over me!"

His head came up. He looked at her, and

384

he didn't appear lashed. He appeared angry and . . . well, angry, but that wasn't all.

He started toward her. She backed up, heading toward the door. He swerved, herding her into the stall where she'd dressed. Dragging his cloak off the wall, he threw it over the pile of straw — and his eyes glinted with intention.

"You have the *gall.* Do you really think you're going to . . . to . . . couple with me?" She made a dash around him.

He caught her around the waist. "I *have* this right. I *take* this right!" He tossed her on top of his cloak and followed her down.

Straw crackled. Dust flew.

"Don't you even think of it!" As hard as she could, she slapped the side of his head.

He captured her wrist and pressed it over her head, then caught her other wrist and imprisoned them together, controlling her with one hand while he used the other to . . . to grope her. The sensitive skin of her inner elbow and wrist. Her long throat. The swell of her breasts beneath her soft chemise.

With the exaltation of her ride still surging in her veins and her fury to back her up, she struggled against him, flinging herself against his strength, snapping her teeth toward his face . . . yet being careful not to hit his wound.

And why not?

Did he really imagine she would submit to him? To this? Now? After he had made his opinion of her so dreadfully, distressingly clear?

Apparently he did, for he sat up, caught her petticoat, and dragged it up, baring her to the cool air. With his hand on her thigh, he pushed it all the way up. He used his knee to separate her legs, and when she kicked at him, he employed his thumb with wicked intent, sliding it along the crease between her legs, fondling her clitoris, then thrusting his thumb inside her.

Looking into her face, he chuckled. "Why are you fighting? You're damp. Yielding. Ready."

"I hate you!" Stupid, petulant, childish thing to say — and the best she could do right now.

"I love the way you hate."

When he withdrew his thumb, she clenched her teeth to contain her groan of protest.

Somehow he had opened his trousers, for now he wrapped his arm around her hips, lifted her, and positioned them groin to groin.

"Don't you dare do . . . that!" She panted,

trying to sound firm, trying to shut him out . . . trying not to want him.

"What? This?" He barely moved, using a small rocking motion that tested her readiness.

She was ready. Blast him. Her body was softening, preparing, wanting.

"Or this?" The head of his penis pressed into her a single, taunting inch, no more, and then slowly withdrew.

She tried to remember why she was so angry at him. "You are the most ungrateful, high-handed, proprietary man I have ever had the bad luck to —"

"Couple with?" He mocked her. "I am the *only* man, my dear. *You were a virgin.* That first time, you were a virgin, hot and sweet, young and tight, and I thought I was going to die from the pleasure of having you, and from the pleasure I gave you." He took a long breath. "Furthermore, I'm going to be the only man you're ever going to have."

"You have no right —"

He thrust again.

The words choked in her throat.

In and out, that single inch that opened her to him . . . and to desperate craving.

Her legs stirred restlessly as she tried to contain her response.

She couldn't. *Oh, God.* She was halfway to

orgasm, carried there by his touch, his weight, by his relentless, guttural, visceral claim on her.

"You're mine," he whispered. "That's why I worry about you. That's why I dare tell you what to do. That's why I'll take you until you know with your every breath, your every heartbeat, that I own you."

"And I own you!" She laid claim foolishly, without thinking of the consequences.

"Yes." And he thrust all the way, filling her, heating her, finding, as he had before, that deepest place where her secrets resided. And her secret now was that *she loved this.*

She loved the powerful motion; she loved the raw violence; she loved that he stretched her until she was full of him and yet needing more. She loved the way he held her in place; she loved his lawless lack of control; she loved her own rebellious submission.

She loved that although she tried to hold off, he wouldn't allow it. He lifted her feet and wrapped them around his back, so she could do nothing but what he forced her to do. Then as he thrust and thrust, he ground his hips in a circle.

She liked being part of the night, swooping along the roads, her costume fluttering, exultant in her freedom.

She liked this better.

She came hard and fast, helpless before the onslaught of love, of lust, of desperate need and glorious release. And as she did, her inner muscles held him captive and massaged him.

He groaned, holding himself rigidly still, letting her use him until she collapsed.

Then he pulled away and thrust again.

And they were moving together, riding wildly, a ferocious hunger driving them.

His cloak twined around them, frustrating them, holding them back.

She kicked it away.

He propelled himself into her blindly, savagely, a man intent on branding himself on his woman.

She came again and again, crying out in ecstasy, filled with him and with satisfaction, yet always wanting more, wanting him.

The rhythm grew faster, the sensation more intense.

She watched his face, saw his eyes glitter with heat, his muscles grow taut with desperation. She was going to die of this pleasure, so much like agony. She was going to kill him, if he didn't kill her. She wanted it to end. She wanted it to go on forever. . . .

And then he convulsed, pouring himself into her, thrusting in a fury and groaning, "Emma. Emma."

The wildness of him poured into her, and she came, too, one final, glorious release that carried her from one peak to the other until she fell, broken and healed, into his arms.

He sank down atop her. They breathed together, heavily, recovering and returning, becoming two people again, Michael and Emma, complete and whole in themselves.

She remembered — he had insulted her. He had forbidden her. He had taken her.

And he would pay.

"Did you tear open your wound?" She pushed at him.

"What?" He lifted himself onto his elbows and looked down at her.

She was pleased — no, delighted — to see that he looked dazed. "Did you tear open your wound?" More forcefully, she shoved at him.

He let her, rolling onto his back and taking her with him. "I don't think so."

She slid his shirt off his shoulder and looked. No crimson stained the white bandage. "You're sure you didn't hurt anything?"

"I'm fine!"

Taking both sides of his shirt in her hands, she ripped it apart. "Stay absolutely still and I won't hurt you now." Putting her mouth to his, she kissed him hotly, deeply, and when he groaned, she knew she was going to win this time.

They were both going to win this time.

As they dressed, she couldn't meet his gaze. She had been wild with him, taking charge, riding him hard, riding him fast, making him carry her where she wanted to go.

She needed to remember more than those moments. She needed to remember what had come before, in all the days of their acquaintance, and what he'd done to her — seduced her with a lie, laughed at her behind her back.

But this didn't feel like a lie, like seduction, or like laughter. It felt like . . . union. It felt like a meeting of souls.

"Emma?"

His deep voice made her want to hide. "Yes?"

He put one hand on her shoulder, used the other to tilt her chin until she *had* to look at him. "Marry me."

"What?" She looked at him now, all right. Looked to see if he was serious.

Her shock must have been all too apparent, for he laughed reluctantly, and repeated, "Marry me. Please."

He looked serious. And she couldn't figure

out why he would propose as a joke. After all, he'd already done with her what he wanted . . . what they both wanted. A little curl of panic started in her belly, so she took a moment to hide her face, and pulled her dress on over her head.

He moved behind her and started fastening her buttons.

Briskly and sensibly, she said, "I'm a paid companion. A rector's daughter. I can't marry the heir to the dukedom of Nevitt."

"What a snob you are." Using his fingers, he combed the hay out of her hair.

"A snob!" His casual dismissal of her background took her breath away. She twisted around to face him. "I assume that someday you want to return to England?"

"Someday very soon." She heard the hitch of homesickness in his voice.

Homesickness was catching, apparently, for she felt it, too. But that made his proposal even more ludicrous. "I remember England if you don't. I'd be shunned. You'd be embarrassed!"

He drew himself up, and for the first time she saw the visage of the nobleman that lay at his core. "I would not be embarrassed, and you would not be shunned. You would be a Durant."

His arrogance took her breath away. But

when she got it back, she retorted, "Not for long. Your father would have the marriage annulled."

"My father would joyously click his heels to know I was marrying at last."

She laughed reluctantly.

But he looked more and more earnest. "More important, when he got to know you, he would slap me on the shoulder and tell me you were too good for a wastrel like me."

"You're not a wastrel," she said automatically.

"Not any longer. But I was. I was a lot of things. A spoiled brat, a wastrel, and an adventurer. Then a prisoner." His eyes grew dark. "Nothing more. Even after I was released, my soul still cowered behind bars and in the dark. Until you came, Emma, and rescued Elixabete. Then I saw kindness still existed in the world, and it was the start of healing."

"No one can stand by while a child screams in pain!"

"Actually, most people can. Then you saved me from Prince Sandre and his thugs. Well" — he waved a dismissive hand — "not me, really, but the Reaper."

"You saved me first!"

He viewed her as if he saw something in her she couldn't imagine. "You repay your debts, even to a crazy man in a costume, and you kiss him in gratitude. Both parts of me — Michael Durant and the Reaper — fell in love with you."

Love.

No, not really. He was still suffering from prison-induced delusions.

She didn't believe him. Or rather, she didn't dare believe him. "You're insane."

He laughed a little. "Possibly. But what I want to know is, who are you, Emma Chegwidden? What will you do with your life? Become the princess of Moricadia?"

"No!" She shuddered in revulsion. "No."

"You could do a lot of good here, use your influence on Sandre to soften his policies. Sacrifice yourself for the good of others."

"No. I won't!"

"Or you could be the Duchess of Nevitt."

"You taunt me."

"Do I look like I'm taunting you?"

She turned her head away, because the idea of being his wife, at his side for his whole life . . . It pulled at her with all the power of the North Star to a magnet. How she wanted him!

"Or you could do whatever you want."

She looked back at him. "What do you mean?"

"You're not the same timid little companion who came to Moricadia and got lost in the woods. You've had a rebirth, Emma Chegwidden, and now you're an Amazon, doing what you believe is right no matter the opposition."

Was that how Michael saw her? As an Amazon? Right now, she didn't feel like an Amazon. Her legs felt like noodles from riding as the Reaper, and from riding Michael, and from orgasms so intense she cried with joy.

"Think about it. You are afraid of nothing, and you can be whatever you want. So be mine." He kissed her lightly on the forehead, on the cheek, on the lips. "Marry me."

CHAPTER
THIRTY-NINE

"This was my father's." Aimée showed Elixabete the small figure of a horse, intricately carved and polished. "One of our Moricadian workers made it from an oak stump, and Father bought it from him. The family had been turned off their land by . . . well, you know."

"By the de Guignards."

"Yes. Look at the workmanship on this." Aimée held the statue in the sunlight coming through the window. "Moricadians don't get to ride anymore, most of them. They don't have the money to feed and stable their horses."

"I love them," Elixabete said fervently.

"Yes, Moricadians have a feel for horses, and the horses know it. In this piece, you can see respect and adoration for the beast." Aimée stroked it affectionately, taking pleasure in the smooth ripple of bone and muscle.

Her bedchamber, the whole house, was draped in sheets. The servants had been dismissed. The cart was coming for Aimée's last load before she closed the house and left.

She hadn't told anyone, most certainly not her dear friend Eleonore, but Rickie's death had freed her. She wasn't ever coming back.

Impulsively, she handed Elixabete the horse. "You keep it."

"No. No, it's yours. Your father gave it to you!" Elixabete tried to hand it back.

"I'm going to Italy, and a Moricadian horse belongs in Moricadia with a Moricadian child." Aimée ruffled the girl's hair. "Keep it in memory of me."

A thump toward the front of the house rattled the windows, and the lady and the girl looked at each other in alarm.

"There's no one here," Elixabete whispered. "The house is empty."

"Fanchere's men were supposed to bring the cart for my last load. Do you suppose they drove it into the foyer?" Aimée crinkled her nose in disgust. "That would make a mess, and I don't want to stay to take care of it." She looked at the last trunk. "I'm almost done here. Dear, go and look for me."

"No. Please, Lady de Guignard." Elixabete huddled close, clutching the horse to her skinny chest. "I don't like this place."

Aimée looked around at her washed-out bedroom. "But why, child?"

"There are ghosts here."

Aimée laughed, then realized she was being heartless. Elixabete was truly frightened. So in a comforting tone, she told her, "No, I swear, there are no ghosts here. No one has died in any of the rooms. The house is new, and even when we lived here, no one *lived* here."

Again they heard a thump from the front of the château.

"It's the house itself then," Elixabete whispered. "The house is *bad.*"

"Darling, that's not the house that's making all that noise. That's not ghosts. Either they drove the cart into the foyer, or" — Aimée brightened as another option occurred to her — "or someone's out there trying to get our attention. Go see why and let me know."

Elixabete stared in wide-eyed fright.

"Go on now." Aimée patted her bottom. "I promise no one will jump out and say, 'Boo!' "

Elixabete curtsied and sidled out the door.

Aimée finished packing and looked around the room, and chuckled. Elixabete was frightened by the spirits in this house. Aimée had been frightened by the man who dwelled here with her, and now that Rickie was gone, Aimée knew the place was safe.

When she thought about Italy, about the sun and the grapes and the art and the music, she wanted to cry for joy. She wanted to kiss Emma for thinking of it, and embrace Fanchere for making it possible. Mostly she wanted to hug Eleonore and pray she could keep her illusions about Sandre and Moricadia, because if Eleonore ever found out what her dear cousin was truly like . . . Well, Eleonore was too kindhearted and didn't deserve that kind of upset.

Aimée glanced toward the door. She had thought Elixabete would be back by now.

Had the child fallen and hurt herself?

Aimée frowned.

And what *was* that thumping they'd heard? It wasn't . . . She hadn't sent Elixabete out into the hands of thieves?

"Oh, Aimée." She walked out into the corridor, scolding herself all the way. "You are such a silly fool. Why didn't you think of that first?" She hurried toward the stairs that curved down toward the main floor. As with the Fancheres', this house had a long, high gallery overlooking the marble-floored foyer.

Unlike the Fancheres', everything here was white, unmarked, colorless.

Ah, when Aimée got to Italy, she would have color everywhere. Lavender blossoms in her vases, walls painted terra cotta and gold, curtains of rich crushed velvet in royal blue. She would be warm and she would be happy. . . .

A child's body lay facedown on the gallery floor.

Elixabete's body.

"My God!" Aimée ran to her. "What happened? Did you fall? Can you speak?"

Elixabete groaned. Her eyes fluttered open.

Blood oozed from a crescent-shaped wound on her forehead.

Aimée traced it with her finger. It looked almost as if the child had been hit.

Elixabete gazed at the horse still clutched in her hand and frowned, her eyes unfocused and confused.

"Do you remember what happened?" Aimée asked.

Elixabete looked up. "Lady de Guignard . . . where did you come from? How did I get here?" Her eyes shifted, focused on something over Aimée's shoulder. Giving a scream, she struggled to sit up.

Aimée half turned. She caught a glimpse

of someone — a man, strong and tall.

He grabbed her from behind by her collar and her waist.

She yelped. He had her hair. "What are you doing?" she shouted, twisting, trying to get a good look at him.

Elixabete gave a grunt like a dog about to sink its teeth into a bone, and grabbed his boot.

He kicked the little girl in the head, knocking her backward across the floor.

Aimée shrieked. She fought.

He lifted her up and over the balustrade.

For one terrifying moment, she stared down at the marble floor so far below.

He let her go.

And she screamed all the way down.

Jean-Pierre heard her land, heard a single groan, and looked over the edge.

Aimée had landed facedown, her hands outstretched in a futile attempt to catch herself. Blood sprayed across the floor and stained the white marble. She didn't move. She was dead, and could no longer fuel the fire of scandal surrounding the Reaper.

That was a job well-done.

He'd found that once he'd shot a few women and children, murder wasn't so hard anymore.

CHAPTER FORTY

Lady Fanchere drove up to the front of Aimée's château, stopped the pony cart, and lifted the picnic basket out of the back. Aimée would be so glad to see her, and this was the least Eleonore could do — help Aimée with the final closing of the château she had shared with Rickie, and wish her Godspeed as she left to start the rest of her life.

The place was quiet. Too quiet. No birds sang in the trees. Nothing moved in the landscape.

No one came out to welcome her, and no servant came to assist her, because Aimée had dismissed them all. She'd given them money, good wishes, and recommendations, and sent them on their way.

So there was no reason to feel unease.

Eleonore lugged the basket to the front door, opened it, and walked in. "Aimée!" she called. "Elixabete!" Her voice echoed up and down the stairways and throughout the empty house.

She was so preoccupied with that stupid basket that at first she didn't see what was there in the middle of the floor.

Then she did.

A body, shattered by the fall, lying there in Aimée's gown, with Aimée's bright ribbons threaded through the bloody hair and the broken skull.

Eleonore screamed and ran, picked up Aimée, and cradled her in her arms.

The body was still warm.

She screamed again.

"Eleonore, why have you come here?" Fanchere hurried to catch up with her as she strode through the palace toward Sandre's office.

She didn't glance at him. He was her husband, and for the first time in her life, she was embarrassed to have him know her.

She was, after all, a de Guignard.

But he must have caught sight of her expression or her bloody hands or . . . or other things, for he forcefully stopped her, looked her over, and asked, "What's wrong? What happened?"

"Aimée was killed. Aimée was killed." Eleonore repeated it as if that would somehow make her realize that it was true.

"Are you sure?" Fanchere shook his head as if embarrassed by the question.

Eleonore's gown, after all, still bore the stain where Aimée's shattered skull had rested against her bosom. "Aimée was killed, and I'm going to report it to Sandre. He's going to want to catch the killer. I know it." And she started for Sandre's office again.

Fanchere didn't try to dissuade her. But he kept pace with her.

The double doors to Sandre's office were closed, with guards on either side.

Eleonore didn't care. She looked at them and, in a tone she'd never used in her life, she said, "I am the prince's cousin Eleonore. I'm going in."

They moved to stop her.

"Do you really want to be responsible for forcibly restraining me from entering Sandre's presence?"

The guards moved aside.

Fanchere opened the doors for her.

She entered without hesitation.

Sandre was sitting with one hip on his desk, talking to Jean-Pierre, laughing.

They were both laughing.

When they saw her, they stopped.

"What happened to you?" Sandre asked,

but he didn't sound surprised.

So she told him, told them both what she'd found in Aimée's house.

Aimée's body, smashed on the marble floor.

Elixabete, her skull creased by a nearby silver candlestick and her nose broken by a boot.

Sandre gave a good imitation of grief. "Poor Aimée," he said. "I was afraid of this. She couldn't live without Rickie, so she tried to kill this Elixabete, then flung herself off the gallery."

"Aimée would never hurt a child!" Eleonore said.

"She really believed the Reaper was a ghost. She was haunted by fear. She went mad!" Sandre acted as if he believed it.

Did he? Eleonore was hard-pressed to believe him, and she fought against the fountain of invectives that threatened to pour forth. That would never convince Sandre of the justness of her suit.

But she knew him. Sandre was logical. So she possessed herself of patience and tried to explain the truth in a way he would comprehend. "Do you remember when we were children together?"

"Of course," Sandre said.

"For fun Rickie used to pull one leg off a

frog and let it go, and wager on whether it would die before a predator ate it."

"Boyish mischief." Sandre dismissed it with a wave.

Vehemently, she said, "He got worse as he got older, not better. Aimée was *not* mourning Rickie's death. She did not go mad with grief. Someone killed her!"

"We will of course bury her next to him," Sandre said. "It's what she would have wanted."

"No, she wouldn't! What she wanted was to go to Italy." Eleonore couldn't believe Sandre could be so blind. "She was murdered!"

"You're distraught. It's your condition." Sandre came to her, tried to make her sit in his chair.

She resisted, her arms stiff and her fists clenched.

Still in that soothing tone, Sandre said, "We are so pleased that at last you're increasing, and you know how dangerous this fretting can be to your health and the health of your child."

"I am not fretting." Her voice rose. "I'm telling you one of Rickie's comrades killed your cousin by marriage. You're the prince. Seek justice!"

"Yes, of course I will." He took her hand,

her *fist,* and led her toward the door. "Now, you go home and rest. Fanchere, you take her. Eleonore, when you come back, make sure you bring Miss Chegwidden. It has been far too long since I've gazed upon her face. I would hate to think she was avoiding me." He patted Eleonore on the shoulder, then turned to his desk.

He was dismissing her.

And she realized . . . he had done it.

He had murdered Aimée.

Maybe he'd thrown her over the balustrade himself.

Maybe he'd had his men throw her.

But he had murdered her cousin and his, a silly woman with a kind heart, because Aimée believed the Reaper had the power to topple his regime and spoke of it too freely.

Aimée was right: The boy Sandre, Eleonore's playmate, was gone forever, replaced by the venal creature hated across the length and breadth of Moricadia.

For possessing that knowledge, Aimée was dead — and for that, Eleonore was responsible.

Her head swam. Her knees collapsed.

Fanchere put his hand around her waist and supported her into a quiet library down the corridor from Sandre's office. He found her a seat and brought her a glass of water.

She sipped it, wishing it could wash away the taste of murder. "I can't raise our child here. I can't."

Quickly he stood, shut the door, turned the key, and came back to her side.

"I know how much you value the de Guignard connection, but I can't live in a land where murder is winked at and corruption stalks the streets." She blinked, trying to clear the tears from her eyes. "I'm sorry."

"Don't be sorry." He went down on one knee before her and chafed her hands. "I have a confession to make. When you told me about the baby, I surreptitiously began moving our money out of Moricadia and into foreign banks — the Bank of England, Banque de France, even an American bank. Because I knew this baby would sooner or later force you to face what you didn't want to see, and I knew we would want to go somewhere where we can raise our child without fear."

She stared at him, disbelieving.

He had known something like this would happen? How was that possible?

Because . . . because he knew the truth about Sandre. The truth she had ignored.

"We'll lose our home," Fanchere said. "But don't fear. I have connections all over the world, and we will not starve."

She couldn't hold back the tears. She and Fanchere had had a good marriage, always, respecting each other and their contributions to the union. He had brought a fortune made in merchandise. She had brought an ancient, noble name and the connections and influence that went with that. But they had never spoken of love. She had thought it was a partnership, nothing more. Now she discovered he was willing to leave Moricadia for her, and for their baby.

Looking into his thin, droopy, adored face, she put her hand to his cheek. "You are a dear man, and I thank God for the day my father picked you as my husband."

He turned his lips into her hand and kissed her palm. "I love you, too."

They basked in the warmth of the unexpected moment.

Leaning close, she whispered in his ear, "One more thing. I would like to somehow speak to the Reaper. Do you know how to reach him?"

He smiled. "As a matter of fact, I believe I do. Come, Eleonore. Let's go home."

CHAPTER FORTY-ONE

A knock sounded on the door, waking Emma from her afternoon nap, the one she substituted for her nighttime sleep.

"Come in," she called, and then she stared at the ceiling and thought, *He wants me to choose him. He wants me to marry him.*

Michael thought she was an Amazon. He saw her as brave and strong, someone who could do anything she wished with her life.

And he wanted her to marry him.

"Miss Chegwidden?" Tia advanced cautiously into the room.

"I'm awake." Emma didn't know what to do with Michael's proposal. Since her father died, no one had wanted her, and now Michael said she had choices. And maybe she did.

What did she want?

What was the right thing to do?

She had loved the Reaper, dark, mysterious, beckoning.

Did she love Michael Durant?

She sat up in bed and rubbed her forehead with the heels of her hands, and glanced out the window. The sun was setting. "It's late. I've got to get dressed!"

"If you would, Miss Chegwidden. We've got an emergency downstairs." Tia stood at the bedside.

For the first time, Emma looked at Tia.

Tia's face was red and blotchy, her eyes tearstained. "It's not Durant," she said.

Emma came off the bed in a rush. "Something with Brimley's finger?"

"His finger is fine. Mending. A miracle. No." Tia shook her head and started crying in earnest. "It's Lady de Guignard and Elixabete."

No. *No.*

As she dressed, Emma questioned Tia.

Tia didn't seem sure of anything except that the men were carrying Elixabete back to the Fancheres'. But she wouldn't speak of Aimée, and she was crying so hard, Emma felt a hard lump settle in her stomach.

Not Aimée. Not dear, kind Aimée, who stood poised on the verge of happiness.

Emma rushed downstairs.

The men were carrying Elixabete into the house on blankets stretched tightly between

411

them. "Put her down," she commanded, and they gently placed the blankets, and the child, on the floor.

She knelt beside her.

Elixabete lay on her side, curled into the fetal position, eyes closed. She clutched something close to her chest. Her face had been kicked, her nose broken, but it was the mark on her forehead that concerned Emma. She had a dent in her skull, and that was the kind of injury that could kill.

Servants crowded around.

"Step back," Brimley ordered. "Give them room to breathe."

Emma touched Elixabete's shoulder.

The child's eyes fluttered open.

"Elixabete, can you hear me?" Emma asked.

"Yes." The girl focused on Emma, then on the people standing around her.

"How many fingers am I holding up?"

"Three."

"Good." God willing, Elixabete would recover. "Can you move your fingers? Your toes?"

"Yes. Yes. Oh, Miss Chegwidden." She gave a wrenching sob. "Why did it have to happen to *her?*"

That lump in Emma's stomach grew heavier. "What happened?"

"He threw her over the edge. She screamed, but he threw her over the edge. I tried to stop him, but he kicked me and threw her over the edge." Elixabete brought her hand up, and in it she clutched a carved horse, polished and exquisite. "She gave me this. It was her father's. She wanted me to have it. And she's *dead.*"

In a soft, soft voice, Emma asked, "Who's dead?"

Elixabete trembled and cried.

"Is it Aimée?" Emma asked.

Elixabete nodded, then curled up around the horse again. "I want my mother," she wailed.

Emma stroked her forehead, then stood up and told Brimley, "Put her to bed. Don't let her get up. Put cold rags on her face to bring down the swelling. Talk to her. Give her water. And for the love of God, bring her mother here." Turning away, she started to make her way through the crowd.

"Miss Chegwidden." Brimley's voice brought her to a halt. "What are you planning to do?"

"I'm going to make them pay."

"Durant, something's happened in the main house."

Michael put down his pen, glad to procrastinate on that difficult letter to his father, the one that told him that the prodigal son was alive and needed help, and raised an inquiring eyebrow at Rubio.

"The child Elixabete was hurt and Lady de Guignard . . ." Rubio shook his head, and his eyes looked the way they had when he'd first come out of the dungeon. Dull. Resigned. In pain.

Michael came to his feet. "Where's Emma?"

"They called her to care for Elixabete."

He wasn't finished speaking before Michael was racing for the house. He ran inside, grabbed a footman. "Where is Elixabete?"

"They carried her upstairs. Did you hear . . . ?" He was a young man, and he had to clear his throat. "Did you hear about Lady de Guignard?"

Michael took the stairs two at a time, followed the trail of weeping maids and medical supplies up to the third level, and rushed into Elixabete's bedroom.

Emma wasn't there.

He grabbed Brimley by the lapels. "Where's Emma?"

Brimley grabbed him right back. "She gave us instructions on how to care for Elixabete; then she left."

"Where did she go?"

"I think she went . . . She said she went to make them pay."

"To make them pay? No. She went to ride? Why didn't you stop her?"

"I have a situation here, Durant. And I can't lay hands on a lady!"

"How long has it been?"

"A quarter of an hour, perhaps more."

Michael's mind raced. Emma's path and his hadn't crossed when he'd run to the château, so it was too late to stop her at the stable. But if he cut across the front and into the forest, he might catch her before she reached the road.

He was running again, down the stairs and out the door. He sprinted along the drive.

The Fancheres' carriage turned into their gate.

He swerved, jumped the hedge, and ran across the lawn.

His lungs hurt. His legs hurt. His shoulder hurt.

He headed up a rise, cut into the forest. The branches smacked him. The brush cut at his legs.

He couldn't run fast enough.

He wasn't going to make it.

Then he did. He broke out of the forest and tottered on the edge a twenty-foot embankment. The road was below — and he was too late. He was too late!

Old Nelson was galloping into the woods, riderless.

Prince Sandre's guard surrounded a white-clad figure in the brush at the side of the road.

She struggled to sit up.

She was alive!

Michael started down the embankment after her.

And someone grabbed his arm.

He came around, fists up.

Fanchere shook him. "No!"

Michael tried to fight him off.

"No. Look at them!" Fanchere said softly.

Michael looked. The guards were mounting their horses. They had guns, swords, knives. They looked surly and angry, ready to kill.

One of them picked her up and flung her onto his saddle.

"Sandre's killing their wives and children," Fanchere said, "and if we try to take the Reaper away, they'll kill us."

"She's dead if she gets to the palace. Or worse." Michael started forward again.

"Eleonore has a plan."

Michael looked back. "She didn't know this was going to happen."

"No. But we can change the plan, make it work. For God's sake, Michael, getting yourself killed won't help Emma escape, or get your revenge on the prince." Fanchere spoke urgently. "And it would break Eleonore's heart, and her heart is already broken enough."

Michael knew Fanchere was right, but bile was sour in his mouth as he watched the guard ride away, Emma sitting behind the leader, holding on to his waist.

"All right." He turned back to the house. "What's the plan?"

Chapter Forty-Two

The guard pushed Emma into Prince Sandre's office.

She knew she would be sorry later, but right now, in the grip of grief and rage, the look on Sandre's face when he recognized her was worth all the gold in his coffers.

He came to his feet with a bound. "What's going on here?" He turned on the head of the patrol. "Quico, what have you done?"

In a rough, deep voice, Quico said, "I don't know if she's the Reaper, Your Highness. It's not my job to answer that question. But we caught her riding in this costume and we brought her to you."

"She's a lady!" Sandre said.

When he spoke, she remembered Aimée. She remembered Elixabete. She remembered how much she hated him. In a rage, Emma leaped at him. "No, I'm the Reaper, you murdering freak!"

Quico grabbed her arms and yanked

418

her back.

"I'm the Reaper," she shouted, straining against his hold, "and everybody's going to know you were chasing after a man, while all the while a mere woman was making a fool of you."

Sandre had clearly been caught by surprise, and he was still trying to save the situation. Save face. "That's impossible. You weren't even in the country until recently."

"I've been hiding out, riding from my secret den."

"Where's your secret den?" He cajoled her as if she were a two-year-old.

"Under the grave of King Reynaldo." She hated him. Hated him with all the clawing anguish of her grief.

"What do you want me to do with her, Your Highness?" Quico pushed her toward two of his men.

They caught her arms.

She struggled against them.

"Let her go."

They did.

Sandre walked toward her. "Now, Miss Chegwidden, let's sit down and talk like reasonable people —"

She lunged at him, fingers clawed, aiming at his eyes.

Sandre turned his head at the last second.

He staggered back, blood running from his ear.

That was even better than riding through the night as the Reaper.

The guards seized her before she could strike at him again.

Sandre stormed forward and slapped her hard enough to snap her head back and wrench her neck, and only the men holding her kept her on her feet.

"I'm sorry you made me do that," he said.

"I didn't make you do anything. You love hurting people." For a moment, she remembered how he had hurt Aimée, and tears threatened.

Then he said, "You will treat me with respect!"

Rage swept away the tears. "You murderer. You killer! No one respects you. You're supposed to be just. Instead you kill people for telling the truth." She strained against the guards, wanting nothing more than to attack him again. "You're a travesty."

His guards stirred restlessly.

His hand came up again.

She braced herself.

He stood, frozen in place, then lowered his hand, very controlled. "Tell me who the Reaper really is and we'll have no more unpleasantness."

"I told you. I'm the Reaper." Obviously he didn't believe her, but that gave her a savage satisfaction, too. "I'm the Reaper, and I will have vengeance for Aimée."

"Perhaps a night in the dungeon will cool your temper and remind you of the proper behavior of a future princess."

A future princess? What did it take to discourage this guy? Repulsed, she said, "I would never marry you!"

"We'll see." The blood from his ear showed red on Sandre's pale neck, and he scrutinized her as if weighing her reaction.

"And you would never marry me. I'm not proper. I'm not docile. *That's* what you want."

"You don't know what I want."

"Yes, I know. You want a young woman from a foreign country with no family to protect her. You want to be able to abuse her, cheat on her, force her to do anything you demand, and know she has no way of fighting back." In a lower voice, she said, "When you're finished with her, you can do to her what you did to Aimée and no one will notice or care."

Sandre lifted his eyebrows as if astonished at the idea.

With a sinking heart, Emma realized she was *still* his ideal wife. "Aimée warned me about you," she finished.

Sandre's phony surprise vanished, replaced by easily stirred ferocity. "Take her below."

She walked between Quico and one of the other guards down to the ground level, then through a stone arch and down a dark flight of stairs lit only by torches on the walls.

A short, fat little man sat there in a chair, whistling tunelessly. When he saw her, he smiled with a mouthful of black teeth and started to chuck her under the chin, then stood at attention when he realized the prince walked behind the grim little party.

The prince held up a big black iron ring with two keys on it. "Gotzon, this prisoner is mine."

Gotzon scowled, but he nodded, and as soon as the prince passed, he started that tuneless whistling again.

They descended another flight of stairs. The torches were farther apart here, and at the bottom, Prince Sandre took the last torch. "We don't waste light on our prisoners," he said, and led the way down the corridor.

She stumbled on the uneven stones under her feet, and as she passed, she glanced in the cells. The bars were thick, black and shiny, as if someone cared for them weekly.

Prince Sandre stopped in front of one door and pushed it open with his foot. "This is a very special cell. We save it for our most important visitors. It's said that King Reynaldo himself spent his last days in here. As you can see" — he waved the torch inside — "it's quite luxurious, and has a cot, which most of the cells do not."

"It's a pit." She had never meant anything so much.

"You should see what's below this. But perhaps you've changed your mind and want to return with me upstairs?"

Shaking off the guards, she walked inside.

Sandre nodded as if not surprised.

The guards shut the door behind her.

He stepped up and turned the lock. Still in that awful, conversational tone, he said, "The true advantage is — I alone have the key for it. But, oh! You despise me. Perhaps you'd rather be in a cell that Gotzon controls?"

Bile rose in her throat. "No."

"You see, I'm not as bad as you've suggested. Now you might want to go sit on the bed. It's dark down here when the light is gone." Sandre turned away, clapped Quico on the shoulder, and asked, "How's your wife? Has she recovered from that bullet wound yet? My office is dusty without her."

As they left, the guards walked behind the prince, and Emma saw the sympathetic glances they sent her.

All except Quico. He shot her a venomous look that made her want to shrink back.

Before the light disappeared, she hurried to the bed and eased herself down.

Here, in the cool damp of the dungeon, her tumble from Old Nelson's back came back to haunt her. She'd managed to get her arms up to protect her face, but nothing protected her arms, and they felt like one big bruise. Her knee hurt as if, even through the costume, she'd scraped it, and she wasn't sure, but she thought she'd probably done something to her hip. It burned like fire.

The cot was narrow, the blanket thin, and the dark was so absolute she could see nothing . . . and hear everything. The rats as they scampered across the floor. The drip of water as it ran down the walls. Far above, the guard's tuneless whistling.

Her stomach growled, reminding her she had eaten only one meal today. But she wasn't really hungry; somewhere close, something had died and was rotting. The smell made her want to vomit.

Michael had lived here for two years.

Where was he now? And how long would it take him to come and get her?

The next day — at least, she thought it was the next day — the light of a torch announced the arrival of Prince Sandre.

He had come for her. Prince Sandre with his cousin Jean-Pierre. "Are you ready to remember what you owe me?" Sandre asked.

She clutched at the cold metal pipe that formed the side of the cot. "I owe you death."

He unlocked the door. "Come out," he said.

"I haven't changed my mind. I'd rather be here than with you."

Jean-Pierre strode in, grabbed her bruised arm, and dragged her out the door. "You don't talk that way to your prince."

She rammed him with her elbow. "He isn't my prince. I'm English. Queen Victoria is my prince, and she's not a coldhearted murderer."

Prince Sandre pinched her chin and turned her face to his. "Are you hungry? Upstairs I've got food for you . . . if you behave."

"What are you going to do, starve me into

submission?" As long as it had been since she'd eaten, she thought it was probably a good strategy.

"Starve is a harsh word," Sandre said kindly. "But I do know how to use food as encouragement for good behavior."

She spit in his face.

In less than a minute, she was back in the cell, alone, but this time her arm was chained to the wall.

By the next time the light appeared down the corridor, she definitely understood what Sandre meant about food encouraging good behavior. She had been sipping water off the slimy wall, and was so hungry that when Jean-Pierre came in to get her, her legs collapsed, and her arm hung limp, cold and numb from the wall. He had to carry her into the corridor over his shoulder.

She thought Sandre was smiling.

Jean-Pierre carried her all the way up to the prince's personal quarters and placed her in a chair before a table of bread and cheese.

But when she reached for it, Sandre slapped her hand. "I'll feed you," he said. And he did.

She let him because her hands were shaking so much she didn't know if she could get the food to her mouth. And no matter the temptation, she didn't bite his hand.

She'd had only a few tastes when he pulled back. "That's enough."

She glared like the wild creature she had become.

"Go change your clothing," he told her. "You reek, and I'm not going to look at you in that ridiculous attire."

She glanced down at the filthy, damp remnants of the Reaper's costume. "This seems an appropriate outfit for the dungeon."

Sandre leaned down and smiled at her. "You don't have to stay in the dungeon."

If she hadn't known the truth, she would have seen only the kind, urbane, princely image he projected. "Yes, I do."

He straightened. "You can change yourself or I can do it for you, but you're going to wear a woman's proper outfit." He pointed at the screen in the corner. "The clothes are there."

She stood.

Jean-Pierre said, "But first —"

He wanted to see her bare shoulders.

She refused.

So they wrestled her to the floor, both of them, uncaring of her aches and her bruises. She burned with mortification as Sandre held her face down on the richly colored carpet while Jean-Pierre examined her skin.

"She might be *a* Reaper, but she's not *the* Reaper. I shot the Reaper." Jean-Pierre dusted his fingers with satisfaction. "She probably knows who he is. With your permission, Highness, I could get the information out of her."

"No. No torture. It's not necessary." Sandre brushed her hair off her neck in a parody of loving kindness, and helped her up off the floor.

Holding her costume over her breasts, she scuttled behind the screen, sickened by his touch.

"There's a comb, and a basin of water and towels," he called. "Avail yourself of those before you dress."

The petticoats were thick, the chemise fine, and the gown that waited for her was a serviceable dark blue wool. These clothes would be good in the dungeon . . . which meant Sandre expected that she wouldn't yet yield.

He was a bully, holding all the trumps in his cruel, jeweled hands, and he relished this struggle, and her eventual downfall, all too much.

Then what would happen? She would rail against the necessity, but in the end, he would prevail. She would marry him, and the years that would follow would be lived one miserable moment after another. She would shudder in his bed. She would cower under his whip. She would know he lived off gullible gamblers, killed and tortured innocent people, and all the while, she would be helpless to stop him. Finally, her very *self* would wither away, and she would kill herself.

She leaned against the wall.

Kill herself? Unlikely. No, he'd kill her first.

She had only herself to blame. She'd heard how Aimée died. She'd lost her temper. She'd ridden out and been captured by the prince's guard.

She wished she could tell Michael how sorry she was, what a fool she'd been. She'd put herself in this mess, and she knew it . . . but every minute that she was down in the dungeon, she prayed that someone — she, Michael, Raul Lawrence — would get revenge for Sandre's murder of Aimée.

She wanted to see Sandre burn in fire and brimstone.

"Miss Chegwidden? Are you ready?" the prince called.

She was as ready as she would ever be. She walked out looking more like herself, with a renewed defiance . . . although her gaze lingered on the table where the food was still stacked.

Sandre held out her chair. "Sit down and eat, Miss Chegwidden, while I tell you our plan."

She didn't hesitate, but seated herself at once.

Yet she flinched when he put his hands on her shoulders, then held herself perfectly still and rigid with rejection.

He pressed his fingers into her flesh, digging them into her muscles; then, when she squirmed, he laughed and let go. "Tell her our plan, Jean-Pierre."

"You know who the Reaper is, Miss Chegwidden," Jean-Pierre said.

"Yes, I do." She ate a grape, then another, and drank a glass of clear water and sipped at the wine. Glancing up, she saw how the men waited for her next comment. "I'm the Reaper."

She thought they would remove the food now, but Jean-Pierre turned away in disgust while a slow smile curled Sandre's lips.

"I told you she wouldn't yield, Jean-Pierre." Sandre pushed the bread closer to her elbow. "We're watching your friends. Brimley is a good choice, we think, and that footman, Henrique. Jean-Pierre thinks it's

430

Fanchere, which I think is patently ridiculous, and he thinks it could be Michael Durant, which is a possibility, but not a good one. I still say he's a broken man, too ashamed to even write to his father to bring him home."

She ate a triangle of Brie and drank more water.

"But whoever it is," Sandre said, "we know he's got to be perturbed that you've been captured."

"What about Lady Fanchere?" Emma wondered what her kind patroness was doing without Aimée or Emma. "Isn't she perturbed?"

"She isn't well," Jean-Pierre said.

Emma dropped the bunch of grapes. Loose ones rolled across the table and onto the floor, but she didn't care. "Is it the baby?"

"So we're told." Jean-Pierre looked different than he had when he'd visited the Fancheres' château. His pale eyes were paler, almost as if the soul within had escaped, leaving only the bits and pieces of a man inside.

"If you'd been a good girl, you'd be there to help dear Eleonore," Sandre told her.

"If you hadn't killed Aimée, she wouldn't be ill with grief," Emma retorted.

Sandre grabbed her braid and yanked her head back. "Miss Chegwidden, you are asking for trouble."

"No, I'm asking for justice."

"Take her food away," Jean-Pierre advised.

She crammed what remained of the bread into her pocket.

Sandre handed her an apple. "Listen to me. Jean-Pierre and I have told the world that we captured you in costume. We've said we're going to hang you on Sunday."

A chill ran up her spine.

"We're not really going to hang you on Sunday," Sandre assured her.

"We're not?" Jean-Pierre grabbed an apple, too, and crunched into it.

"No, we're not. Be civilized, Jean-Pierre," Sandre reproved. Turning back to Emma, he said, "You're bait. We think the real Reaper will try to rescue you, and then we'll have him. Simple!"

"It is simple," she said. "But it won't work. There's no one to rescue me. I'm the Reaper."

"Have you ever seen a hanging, Miss Chegwidden?" Sandre asked in a conversational tone. "Very entertaining. If done right, it can go on for hours."

"Thank you for letting me know." Her heart beat slowly, chilling with her blood.

"Actually, we don't have to hang you. There is another alternative." Sandre sounded so charming.

She wanted to stick her fingers in her ears.

"You can marry me on Sunday instead."

"Marry you? A coldhearted murderer of his own family? Of a dear, sweet, kind woman whose only sin was silliness? No. No. Believe me, Sandre: I may be only a paid companion, but I would never stoop so low."

When she was back in the dungeon with both hands chained to the wall, she wished there were a way to hurry this along. Eventually, she knew, Sandre would grow tired of her defiance. She knew he'd do to her what he'd done to Aimée, and someone would find her body broken on the rocks below the palace terrace.

The sooner, the better — because like Sandre and Jean-Pierre, she knew the Reaper would come to rescue her, and he could attack the royal palace and Prince Sandre . . . but he couldn't win.

Durant had already escaped from this hell once, and she never wanted him to have to return.

Next time, he wouldn't come out alive.

CHAPTER
FORTY-THREE

It was late Saturday afternoon when Prince Sandre walked into Jean-Pierre's rooms, holding a paper pressed with a red seal, and frowning.

Jean-Pierre straightened from his concentrated examination of a Moricadian map, bowed, and said, "How may I help you, Your Highness?"

"I have here a letter from our cousin Eleonore, saying she has heard rumors that tonight the Reaper will appear to the people of Moricadia and raise a rebellion against me sure to shatter my control."

"Your Highness, we've heard that rumor before." Jean-Pierre had ignored those rumors, choosing instead to search the nooks and crannies of Moricadia, seeking the Reaper's hideout.

"Eleonore is most insistent and most concerned for my safety, and she is not a woman to take alarm without reason."

"Shall I send someone to bring her to the palace so we may question her?"

Sandre tapped the letter against his fingertips. "No. Eleonore's the only one who . . . No, I can't question her as if she were a criminal."

Jean-Pierre understood why Sandre hesitated. He'd killed Aimée and insulted Eleonore to her face, and he had feared that at last he'd lost Eleonore's love. This letter was a sign she still believed Sandre was a good man, much maligned, and in the depths of Sandre's corrupt soul, he needed her to continue in her innocent faith.

Personally, Jean-Pierre thought she was an idiot.

"Shall I go visit her home and question her?" he asked.

"No! Fanchere would take that ill, very ill."

"Why should you care?"

"He's quiet, but powerful. I don't choose to anger him."

Jean-Pierre's nimble mind had considered Fanchere as a prospect for the Reaper, and now he considered him again. Fanchere spoke so seldom, he was certainly silent enough to play the role. "Then what are your orders, Highness?"

"Take your men. Ride the roads. See if

you can find the Reaper. See if there is any truth to this rumor."

Jean-Pierre wanted to point out how much more useful he would be ferreting out suspicious behavior among the rich. But Sandre continued to shackle his hands, citing the income brought by affluent gamblers and partygoers, and Jean-Pierre had not yet secured his position as Prince Sandre's right-hand man, and the fortune and influence that accompanied it. To do so, he had to discover who harbored the Reaper, and he would — after he had searched the roads this night. He bowed. "As you command, my prince."

As Michael rode Old Nelson toward the palace, he smiled beneath the black mask that covered the upper half of his face. It was Saturday night, the full moon floated in a cloudless sky, lighting the road like a benediction, and he heard the sound of many hooves galloping toward him.

The palace guard was on the move.

Eleonore's plan was in motion.

Michael dared not falter now.

Around the bend, a dozen horses rode toward him, surrounded him, and Jean-Pierre de Guignard pointed his pistol at Michael's heart. His voice was cool, his hand steady. "Reveal yourself or die."

Michael pushed his mask up onto the top of his head, then left his hands in the air in a gesture of surrender. "What's wrong, de Guignard? Is it now a crime to attend a party in Moricadia?"

"A party?" Jean-Pierre looked him up and down. "What party do you attend looking like that?"

Michael glanced at his outfit — black riding breeches and riding boots, ruffled white shirt opened halfway down his chest, a black cravat ticd at his throat, and a black knee-length riding coat. He looked down at Old Nelson, done up with bows in his braided mane and white ruffles sewn onto his saddle blanket. "What's wrong? I thought my costume very dashing, and my horse's, too."

Jean-Pierre all too obviously believed not a word. "Dashing, yes, if you're dashing out of the country."

"I thought you were Prince Sandre's top man . . . now that Rickie is dead?"

That barb dug smoothly under Jean-Pierre's skin, making his eyes glow white with an inner fury. "I am."

"Then how is it you don't know about this party? Everyone was invited."

Jean-Pierre paused for a long moment.

"Apparently not."

At Michael's jibe, the guards grew nervous. Their horses sensed their disquiet and moved restlessly. The riders tried to quiet their mounts' agitation.

The men — indeed, everyone at the palace — feared Jean-Pierre. Feared him and hated him.

On that fact rested the success of Eleonore's plan.

"I'm sure your invitation was lost — you know how careless servants are — or perhaps it was simply an oversight." Michael started to lower his arms.

Jean-Pierre cocked the pistol.

Michael hastily raised his hands again. "You can invite yourself. It's a masquerade. No one will know you slipped in without an invitation." He used a soothing tone, all the while aware he prodded Jean-Pierre like a foolish boy prods a rabid dog.

But he needed Jean-Pierre angry enough to take action thoughtlessly.

For Michael's part of the plan to succeed, he needed time.

More important, he needed to behave as if time didn't matter.

"Where is this party taking place?" Jean-Pierre asked.

Michael flopped his hands as if they were

438

dying fishes. "My arms are getting tired. Please may I put them down? I'm not fool enough to try to run. You've got a dozen firearms fixed on my chest."

Jean-Pierre glanced at his men, then at Michael, and nodded shortly. He did not, however, lower his pistol.

Michael dropped his hands with a groan, and rubbed his upper arms as if they ached.

"Where is this party taking place?" Jean-Pierre repeated.

"Would you like me to show you the invitation?" Michael patted his bulging saddlebag.

Jean-Pierre didn't even take a second thought. "Yes. Show me the invitation."

Michael tugged the leather flap open. The strap slapped Old Nelson across his rump, and, right on cue, he danced sideways across the path.

Jean-Pierre snapped, "Control that horse."

"I am!" Michael made a play for grabbing the reins, wavered in the saddle, righted himself, and patted Old Nelson's neck until he calmed. "He's aging and cantankerous, and I'm not the horseman I was two years ago . . . before my imprisonment."

"I don't care about your lack of skill or your stupid horse," Jean-Pierre said. "I want to see that invitation."

"I'm trying!" Michael pulled a wool shawl out of the bag.

"What's that for?" Jean-Pierre asked.

"A gift for my hostess." Michael spoke slowly and carefully, as if Jean-Pierre were a social dolt not to know such a thing.

One of Jean-Pierre's men spoke in a low, urgent tone. "My lord."

Michael pulled out a leather holster and a pistol.

"Is that also a gift for your hostess?" Jean-Pierre asked.

"Not everyone I might meet on a dark road is as charming and kind as you, de Guignard." Now Michael allowed himself sarcasm. "Some are actually robbers and thieves, and, of course, there's the legend of the Reaper, with his habit of hanging noblemen."

"My lord," Jean-Pierre's man said again.

"Shut up, Quico," Jean-Pierre snarled in his direction. Then to Michael he said, "You don't believe the Reaper is a ghoul?"

"Of course not. I'm not a child or a fool to believe the ghost of a long-dead king roams the roads of Moricadia." Michael's black leather hat was wide brimmed, shading his face and keeping his expression private, even under this full moon. "The Reaper is most definitely a man."

440

"So you don't believe the Reaper is Miss Emma Chegwidden?"

Michael locked gazes with Jean-Pierre. "How would a woman with the build of Miss Emma Chegwidden hang a man the size of Rickie de Guignard?"

"Yet she rode in the Reaper's costume, and we will hang *her* tomorrow for the crime."

"So I hear."

"You know this Englishwoman. She seemed fond of you. Don't you want to save her?"

"Of course I do. But do you really think I would descend into that dungeon to free her?"

"My lord!" Quico sounded desperate now.

"What?" Jean-Pierre turned ferociously on Quico.

Quico pointed soundlessly up the road.

Galloping down the road toward them on a large white horse was . . . the Reaper.

With a shout, Jean-Pierre and his men spurred their horses toward the ghostly, fearsome figure.

Michael watched long enough to see Jean-Pierre launch himself out of the saddle and bring down the Reaper.

Then, quietly, quickly, he stuffed the pistol

and Emma's shawl back into his saddlebags and rode hell-for-leather toward the palace.

CHAPTER
FORTY-FOUR

Michael lifted his gaze to the palace rising out of the rocky outcrop like a giant, medieval stone crystal growing from the earth. Within its narrow, towering walls, stairways wound up from the kitchens at ground level to the communal areas above that, and to the royal living quarters above that.

And he had personal reason to know those same stairways twisted their way down to the dungeons, deep into the murky caverns beneath the ground.

The palace had been constructed, dungeons and all, by Moricadia's long-dead kings, but when the de Guignards had dispossessed and killed them, the building had taken on a sinister aspect. At night, the cooks banked the fires and fled the kitchens, but occasionally visitors stumbled down in search of hot water or food or a toothache remedy, and even the most pragmatic whispered of ghosts drifting up from the dark depths, their mouths perpetually open to scream in agony.

The postern gate, a small entrance where the servants came and went with supplies for the kitchens, was accessed by a steep, winding path treacherous even in daylight, and there Old Nelson could not go. Slipping from the saddle, Michael took his companion of so many missions into the woods and tied him to a branch. "Wait here. It'll take as long as it takes, but then we'll need you. So, patience, my friend." He looked up through the fluttering leaves at the palace. "I promise I will not linger any longer than I have to." He loosened the reins a little. Just in case.

He climbed the postern path with a loaded pistol in each of his coat pockets, a sword strapped to his belt, one knife in his boot and another up his sleeve. Yet nothing he could carry — no firearm, no blade — could make him secure enough for the task ahead. All he truly had was this plan and the knowledge that he should have been dead a thousand times before. What matter if he died today, as long as Emma lived?

He had been promised that any guards would be otherwise occupied, and it appeared they were. He had been promised the postern door would be left unlocked, and it was. He walked into an empty chamber filled with the deliveries of the day. A crate of fresh strawberries. A dozen sacks of white flour. A crate of live chickens, squawking in protest of their fate. Through the open door, he heard the hum of the kitchen staff as they prepared tea and cakes. He listened to the cook shout at the footman, "For the prince. At once. At once! Else you go the way of the others." She stomped her foot on the floor and indicated the dungeon, then wrapped her hands around her neck and bugged out her eyes.

Lovely female, but at least she had provided Michael with an easy way to find where Prince Sandre was spending his evening.

Michael followed the footman up the stairs; then, in a swift move, he removed the tray from his hands, thrust him into a closet, and pushed a chair under the door handle. The tea steamed in the ceramic pot, the buttercream frosting roses decorated the cakes, the footman thumped and shouted, and Michael balanced the silver tray with a sure hand as he strode toward his destiny.

The de Guignard shield decorated the double doors at the center of the corridor; he gave a brief knock, then entered at Sandre's call.

The office looked different in the candle-light, all polished walnut wood, gilded plaster, fringed oriental rugs, and velvet drapes closed against the night: a hushed, luxurious den where the prince could work and relax . . . alone.

Sandre was indeed alone, sitting at his antique desk in a pool of light provided by a candelabrum of lit beeswax candles. He dipped his pen into his ornate silver ink-well, then wrote studiously on some official document. An Italian glass bowl filled with candy sat at his right hand. A brass sculpture of a noble eagle posed on one corner as if to remind the visitor — or perhaps Sandre — that here was royalty.

Without looking up, he said, "Put the tray on the table."

Michael shut the door behind him, turned the key in the lock, and walked to the desk. With a thump, he deposited the tray at Sandre's elbow.

Sandre stiffened, then slowly ran his gaze from Michael's boots all the way to the brim of his black hat. He sighed. Fixing his eyes on Michael's, he leaned back in a show of careless disregard, and smiled. "You English are so predictable. You've come to save the girl."

"More than that, I've come to confess my

crimes. I am the Reaper."

"Of course you are." Sandre's tone was disbelieving.

"And I do know the true heir to the throne of Moricadia, where he is, and how he intends to bring about a revolution."

"Of course you do," Sandre drawled, and casually moved his hand toward the drawer where he kept the loaded pistol.

Michael pulled his own pistol and cocked it. "I don't think so, Your Highness."

With equal casualness, Sandre moved his hand away. Still pleasant and disbelieving, he said, "This is a rather sweet effort on your part. Sweet . . . and worthless. What do you think you're going to accomplish by this except another, permanent visit to my dungeons? You may have gotten into the palace, but you'll never get out again. You can't take Emma away; she's grown fond of me. And what's more pathetic, no one would ever believe you have the intelligence to nightly escape your house arrest at the Fancheres', much less the guts to defy me, kill my cousin, and ride through the night dressed as the ghost of Reynaldo."

Michael smiled at him with genuine amusement.

Sandre jerked his head back as if he'd been slapped. "You don't . . . You

447

haven't . . ."

With one hand, Michael untied the black cravat, pushed his shirt off his shoulder, and showed Sandre the red, puckered, painful gunshot wound. "If Jean-Pierre were a better shot, you would be rid of the Reaper. Better yet, no one would ever know it was the cowardly, broken Englishman whom you dismissed so casually. Now everyone will discover the truth — that Prince Sandre is an overconfident imbecile."

Sandre sprang up and lunged at Michael.

Michael met him with a fist to the chin.

Sandre fell backward into his chair.

Michael stepped out of reach, leveled the pistol between Sandre's eyes. "You left her in the dungeon, day and night, hoping to break her spirit, make her yield to you."

"How do you know that?" Sandre snarled.

"The *true* king of Moricadia has returned, and he has spies everywhere. In your bedroom. In your kitchen. Among your guard."

A bruise was forming along Sandre's jaw, but he laughed unworriedly. "If that were true, I would have been dead yesterday."

"No, they want *you* in place. There's no reason for a coup d'état against a *just* monarch."

Sandre still smiled, but where he grasped the chair arms, his knuckles were white.

"Are you so jealous of me and my darling Emma that you must try to tear us apart?"

With exaggerated patience, Michael said, "Sandre, you're keeping her in the dungeon. If that's what you do with a woman you love, what do you do with a woman you hate?" When Sandre would have answered, Michael held up his hand. "Don't tell me. You hang her on Sunday morning as a lesson to any person who dares defy you."

"I am willing to show clemency."

In a staggering moment of clarity, Michael realized Sandre really did love her, or as much as a creature like him could love.

Sandre continued. "Emma can save herself if she will. All she has to do is marry me."

"She doesn't have to save herself. I'm going to save her." Michael pushed a sheet of paper toward Sandre. "Write out a pardon and stamp it with your seal."

"No."

"I was hoping you would say that." Michael grabbed Sandre by the shirtfront and pulled until he stood. "For over two years, I've been waiting for this, and I intend to enjoy every moment."

"I will die bravely." Sandre fixed his gaze on the gun still trained on his head.

"This? No." Michael slipped the pistol

back into his pocket. "Nothing so easy for you."

"Fencing? A duel?" Sandre sounded hopeful. Superior.

"I'm going to beat the hell out of you." Michael lifted his fists. "Somebody had better."

Before Michael had finished speaking, Sandre grabbed his silver inkwell and threw it at him. The heavy metal smacked him on the cheek; ink splashed his eyes and hair; the tarlike smell filled his nose. Leaping up, Sandre grabbed Michael at the site of his wound and brutally twisted.

The still-healing flesh tore. Pain ripped through his nerves. Michael's vision swam with red dots. He fell to his knees.

Through the buzzing in his ears, he heard Sandre say, "You Englishmen with your fair rules of boxing. So easy to defeat!"

Lowering his head, Michael rammed it into Sandre's belly.

Sandre fell backward against the desk, gaping like a hooked fish.

Papers flew.

Hours of torture had taught Michael one lesson — he could endure anything. He got his feet under him and body-tackled Sandre, bringing him to the floor with a thump that shook the glass windows.

Sandre gasped painfully.

For one moment, they were face-to-face, and Sandre's blue eyes blazed with maniacal fire. Then Sandre's elbow slashed up, catching Michael in the ribs.

Michael doubled over.

Sandre rolled.

Michael grabbed for that carefully coiffed head of silver-touched hair, and rammed Sandre's head into the floor.

Sandre's eyes swam. He closed them as if too dazed to focus.

Michael asked, "How's that for fair rules of boxing?" Panting, he allowed himself a moment of recovery — for himself and Sandre.

He wanted to feel the crunch of Sandre's bones beneath his fists. He wanted to savor Sandre's pain and frustration.

Maybe that made him as twisted as Sandre. He didn't care. Through the endless days in the dungeon, dreaming of this moment had kept him alive.

Still holding Sandre by the hair, he dragged him to his feet.

Sandre's eyes sprang open, full of sly cunning and desperate intelligence. Grabbing the ends of Michael's cravat, he wrapped it around Michael's neck, cutting off his air, crushing his already damaged windpipe.

451

Michael grabbed for his throat, gagging, choking, while Sandre laughed with pleasure, shoved him, got behind him, and *pulled.* Michael slammed himself backward, knocking Sandre off his feet. He landed on top of Sandre, and when the cravat loosened, he slid out from its deadly grasp.

He tried to recover, but his trachea spasmed, fighting the all-too-familiar sensation of being hanged.

Vicious and intent, Sandre put his knee into Michael's belly and again wrapped the cravat around his neck.

Michael punched blindly, and felt Sandre's nose break.

Blood sprayed them both.

Immediately, Michael caught his breath and felt better.

Sandre grabbed for his own face. "Curse you!" he said, muffled behind his hand. He was finished playing. He spun away, skidded across his desk flat on his belly, and groped for the drawer. Pulling it open, he extracted the pistol.

Michael lunged for Sandre, landed atop him, and grabbed his arm. They slid across the desk, grappling for the weapon.

The glass bowl flew across the room, shattering against the wall, candy taking temporary wing. The heavy gold candelabrum smashed into the carpet, extinguishing the candles and plunging Michael into a dim, surreal cavern where blood and violence reigned and the only sound was the panting of their breath.

Sandre slithered out from underneath him and free-fell toward the floor, his tumble broken by the open drawer. The wood snapped and splintered. Sandre yelled unintelligibly, whether from pain or the desecration of his desk, Michael didn't know.

Rolling onto his back, Sandre pointed the pistol up at Michael.

Michael grabbed the brass eagle and swung. The eagle connected with Sandre's head.

The shot shattered the quiet.

Michael flinched.

Sandre went limp.

Plaster showered from the ceiling, filling the air with dust, covering Michael with chunks of pure white and glittering gilt.

He opened his eyes. He was alive. The eagle had knocked Sandre out and his aim askew at the same time. Michael was alive . . . and he'd won.

Opening the desk drawer, Michael retrieved the keys to the dungeon and put them in the inner pocket of his cloak.

Now he had only to free Emma and, finally, to finish his revenge and force Sandre to face the thing he feared most.

Humiliation.

He went to work on Sandre.

CHAPTER
FORTY-FIVE

"What do you imagine you are doing?" the delegate from Spain bellowed so loudly his round belly quivered.

Jean-Pierre brushed the road's dust off his riding breeches and said, for the fourth time, "I'm sorry, my lord, but you were dressed as the Reaper."

"I have never been treated so badly in my life!"

"Yes, my lord." Jean-Pierre took the reins, mounted his horse, and tried again to take command of the situation. "I'm sorry, but why are you dressed as the Reaper?"

Lord Torres-Martez was having nothing of Jean-Pierre's apologies. "I'm going to tell Prince Sandre what you've done and he will take appropriate steps to discipline you, you . . . you . . . son of a whore!"

Jean-Pierre stiffened. He wanted so badly to take the pompous bastard down onto the road again, shove his face into a pile of horse shit, make him sorry he'd ever dared to make derogatory comments to Jean-Pierre de Guignard about his whore of a mother. He wanted to —

One of his men said, "My lord!"

This time Jean-Pierre wasn't so imprudent as to dismiss that urgent tone of voice. He looked up to the top of the hill behind them . . . and there, chasing a noble carriage, rode the Reaper.

This time the Reaper would pay.

Everyone was invited.

As Jean-Pierre galloped at the head of his troop, whipping his horse up the rise, Durant's words echoed mockingly in his ears.

How is it you don't know about this party?

Jean-Pierre cursed smug Michael Durant and deceitful Prince Sandre, who had so artfully *not* told Jean-Pierre of the event tonight. He cursed whoever had planned a masquerade party this night, and every blasted nobleman in the country.

You can invite yourself. It's a masquerade. No one will ever know you slipped in without an invitation.

Someday they would all pay for their neglect and prejudice against Jean-Pierre. He would make them pay.

Like a bullet, he aimed his ire at the pale, masked Reaper. Shouting, he spurred his horse onward.

The Reaper made a squawking noise. He tried to turn his mount, aim the creature back down the road.

With a roar of fury, Jean-Pierre launched himself out of the saddle, tackling the Reaper, knocking him to the ground. The two tumbled end over end, and when they stopped, Jean-Pierre tore off the villain's white mask — and found himself on top of and staring at a terrified Lord Nesbitt. "My lord. What are you doing here?"

Lady Nesbitt's sharp, high voice sounded behind his left shoulder. "What is he doing? What are you doing, you upstart excuse of a de Guignard peasant?"

Jean-Pierre turned and snarled.

"Don't you dare speak to me in such a manner." Her face was covered in pale powder, and she, too, wore tattered white lace similar to a shroud, but there was no mistaking Lady Nesbitt's finger as she shook it in his face. "You attacked my husband!"

"What is he doing dressed like this? What are you doing dressed like this?"

"We're going to the prince's party."

"What?" Jean-Pierre loosened his grip on Lord Nesbitt's cravat.

"The prince's party. His masquerade party. Tonight. I thought you were Prince

Sandre's cousin and bodyguard, but obviously you know nothing."

"The invitation. Do you have the invitation?"

"Why? Do we need it to get into the palace?" Lord Nesbitt's voice quavered.

"No, we do not!" Lady Nesbitt's voice rose. "We are Lord and Lady Nesbitt. Even the prince knows that!"

"I want to see the invitation," Jean-Pierre repeated. "Do you have it with you?"

Something of his urgency must have penetrated Lady Nesbitt's righteous anger, for she observed him more closely, then nodded regally. "I do. Come with me."

Jean-Pierre stood and gestured to his men. "Get Lord Nesbitt cleaned up and on his feet." He followed Lady Nesbitt to the carriage.

She reached inside, pulled out her reticule, and found a stiff piece of paper. Jean-Pierre tried to take it, but she pulled it away, gestured to her outrunners to come close, and by the light of their torches, read, " 'To celebrate the success of our pursuit and capture of the Reaper, by the order of Prince Sandre, come to the palace for a masquerade, and wear your rendition of the Reaper's costume. Stamped with the royal seal, this eighteenth day of September,

1849.' "When she was finished reading, she extended the invitation to him.

Taking it, he reviewed the words with disbelief. This party . . . the *prince* was giving it? Without a word to Jean-Pierre, Prince Sandre had invited every nobleman in the entire country to come to the *palace?* To come dressed as the *Reaper?* Then he sent Jean-Pierre out onto the roads to apprehend them?

No. That didn't make sense.

But the royal seal looked authentic.

And what about Michael Durant? He had mentioned a party, a masquerade, but he was dressed in a buccaneer's clothing. He carried a weapon. He . . . Jean-Pierre looked over the countryside, to the road where he'd apprehended Durant . . . the road that went to the palace. Realization of the truth overwhelmed his rage, and he saw his mistake.

"My lady, I suggest you go home. The invitation is a fake, and if you go to the palace tonight, all you'll see is horror and bloodshed."

Her mouth dropped open.

With a bow, he handed her the invitation, mounted his horse, and rode to the palace — where he intended to kill Michael Durant.

As Lady Nesbitt stepped into the carriage, she told the driver, "Whip up the horses. We're going to the palace. This should be very interesting indeed."

CHAPTER
FORTY-SIX

Michael stood at the gaping black entrance to the dungeon . . . at the entrance to the abyss. The exhilaration of defeating Sandre and leaving him to his fate was subsiding, and in its place came a creeping paralysis, a fear of darkness and cold, of slime and rats and a death so gradual a man could pass from this life to the next and never realize he had changed domains.

He took the first step down the stairs. He wasn't even to the first gate, yet the familiar scent of dirt and mildew filled his lungs. He could scarcely breathe, yet he took another step, and another.

Emma was down in this place, in this dungeon where hope had died.

Would she be alive?

Of course. Sandre took no pleasure in killing. He lived to torment, and he had his special pets. For them he reserved the royal cell, and Michael knew that was where he would find her.

Slowly he descended, down, down, finally reaching the first level, where Gotzon sat dozing, a hound of hell.

Michael leaned over him, shook his shoulder, said, "Gotzon, let me in."

Gotzon snorted and woke, stared at Michael, and grinned. "I knew you couldn't stay away. Not with that pretty girl in the dungeon."

"That's right." Michael lifted Sandre's keys. "I've come to take her."

Gotzon laughed, a big, jolly laugh, like some perverted St. Nick. "You can't. Tomorrow she'll marry Sandre or she'll hang. Tonight, if she doesn't yield to Sandre, I get her. We all get her. It'll be a lovely party, and I'm not going to miss it by opening the door to —"

Michael stuck his knife into Gotzon's soft belly.

Gotzon's mouth moved and his eyes bugged in surprise.

Michael pulled his knife free and wiped it on his handkerchief.

Gotzon collapsed on the floor. "You," he whispered. His eyes rolled back in his head, and he died at Michael's feet.

Justice done.

Michael stepped over the body and took

the ring of a dozen keys off the wall. He tested the largest; the third opened the first gate. He started to discard them. But no. He dared not take the chance someone would come behind him and lock him in.

So with Prince Sandre's personal keys in one hand, and Gotzon's keys in his pocket, he descended.

Torches smoked on sconces set high on the walls. He grabbed one and walked along the dark steps, the puddle of feeble light moving with him valiantly battling the grim darkness. Dampness dripped from the ceiling. Panic closed Michael's throat, making it hard for him to breathe, to swallow. Each step echoed along the stone walls, and landmarks appeared and disappeared like truth encased in nightmares.

There. Sandre had placed the brand on his shoulder.

Michael's steps slowed.

There. Rickie had lashed him with a whip until blood ran down his legs.

This place reeked of horrors.

There. Gotzon had wrapped a rope around his neck, flung it over the rafters, and hanged him. Sandre and Rickie laughed while Michael kicked and clawed at his throat. Then he passed out. Then when he awoke, they did it again. And again. And again.

In all the time since he'd left the dungeon, he had been focused on his corrosive hatred of Sandre. He hadn't realized that the place where he'd been imprisoned still held his soul in thrall.

The dungeon was too deep for any but the most loathsome insects, and not even the largest palace cats would attempt to kill one of the rats that slid furtively along the walls.

Emma was down here. Down here somewhere.

Still the corridor extended downward into the depths, and he walked in an unending nightmare.

"Michael." A soft voice whispered his name. *"Michael?"*

With a start, he turned toward that beloved sound. "Emma?"

"Here!"

Her voice, so eager, yet so quiet, rasping as if . . . *Dear God.* Had they hanged her, too? Cut her down and hanged her again?

"Say more." He waved the torch down the row of bars and doors.

"To your right and back. Please. Please, Michael. This time, don't be a dream."

He followed the sound of her desperation,

thrusting the torch at the bars until the feeble illumination touched her, a small, dim figure huddled on a cot against the far wall.

The sick bastard had placed her in the royal cell — the same cell Michael had inhabited for two long, despairing years.

Using Prince Sandre's keys, he thrust first one, then the other into the lock. The second turned; the door opened with a creak. He beckoned her. "Come on. Hurry!"

Chains rattled. "I can't."

They had shackled her. Of course they had.

He closed his eyes in a single moment of anguish for her. For her helplessness.

Then he opened them. The anguish remained, tasting sour in the back of his throat.

It tasted like fear.

"Michael?" Her voice trembled. "You have the keys."

"Yes." He held Sandre's keys in his hand. He pulled Gotzon's iron ring from his pocket. They were heavy and cold in his hand, and he was in the grip of such horror he couldn't move.

How could he walk into this dark womb of earth where hour followed hour, day followed day, without light, without heat, without the sound of a human voice or the warmth of a human touch? Where every moment dragged on for an eternity, until all too soon, Sandre came and had him dragged out, and gave him to Rickie like a mouse to a cat?

"Michael. I need you." Emma's voice was barely a breath.

Emma. Unless he moved, she would die.

He took a step into the cell. Terror brushed his skin like cobwebs. Another step. The familiar smell of mold and damp filled his head. Another step. His mind shouted, *This is a trap. A trap!*

Then the torch flame illuminated Emma's upturned face. She looked thin and tired, but she watched him, eyes shining, as if he were brave and strong.

"Stop," he muttered.

"Stop? Stop what? I can't move." Her wrists were chained to the wall, her ankles chained together, then chained to her wrists.

Falling to his knees, he carefully placed the torch on the floor and used its light to search for a smaller key on Gotzon's ring, a key that would fit her shackles. "Stop looking at me like that. Like I came fearlessly to save you." He found the key and tried to fit it into the lock at her ankles.

His hands shook, and the key clinked

against the metal.

"Sandre told me this was your cell. He told me what he did to you. Oh, Michael." Her hand lifted. She tried to touch his cheek, but the chain clinked as it reached its limit inches from his face. "You knew when you came down here what they had done to you. You knew you could be captured and tortured once more. You knew you could be killed. Yet you came anyway. I hope you came for my sake, but also — I know you came because you always do the right thing."

Once again he tried to put the key in the lock, but his tremors were too violent. He couldn't, he just couldn't make the final gesture to free her.

He was a failure.

"I don't do the right thing," he said in a low voice. "I do what I have to."

She laughed. She actually laughed — a sound that had never been heard down here before, a sound that chased away the darkness. "You didn't *have* to do any of this. After you were released from this dungeon and discovered your way out of your cell at Lady Fanchere's, you could have gone home to England. Who would have blamed you? Instead, you donned the costume of the Reaper and rode for justice. When you discovered I had been captured — captured after you told me not to ride — you could have let me take the punishment meted out to me. Instead you faced this horror. Right now, you have to be petrified, yet you came in; you came after me. Honor is a choice. Bravery is a choice. And you are the bravest man I know!" She tried to touch him, but again she reached the end of the chain. "I wouldn't have stayed sane, but I always knew you were coming after me."

As she spoke, the shaking of his hands eased.

He opened the shackles, her feet first, then her hands.

He wrapped her in his arms for one minute, only one, for he kept in mind the barred door on the cell, the long corridor they had to traverse, the stairs, the gate, and the palace full of the prince's servants and the prince's soldiers.

He and Emma had to get out of here before the prince was served.

But, *oh.* That one minute when he held her and she held him . . . it was life and light and love renewed.

"Can you stand?" he asked.

"Yes." She hobbled to her feet. "I just . . . When I fell off Old Nelson I bruised myself, and I haven't healed well."

"Of course you haven't." He kept his voice soothing, but if he had known . . . would he have been able to restrain himself? Or would he have killed Sandre when he had the chance?

He picked up the torch, moved to help her, but the iron rings with their heavy keys hindered him. He stared at them, wanting to fling them away, knowing such a move would be stupid. Before he and Emma were out, he might need them. . . .

"Here." She lifted the dirty, thin mat that Sandre mockingly called a mattress. "Put them here."

The bed frame was constructed of rusty iron pipes and twisted metal wires — wires easily twisted into hooks for the keys. He handed her the torch and, in moments, the keys were hidden, yet accessible to them and perhaps . . . to some future prisoner?

Taking the torch, he wrapped his arm around her waist and helped her to the door.

She was limping, favoring one hip. "I'll work it out," she assured him. "It gets better when I walk."

She did seem to improve as they moved along the midnight corridor.

With his hands around her ribs, he discovered how very thin she'd grown, and his temper sizzled. "Did he starve you?"

"If he did, it's my fault." She stopped him on the first step of the stairs. "I can't go on without begging you to forgive me. All I could think, during the dark days and nights, was that you and Lady Fanchere would do whatever it took to save me. And it was my fault that I was here. I lost my temper and I rode stupidly, without thought to anything but my own satisfaction. It was one thing for me to pay for my thoughtlessness, but to put you in danger . . . Oh, Michael, I'm so sorry."

He felt . . . well, he felt sheepish. "I can't believe you're asking forgiveness after I deceived you so terribly."

"But I don't want to forgive you." Her voice rang with sly humor, and she kissed him once, just once, with all the passion in her soul. "I want to make you pay for the rest of your life."

He chortled, then caught his breath. "So you're going to marry me?"

"If you still want me. Michael . . ." She stroked his cheek. "I love you."

That was all he needed to hear. "Come on. We've got to get out of here. This is no place to make love."

She was laughing as he half carried her up the stairs. They went through the top gate; she didn't even glance when Michael dropped the torch beside Gotzon's body. A row of torches lit the next flight of stairs, and at the top he could see the softer candlelight of the palace.

They were moving faster now, almost out of the dungeons. They reached the top step. . . .

And Jean-Pierre stood there, sword in hand, blocking the way.

CHAPTER
FORTY-SEVEN

Michael's hands were empty of weapons —
because he'd been helping her, Emma, up
the stairs.

Now they were helpless, facing the pale,
lethal gaze of Jean-Pierre and his sharp,
well-honed sword.

Jean-Pierre glanced at her and dismissed
her. He focused on Michael and asked,
"Where is my cousin? Where is Prince Sandre?"

Michael widened his eyes. "How would I
know?"

That tone would never convince Jean-
Pierre.

"You did something with Sandre?" she
asked.

Michael glanced at her and inclined his
head.

"I hope it's something awful."

The faintest smile played around Michael's lips.

"His study is a wreck. There's blood on the carpet." Jean-Pierre straightened his arm and pressed the tip of his sword into Michael's breastbone. "Tell me before I skewer you — where is my cousin?"

Michael replied with an insouciance that took her breath away. "If you're going to skewer me anyway, I'm not telling you a thing."

She wanted to fall to her knees, to beg for Michael's life, when Jean-Pierre pulled the sword back and asked in frustration, "How did you do this? Make up a party, send out invitations stamped with the prince's own seal?"

"It was not the prince's own seal," Michael said gently. "It's the seal of the family de Guignard. You probably have one somewhere yourself."

"You threw a party for the prince? You threw a party so you could rescue me?" Emma could scarcely believe the cleverness of the ruse.

"You lived with the Fancheres — and you stole Eleonore's seal?" Jean-Pierre's voice rose.

"I didn't have to steal it." To Emma, Michael said, "I didn't even come up with the idea. The party, the masquerade, all of it was Lady Fanchere's idea."

Emma laughed, low and long. "I knew when she discovered who had killed Aimée . . . I knew she wouldn't allow Sandre to escape unscathed."

"She coordinated everything — the food, the decorations, and the orchestra. She instructed the prince's servants. She wrote out the invitations with her own hand. She heated the wax. She sealed the invitations with her own seal." Michael sounded cocky, and stood with all the confidence of a young stud rooster. "She is gone now, she and her husband, gone to stay in the Italian villa Fanchere rented for Aimée — and their money went with them. A sad loss for Moricadia, wouldn't you say?"

"Eleonore betrayed us," Jean-Pierre breathed.

"No. She discovered the truth. About you, and about Sandre," Michael said.

"You should never have killed Aimée." Emma's anger rose, as fresh and clean as the first moment she'd heard the news.

Jean-Pierre's gaze shifted from Emma to Michael and back. "He demanded that I do so."

"When the devil commands, you don't have to listen." She tried to spring at Jean-Pierre.

Michael restrained her. "You're going to

hell, Jean-Pierre, and you're carrying Sandre on your back."

Jean-Pierre's sword flashed up toward Michael's throat.

Emma screamed.

A flash, a sharp explosion, and Jean-Pierre staggered back. He dropped his sword, and clasped his bleeding hand.

Three men stepped forward, hats pulled low, scarves wrapped around their faces, and pistols clasped in their hands.

From one, the faintest curl of smoke rose.

Although Emma had never met any of them, she recognized two. They both had blue eyes, and the younger had brown hair that swept his collar, but something about these men — the way they moved, or perhaps their cool attitude — reminded her of Michael.

His brother. His father, the marksman who had shot Jean-Pierre.

The other man resembled no one here. He was a man at home in the shadows . . . and a man used to being in charge.

Regardless of their disguises, Michael obviously knew who they were. He whooped; then in tones of delight, he said, "Father! Throckmorton! Jude!"

The man he called "Throckmorton" never allowed his cold gaze to wander from Jean-

Pierre. Keeping his pistol aimed at Jean-Pierre, he said, "Disarm him."

"I'll do it." Clumsily, slowly, using his left hand, Jean-Pierre pulled a pistol from his belt and placed it on the floor.

"He'll have a knife, too," Michael said. "Perhaps more than one."

Jean-Pierre pulled a knife out of his sleeve and one out of his boot, and dropped them on top of the pistol.

"Tie him up," Throckmorton ordered.

Jean-Pierre cast Throckmorton a loathing glance.

The atmosphere grew dark, tense, reckless.

Emma could barely breathe as she waited to see if Jean-Pierre would attack like a rabid dog.

But no. He turned with his hands behind his back.

Jude used the coil of rope at his belt to secure Jean-Pierre's hands and tie him to the bars over the window. "More?" He raised an eyebrow at Throckmorton.

"That'll keep him." Throckmorton turned away. "Let's go."

"Yes." Michael put his delight on hold and pulled Emma close. "Let's get out of here."

He led the way with Emma. The other men closed ranks behind, and right before they turned the corner, Emma glanced back.

Blood soaked the handkerchief Jean-Pierre had wrapped around his hand. He twisted in the restraints, and those pale eyes turned toward them and shone like beacons of pure malice.

She shivered and walked with increased speed.

They rushed down the corridor and toward the kitchen.

"How is Mum?" Michael spoke as he walked. "And Adrian?"

"Both well. Both waiting for us to return with you," Nevitt answered.

"They'll be pleased to find there's a bonus." Jude glanced at the hold Michael had on Emma.

"Yes," Michael said. "They'll like my Emma."

Emma wanted to tell him he was saying too much, too soon. If they were going to do this properly, she should put on her best clothes, go to visit the Duke of Nevitt and his family, and be introduced in a drawing room in England.

But perhaps it was too late for that. Perhaps it had always been too late for that.

"How are we getting out of here?" Michael asked.

"The same way we came in," Michael's

father said. "Through the front gate."

"Of course." Michael laughed. "You're the Duke of Nevitt. Where else would you enter and exit?"

"Exactly." Nevitt pulled the scarf away from his face.

Jude did the same, and Emma saw the striking resemblance between the father and his sons.

Liveried servants bustled past, carrying platters of food and bottles of wine up to the next level. Emma expected one of them to speak, to ask where she and her four rescuers were bound, or perhaps to direct them elsewhere, or to call for help because one of the prisoners had escaped.

Instead, they seemed oblivious to Michael, to Emma, to the other men.

Prince Sandre's servants were preparing for a party . . . and they were smiling.

How strange. She had never seen any of them smile before.

"Throckmorton arranged for the stable boy to hold our horses," Jude said. "There's something odd about this palace and this party. And this country, for that matter — they're having some kind of weird costume party. They're all dressed as ghosts or some-thing."

Emma realized what Michael and Lady

Fanchere had done, and chuckled deep in her throat.

Michael grinned down at her.

"I don't suppose you know anything about that, Michael?" the other man asked.

"Yes, Throckmorton, I might." Emma loved the way Michael's voice sounded while he was smiling: warm, amused, smug.

They reached the massive front door. The men placed their pistols in holsters strapped to their sides, a futile attempt at discretion, and walked out into the courtyard.

The night air was smoky; torches lit the perimeter of the walls.

Carriages were rumbling across the cobblestones and up to the steps. Men and women dressed as Reapers were descending, stopping and mingling with the other guests, then laughing as if they all enjoyed this masquerade more than they should.

No one seemed at all interested in four men dressed as travelers and a young woman in damp, dirty clothes.

"An odd and peculiar place you chose to inhabit, Michael," Nevitt snapped.

"A good part of the time, sir, it was not a choice," Michael said firmly.

"Over here." Throckmorton led them toward the stables, then beckoned, and a boy came forward, leading two horses. He handed reins to Throckmorton and to Jude, and went back for the other two horses tethered nearby.

"I've got another mount below," Michael said. "We can stop and get him on the way."

"Old Nelson." Emma sighed with delight. "I'm so glad. I would hate to leave him behind."

"In the meantime, can the young lady ride with you, Michael?" Throckmorton asked.

"Throckmorton, I wouldn't have it any other way." Michael flashed him a grin.

Emma didn't like being demoted to mere saddle luggage. "Or perhaps, Mr. Throckmorton, Michael can ride with me."

"Who is this saucy wench?" The Duke of Nevitt sounded stern, but one side of his mouth twitched as if he were fighting a smile.

"Let me introduce you." Michael took her by the shoulders and turned her to face the Duke of Nevitt. "Father, this lady is Miss Emma Chegwidden."

She curtsied as correctly as she would in any ballroom.

Michael continued. "She saved my life when it was in danger. She saved my heart when I thought it was broken. She saved my sanity . . . for what that is worth."

Jude snorted.

Michael never turned his gaze away from his father, but his fist flew out and punched Jude in the arm. As calmly as if nothing had happened, he continued speaking to his father. "She has consented to be my wife, and I'm going to marry her as soon as I can. Pray give us your blessing."

Nevitt accepted the reins, put his boot in the stirrup, and lifted himself into the saddle.

Emma tensed. *Oh, God.* He was going to refuse.

He looked down at them. "If she did all those things, then she's more than you deserve, boy. Of course you have my blessing."

Emma almost collapsed with relief . . . and surprise.

"Father recognizes an Amazon when he sees one," Michael said in her ear.

"I'll help you up, Miss Chegwidden." Jude put his hands on her shoulders. "Michael, hurry up."

Michael mounted and held out his hand.

Emma put her hand in his, her foot in Jude's cupped palms, and scrambled into the saddle behind Michael, flashing, she was sure, bare legs as she wrapped them around the horse.

She had been the Reaper; she was *not*

riding side-saddle.

The men noticed, of course. They were men. But there was no censure in their gazes.

Nevitt wheeled his horse away, then wheeled it back. "Michael, you should worry more about Miss Chegwidden's father's blessing."

"My father is deceased, sir," she said.

"I always said Michael had the devil's own luck," Nevitt said gruffly. "But I'll stand in for your father and tell you — you don't have to marry this reprobate. You've saved his life and I owe you for that, and I can settle a sum on you that would enable you to be an independent woman."

"Father, for the love of God, shut up!" Michael pulled her arms tightly around his waist. "She *wants* to marry me."

Jude laughed and mounted his horse. "Probably just for your position as the future Duke of Nevitt."

Throckmorton chuckled, but his gaze wandered, scrutinizing the gate and the guards, before he also mounted his horse.

"I don't care why she wants to marry me," Michael said. "She can have my every penny; she can flaunt the title when she gets it, as long as she stays beside me and keeps the darkness away."

Emma realized she needed to make her position clear now, before they rode away and conversation was no longer possible. In her firmest tone, she said, "I intend to marry Michael, and squander all his money and run his life, and make sure he never again consorts with wicked women or gambles with licentious men. I promise I will henpeck him until he has no life beyond what I allow him, and when we die, I will lie in his arms through all eternity."

For a moment, the men were silent.

Nevitt took out his handkerchief and blew his nose with a honk.

"There you go. I've lost all control of my life." Michael sounded cheerful, and he picked up her hand from around his waist and kissed it.

"It's about time. You were never good at control, anyway," Nevitt said.

"Bravo, Miss Chegwidden!" Throckmorton urged his horse forward. "Well said. Now let's go."

Michael replaced her hand on his waist. "Hold me tight. Never let me go."

He and Emma followed Throckmorton out the gate and down the steep road. Nevitt and Jude followed them. They avoided oncoming carriages, riding into the darkness and the forest below.

Michael led them into the woods to Old Nelson.

As Michael adjusted the stirrups, Emma greeted the gelding with delight, then mounted him and sighed with relief. Now she felt at home. She felt free.

Michael looked up at her. "You can't ride the roads of England righting wrongs, you know."

"No?" She smiled down at him. "I can't?"

"You're going to lead me a merry chase, aren't you?" He sounded resigned. And delighted.

Nevitt watched and announced, "We'd better get these two married in Spain. Michael was always an impatient lad."

Emma glanced at her future father-in-law in dismay. How much had they betrayed with a glance and a few words?

Nevitt chuckled. "Don't worry, lass; the first child can come at any time. The rest of them take nine months."

Michael mounted his horse. "Father, stop embarrassing Emma and *ride.* We want to be well away from Jean-Pierre by morning."

"He's a coward," Jude said.

"He's not a coward." Michael led the way back to the road. "He is the most dangerous man I know. Throckmorton's right: We should get out of Moricadia as fast as possible — before he discovers what I did with Sandre, and before all hell breaks loose."

"So my sources are right?" Throckmorton asked. "Trouble is about to visit the de Guignards?"

Michael's gaze grew cold with satisfaction. "Sandre should have paid attention. The appearance of the Reaper was a sign. The king has returned."

The party at the palace was in full swing. Guests dressed as the Reaper danced with abandon, disguised by their masks, their makeup, and their costumes. When asked, they said they were half-mad with the joy of knowing the Reaper had been captured and tomorrow would hang.

Jean-Pierre believed they behaved like children let out of school because Prince Sandre was nowhere in sight.

Jean-Pierre stood on the balcony, his hand wrapped in a bloody napkin, his wrists torn from his wrestling with the ropes, watching the crowd and wondering where that cursed Durant had hidden Sandre. He'd sent the guard everywhere, into every room, every closet, every cupboard. They hadn't found him . . . or they said they hadn't.

He didn't trust them. Their hatred had gone beyond fear. If one of them had found

Sandre bound and gagged, Jean-Pierre was sure that guardsman would have slit Sandre's throat without compunction.

Jean-Pierre didn't trust the servants, either. They set up a long table on the edge of the dance floor and filled it with dishes of exquisite taste — a peacock with its tail feathers attached, an aspic in the shape of a red rose — and while they did, they smiled. Smiled! That wasn't the way Sandre's servants behaved.

And where were the keys to the dungeon? Sandre's keys had disappeared. Gotzon's keys had disappeared. Were there more? Jean-Pierre didn't know.

Curse Durant all to hell.

The small orchestra stopped in the middle of the dance, and blew a fanfare.

Jean-Pierre leaned over the railing.

Two hefty men carried out a huge covered silver salver. Pleased chatter swept the dance floor.

"The pièce de résistance!"

"A whole roasted pig!"

The guests crowded around.

The men hoisted the platter onto the table.

Jean-Pierre's eyes narrowed on them.

Those guys looked more than just strong. They were rough, bearded, and neither of them wore the palace livery.

His gaze fell on the dome-covered salver again. He realized the contents. He straightened. He shouted, "No!"

The men glanced up. They met his gaze — and grinned. They whipped off the lid, stepped back — and there was Prince Sandre, naked and trussed up like a chicken, his butt in the air and a lit candle between his hairy cheeks.

A moment of shocked silence. Then — a hundred Reapers roared with laughter.

Jean-Pierre sprinted down the stairs, shouting at the men who had carried Sandre to remain where they were. He would get to the bottom of this, he shouted.

The Reapers laughed harder.

Jean-Pierre pulled his pistol and pointed it at one of the intruders who had carried in the prince.

The man froze.

Then Sandre screamed.

The candle burned down; Sandre's butt hair was on fire.

Jean-Pierre forgot the laughing guests, forgot the treacherous men. He raced to Sandre's side and blew out the candle and the other burning parts, and when he straightened, the crowd had vanished as if it had never been.

The party was over.

The laughter was ended.

Prince Sandre's much-cherished pride was ground into dust.

From a dark corner, Raul Lawrence watched and smiled, then turned away to go back to his home, to his people . . . and to the secret he had hidden so well.

The rumors were right. The true king had indeed returned to Moricadia.

ABOUT THE AUTHOR

New York Times bestselling author **Christina Dodd** builds worlds filled with romance and adventure and creates the most distinctive characters in fiction today. Her forty novels — paranormals, historicals, and romantic suspense — have been translated into fifteen languages, featured by Doubleday Book Club®, recorded as books on tape for the blind, given Romance Writers of America's prestigious Golden Heart and RITA awards, and called the year's best by *Library Journal.* Dodd herself has been a clue in the *Los Angeles Times* crossword puzzle. Dodd invites readers to enter her worlds and join her mailing list at www.christina dodd.com.